Brianna walked to the long window overlooking the drive and pulled back the heavy velvet draperies.

Major Fallon had just mounted a spirited bay. Gripping the reins with a gloved hand, he swung the horse around and raised his gaze to the long window where she stood—as if he'd know that she'd be there—the small turn of his mouth his only concession to her presence. Brianna stared back, making no outward show that her pulse raced, and that they had just agreed to become lovers.

Her whole body hummed.

Michael Fallon was arrogant and annoying, and positively the most exciting man she had ever met.

Indeed, there was something that drew her into his flame. And heaven help her, when she stepped into his smoky gaze, she burned.

Other **AVON ROMANCES**

Coming Soon

And Don't Miss These
ROMANTIC TREASURES
from Avon Books

MELODY THOMAS

Must Have Been The Moonlight

AVON BOOKS

An Imprint of HarperCollinsPublishers

This is a work of fiction. Names, characters, places, and incidents are products of the author's imagination or are used fictitiously and are not to be construed as real. Any resemblance to actual events, locales, organizations, or persons, living or dead, is entirely coincidental.

AVON BOOKS
An Imprint of HarperCollins*Publishers*
10 East 53rd Street
New York, New York 10022-5299

Copyright © 2004 by Laura Renken
ISBN: 0-06-056448-2
www.avonromance.com

First Avon Books paperback printing: December 2004

Avon Trademark Reg. U.S. Pat. Off. and in Other Countries, Marca Registrada, Hecho en U.S.A.
HarperCollins® is a registered trademark of HarperCollins Publishers Inc.

Printed in the U.S.A.

10 9 8 7 6 5 4 3 2

To my daughter Shari,

for the gift of your youthful insight and wisdom.
Your laughter and your smile add
the most wonderous color to my world.
How did I ever get so lucky?

I love you.

Chapter 1

Egypt
1870

Major Michael Fallon squatted on his heels, his face dark with a beard, and squinted against the harsh glare of the Western Sahara. He looked for the object that had caught his eye when he'd crested the last dune—a dark flutter of silk on sunlight. Finding it now amid the loose clutter on sand—a wisp of cloth snagged on rock—he brought the veil to his nose. English roses and something else uniquely feminine touched his senses. Turning the cloth over in his hands, Michael turned his attention to a steel-dust Arabian trailing its reins some distance away. Where was the second rider he had been following?

Bending over the field glasses beside him, he adjusted the leather hood over the lenses to prevent the fading sunlight from reflecting off the glass. An ancient watchtower and stone wall, relegated back to the desert some centuries before, made a somber landmark against the indigo sky as nightfall lowered its sleepy eye over the terrain. He knew that good rifle scope would pick him off at this range if he stepped into the open.

He swore softly as he looked back at his white camel, couched in the sand like some bored Sheba oblivious to the growing chill. He pulled out a tin of peppermints, slid one beneath his tongue, and again brought the veil to his nose before shoving it into his shirt.

Holding the carbine in one hand, his burnoose slapping at his boots, he remained on the backside of the dune and trailed the Arabian on foot through the growing darkness to the outer perimeter of the watchtower. Three days without sleep—or perhaps it was the beating three Kharga slavers had given him last month—made him feel every muscle in his legs as he kept low to the ground.

The horse ambled up a path—and stopped.

Michael dropped to his haunches, his fist tightening around his rifle. He carried a brace of pistols across his chest and a knife in his other hand. Such ancient watchtowers had been built around springs. He didn't see any livestock, but guessed they were corralled behind the tower against the rocks. One small heel print crossed the worn path almost at his feet. Shifting his weight, he raised his eyes to the rocks a heartbeat before he heard the click of a pistol behind him.

And froze.

"The only reason you're still alive," said a decidedly feminine voice, "is because my rifle is out of bullets."

Michael rose to his feet and turned slowly. His tagilmust hung loose and draped his shoulder. Each hand gripped a weapon. Their eyes met, and for a breathless heartbeat they faced each other. He wasn't sure how many people were present in the camp. Whatever he'd expected to find, it wasn't a blue-eyed houri in the Sahara Desert holding a lethal-looking revolver on him.

Wearing a dark robe, half draped in moonlight, her body was detailed against the flimsy cloth as she stood between two boulders. Her cheeks were pale, and a wisp of dark hair had fallen from the wild braid down her back.

His gaze glinting with hard humor, Michael respected grit as much as he did the seven-inch barrel aimed at his chest. "It is fortunate for me that your rifle had no bullets, *amîri*," he said impassively, raising his arms in a gesture of submission.

His movement revealed to her the baggy white *sirwal* beneath his robes, trousers tucked in soft leather knee-high boots.

Her light-colored gaze held his. Those striking eyes had kept him from possibly killing her. That and the fact that she'd spoken in English—and he'd answered in kind.

He didn't hear movement behind him, only felt the stars explode in his head. Then he was falling, and his face hit the sand.

Brianna Donally could barely breathe as she held the field glasses to her eyes and scanned the desert, the sick feeling in her gut increasing with every moment. The white camel she'd been watching earlier had not moved from its solemn place in the sand. She would have to go out there. Yet, she knew there was someone else in the darkness. Somehow, despite all of her efforts, they'd been tracked. First by the pair this morning. Then by the man on the white camel.

She knew that one man lay on the desert floor because she'd put him there earlier that morning, and the man on the white camel lay behind her.

Her sister-in-law slumped against the stone wall, her breath coming in quick heaves. They'd both been running.

"Do you think that I killed him, Brea?" Lady Alexandra removed the wide-brimmed beater hat from her head and dropped it onto the sand. A visible bruise marred her cheek. "We can't just leave him to . . . to the scavengers. Like the other one."

They had escaped two assassins. Closing her eyes, Brianna lowered her forehead against the stone wall. It was cold against her cheek. How long would it be before those who had pillaged the caravan sent more people to hunt down the two Inglizi missies who had escaped the massacre? She would not allow Lady Alexandra's compassion to intrude on her conscience. Nor was she going to expend her energies to bury murderers. Some things were better left alone.

Unlike Brianna, her sister-in-law wore a long-sleeve cotton shirtwaist and collared jacket over a divided skirt, the blouse and jacket torn and spattered with blood. How much came from the wound on her mouth or shoulder, or from the soldier who'd been beside her when he was shot, Brianna didn't know.

"If that man wished to be buried in accordance to his custom, then he should not have attacked us, my lady."

Blinking to clear her vision, Brianna forced herself to refocus. The moon was a scimitar in the sky, lying over the desert terrain like a half-lit lantern. Nothing moved in the pale stillness, the stark beauty made more terrifying by the absolute silence. They were vulnerable if they stepped out onto open ground. Surely, they would be just as dead if they did not.

"Lord, Brea," Lady Alex whispered in the heavy stillness that surrounded them. "I think I'm going to be sick again." She leaned her forehead against her knees.

Brianna wrapped her sister-in-law tightly in her arms. "Me, too, my lady. But we have to remain strong."

A gust of wind blew sand in her face. She'd never been anyone's caretaker. It frightened her to think that the intrepid Lady Alexandra might need her when they'd both been strong for so long. That she might somehow fail this moment.

That she already had.

If Alex collapsed, that would leave only her to see them through.

They'd added two pistols to their arsenal and a very ugly knife—what kind of man carried a lethal weapon of that size?—that she had no idea how to use. Their rifle broke when Alex had hit the man, and she could barely lift the rifle he'd carried, which made it practically useless to her in defending off an attack from any distance.

If only one could eat gunpowder, she thought, they'd have a feast.

She knew she should retrieve the camel, but was afraid to go out there—aye, frightened. Brianna Donally, legion activist for all manner of political anarchy, was afraid of the night.

How infinitesimal her problems in England had been, compared to now. How trivial, when everything in her life had come down to murdering another human being for survival.

Starvation was a very real possibility. They had no food. She didn't know how to hunt in the desert. And the only water they'd found in days sat on a patch of land that wasn't safe from intruders.

Brianna laid her palm across Lady Alex's brow. "At least you do not have a fever." She gave her sister-in-law the waterskin and helped her sip.

"Lord, I feel like I'm chewing sand." Her eyes were in the shadow of her tangled hair. "I probably just killed a man. I should be thinking what it's going to be like seeing him in hell."

Brianna stood. "Then we'll see him together, my lady. Along with all the other murderers who raided our caravan." She hadn't meant her voice to be so sharp. "You did what you had to do tonight because I didn't pull the trigger."

"Brea—"

"We can't stay here. I know there are more men out there."

Brianna took one of the heavy pistols and walked behind the tower to check on the camel and the Arabian that had followed them into camp. It was different shooting a rifle at two hundred yards in self-defense than it was standing ten feet away from a man. He should have been ugly for the kind of killer he was. Instead, his gaze had touched her with something akin to incredulity, something that went beyond the handsome darkness of his face—and she'd hesitated. Fringed in the darkest of lashes, his eyes had been almost silver in the twilight, his rich baritone voice cultured and his words spoken soundly in English. If not for Alex, the tall Bedouin would probably have slain her with that hideous knife he'd carried.

She almost started to cry. She'd been holding it in for days.

Her camel stirred at her approach. "How are you doing, beautiful?" Brianna whispered, rubbing her palm over its long brown nose. The beast growled and protested, but Brianna didn't care. The camel was a notorious windbag. "At least we'll no longer have to ride double. We have a horse now."

She could not have imagined that she and Alex would have made it this far if not for the stout beast. For three days they'd survived the insufferable heat. They'd found a pot-hole of an oasis among the scattered rocks where some long ago tribe had built a watchtower. Perhaps to guard their goats, though Brianna could only imagine what sustained the lot. A dozen date palms and spiny thornbushes struggled for life, like the rest of the oasis inhabitants.

They had to leave. Yet, Brianna knew very well that when they did, she and Alex would probably die. She had no idea how to find her brother's camp.

Christopher would know by now that something was wrong.

Brianna looked over her shoulder. She should go back and make sure that the Bedouin was dead.

It had been at least fifteen minutes. He was tied. She'd wrapped the ropes around his arms and ankles herself. They could perhaps stay one day more to sleep and search for food.

If he were only dead.

Opening her fingers, Brianna stared down at the gun in her hand. His gun. The smooth ivory hilt, made for a man's bigger palm, did not fit hers. She thought of Captain Pritchards and all the others who had perished. The dark-eyed youth whom she had befriended. He had been the nephew of one of the caravan's guides. And all the soldiers who had gone down in the volley of rifle fire. Those images had burned into her head, and she closed her eyes to dispel them.

"Where is my strength?" she whispered, her gaze falling on her heavy box camera, still attached to the back of the three-pronged saddle. She'd come to this country with dreams of making something more of herself. "Where is some sign that after all of this, we're not going to die out here? I'll settle for a lightning bolt, Lord."

Brianna shifted as she tightened the last strap on the saddle. A large lizard shot out of the rocks near her feet. Startled, she watched it waddle, tail flagging in the air, toward the rocks on the other side of the narrow pool of water.

Brianna grabbed her gun and gave chase. This was better than a lightning bolt!

Taking a shortcut to the rock wall, she sloshed through a leg of the freshwater pond, seeking the crevices in the rock wall where the lizard was attempting to flee. If she couldn't catch it with her hands, she'd use her bloody gun. Three lizards scampered out and scattered. Brianna grabbed the tail of the bigger one, more by luck than skill, and wrestled to keep hold of the squirming creature. She lost her gun. Tumbling into the waterhole, she held onto her prize with both her hands. Triumph yielded to an excited cry.

The lizard had stopped writhing. Staring at it, wondering what to do next, she sat in water up to her waist, her hair tangled in her face, and for a moment did not register the man standing at the edge of the pool.

His dark-booted foot was propped on a rock, a rope dangling from fingers. His baggy trousers were tucked in soft leather knee-high boots. Heart pounding, she raised her gaze higher, past his thighs. His long hooded robe was all that moved on his body as she met the soft glitter of his silver eyes.

Good God! It was he!

A hint of white flashed in the shadows. "Get up, *amîri*," he said in a perfectly affected British accent. "Before I drag you out of there."

She looked at the lizard in her hands, barely aware that a part of her decried letting it go. But she did.

Brianna dove backward in the water. Her hand wrapped around the pistol an instant before splashing heralded her capture. The man's hand ruthlessly gripped her wrist. She cried out but he dunked her head. Hand over her mouth, he lifted her bodily out of the water, while she kicked and clawed at the arm that tightened around her waist. Her hair tangled around him like a net. He slipped on the muddy incline then fell. He would have landed heavily on her had he not caught himself.

Her palm still gripping the pistol, she spat obscenities in Arabic. She called him a *hâwi*, snake charmer, and a barracuda.

"Indeed." His laugh was unpleasant. "You have no idea."

In one furious movement he flipped the little wildcat on her back and slid her beneath him, dragging her robe up to her hips. His thighs imprisoned her naked flanks; his hands held both of hers above her head.

"Drop it." His voice was deadly calm. He squeezed his hand over hers, in no mood to grant her clemency. "Or I *will* break your bloody wrist."

Defiance flashed in her eyes. A reluctant smile tilted Michael's mouth. He respected courage. But there was also the matter of why she'd tried to kill him, and what had happened to the rider on the steel-dust Arabian—and who the hell was she, anyway? He trusted her as far as he could chase her, which, at the moment, wouldn't be far. His skull throbbed. Someone had hit him. And that someone was still about.

Conscious of her hot breath on his chin, he dropped his gaze to her mouth. Stretched over her the way he was, he could feel the softness of her breasts. She looked like a drowned squirrel, but her squirming, rounded body, which even the voluminous robes couldn't conceal, felt purely female.

He made no effort to mask his reaction, one that she clearly recognized, for she stilled her wriggling. Her large eyes reflected the wild tempo of her heartbeat. "Go away and pretend you never found us," she said. "No one need know." Her tongue ran had her dried lips. "We haven't eaten in days. We'll probably die of hunger any way."

Michael yanked the gun away. His clothes were soaked. "Forget the lament. You're bloody lethal." With her wrists pinioned above her head, he frisked her thoroughly, including her backside and her legs. She tried to strike him. He yanked her to her feet.

At once, she shoved away from him and stumbled. Her hand came away with his blood, and he saw that she was finally afraid. She should be. The fact that he hadn't been braced for the blow to his head had probably kept him from getting his brains splattered. "Aye, you cracked my skull. By all rights, any other man would have killed you. How many more of you are there?"

"Five."

"Wrong answer." He checked the load in the pistol; *his* pistol. "You're on one camel. There must be only two of you." He shoved her toward the camp. "Move—"

"Don't . . . please." She flung herself into his arms. Her body was warm beneath her wet robes. "You can be rich if you choose. I'm wealthy. My brother is wealthy. You don't have to do this."

He could only stare down at her tangled hair as she babbled in English about ransoms, her words tinged with an Irish accent so faint it could almost pass for cultured.

In the distance, his camel chose that moment to bellow: a sound that resembled a tortuous scream. Magnified by the emptiness of the desert, it ricocheted against the rocks.

Whatever courage the girl had momentarily lost reappeared tenfold in its echo. He barely evaded her knee, and then only because he'd felt her body tense. She sidestepped him, but he caught her easily in a few steps.

"Let go!" Her feet flailing in the air, she kicked wildly at his legs. He saw the shadow of a woman slumped against the far rock wall the same instant the terrier in his arms did. "Oh, please"—her fingers tried to pry him loose—"something has happened to her."

There were tracks in the sand made by stout English boots, clearly female. No fire lit the clearing. He saw no packs, no food, nor any knapsack that might carry utensils, only one waterskin, all of which he glimpsed as he let go of the struggling woman in his arms.

The second woman was lying unconscious with her back to the wall, her pale cheek resting on her outstretched arm. She was also European. Her torn clothes bore the evidence of her flight these past days.

Watching as the dark-haired houri spoke to the woman, cradling the faintly blond head in her lap, he slowly approached.

And stopped.

Michael recognized the unconscious woman.

What Englishman in Egypt didn't know the aristocrat wife of the minister of public works? Though Michael had been present once or twice at a function that included Sir Christopher Donally, not in the three years since his arrival in Egypt had he personally had an occasion to be introduced to his archeologist wife. Like most men, he had admired the lady from afar. From his sources in Cairo, he'd known that Donally's sister had arrived in Egypt some months ago.

These two must have been on the caravan due at Donally's base camp.

The caravan he'd been going to meet.

Michael lifted his gaze—straight into the muzzle of another one of his own damn guns. "Shit!"

The girl reached one trembling hand to cock the revolver. "I swear . . . I'll shoot." The hand holding the weapon shook. Lady Alexandra's head rested protectively in her lap. "Go away and leave us alone."

"I can't do that, *amîri*."

He could have attempted to take the gun—and might have been killed for the effort. Hunched on his calves, Michael stayed where he was. His burnoose folded around his knees, the tagilmust fell forward off his shoulder. He braced one elbow on his knee and lay one hand across the other. "There was a second rider trailing you," he said, keeping his voice level. "I am not he. I am not your enemy, Miss Donally."

Her breath caught at the sound of her name. "Don't come near us. I mean it. How else would you know who we are if you're not one of them?"

Donally's sister hadn't been in Egypt long enough to know who he was. She probably wouldn't believe him anyway. Hell, he wasn't exactly pristine in appearance. "Like your brother, I, too, work for the khedive," he quietly said.

The muzzle wavered slightly, but now when their eyes held, he saw that she was confused. "Anyone c-could say that." She started to shake from the shock and her wet clothes. The gun was too heavy for her to hold steady. He patiently waited for exhaustion to overtake her.

"Ask me where in England I'm from," he said, to keep her talking.

"You speak perfect English." Her whisper had become strained. "Obviously you've l-lived abroad. That's c-common."

Her head held high, the dark tangled ebony of her hair framed her face. Michael felt tight and strange inside. She'd been through hell, and she still fought him like a tiger-cat. For a man who'd known little tenderness in his lifetime and who'd found only mystery in his emotions, he was deeply moved by her courage.

Unfortunately, it was a battle of wills that she would lose. But then, the Irish always were tougher than they looked.

She hung on a half hour longer than he'd expected.

* * *

Brianna opened her eyes and lay still for a time, listening. She was lying on her back inside a tent with both flaps raised. The breeze stirred the striped canvas walls of her shelter. She turned her head. A fire outside the tent had burned low, and the aroma of coffee mingled with the night. Someone had set a kettle and coffeepot atop the heat.

Brianna sat up, the blanket slipping to her waist. Her hair was a tangled mass. She wore only a thin cotton chemise, still damp from her trek through the pond. For a moment she sat unmoving and confused.

Someone had removed her outer clothing and laid a blanket over her.

She twisted to find Alex asleep beside her, her skirt and jacket torn and stained with dust and dried blood. The blanket had slipped to her side, and Brianna covered her. Alex mumbled something, her dreams unsettled, and Brianna realized her sister-in-law's restlessness must have been what awakened her. At once, her heart raced.

She moved to the tent's entrance to look out. They were camped against a pair of bent trees near the pool. The English-speaking nomad was nowhere in camp. Neither were any weapons that she could see after she'd rummaged through the packs a moment later. But there was food, and Brianna burned her hand lifting the kettle from the fire when she tried to see what was in it.

With a cry, she sucked at her finger. She saw a discarded tin plate and utensils. Grabbing the fork, she dipped it inside the kettle and speared what looked like a piece of meat. She carefully put her tongue to the food to test for heat, then shoved the piece in her mouth. The food was heaven. Delicious beyond anything she'd ever had. She ate, shoveling forkfuls into her mouth. She guessed the lizards in the rocks had made it into this pot with the rice.

Bent over the food, she didn't hear the movement until she looked up, her cheeks bulging with food, and saw her captor enter camp. Carrying a spade and rifle in one hand and a knapsack slung over the other, he slowed when he saw her.

Noting that she'd gone through his packs, he brought his eyes back to hers. With his other hand, he pulled his wickedly sharp knife from beneath his burnoose and stabbed it in the tree, just out of her reach. "Not that I would give you any ideas," he said. "I see that you already went through my bags."

Brianna swallowed the chunk of food in her mouth. The blanket had fallen around her hips, and conscious of his male presence, she brought it up to her shoulders. Coming to her feet, she told herself that if he'd wanted her dead, she would already be buried. He was taller than most men and broad of shoulder. He and his knife certainly looked capable of carrying out the deed. The growth of beard shadowing his face didn't hide the kind of decadent looks that a woman noticed. Not that it mattered. And she was appalled that she'd noticed it at all.

Her chin went up. "Where are my clothes?"

"Spread on the rocks to dry." His footsteps made no sound in the sand as he walked to where she was standing and dropped the shovel and pack. "They'll be dry sometime after the sun rises."

He slid a hairy waterskin off his shoulder. "Drink," he offered. "It will help with your hunger."

Reluctantly, Brianna placed her lips to the malleable opening. She tasted coffee and a faint hint of something like peppermint where his mouth had been before hers. Her eyes moved to his. Tipping the skin, she drank the warm milk inside—and nearly gagged.

"It's something to which you have to become accustomed," he said, his eyes faintly amused. "But it will give you back your strength."

She did as she was told, only because she'd oft heard that camel's milk was a life-giving meal. After she drank, she returned the skin to him and wiped her mouth with the back of her hand. That he had undressed her seemed only logical and of no concern to him at all. At least he'd left her with some modesty intact.

Tugging the blanket closer, she watched him move around the camp. Moonlight spread silvery ripples over the sand. "What do you intend to do with us?"

"Return you to your brother," he said without looking at her. He'd knelt and was pouring himself coffee.

"Christopher? You know where he is?"

The firelight caught in his eyes when he raised his gaze. She'd noticed that he seemed to have a perpetual glint of amusement when he looked at her, as if he knew the source of her discomfiture. As if he were used to the way women acted around him. "If you'd ridden south instead of north, you might have hit his camp." He looked at her from over the top of his cup. "Are you the one who shot that man out there?"

Without moving nearer to him, she felt her hands clasp the edges of the blanket. "I am an excellent shot. Much to my family's chagrin, I used to attend the country fairs back home." She hesitated as she felt her chest tighten. "Did you bury him?" Her gaze dropped to the spade.

"No one will accuse you of murder," he said softly, as if reading her mind. "I buried him because I don't want his trail leading back to us."

Brianna wasn't naive. She didn't dare trust him, and find herself sold to some slaver somewhere, or dead. She'd not come this far to throw herself on the mercy of any dangerous-looking stranger with smoked crystal for eyes and a demeanor that compared to his lethal knife. How did she even know that he wasn't the second man who'd been following them?

"Are you really English?"

"Born and bred." The succinct clip in his tone bore a faint hint of irony. "And here I am in the Sahara talking to a fellow countryman. Who would have thought?"

"Where did you attend school?"

Behind her, Alex made a noise, as something she was dreaming clearly became a nightmare. He sipped his coffee and looked at her consideringly, before tossing the remains of his cup into the sand and standing. "How long has she been like this?" he asked, reaching behind him for the skin that contained the camel's milk.

"She needs food."

Brianna also suspected that Lady Alexandra might be pregnant.

Alex was sitting up when the man ducked into the tent, fear evident in her sleepy gaze, until she saw Brianna. Alex looked at the man as he knelt, and she spoke to him in Arabic, to which he responded in kind, his deep voice strangely mesmerizing. She had a wound on her arm, and he checked the makeshift bandage, helping her to sit straight so he could give her the milk.

"The milk should help you, my lady."

Brushing the long end of the tagilmust off his cheek, Lady Alex looked up into the Bedouin's face. "Major Fallon?"

Brianna's gaze shot to the man's profile. He didn't seem surprised that Lady Alex would know him. "It's unfortunate that we could not have met under better circumstances, my lady."

A shadow seemed to cross Alex's face as the memory of the last few days ripped away the gauzy peace that had momentarily enveloped her. Dropping her gaze to her blood-splattered clothing, she wiped her hands over her torn blouse. Brianna, too, felt the terrible sense of desperation drive like a sword thrust into her lungs.

"I don't think that I'll ever close my eyes again and not remember," Alex whispered, raising her gaze to the major's face. "Are you as dangerous as they say?"

Major Fallon tipped her face into the light to look at the bruise. "I should be asking you that question, my lady."

Brianna could hear the seriousness in his voice, yet, there seemed to be a hint of deviltry in his words. "I think it is I who will have a headache to remember this meeting."

Wiping the strands of damp hair from her eyes, Brianna let her gaze stray to his unshaven profile as they continued to speak.

She'd heard his name mentioned more than once since her arrival in Egypt. Though she'd never actually met the British officer whom the khedive called El Tazor, the Barracuda, she'd not been immune to the lurid gossip in the ladies' parlor at the consulate.

Infamous for his war against the slave and hashish trade in Egypt, Major Fallon was a legend in some circles at the British consulate, heatedly despised by others. To the priggish, he was the man who openly cavorted with a native mistress.

Lady Alex's eyes did not leave Major Fallon's face, bent so near to her own. They seemed to have forgotten Brianna's presence as he dabbed at her mouth, like some nomadic Prince Charming, which was probably not far from the truth, considering who he was.

Brianna left the tent.

Clasping the blanket, she stood immobilized in the clearing before lifting her face to the cool desert breeze. A morass of glittery stars filled the velvety sky, the beauty a harsh contradiction to the horror it shielded. To the horror inside her.

Afraid to leave the comforting glow of the fire, but ashamed of that fear, Brianna sat on a pack and buried her chin in a blanket.

She and Alex had endured the terror of being chased by murderers. Even now, as she looked out over the desert, she still felt as if she were running for her life.

Behind her, she sensed rather than heard Major Fallon's approach. The dusty toe of his boot came into focus. She raised her head. He looked at her sitting near the fire. For a moment she sat frozen beneath the weight of his stare. Then she watched his gaze take in the surrounding area before he crouched in front of her and poured a cup of coffee.

"She has a fever." He handed Brianna the cup. "But she'll

sleep better now that she has something in her stomach. She's been shot."

"Yes, I know," Brianna said, her hands wrapped around the cup. "Lady Alexandra wanted photos for her book." For a long time she said nothing else, then suddenly the words were on her tongue, and she couldn't pull them back.

"We weren't in the camp when the raiders attacked," she explained, holding the cup in her hands. "We'd gone to find the Coptic temple that we'd glimpsed that day. The temple had never been documented. This was to have been a big opportunity for her. We'd left with one of the guides and a soldier to escort us." Brianna drank. "We were there longer than we should have been. We must have been less than a mile from the camp when the attack came."

She looked up to find Major Fallon's gaze intent on her face. "One always imagines how one would react when faced with danger. It wasn't how I'd ever expected. I could only stare in frozen horror as riders swarmed over the dunes from the west. I don't know how long we all sat on our camels. Maybe ten seconds, maybe five minutes. I don't know.

"Then the man—our guide—raised his gun and shot the soldier in the back of the head. He turned his gun on Lady Alexandra. But she'd pulled the camel around and the bullet hit the camel's head. The shot must have grazed her arm. When she went down, I thought the fall had killed her. When the man turned on me, I already had my revolver in my hand. I shot him." Her hands held the tin cup tightly. Much needed heat infused her. "After that . . ." Brianna raised her gaze. "I took the rifle the soldier had been carrying and managed to get Lady Alex from beneath the camel. We rode away on my camel. I stayed to the harder ground for a day. When we reached the sand, I dragged the canvas tent that I'd used to develop my photographs to hide our tracks. The sand shifts so fast, you see . . ." she said, her voice trailing away. "There were merchants' families traveling with us. Children."

"Who was the officer in charge of the detail, Miss Donally?"

Brianna remembered the dashing officer in charge with the sunburn on his nose. "Captain Pritchards."

His quiet oath focused her gaze on his. "You knew him?"

He was looking at her, or rather, through her, when she felt herself come into focus in his gaze. The contact brought breath into her lungs.

"You should sleep before we leave in a few hours."

She stood when he stood. He hesitated when her palm touched his forearm. She felt the coiled strength of him beneath her fingertips. "What about the other man who was trailing us?"

Major Fallon looked down at her hand before raising his gaze back to hers. She felt her pulse quicken. His expression was half indolent and half . . . something no decent woman should ever think about with a stranger. Brianna could feel it pulsing through her.

With a hot flush, she removed her hand and stepped away.

"The second man is no longer a threat, Miss Donally."

His footsteps made no sound in the soft sand as he walked fifty feet to a place at the wall to set up watch.

She'd heard no gunfire. But then, gunfire would carry for a long distance, and Major Fallon didn't seem the kind of man who would advertise his presence. Brianna remembered the lethal-looking knife.

Later, when she lay down to sleep, she tried to find comfort from her position on the sand. The tent remained open to the breeze. She smelled Turkish tobacco. Turning into the crook of her arm, she found the robed figure of Major Fallon. He sat against the stone wall, the rifle casually drawn against his knees. He was half facing the tent. The tip of a cigarette glowed orange as he inhaled. As if sensing her eyes on him, he turned his face, and she felt the strange impact of his gaze.

It was a long time before Morpheus claimed her in his arms.

Chapter 2

"**I** know that the captain was a friend, Major Fallon."
Halid al-Nahar's shadow lay over the perfectly
square hole painstakingly dug in the hardened earth. He'd
spoken the words in Arabic.

"What of the women and children who belonged to the
merchant families on that caravan?" Michael observed Halid
from over the tagilmust that covered his mouth and his nose.
"Miss Donally said there were many."

"We found only the men." Glancing up the horseshoe-
shaped berm behind them, Halid's fingers tightened on the
serviceable-looking talwar at his side. "The jackals uncov-
ered the mass grave, or Donally Pasha's men might have
missed it entirely."

"It would have taken hours to prepare such a pit." The
ground was hard. Inhospitable. The dry wadi bed fraught
with long-thorned fragments of dead Loranthus. "Why
spend the time to bury the men at all?"

And with every question, Michael wondered what had
gone so wrong that an armed escort could be ambushed,
where only two English women had survived against all
odds. Climbing the steep grade past a dead olive tree, he let

his eyes go across the barren landscape and waited for instinct to whisper into the silence. Out here, living or dying depended on seeing with more than his eyes. The site had already become known as the Well of the Dead. There was no well or water, though, the most numerous living inhabitants being the black flies thick in the air.

Donally's camp had been the caravan's destination. Tents of the workers, laying the telegraph, pocked the distant landscape like termite mounds. Thanks to Donally's efforts, modern technology would soon stretch from Cairo to this outer desert oasis.

Except a week ago, Donally's base camp had been forty miles southeast of this place. The thought stopped him cold. The caravan had been miles off-course.

"Who hires the guides, Halid?"

"Most probably the arrangements come from the chief of the general staff. Donally Pasha might know," he said mildly. "You could ask him, if he had not left here yesterday."

Michael turned. "Donally left? Where?"

Halid's shrug was as elegant as his clothes. The son of a wealthy sheikh, Halid savored the unlikely conviction that civilization sprouted from men who sported fashionable attire. Educated in England, he commanded the outpost near this oasis.

"I only know that when the caravan was overdue, he sent out patrols. After his men found this site, I am told that he went mad. He then gathered two rifles, a pistol, and supplies and headed to El-Musa."

"Not Cairo?" Staring across the sands, Michael no longer saw the swirling hot currents. "What would compel a man like Donally to go racing across the desert wasteland to a town where the reigning sheikh is a notorious hashish smuggler?"

"No man who works as hard as Donally Pasha does for the fellaheen can be a thief or murderer. I believe he has a reason."

"I want men sent to the outer oases to search for those

missing from this attack." Michael maneuvered downhill, his burnoose sailing outward with his pace. "Follow the old slave route—"

"It has been too long"—Halid caught up with Michael's long-legged stride—"even if the women did survive, everyone knows what befalls those the slavers bring to market."

Michael despised the didactic drivel that hovered over female chastity as if virtue alone elevated women to the status of sainthood, or the lack of it denied them. "Who can account for the intrepid compassion that weighs moral convenience above life? Give me justice, Halid. Not sanctimonious fervor."

"You are angry. This is not your fault."

"Captain Pritchards was carrying payroll currency that Donally was supposed to use to pay those workers out there. Currency that you are supposed to use to pay your own troops. Information about that shipment was classified, Halid. How many people knew? Think about what that means."

The implication was as far-reaching as the moon, too dangerous to ignore. How many other caravans had vanished carrying governmental stores and precious antiquities? Just enough that until now the attacks had looked random.

"Major . . ." Halid placed a restraining hand on Michael's arm, stopping him before they reached the other men. "Without proof, they will court-martial you if you so much as make an insinuating remark against any high public official."

"Spare me your Byronic version of decorum, Halid. You speak the Bedouin dialect. Your family lives in the desert. Find someone who might know someone's cousin or uncle. These raiders have to hide somewhere. The prodigal son needs to return and ask some questions."

A faint flush spread across Halid's face. "I think that you are a—" He waved an indignant hand about the air in front of Michael's nose. "What is a more descriptive word for the penis of a donkey?"

"The word is ass, Halid. A-S-S."

Unamused, Halid spat in the dirt. *"Wā hasratan*, God has afflicted you, O Acerbic One. It is fortunate for you that I am your friend, Englishman. Or you would have nothing left but your barren soul to rule."

Watching him swing onto his mount, Michael reached into his robe and pulled out the makings for a cigarette. "Wear blue," he called. "I wouldn't want your relatives to mistake you for an Englishman and shoot you."

Halid's arm shot up in a universal gesture that needed no interpretation. Staring moodily at the cigarette he'd rolled, Michael struck a match to the tip. His gaze went to the sky. The day had already turned to leaden gray, and he'd learned one thing since his arrival in Egypt. Out here in the desert, sanity was relative to the heat.

Discounting any excuse for his black mood, Michael knew he wasn't decent company for anyone. Besides, Halid no doubt noticed that the imposing effendi, lord of a million souls in his jurisdiction, had nearly lost his stomach back there at the pit.

Nor was he indifferent to Halid's words. Halid had erred if he didn't think he understood military bureaucracy. The military was no different in its moral perception of justice from any other establishment in Britain.

But this had become personal in a way he'd not expected.

The British captain buried in that mass grave had not only been his friend since Eton, but his colleague. Michael had served with Captain Pritchards in China before they'd both come to Egypt almost three years ago. He'd made a toast at Pritchards's wedding last year.

Michael drew deeply on his cigarette before tossing it in the sand. Mounting his camel, he went in search of the site foreman. Later, he interviewed the five men who had found the gravesite. The foreman then took him to Donally's tent, an hour away. No one questioned Michael's motives for asking to go there. Hospitality was as automatic to a man of his rank as it would have been to the sultan himself.

A striped awning stretched the length of the entrance where a table and chairs remained on a carpet overlooking a small pond. It was the first touch of greenery Michael had seen in months. Cautiously, he stepped through the entryway. The skirt of the tent was raised to let in the desert breezes. His gaze scanned the strewn cushions, the shelves filled with photos, books, and maps. A red carpet covered the desert floor. It was unbelievable that so bare a place could be made to look like a home.

"I will have your personal things brought in here, effendi," a servant said.

"No." He turned. "Where are Lady Alexandra and Miss Donally?"

The servant waved his hand over the sheet of heavy silk that divided the room. "They are asleep. They have not moved in hours."

Michael's gaze went to the screen. He stopped the foreman as he turned to leave. "Is someone attending to my mount?"

"Yes, effendi." He bowed slightly before he left.

The lamplighter, who also served as Donally's personal steward, sidled apologetically around the close quarters to light the paraffin lamps. Waiting for the servant to leave, Michael leaned over the maps on the desk. Dust had already settled over everything. Behind him, photographs lined the makeshift shelves. One picture caught his attention.

Drawn by some elemental response he couldn't name, Michael picked up the image of a man and woman atop a camel, his arm around her waist in a racy pose. Her face was turned adoringly toward his profile. In the background, seen through a gossamer halo of light, the shadows of an approaching eclipse stretched across the pyramids of Giza.

Compelled by a combination of interest and admiration for the photographer, he held the photograph nearer to the paraffin lamp. The photograph was arresting. Poetic in its contrasts of past and present, darkness and light. Michael switched his attention to the bottom of the frame, where

another photo was wedged inside. Edging it out, he found
that it was Alexandra Donally, wearing a veiled costume of a
belly dancer. The daughter of an earl, Donally's wife was an
interesting study in cultural diversity. Amused, Michael
shoved the photograph back into the frame. He again considered her husband and the questions his absence raised.

"The Donally Pasha's sister, she is a good image taker,
yes?"

Michael returned the frame to the shelf, the visual memory of the girl standing unflinchingly with a gun trained on
him predominant in his thoughts. "Miss Donally took all of
these?"

The servant tipped his head toward the photograph that
had been taken in Giza. "Lady Alexandra has been traveling
Egypt writing a book for the British Museum. You know her,
yes?"

By choice, Michael didn't walk the same social circles of
Egypt's anointed elite. Having had enough pomposity in his
life to last until his eternal leap into purgatory, he'd left Captain Pritchards to stoke the home fires of social fortitude.
Now, he regretted the neglect.

"Why did Donally go to El-Musa?" he asked.

"Donally Pasha was not himself, effendi. When he
returned from the gravesite, he was a man possessed. He
packed only a few of his belongings, took his rifle and pistols, and left."

"Alone? Over a hundred miles across the desert with no
guard?"

"You travel alone. What does it matter when numbers do
not protect a man? He speaks the language and has traveled
much."

Finding no logical argument, Michael dropped his gaze to
the photograph. Maybe Donally was no milquetoast Euro-
crat. If he possessed half the courage of his sister, then he
was a man who could survive hell.

Michael certainly appreciated his taste in photography.

"I will bring lamb stew." The servant bowed.

"That will be fine," he told the servant.

"I am Abdul," he said. "I will revisit this evening with dinner."

Returning his gaze to the loving pair in the photograph taken in Giza, Michael started to roll a cigarette before he caught himself. It wasn't smoking the Turkish tobacco that had stopped him. It was the craving that he refused to let control him—and something else that he hadn't felt in a long time as he looked at the photograph.

Lady Alexandra had been raised in the same elitist society that had surrounded him his whole life. That she had somehow escaped the narrow confines of her world intrigued him. That she'd married an Irish commoner impressed him.

Hell, Pritchards's death had unhinged him. The man the last ten years had shaped was not prone to either whimsy or regret. Michael lay on the cot, both feet rooted to the floor, a position he favored. With one hand behind his head, he closed his eyes. He never wanted to get too comfortable, as if staying in one place for too long would somehow grow on him. He was bone weary in every part of his body. He should be thinking about his plans to get back to Cairo. To hunting Donally down, if only to return the man's sister and his wife to him. A position that had fallen to him by virtue of default.

But for just a moment he would remain here.

He didn't awaken when Brianna approached that evening, as the sun had set and the air grew cold, with a blanket. She looked down at his unshaven features refined by the shadows, the dark smudge of his lashes resting on his cheek. Even in repose he exuded a vibrant, male vitality that contradicted the vulnerability she saw.

Lying on the cot, Major Fallon looked uncommonly long and lean, with broad shoulders that she remembered all too well when he'd fairly frisked her bones. His burnoose had fallen open, revealing the knife tucked in the crimson sash at his hip. His thighs were well formed beneath the once silky white *sirwal* trousers. They had ridden for three days in the dirt and the grit. They had ridden when she thought she could go no more, and he'd carried Alex when there had been no more strength for her to sit atop a camel.

Brianna covered him with the blanket. Then, turning, she started to extinguish the lamp beside the cot, and felt his fingers wrap around her wrist.

With a start, her gaze slammed directly into his.

His eyes, half lidded and astonishingly silver in the light, eased over her. He was still asleep, settled in the shadows of some dream.

Brianna held her hand still and returned his look, but for all of her talk about equality for women, and her emboldened demeanor, she still possessed more Victorian mores than she cared to admit. Michael Fallon made her nervous. And she was never nervous around men.

For the most part, members of the opposite gender annoyed her with their condescending nature and patronizing platitudes, and she'd never had a problem dismissing them. Except for Stephan. Her once betrothed.

There had been security in the predictability that she'd found with Stephan. Security that she'd never appreciated, and on more than one occasion taken for granted. At twenty-five, he was three years older than she, and studying to become a barrister, a crown jewel in England's justice system. She'd never loved anyone but him. They might have been married upon his graduation, except for one fatal flaw in her plans.

Stephan had wanted children and a wife who would make him a home in his perfectly respectable, sedate life. Yet, for all her dreams of being in love, not once had she looked upon Stephan Williams with anything more than a girlish adoration—which faded immeasurably compared to the curious intensity she felt when she looked upon Major Fallon.

A dangerous thrill ran through her.

Dangerous because she'd had her hands on him before and ached to do so again.

He pushed up on one elbow and looked around the tent. "What are you doing here?" His voice was raspy, awake now.

She raised a brow fractionally and her gaze dropped to the band of steel still holding her wrist. "Are you going to kiss me, Major? Or let me go?"

She'd seen the look in his eyes when he first touched her, and wondered now, as he awakened fully, who he'd been thinking about.

Their eyes held for a fraction longer before he looked around again as if to reaffirm his surroundings. "I've been asleep."

He released her. "For the whole day, it would seem, sir."

Her hair had come undone, and she tucked a wisp behind her ear. She'd given up trying to comb it out and had tied the mass off her face with a leather thong. "Where do you have to go, Major?" she asked readily. "Why don't you remove your boots and sleep?"

The tent flap opened and Christopher's servant entered. He stopped when he saw her standing beside the cot, and a smile lit his bearded countenance. "Sitt Donally, I am so glad that you are well. I did not get to see you when you arrived."

"Abdul." She took the wizened hands clasped in front of him. "It's good to see you as well."

He wore his white turban and a belted long-sleeve tunic that reached his knees. "If only your brother had waited another day before he left. You would not have known him, Sitt."

His voice was quiet, and afraid that Alex might be awake, Brianna turned to Fallon, who'd not moved from his position on the edge of the cot. "Abdul, please bring in his gear. He'll be sleeping here."

"But he asked that I not do so."

"Do it, Abdul," Fallon said tiredly, one eye squinted up at her. "And a bowl of water if you will. I need to wash."

"And to shave as well, Major." Brianna smiled after Abdul

scurried out. "Pity the poor woman you'd kiss tonight, other-wise."

A slow grin curved the edges of his mouth, a flash of white in the shadows of his face. "Are you always so bold with men, Miss Donally?"

"Only with those who have already seen me undressed. We've rather bypassed polite formalities, have we not, Major Fallon?"

She could tell by the wary look that came into his eyes that she wasn't at all what he'd expected. That was just fine with her. There was nothing worse than being predictable. Putting space between them, Brianna escaped the tent when Abdul entered with a tray of food.

Christopher's tent had been erected near a large pool of water. An enormous star hung low on the horizon. It was ironic that such stark beauty gave life to a barren plateau of sand. Some distance away, a boy herded bleating goats. Behind Brianna, the tent flap opened. Major Fallon's robed figure filled the opening. His gaze found her standing near the fire. Then she watched him take in the surrounding area.

He didn't like their neighbors; she could see that in the narrow look that came into his eyes. Turning her head, she tried to see what he saw. Did he think they were still being followed?

Abdul squeezed through the opening. "I have dinner pre-pared, Sitt. Shall I have food brought to her ladyship?"

"Only if she's awake. Where has the baggage that was brought in on my camel been stowed? I haven't found my camera."

"Come with me, Sitt."

Without a backward glance at Major Fallon, Brianna fol-lowed Abdul. She glimpsed a woman leaving the pond. "Why aren't some women veiled?" she asked as he led her around the larger tent to one in back.

"It is not uncommon among nomadic women to go unveiled." Abdul held back the flap and Brianna's heart leapt. She'd found her camera.

Nothing seemed broken in the trunk holding the photo chemicals, black cloth, and plates. She'd been carrying that trunk with her since the day she and Alex had left to photograph the temple. "You're from the desert, aren't you, Abdul? Doesn't that make you a nomad?"

"Pah!" His large black eyes rounded with insult. "I am the son of a merchant," he said, as if speaking to someone whom Allah had afflicted with feeble-mindedness. "I used to travel often from the cities to the oases to trade, and would be rich from the Damascus silk that my father sold had he not a problem with dice. Alas, I am now a steward. But your brother pays his staff well. That is good for me."

Abdul was also one of the few men she'd seen in this country who treated women with any respect. Not that her own countrymen behaved any better most of the time. She'd gotten to know Abdul in Cairo and was glad that he was here. Brianna lifted her camera.

"I will carry that, Sitt Donally."

"Take the trunk, please."

She set her camera outside as he dragged the trunk to her feet. Kneeling, she worked the knots out of the leather straps that bound the chest lid. "I'm lucky that I have anything left at all, I suppose."

"You are most fortunate that it was El Tazar who found you."

Still crouched, she braced an elbow on her knee. "How is it that you're so familiar with someone called the Barracuda, Abdul?"

"My cousin, he gives Fallon effendi information. The major, he allows my cousin to live another day. It is a simple trade."

"Simple?" She was appalled.

At which point he smiled. "The major could have left my foolish cousin to rot in the gaol last year." Abdul shrugged. "He did not."

She lifted the trunk lid. "No doubt extortion is an acceptable road to paradise."

He looked offended. "Show me a man without vice, missy, and I will show you a man who does not breathe."

Her attention was drawn to the top photograph in the pile. One of the few that came from the positives that had survived the massacre, only because she'd developed the plates, along with the others that she'd taken at the Coptic temple. It was the reason she and Alex had returned late to the caravan that fateful evening.

Leaning closer, Brianna pulled a photograph off the pile and held it to the light. The young man featured was posed with his rifle across his chest. She'd only known him as Selim. Wearing the loose-fitting, ankle-length garment and headdress of his people, he stood with Napoleonic fervor beside a camel. He'd befriended her over a meal of couscous, joking because men did not do the cooking. Yet, he had shown her how to prepare the meal. And now he was dead.

"Will her ladyship be all right?" Abdul asked after a moment.

Replacing the photographs, Brianna looked across the desert. If only Christopher had been here. Tension that had gripped her since the attack tightened. She worried about how she would get Alex back to Cairo. Aristocrats were inherently helpless by birth. It was natural that she felt protective of her sister-in-law, considering all they'd been through.

"You just find a way to get us back to Cairo. I don't know if Major Fallon will see us that far. I only know that I can't stay here."

"Do not worry, Sitt." His arms filled with her camera pod, Brianna watched him weave a path around the cooking fire, before dragging the trunk filled with her chemicals back inside the tent. She wasn't worried, she told herself.

Major Fallon was leaning with his back against a tree when she passed the corner of the tent. She didn't see him in the darkness until he spoke. "If you insist on walking around out here," he said, and she swung around, "I suggest that you go armed."

It piqued her that he'd startled her with such ease. Unfolding his arms, he stepped toward her. She dropped her gaze to his hand. "It's loaded." He handed her the revolver that he'd taken from her at the watchtower. "Vigilance is the way of life out here, Miss Donally. I'd hate to see that with everything you've survived, you end up getting yourself killed because of negligence."

The message of his warning was punctuated by the glimpse of two guards standing at the camp's edge. "Major Fallon?" She grabbed his forearm as he'd started to turn. "Thank you for everything that you've done. We would not be alive but for you."

The corners of his lips relaxed. "You're no quitter, Miss Donally. I'll give you that much."

"With five older brothers, if I'd have quit at anything, I'd have been trampled. One learns to survive."

His gaze went over her. They weren't separated by more than a hand's width between his arm and her shoulder. His tagilmust hung loose. "The beard bothers you, does it?"

"Excuse me?" Amusement lurked in his gray eyes as he watched her flustered response. The unexpected question had thrown her off her guard, and her heart did a ridiculous flutter in her chest.

"Did you want me to kiss you, Miss Donally?" he asked clearly, reading the look in her eyes, and remembering her comment in the tent.

"Don't be ridiculous. I don't know any woman who finds facial hair inviting, Major Fallon."

"Then you speak from experience?"

"You won't shock me." She crossed her arms beneath her breasts. "I've kissed many times."

"Aye, *amîri*." Brianna felt his gaze go down the front of her caftan, the part not covered by the dark robe. The part only he could see. And she wasn't wearing underclothing. "But how many were grown *men*?"

Her fingers thrummed her elbows, waiting for him to return his attention to her face. "Come to think of it"—she flashed him a cheeky smile—"only one. But I fear he spoiled me for life."

She dismissed him and walked back inside the tent.

Stroking the offending beard in question, Michael grinned appreciatively into the darkness. Miss Donally had a nice body.

"How do you do it, Brea?" Alex said for the fourth time that morning, listlessly stirring a fork around in her bowl.

"I don't think about it, my lady." Sitting on a carpet, legs crossed, Brianna continued to rub at the camera lens.

"I wish there was some way Christopher knew that we were alive. I can't bear to think what he's going through."

This was a conversation they'd had a hundred times in the two days since they arrived. No reassurances seemed to soothe Alex. She'd wept, argued, and slept, all in the hopeless human need to do battle with forces over which she had no control. Clean from her bath and wearing a dark red caftan, at least she was finally eating something. "Do you think Major Fallon will get us back to Cairo?" she asked.

Brianna looked up from beneath her caftan hood toward the pool where the subject of their conversation was bent over a small square mirror. A long rifle leaned against a date palm beside his burnoose. He'd ridden into the camp earlier and, after handing off the horse, walked straight past them to the pond. Her camera lay beside her, and her hands paused in their cleaning.

He'd tried to insult her last night by suggesting she'd never kissed a real man, only boys. Though the insult hadn't worked—*mostly* it hadn't worked—he'd had nerve to imply that a man's facial hair was a measurement of his masculinity.

Yet, that side of Major Fallon had caught her pleasantly by surprise, contrasting 180 degrees to the man who wielded a knife with ruthless proficiency.

To the man she watched shaving now.

He'd removed his shirt and turban. Brianna raised a cup

of tea to her mouth and took a drink. His hair was not nearly as black or as long as she'd expected. Indeed, it was cropped to his nape, thick and wavy at the top, shorter on the sides. His chest was tan, as if he spent a lot of time without his shirt. The defined, corded tendons and muscles of his shoulders were visible with each swipe of the razor.

Brianna knew she should have been appalled that two grown women would be observing a man performing so intimate an ablution as shaving. Except she wasn't finished looking. "Do you know him well, my lady?"

Alex turned her head. "Do I detect a hint of malcontent, Brea?"

Suddenly annoyed with herself, Brianna returned her attention to her camera, where she'd removed the outer box casing. "I think that I'm dissatisfied with the whole world order of things."

"You always are." Alex's voice seemed to smile. "I've seen Major Fallon at various functions since we've been in Egypt. But no one knows anything about him. Women have tried." Lady Alex studied her fork with an intensity borne of a new perception. "It's better they pant over him rather than my husband." She resumed eating. "Cairo pulls in quite a winter crowd. Fortunately, this is also the time of year when sites open for excavation and I spend most of my time out of town. I try to stay busy and not think about anything else."

All of which Brianna understood. God only knew that she'd made her fair share of mistakes to end up in Egypt in the first place, but the thrill of adventure had waned considerably since her arrival.

It didn't help that a derailed train had stranded them in an antiquated village for a week in September. Then there had been that dangerous altercation with their camel driver in October. As there was no notoriety in falling sacrifice to anyone's brutal passions, Brianna had actually drawn her pistol on the turbaned brigand who was supposed to have been their guard. Then there was the horrible event last week . . .

"Major Fallon was very disturbed when he'd heard that Captain Pritchards was the officer in charge of the caravan," Brianna said.

"The major was supposed to have been in charge of the caravan."

"I see." Brianna focused on the lens in her hands.

"Christopher didn't want me to make the trip," Alex quietly said. "You wouldn't be here now if not for me, Brea."

"I'm here because I choose to be, my lady." Finished cleaning her camera, she began to put it back together. Although the morning was crisp, the air was rapidly becoming hot. Within an hour they would have to return inside. "Does Christopher know about the baby?" She changed the subject.

"No." Alex dabbed the edge of her sleeve against her eye. "I'm thirty-two years old. Neither of us ever thought it possible."

"My lady—"

"Brea . . ." There was unexpected affection in Alex's tone. "Why do you remain so stubborn? You've always had permission to use my name."

Brianna respected her sister-in-law more than any other person in the world. Alex was everything that she struggled to be. Intelligent. Daring. Independent. She'd made people proud of her. "Be still, my heart." Brianna laughed. "Your real name? All ten of them?"

"You're such a fraud, sister-of-mine. And far more headstrong than you should be." Alex thrust her fork into her bowl and speared a piece of meat. "Did you know that this tastes almost as good as Major Fallon's chicken stew?"

"Truly, my lady"—the absurdity of the statement coming from someone so worldly hit Brianna—"did you see any chickens clucking about the watchtower?"

Alex's green eyes widened. Suddenly they were both laughing. Hysteria bubbled at the surface, but Brianna didn't care. They were raving lunatics in a hostile world. Heaven only knew their will to survive had been all that had stood between them and vanishing forever in the desert. Better to lose one's mind now. Instead, it was as if a safety valve had suddenly opened to let out the steam.

Alexandra lay back on the sand. "It hurts to laugh."

Brianna fell beside her and nearly on top of the pair of dusty boots that had suddenly appeared. Major Fallon was looking down at them. He no longer had a beard, and if he had been noteworthy before, he was devastating to her female psyche now. Brianna turned on her stomach. A woman could drown in eyes like his.

"Major Fallon." Alex struggled to her elbow. "We were just touting your culinary expertise."

"Your praise is obvious." If he felt insulted, it didn't show.

Beneath an open caftan that hung to his knees, his torso was bare save for the dark thatch of hair that narrowed and disappeared in the low waist of his baggy pants. In one hand he carried the long rifle. He knelt, bringing with him the scent of his shaving soap. Fine black hair shadowed his armpits.

"I'm glad to see that you've both recovered, *amîri*." His eyes seemed almost a caress on hers.

The feeling inside Brianna was so unexpected, she wondered what was wrong with her. "We Donallys are forged in iron, Major," she managed in the spirit of the moment.

"That's reassuring," he said, his voice silky dark. He stood. "Because I'll be needing your clothes. Tomorrow night we're riding back into hell."

Chapter 3

"It's never my luck that anything might be simple."
Alex wrinkled her nose. "Or that Major Fallon
couldn't have found clothes from a man who'd bathed
within the last year."

Brianna struggled with the binding around her breasts,
then slid a robe over her head. "I only hope he knows what
he's doing."

"My lady, are you prepared to leave?" Abdul said from
the other side of the screen after they'd finished dressing.

Brianna looked up to find Alex working the turban over
her head. A strand of Alex's hair, bleached honey by the sun,
had escaped captivity, and Brianna tucked it behind her ear.
She worried that Alex felt feverish. "Walk with stride in your
step, my lady."

Major Fallon entered the tent as they stepped out from
behind the partition. Earlier, he'd stopped to say something to the feminine versions of themselves, eating dinner
outside beneath the awning. Their disguises complete, people had to believe Brianna and Alexandra were still in
camp or Major Fallon's plan would fail. The night was
still.

The very image of a desert warrior, Major Fallon turned when Alex approached, and the front of the tent flap dropped as he stepped inside.

He'd been implicit in his instructions. Alex would leave first. She was dressed as one of Christopher's cooks.

"You'll be staying with the foreman's family for two days before the caravan leaves. Everything will be packed," he said, when he caught Lady Alex's gaze going over the photographs on the shelves.

"I'm sure you've seen to every detail, Major Fallon." Alex's reply was every bit that of a lady. "I'm not worried for myself, only for my husband."

"Five armed men from the outpost will be traveling with you. It will look like you're part of your husband's staff. If anyone is watching tonight, they will see me leaving with you and Miss Donally."

"I don't have to tell you to be careful." She held out her hand, and he brought it to his lips. "*Salaam aleikum*. Go in peace."

Bowed over her hand, he responded in kind. Abdul gave her a silver tea tray. Together they walked out of the tent.

Brianna remained where she'd been left as she watched Major Fallon observing Alex's departure. A skein of jealousy lifted her chin. The strength of it caught her by surprise. A single tallow lamp lit the cavernous space of her brother's desert abode. The plan was that she would wait thirty minutes. A guard would ride into camp, enter the tent, and she would ride out in his place.

Abdul had promised earlier that her photography equipment had already been packed. She didn't want to fret over something so frivolous. She shifted her thoughts. The way Major Fallon had looked with his robe off that morning came to mind as she found herself alone with him. Brianna caught him regarding her, his expression indolent. And her heart did that strange flutter that she didn't like.

His eyes went to the long winding cloth in her hands. She'd been unable to make the turban stay on her head. "I'm afraid my hair is not the sleek, glossy tresses of which legends are made." With one hand, she whirled her braid like a lasso. "I swear, I'm cutting it off when I return to Cairo."

"That would be a shame."

"Why?"

His soft leather boots making no sound on the carpet, he took the cloth from her hand. "I imagine it looks decent when brushed."

"Goodness, Major"—she flapped a hand in front of her face in a mock swoon as he stepped closer—"you have a poetic way with words."

He was taller than Christopher, who stood inches above most men. "Turn around."

"My mother's hair was blond and wavy," she said.

His hands worked the turban around her head with deft ease. Unsettled by the novelty of her sensual interest in him, she schooled her features, ignoring his warmth against her back. "Not one person in my family inherited anything from her except the predisposition for wavy hair. She was English. Her family disinherited her when she married Da."

Now if he'd been any other man, he'd have offered her condolences or sympathy and they might have diverted to a topic of dialogue. "British families are like that," he said.

He suddenly became more fascinating. "What horrible sin did you commit that your family would disown you? Or did you disown them?"

The dark look he slanted her told her that the topic wasn't up for discussion. Normally, she wasn't so easily cowed, but these weren't normal circumstances. Sizing up his mood, she elected to abstain from questioning him. Whatever softness might lie inside him was guarded and deep, and he had a way of closing himself off; except from Alex, she realized.

"As much of an aggravation as my family is, I love them very much," she said quietly. "Stand against one Donally and a person stands against all." Brushing her hands over the robe, she felt the push of her breasts against the tight bindings. She didn't know how she was going to manage the constriction all the way back to Cairo.

And that was when she felt it all over again, the sense of dread that kept dogging her. She was comforted to know that she and Major Fallon were allies, so to speak. He'd shared her outrage, had a personal connection to the victims, and she welcomed his ability to think rationally. "Will there be a cart to take Lady Alexandra into the village?" she asked. "I'm concerned about her walking."

"How far along is she?"

"I . . ." Brianna flushed hotly, and was glad he was hovering over her head and couldn't see her face. She didn't make the mistake of accidentally touching him, and kept her hands at her side.

"Surely someone who is never shocked isn't struck speechless?"

"I'm not speechless." Her nose was pressed to his chest as he tugged and looped the cloth around her head. "Nine, maybe ten weeks," she said. "A logical conclusion, considering she didn't know when we left Cairo. I mean, the last time she and my brother . . . they were together in Giza. They shared the same camel, all right?" She could feel his grin as she stumbled along making a fool of herself. "Are you sure this plan will work?"

He tipped her chin and looked down into her eyes. "My presence on that caravan will not make you any safer." He returned his attention to her turban. "In fact, it'll probably make you less safe. At least this way, if someone is out there watching us, they'll be following me."

As well as the two men outside, who were dressed up like women. They were setting an ambush. "Naturally that makes me feel more at ease. Who protects you?"

"I know what I'm doing, *amîri*."

Their faces were close as he worked the turban. So close she tasted the scent of peppermint on his breath, which was pleasant.

It occurred to her in her musings and admiration that he'd experienced worlds she'd only glimpsed in novels and photographs. He spoke the language, had acquired the mannerisms of the people, and hadn't seemed to fret that two proper English women had gawked at him while he shaved. Her gaze slid past his tanned throat to touch the firm square of his jaw and she focused on his slightly parted lips, which showed the edges of straight white teeth. Her feelings were potent because he'd kept her safe, and he was risking his life to continue to keep them safe. What woman wouldn't find that a weight on her emotions? It wasn't as if she were attracted to him. Completely, swooningly attracted, anyway.

She knew when he became aware of her eyes on his mouth. Her lashes lifted another notch, and she found herself staring into eyes the color of fine sterling. A smile was in his gaze and on his lips. Her mind had turned carnal. Curiosity more than anything kept her legs immobile.

"Stay with Abdul," he said, his voice laced with gentle humor. "I don't want to get back to Cairo and learn that you've been thrown into someone's harem."

"I'll do my best, Major," she said, her guilty thoughts making her response testy. "Though I have no idea how I'll possibly control my urge to fraternize. I mean, it's an awfully long trip."

His gaze slid over her lips. In the silver glitter of his eyes, she recognized the challenge that she'd thrown at him last night. Indeed, ever since she'd told him that she wasn't easily shocked, it seemed as if he went out of his way to shock her on purpose. Now that her ladyship wasn't present, he was behaving obnoxiously.

He splayed his chin. "I did wash and shave."

"Now you wish me to tell you if your kiss is memorable?" she brazened, unwilling to allow him to intimidate her.

A charged silence filled the empty space between them, forged on her part by recognition that unlike Stephan Williams, this man was not afraid of Christopher. The shock was exciting.

Dangerous.

Unexpected.

She knew she was insane to find him attractive, or to even think about involving herself with someone the khedive called the Barracuda. Yet, she'd discovered to her horror that she wanted him to kiss her.

"How old are you?" he suddenly asked.

"Excuse me?" Her head oddly dizzy, she only knew that she was old enough to kiss a man. "Twenty-two. In six months. Why?" She thought she'd heard an oath. "How old are you?"

"Much older than you are."

"How much?"

"Eleven years. A decade . . ."

Her eyes widened in mock horror. "Four thousand days, plus or minus a few weeks." She despised the implication that she was a child. More so now, because she was feeling her inexperience. Maybe it came from being the youngest in a family, and having to fight for every inch of respect she'd ever received. Or getting no respect at all. "Goodness, Major Fallon." Stepping away, she put the space of the desk between them. "I still would have been wearing pinafores when you were off doing . . . whatever it is boys who think they are men do."

He was leaning against the desk. "While you were wearing pinafores, I was fighting with Gordon in China."

"I see." Lord, how had they gotten to this point anyway? "I'm quite capable of making my mind up about men, Major."

"No doubt you are."

"It isn't as if I haven't seen enough pictures and statues in my lifetime to know what happens between a man and a woman. Christopher collects some of the most erotic eastern artwork I've ever seen." Finding new purpose for her turban, she raised the heavy cloth over her mouth. "It is only art, after all."

Major Fallon had not responded except to arch one brow.

"And here I was thinking, with the ten minutes we have left, we could have all-out lusty sex in the back room, just me and the desert breeze against your hot naked skin." Exuding potent sexuality, he leaned toward her. Brianna flushed to the roots of her dark hair. Only her blue eyes shone above the tagilmust. "Trust me, Miss Donally, I may be a cad, but I am somewhat discriminating about the women I choose to take to bed."

She laughed, rolling her eyes. The man had the morals of a camel. Not in her whole life had anyone ever spoken such candid filth to her. Her reaction was purely self-defense. "I happen to know that you have a mistress. So, you're quite safe from me and my cap."

He'd crossed his arms. His heavy sleeves covered his hands. "You mean Yasmeen?" He gave her a wicked smile that did not reach his eyes—a perfect sphinx version of his usual grin. If he was disconcerted that he was a familiar topic among the ladies at the consulate, it didn't show. "It seems that you have me at a disadvantage. I don't know anything about you. Except that you're a photographer."

"A very good one, too." She released her turbulent exhalation. How many people in her life actually knew her? "I like the sunrise and the way the air smells in the morning. I love roses. I miss the rain." She'd left her self-extolment a trifle seraphic, for she was also a member of the temperance society for city children. She'd marched in London with the ladies of suffrage, had seen the inside of more than one gaol, and, after having had her most recent publication banned in England, found herself exiled by her family to Egypt. Now, for someone who was supposedly in love with another man, she was experiencing myriad feelings that she didn't understand. "And I think that you have the most beautiful eyes I've ever seen," she finished by saying, and watched the mockery slide from his gaze. "They're not quite blue. They are . . ."

"Gray, ashen, stormy?"

"One might even say they're very nice to gaze into."

"And what do you say, Miss Donally?"

"I say that it's unfortunate you only want what you cannot have, Major." She'd seen the way he'd looked at Alex on more than one occasion. "But I suppose, wanting what you cannot have gives you a reason to remain angry with the world."

The silver gaze he fixed on her didn't waver, and where his formidable authority had lent him only certitude moments ago, she now glimpsed something else in his expression that defied description. It pleased her that the intrepid Major Fallon was human after all.

The sound of an approaching horse intruded. Her heart began to beat harder. Her body double had arrived and, at any moment, a servant would be walking into the tent to announce his arrival.

"I don't suppose I'm going to get that kiss after all?" She just had to be cocky. It was in her nature: when things got tough, she turned into an ass. Clearly not amused, Major Fallon pushed off the desk and walked to the cot, where he retrieved a rifle.

"You aren't going to shoot me, are you?"

"Now there's a thought that never crossed my mind."

The servant entered then, bringing the guard with him. Their places now exchanged, Brianna listened to the Arabic discourse. Excluded by virtue of her ignorance, she glanced briefly at Major Fallon. Her gaze traveled from the tensile strength of his hands as he spoke, the rifle gripped in his hand, before rising to his profile, and found him watching her.

For an instant he held her pinned with his gaze, and she forgot the other men in the tent. "The moon is waning, so the light won't help you much tonight." His voice was sure, in control again, having relegated whatever had just passed between them someplace else. "Abdul will be waiting for you when you get to the edge of the camp. The gray horse is yours," he added. "The Arabian is valuable and probably once belonged to some sheikh before she ended up where she did. You might find that you want to keep the mare."

The horse was hers by right of conquest. She'd not asked about it before because she was unsure of her emotions on the topic. The Arabian was one of two horses that Major Fallon had been unwilling to leave at the watchtower oasis. There was something undefined about a man who had no qualms in killing another human being, yet, at great risk to himself, could bring an animal and two strangers three days across hostile territory. Knowing it wasn't over yet brought a shock of tears to her eyes. She was suddenly afraid for him.

He lifted her tagilmust as it fell lose. "I meant what I said about maintaining your disguise and staying with Abdul."

"The last thing I want is for you to worry, Major." Then, knowing she might never see him again, Brianna did something she knew she shouldn't have. *Goodbye.* She stepped forward on the balls of her feet and kissed him.

Without waiting for the drumming in her ears to subside, she pulled away to leave, only to meet the steel of his hand at her nape. Her gaze snapped up to his. He'd gathered the cloth of her turban and tipped her head back, his silky eyes sliding to her mouth. Her lashes drifted shut the moment his mouth touched hers, feather light at first, inquiringly, as if tasting her, testing her response with solicitous efficiency. Altering his lips subtly, he touched his tongue to the full curve of her bottom lip, and the kiss that had been chaste before began to burn with a strange exotic blue flame fanned by her racing heart.

He slipped his tongue between her lips to dance with hers, the cadence between them becoming a beat, a velvet rhythm that only they heard in the dimness of the night.

She had no idea what her body was doing. Sliding her hands to his neck, she rose on her tiptoes, seeking more of the heat that enveloped her. He held the rifle gripped in one hand; his other had drifted down the curve of her back. Heat branded her flesh. She became lost and alive at once, every sense heightened to the body pressed against hers, singularly aware of the contrast between the softer burnoose he wore and the hardened male beneath. Then, as if by mutual assent, the kiss deepened and flared into something more primal.

There was no gentleness in his possession as he deliberately dragged her into a sensual tide so elemental that any sense to protest was swept away by the roaring in her veins and her groan of surrender. Or did that sound come from him?

She basked in the sensual feast, teetering on the brink of a shivery exhalation, a miasmic bog clouding her brain, when reality intruded. Some noise outside the tent reminded them where they were.

She opened her eyes to find him looking down at her. Her lips throbbed. Beneath her fingertips she could feel the slight bump on his head where Alex had hit him with the rifle. She withdrew her arms.

His thumb eased over her bottom lip. "This will make for interesting gossip," he said, referring to the other men in the tent.

A keen sense of horror fell over her. Although there was no amusement in his eyes, neither was there admiration or devotion. Where she had lost control, it was clear that he had not. This was probably regular fare for him, the ladies throwing themselves into his arms. He'd only answered her challenge, granting what she'd sought. Major Fallon was no innocent, and she'd stumbled before the dance had even begun.

He held out the rifle. "If you ride past Abdul in the darkness, one of my men will let you know."

She reattached the tagilmust with trembling fingers before she took the rifle. "Will your man whistle, Major?"

"Would you come if he did? Somehow I doubt obedience is in your nature, *amîri*. Or that you're as easy as you seem."

Brianna had no problem affecting the walk of a man, especially in her agitated state. Men had surrounded her entire life, men who could have invented the masculine persona for Irish arrogance—none of whom held a candle to the very British but not so very proper Major Michael Fallon.

Michael motioned two men standing near the fire to follow Brianna. Without taking his eyes off the pale figure riding like the wind away from him, he reached beneath his burnoose and withdrew his tin of peppermints. "Is everything ready?" he asked the guard behind him.

"Yes, effendi," the man said, then added, "Do not worry. The men will die before they allow anything to happen to Donally Pasha's family."

The idea was not comforting. But if he was to have any hope of protecting them, he had to do his job. The caravan leaving from Baharia was over seventy strong. Many were on their annual pilgrimage. Brianna and Lady Alexandra would be with Donally's returning staff and the physician who would accompany her back.

Out of the corner of his eye Michael caught the movement of the two men dressed in Lady Alexandra's and Brianna's clothes. They were talking. He thanked God for thick veils and darkness. The two made the homeliest pair he'd ever seen. But they knew how to use a knife, and that's why he'd brought them from the outpost.

Michael dropped the tent flap. The faint scent of roses lingered in the tent. A vase of flowers bloomed on the shelves next to the photographs. He held the photograph that Brianna had taken in Giza to the single lamp.

Brianna had not read him as thoroughly as she'd thought. He'd been drawn to Lady Alexandra's softness and grace. She reminded him of home, of something gentler than he was. But where he was wont to treat the one like a lady, the other made him believe in sin. Some women just knew how to move in their bodies, some innate sense that had little to do with experience and everything to do with lack of inhibition. Brianna Donally was earthy and sensual, a rarity in the western world. He hadn't expected it from Little-Miss-Spoiled-For-Life-With-One-Kiss.

Smiling to himself, Michael pulled the cork from the wine bottle sitting on the desk. He'd leave the moment Abdul returned with word that the two women were safe. He had business to take care of in El-Musa. And with any luck, he'd be followed all the way there.

Chapter 4

❦

There was no dawn like the sunrise that rose over the desert. Crisp air still cool from the night swept off the Nile. Michael eyed the mix of mud houses, minarets, and spires that swam in the misty morning light. It seemed that there was something symbolic in the gentle beauty that illuminated the countryside. El-Musa was not an unattractive town, but Sheikh Omar, the governor-mayor of the region, was rotten to his core. He and the governor-mayor were old enemies. Educated in England, the sheikh was related to the khedive, and in usual political proviso, Michael had been warned after past altercations to leave Omar alone. But somewhere here, Michael was sure he would find Donally.

After waiting for his men to secure the perimeter of the house, Michael signaled them to move inside the courtyard. The neo-Byzantine palace belonging to the sheikh stood at the edge of the town, pale pink in the sunrise. Inside, a muddle of English and opulent native furnishings cluttered every room. Michael's boots made a *tap-tap* sound on the stone floor as he waded through a cluster of irate servants.

Michael motioned to one of his men to remain on the stairway. A rifle braced across his chest like an Egyptian

47

demigod, he halted the progression of panicked servants on their way to the upper level. Without breaking stride, Michael entered the master's chambers, a cavernous room embellished by tapestries, colored marble, and gilt furniture. Red silken drapery the color of blood fluttered in the morning breeze.

Cocking the hammer on his revolver, Michael nudged the sleeping sheikh with the dusty toe of his boot. "Rise and shine, my lord."

Black hair, black-eyed, his beard streaked with gray, the man on the cushions stirred. A naked girl spooned against him opened her eyes and screamed. Sheikh Omar shot straight up.

"Major Fallon!" He slid back against the plush wall of pillows. "Allah save me from crazy Englishmen. Not again."

"Where is he?"

"If you mean that madman Donally, he was here when I returned last night from the camel mart, mind you, on legitimate business."

Michael smiled. "I haven't slept for days, Omar. Do you want to know why I haven't slept?"

"You do not want to kill me, Major."

"Oh, but there you are mistaken. Donally may be willing to overlook certain iniquities to do his job, but I am not."

"He is not above compromise. Have you not noticed? The railroad went through here two years ago. There is no peace for him unless he makes peace with the men upon whose lands he builds upon. My men guard the tracks and the telegraph. Down the river it is someone else."

"Yet, he thinks that you had something to do with the attacks on a particular caravan some weeks ago. Why would he think that, Omar? Why would he ride alone seven days across the desert to reach you?"

Michael spoke over his shoulder. "I want every man present checked for a tattoo. A scarab on the wrist." Omar tried to rise, but Michael trapped him with a boot. "Three men ambushed me on my way here. Unfortunately, two didn't survive. But the one who did brought me straight to you. He had a tattoo." Michael checked both Omar's arms. "A scarab—an insect resembling a cockroach."

"I swear you'll pay for this insult, Fallon."

"Why would Donally think you're involved?"

"He assumed that I knew about the gold because I've occasionally handled stolen goods taken in raids. But that was years ago. Go ask him. He is down the corridor."

"Then who did know about the gold Pritchards was carrying?"

"I don't know. I swear, I am a man of honor."

Michael eased off the revolver hammer. "You feed opium to children, Omar. Where is the honor in that?" He turned to the two men standing behind him. "Stay with him until I return."

"You said that you had a witness . . . the attack on you—"

"I lied. No one survived." Michael shoved the gun into his sash. "My men are very proficient at what they do, Omar."

"Bastard!" Omar spat at Michael's legs.

"Consider us even for the beating your men gave me in El-Kharga last month. Next time I may just accidentally shoot you."

"Laugh, Fallon. I swear it will be your last time. You will pay for this outrage."

The hallway opened to the breeze. Doors were thrown wide to the veranda. It was early morning, and a girl was watering the hanging baskets of bougainvillea. The fragrance stirred the air, mixing with heavy perfume. Ducking beneath the archway at the end of the hall, Michael entered a room. His gaze went to the massive English-style bed. A woman's slim form clearly visible beneath a sheet moved slightly. Michael stripped the cover from her. She shot up with a startled squeal, her body barely hidden beneath a curtain of jet hair. She was naked, her dusky skin unblemished. Glass beads jangled on her ankles.

Michael dropped the coverlet. She looked all of fourteen. "I was told Donally Pasha was here." He spoke in Arabic.

Her head shook. "My sheikh would whip me if he knew that the effendi did not sleep here, for all that he knew I existed." Murmuring, she lifted dark liquid eyes to his. "Please say nothing."

Bloody Christ, Omar was low-brow refuse, Michael thought. Having the greatest respect for Donally's self-control, he wondered how the Irishman had not put a bullet into Omar's head. The sheikhdoms were a medieval frontier answering to no constabulary, or a government that had little ability to enforce its own laws. And Michael had his bloody hands tied. How many young girls had he brought back from the markets to families that ended up selling them into sexual slavery or killing them?

"Where is Donally Pasha now?"

"He comes here last night and threatens to kill my master. It takes many men to pull him away." The girl shrugged toward the veranda. "I think he is going after slavers in Kharga."

Michael left through the veranda. His gaze went over the stone courtyard below where a donkey was pulling a cart of manure. He dropped to the courtyard below and crossed the grounds to the stables.

The man bent over the bay mare wore a black tunic fastened at the waist with a broad leather belt that carried a curved dagger. A tarboosh and turban covered his head. His face, tanned by the sun, contrasted with the stark blue of his eyes as he straightened and met Michael's gaze over the saddle. The first thing Michael noticed, other than the gun pointed at his head, was that Donally's eyes were the same summer blue as Brianna's.

A growth of black stubble had rendered Michael uncivilized, but Donally looked feral. "Fallon." The single harsh word kept Michael's hands from the revolver in his belt or the knife in his sash.

They regarded each other, marking the passage of time since they'd last seen one another. When had it been? Last year at Captain Pritchards's wedding? Donally swung into the saddle of the Arab mare he'd saddled, his hands clenching the reins as he brought the horse around, the pistol still in his hand. "Move out of my way."

Michael had never heard an accent in Donally's voice before. That he did so now told him the man was close to the edge and dangerous. "I've already sent men to Kharga," Michael said. "Your wife and sister were not among those who might have been taken. They're alive, Donally."

The hammer clicked. "So help me, Fallon. Don't bloody tempt me."

"They're traveling with Abdul, a platoon of guards, a physician, and your servants, and are on their way to Cairo as we speak."

Something changed in Donally's harsh features. "What are you talking about?" The gun in his hand wavered. He pulled it back, appeared etched from stone as he struggled for composure.

"Your wife and sister weren't in the camp when the attack came. They survived. And what they want most at this moment is to see you."

Brianna didn't know how long she'd lain in the sand on her back, staring at the sky like a slug in hibernation. Her long dark braid remained hidden beneath her turban. She had yet to feel her feet and derriere. For eight days the caravan had wound over the molten sand like a slow-moving river—and for every one of those eight days, she had ridden Matilda, the racing camel from hell.

Lying beside her, looking like some green-eyed jinn behind the cloth of her own turban, Alex groaned. "Tomorrow we should reach Cairo."

"What missies need is liniment and a soft bed." Abdul chuckled, standing above them. "Of which neither are here."

"Thank you, Abdul. I shall add your advice to my tome of medical miracles." Brianna struggled to her elbow. Will you unpack Lady Alexandra's blankets and bring them to the tent?"

Cooking fires dotted the landscape. Brianna's stomach growled. That was one more thing she was going to have to do. Help Abdul cook, because she'd taken it upon herself to be useful. She collapsed back onto the sand. The early morning sky was hazy and unpleasant. "Do you think Major Fallon's plan worked?" she asked. It was a topic they'd both avoided.

"I think the major can take care of himself." Alex stood and brushed the sand off her hands.

"Christopher can too, my lady." Brianna's voice was quiet.

"I know." Alex's worried gaze paused on Brianna, then abruptly she turned and stumbled through the sand up the hill. Brianna watched her. She turned away, digging her hand in the sand, her own frustration, which had been boiling all week, brought to the surface. Major Fallon was no unseasoned youth, as Stephan had been.

He'd put his tongue in her mouth and shattered every virginal stereotype she'd ever held about men.

Her whole body hummed.

Brianna rarely dwelled on men. She had no divine drive to be anyone's wife, no maternal calling pealing bells over her head. Being the youngest in a family of five domineering older brothers had given her the impetus to make her own way. She was her own woman.

Yet never had she been subjected to such a powerful undercurrent of electricity as when he'd kissed her, which attuned her to her body in ways she'd never felt before. She'd experienced that undercurrent the first time in the pool at the oasis. She felt it again when her body leaned into his.

So had he.

And there had been a moment when Major Fallon kissed her when she wanted to taste more than his lips. To run her hands down his body. He'd had a hard body beneath those robes.

With a start, Brianna forced her attention back to the task at hand. Brushing the sand off her lap, she stood and scanned for Abdul. Her gaze stopped on the corral where her Arab mare had been penned. A man was watching her. Above his tagilmust his black gaze locked briefly on hers before he turned abruptly away.

"We are finished here, Sitt." Abdul was suddenly beside her. "Do you need help moving your camera?"

"Who is that man standing near my horse? Do you know?"

Abdul glimpsed the topic of her query. "I had to run that one away once from your mare." He spat in the sand. "He claims that he is a horse trader."

The young man was gone when Brianna reached the corral of horses. Drawing nearer to where he'd been standing, she tented a hand over her eyes. The wind was gathering force. Her mare whickered restlessly.

"You aren't so evil, are you, princess?" she murmured, her hands going over the mare's long gray mane.

A gust of wind blew sand across the dozing caravan, and shielding her eyes, Brianna turned her face away. A hazy red luminescence radiated from the northeast. "What is it?" She was breathless when she joined Abdul and Alex outside the tent. Transfixed, Brianna watched the sky darken.

"They call it the *sheytàn*—Devil Wind." Abdul's long white robes were flapping in the wind. "It is the *simoon*."

It looked like a monstrous fire. "How long before it reaches us?"

"A quarter hour, maybe."

Riders suddenly appeared like a shimmering mirage running in front of the reddish glow, and Brianna froze. A dozen men on horses and camels were coming toward them at a gallop. One was riding a white racing camel, and her heart picked up pace.

Beside her, Alex took a step. The riders approached.

A small cry emanated from Alex's throat, and before Brianna could catch her, Alex had gathered her robes in her fist. Half running, half falling, she slid down the dune, toward the riders. A black horse suddenly separated from the group, and soon the dark-clad rider swung from the saddle and was on his feet, sweeping Alex into his arms.

Christopher.

Brianna's feet carried her down the dune before she stopped. Alex's arms were around Christopher's neck and her feet off the ground as he wrapped her in his arms, kissing her lips, her hair, her face. Christopher had always been omnipotent in her eyes, invincible, but now seemed only too human as he held his wife.

"Go, Sitt Donally," Abdul said from behind her. "He is your family, too. Bring him back here."

But she didn't run into her brother's protective arms. She didn't belong in that intimate circle. She looked past her brother, directly into Major Fallon's eyes. Sporting a rough beard, he sat atop the white camel, his rifle lying casually across his knees. Brianna saw rather than heard him give a command to his men. They rode past her. The air was growing increasingly hotter. Brianna hadn't realized how far she was from camp.

Major Fallon stopped in front of her, his arm braced across his thigh. "I suggest that you find shelter, Miss Donally."

Her gaze shot to Christopher and Alex.

"Don't worry about them, *amîri*. They'll be all right."

"Did your plan work?" Her voice was quiet. "You're still alive."

"It worked."

Holding one hand over her turban, she turned as he rode past and into camp. Brianna scrabbled back up the hill and ran to help Abdul take down the tent. All around the caravan, people were doing the same. Somewhere, she could hear Major Fallon's voice carry above the wind. Camels stretched out their long swanlike necks to the ground and closed their eyes. The heat continued to rise like the mouth of a hot oven. Brianna saw her mare pacing the corral and ran across the camp. In the chaos, she could hear Christopher calling her name. The horse reared when Brianna grabbed onto the mane, desperate to get the mare to kneel as the others had done. The sky continued to darken with violent, swirling particles of sand. She'd never seen anything so powerful as the darkness that was bearing down on them, and fought with the panicked horse until strong arms suddenly came around her.

"Get back! Major Fallon took the reins" His hand went over the mare's nose and mane. He spoke gently, making a clicking noise with his tongue. Brianna watched the horse kneel. He secured a cloth over the mare's eyes and nose, then reached for her, and caught a jolt of electricity. It arced from his hands, and her eyes shot to his. "We have to get down," he yelled against her ear.

Brianna's gaze swung to the sky. A heavy blanket went over her as Major Fallon took her down into the sand beside the mare.

Her ragged breathing was the only sound in the narrow tomb in which she'd found herself enclosed. "I can't breathe," she whispered in panic.

"You can." Major Fallon's breath ruffled the loose tendrils of hair on her cheek. One of his legs lay over hers to still her panicked movement. "Unless you try to get out of here."

She put a hand between them. "I need a knife. Give me a knife."

He pulled back to look at her. "And have you bleed all over me?"

"I don't want to kill myself. I need to cut my bindings." She shoved against the hard ridge of his belly. "You're too damn close!"

The low sound of his answering laughter filled the narrow space between them. "Unfortunately, we're both going to have to live with that," he said, his voice growing louder above the wind. "I would urge you to be still."

The moaning, howling wind struck them. Brianna covered

her ears and pressed her face against his chest. Michael was conscious of his arms surrounding her in an attempt to keep some of the terror at bay, fitting the softer curves of her body against the harder angles of his. A length of her hair had shaken loose from the turban.

"I swear, I don't cry," she said. "I don't jump at bogeymen in the dark. I don't faint—"

"I'm not accusing you of being weak."

"Yes, you are." She wiped a sleeve on her nose and pulled back to look up at him in accusation.

Michael found himself staring into the most extraordinary liquid-blue eyes he'd ever seen. Her musk filled the enclosed space, no doubt along with his. He shouldn't have been tantalized, he told himself.

"I can feel it." She laughed. "You're being nice."

His eyes dropped to her mouth. Annoyed with the extent of his growing arousal, he removed the knife from his hip. "Do you really want your bindings cut?"

"With that horrible thing? Are you insane?"

He stabbed the knife into the sand to anchor the blanket at his head. "You're going to have to stop squirming."

"I hope Abdul covered my photography equipment."

"You'll probably have to remember where it was and dig it out."

Alarmed, her gaze lifted. "How long do one of these . . . these *simoons* last?"

"Days."

"Days!" she gasped. "We'll die of starvation." Then she saw that he was laughing. Her eyes narrowed to slits. "Truly, Major, you are *such* a bore." Her body relaxed a little as she seemed to compose herself. "You can let go of me."

He complied, and she lay on her back and looked up at him. With her head wrapped in the turban, her Mona Lisa expression in place, she looked astonishingly serene in the dim light. Distracted by the length of dark hair that had fallen from her turban, he propped his head on his hand.

"Maybe a few hours," he rectified.

"Do you think Christopher and Alex are all right?"

"What do you think?"

She propped herself on her elbow and peered up at him in the meager light. "I think a few hours is certainly more than the ten minutes we had the last time we were alone, Major."

The shadow accentuated the provocative curve of her waist. He saw her mouth slide into a smile. "Don't sound so smug, Miss Donally."

"And here I was thinking we could have lusty sex—just me and the desert *simoon* against your hot naked skin."

His eyes narrowed. Little-Miss-Spoiled-For-Life-With-One-Kiss thought she was safe.

She lay back, content to think herself immune from him. "You mean, you don't want to strip naked?" she asked.

His mouth moved into a slow grin. He put his palm on her stomach. "I think it's the best damn idea you've had yet."

She slapped his hand away.

Michael liked that he'd shocked her, and put his hand back, lower this time. He had no idea why anger shot through him, except Miss Donally in all of her restless naiveté was like a shot of brandy in his veins. He bloody should have let her brother deal with her welfare. But when he'd seen her fighting to save the mare's life, he'd only thought of saving hers. Maybe he'd wanted to be tucked in for the day with Miss Donally and her nice body.

"You know what else I think?" he said. "You like the thought of getting your hands dirty. It excites you."

She didn't remove his hand, and he was tempted to move it lower. To move his lips against her slim throat. He tried to stay detached. Except there wasn't anything detached about his erection.

"I'm not going to kiss you," he said, reading the look in her eyes. "If that's what you're wanting."

"Don't disgust me." This time she did remove his hand. "You happen to smell like a camel."

"And you don't?" He laughed. His mouth lowered unwillingly, grazing hers. He could make quick work of her bindings, and had an urge to fill his hands with her breasts.

"And your face is rough," she rasped, her eyes betraying her awareness of him.

"You don't like that, do you?" His thumb slid across her bottom lip. "Have you ever come, Miss Donally?"

"Let go of me!"

He grabbed her hand and pressed it into his other hand, grappling easily with her slim form. He could see her pulse racing at the base of her neck. "What if I don't?" He'd also pinned her with his leg, and if he fought with her anymore, they were liable to lose their shelter.

He thought about opening her mouth and sucking on her tongue like a sweet orange, and might have if she hadn't looked so eager for him to do something. Then his hand was on her again, moving lower over her abdomen.

"You get coy with me, and you'll lose more than you bargained for, Miss Donally."

"You don't make me nervous." Her voice was breathy. Challenging.

Did she think he wouldn't take her dare? With her gaze on his, he could read her defiance and something far more potent conveyed in her expressive eyes, acting like an aphrodisiac. "Not even now?"

Her lips parted slightly. She let him trail his palm over the concave curve of her belly.

Christ, he shouldn't be doing this, he told himself.

He should have stopped there.

He should have stopped before his palm came in contact with the hot juncture between her thighs. He should have removed his hand, but he was suddenly touching her in the most intimate way.

"Have you ever had a lover?" he asked, the intensity in his tone deceptively casual. He pulled back to look into her face.

Her lips were compressed. That *something* he'd seen in

her thick-lashed eyes earlier had wobbled into something else. He wondered if a man had ever touched her at all.

He withdrew his hand. "I've never had patience for a practiced flirt, Miss Donally." His voice was a quiet rasp, more anger-filled at himself for not acting smarter, for putting them both in a place neither had any business delving. "And I never play for anything halfway."

The weighted silence was soon replaced by the moaning wind outside their enclosed sanctuary.

Finally, she turned away from him. "Why did you come back?" she asked. "We'll be in Cairo soon."

Michael didn't answer her.

But his gaze fell on the pale curve of her profile, the bow of her full mouth, the gentle wing of an eyebrow. Not for the first time did he find himself staring at her, caught by her beauty, wanting to see into her eyes. In disgust, he turned his head and stared at the blanket. He was an idiot.

Chapter 5

As was her habit since her return to Cairo, Brianna rode out of the stables before the sun crested the lake. She wore her usual tanned boots and split skirt, her shirt opened at the throat. The air cooled her skin.

Her brother's home overlooked the most beautiful garden this side of the Nile. Beyond the stone walls of his residency, morning mist rose above the lake, one of many throughout the city. All around her, in the tall mimosa trees and sycamores, the world had come to life, and as Brianna left the grounds, birdsong greeted her. Here there was no sense of being shut in, and Brianna loved her freedom.

Western women seldom rode where she went. Though her eyes didn't miss the squalor beneath the ancient magnificence, she loved the city with its eastern flavor and strange language. Cairo appealed to her in a way her own culture with its mode of sterility did not. Maybe that's why she enjoyed photography as much as she did. She had the ability to capture life in its rawest form.

Brianna's Arab mare clip-clopped along the narrow stone streets as she rode this morning to the hot baths. By the time she and her groom returned to the house, the sun had already climbed past the horizon. She doffed the last of her dingy clothes and, slipping her arms into her wrapper, walked outside her bedroom to stand against the granite balustrade that overlooked the lake.

The entire house smelled overwhelmingly of roses and heliotrope since her return, as she'd been deluged with flowers, her room awash in floral tributes from civil servants and military personnel she'd met at the consulate before leaving Cairo with Alex. Cairo's colorful social world was a young woman's dream. But she'd found herself restless and bored by what she'd once found fascinating among the men she met at the consulate.

She had thought of little else but Major Fallon since she'd awakened after the *simoon* and found him gone. She had discovered through some digging that he worked at the ministry.

Behind her, she heard her bedroom door open and listened to the soft pad of footsteps approach. She turned to see her maid. "Mum, will ye be wantin' breakfast up here or in the dining room?" Except for her warm brown eyes, everything about Gracie was as old as the earth. She wore a net over ash curls, a pale apron over a gray dress. She'd looked old when Brianna was three, and hadn't seemed to age a year since.

"I'll dine downstairs, Gracie."

"Ye should not be getting out of bed at such early hours, mum. It's been barely two weeks since your return. You've not gained back the weight you lost."

Brianna leaned her head against the mass of a flowering creeper that clothed one of the marble pillars in scented lilac. "And you worry overmuch." She walked back into her room. "I have work to do today."

"Will ye be going to the consulate with your brother?" Gracie set out her gown.

"Christopher told me to stay home." Brianna slipped out of her wrapper and stood in her chemise and corset. "He said Major Fallon was facing a disciplinary hearing today."

According to the charges launched against him, he'd put a gun to the head of a royal family member and tried to kill him. Brianna wasn't surprised that Major Fallon was capable of inciting an international incident, but she'd also gathered from Christopher's comments that Sheikh Omar was a brutal man.

"Lift your arms, mum." Gracie slid a petticoat over Brianna's head, followed by her gown. "The major has taken over Captain Pritchards's duties at the ministry, which means he'll be staying in Cairo."

Brianna dropped quietly onto the pillowed bench in front of her looking glass. "Do you know that he will be staying for a fact?"

Her maid picked up a brush. "It helps that I share tea every morning with Miss Amelia. She is Lady Bess's parlor maid, and her bein' married to the consul general himself. Lady Bess is hoping to pair one of her daughters with Major Fallon for the upcoming picnic."

Rolling her eyes, Brianna adjusted the décolletage on her bodice. Servants had an intelligen network that rivaled the British government. "Lady Bess's daughter isn't even twenty. He won't do it."

Gracie brushed out Brianna's thick hair. "Most of us think he won't do it for other reasons. It's all very hush-hush in the servants' ranks at the consulate. But he spends much of his time in the old quarter."

Gracie twisted Brianna's thick hair into a French roll.

Brianna lifted her gaze to the mirror. The peacock blue bodice accentuated her eyes. She lacked no illusions about her beauty. Only that she had not been as worldly as she thought she was.

A hairpin tumbled to the floor. Brianna twisted around on the bench and, taking the brush from Gracie, turned her hands over in hers. Gracie's once beautiful hands had gone arthritic years ago and looked swollen.

"Gracie, what are you doing? I don't expect you to be up at dawn to tend to me every day. I can brush out my own hair."

Gracie snatched away her hands and retrieved the brush. "You don't be worryin' none about me. I've been tendin' to ye since you were a wee brat in swaddlin'. I'll be tendin' to your own babes one day."

"Very well, Gracie." Brianna turned to face the looking glass. "But may we please change the subject?"

"I'm sorry, dear. But it's truly hard not to partake in the talk, when Major Fallon is all that is the topic these days since he brought you and her ladyship out of the desert alive."

Indeed, the gossip mill had run on all ongs until Brianna was sick to death of the subject.

After Gracie finished with her toilette, Brianna gathered her collection of photographs from her darkroom. She went downstairs to the dining room, where the light was best this time of the day. She laid each photograph on the dining room table. Yesterday, she'd started cataloging and labeling her work for the book she and Alex were working on—especially since her sister-in-law had been so ill since their return. To Brianna's dismay, she'd discovered that half of her older photographs were ruined beyond repair.

She'd not anticipated what heat did to fragile items that were not properly stored. Added to the photographs she'd lost in the attack, she was acutely aware that she did not have enough for Alex's documentation.

Brianna had not told Alex the news yet.

And had decided that she wouldn't. She'd just fix the problem.

Alex deserved better than her failure. In a profession wrought with peer jealousy, no one labored harder for so little recognition than her sister-in-law did. She deserved to win a professional accolade every now and then, and this book had been a professional coup. For her as well.

Working on the book had given her legitimacy in a career that had caused her nothing but social castigation since the moment she'd discovered soup kitchens and suffrage. But life had a way of veering left when least expected, then crashing into a wall.

Since her return to Cairo, Brianna sought only to regain

her place in her life. She visited the suks and resumed teaching twice a week at the American mission. She'd begun to take photographs again. Nothing had changed, yet everything looked different. Not even Stephan had trespassed in the places that Major Fallon had gone in her thoughts.

It wasn't enough that in a moment of vulnerability she'd kissed him in open-mouthed abandon. No, his presence had been indelibly printed into her head like some photographic masterpiece. She fantasized about him almost every night, imagining what it would be like to have his hands all over her the way he'd touched her that day beneath the blanket. The implied promise of his action rooted deep in her imagination until it began to spill over into her sleep, and she knew that neither hard work nor a busy schedule would cure her deep down restlessness.

The closest she'd ever come to wanting an affair with any man had been with her former betrothed. She'd been in love with him, after all. But Stephan was a true gentleman to the core of his principled being. He'd been scandalized at the idea of "ruining" her.

On the other hand, Major Fallon had no moral reticence against ruining her. He probably figured she deserved it for throwing herself at him. But then, she wasn't attracted to him because he was a gentleman, and she didn't care if he considered her less than a lady.

What she had in her mind certainly didn't make her one.

"Coffee, Sitt Donally?"

Startling her out of her revelry, Abdul bowed beside her. "Your favorite, Sitt."

Steam rose from the warm liquid, a contrast to the chill in the air. "Please." Smiling up at him, she accepted her cup.

The special ground drink was her favorite beverage this time of year. Water never touched a grain of this special blend; instead, milk was served boiling over the beans. Brianna called it her white-coffee drink; a beverage she could only appreciate before the weather grew hot again.

"We have not seen much of you," he said. "You have been

out of the house before dawn every morning. I think no one can keep up with you."

Another white-clad servant entered, bearing a breakfast tray set for one. "Is my brother not attending his meal? I didn't think he had to be at the consulate until later."

"He left an hour ago. Her ladyship is still abed. Would you care to join her this morning?"

"How is she feeling?"

Abdul shook his head. "Very poorly, Sitt."

"How is my brother faring through all of this?"

Abdul shook his head again. "I think that he does not entirely understand . . . the heightened sensitivity that accompanies one's delicate state. It is a balance of patience and fortitude, Sitt."

Brianna laughed at Abdul's apt description, glad that she was living on the other side of the sprawling marble residence. She would rather chew glass than have a baby. She shivered at the thought. "Let her sleep, Abdul. I have work to do this afternoon. It's already past ten."

With the flick of his wrist, Abdul motioned the servant to lay out her breakfast. "I have ordered the cooks to prepare your favorite meal today. As you call it, Eggs Benedict."

"Truly?" Brianna smiled up at him. "I think that you are trying to fatten me up, Abdul."

"You are gaining your weight back most nicely," he said, and returned to take his place at the end of the table.

Brianna sipped her coffee. The dining room was open to the garden, and she glanced over her cup as a burst of cool fragrant air billowed the sheer draperies. The breeze stirred her photographs.

"Abdul?" She looked at him over her cup. "Did my brother say what time the hearing at the consulate began?"

"Perhaps you will have better luck seeing the Fallon effendi at the picnic next week, Sitt."

Brianna set down her cup with a *clink*. "Am I so transparent?"

"Yes, missy."

Abdul continued to stand in the doorway with his hands clasped behind him like a sentinel carved from salt. Brianna fidgeted with her napkin. "You've lived here longer than I have," she said after a moment. "Are hearings of this nature common?"

"This is not the first hearing for Major Fallon, if that is what you are asking. I believe this will be his fourth in three years."

"Fourth? Is he that unpopular?"

"Among a certain sect, I would say that he is."

A servant entered from the opposite doorway. "You have a visitor, Sitt." He bowed over her with a silver tray. "A gentleman."

Turning the card in her hand, she read the inscription. "Charles Cross," she said.

He was the short golden Adonis who worked for Alex at the museum. Brianna saw him on a regular basis, but he'd rarely come to the house. Men just didn't venture into the hallowed halls of her brother's sanctum, especially since Christopher had a way of intimidating the most stalwart of her suitors. "He must be here to see Lady Alexandra."

Mr. Cross stood in the entryway. "Miss Donally." His face lit up when he saw her. "I ask that you forgive my impertinence at this hour—"

"I'm not going to send you away." She approached him. "But I'm afraid her ladyship still isn't receiving visitors. I'll take the flowers to her. Is this call about something at the museum?"

"I came to see you, Miss Donally." His awkward gaze touched two vases of roses and an arrangement of lilies sitting on a table beside the door. "These flowers are yours."

"Oh." She accepted the flowers, and smiled warmly. "Thank you. They're beautiful."

Charles Cross was one of those colorless English gentlemen that she liked wholeheartedly on principle. He was not part of the insular sect. He wore spectacles and behaved with the bookish intensity of one who'd made neatness and subservience a virtue. She had no idea why, of all the women in Cairo to choose from, he liked *her*. She failed neatness and was the least subservient person alive.

Maybe she'd become his friend because he'd reminded her of Stephan. Plus she generally had a soft heart for outcasts. But she'd also seen him feed the stray cats out back of the museum. She liked him for that alone. "Have you eaten?" she inquired.

The invitation seemed to relax him. "I thought perhaps we could take a ride in the park and talk about the book you're working on. I've found the research documents that you asked me for yesterday. Maybe we could have tea at the consulate and talk . . . perhaps."

"Perfect!" Her work forgotten, Brianna held the spray of flowers to her nose. "I'll join you."

Without a word to the uniformed guard who stood outside the consulate chambers, Michael stopped at the desk to retrieve his pith helmet. Sheikh Omar stood with his assemblage of bodyguards, talking to the undersecretary, his dark eyes triumphant as they slid over Michael.

His boots making a *clip-clip* sound on the polished wooden floor didn't slow as Michael passed the flamboyant retinue.

He wasn't surprised that Omar had filed the grievance against him. They'd danced these steps before. The sheikh could rot as far as he was concerned. His job didn't rest on his popularity with the European consortium that seemed to have descended on Cairo in the last decade, especially since the opening of the Suez Canal last year. The British did not rule Egypt. Not yet, anyway.

Michael worked for the khedive in a diplomatic exchange, and ultimately the foreign secretary's office in London. In mutual government cooperation between the two respective countries, and because the khedive was interested in securing British bank money, Michael's job had come about as Egypt attempted to push out of the dark ages. Banishing slavery and seeking to end the lucrative hashish trade had been the first sign of the khedive's goodwill. The push, Michael soon realized, was more show than any serious desire to end either practice. He had become disillusioned with the fight. Slavery was too ingrained in the culture. Over the past year, his job had turned into one of eternal police-man as one caravan after another was plundered. His only goal now was to find those responsible for Captain Pritchards's murder, for in doing that he knew he would also find the men responsible for the murders of countless others.

His white pith helmet tucked beneath his arm, Michael took the stairs. The consulate was crowded, as usual. He slowed and finally came to a halt. The current Public Works minister was awaiting his descent. Standing with his elbow on the newel post, Sir Christopher Donally wore a tailored white linen suit and a loosely knotted green tie.

Michael let no man fight his battles. But he recognized what Donally was doing for him by being here today.

"Sheikh Omar and his bodyguards went upstairs a few moments ago." Donally's gaze lifted to the landing. "But then, there were only four of them. So I thought I'd give the situation another five minutes."

"You left your military calling too soon."

"I heeded my calling," Donally replied. "I'm finished."

"The Crimean, Tangier, India. You were seriously wounded in 'fifty-eight."

"You've investigated me." Donally didn't seem too pleased.

Michael's mouth turned up at one corner. "I've done my best."

"Would you care for a drink?"

They walked into a room off the parlor. In the corner, two men in uniform lounged over a game of chess. A cloud of cigarette smoke hovered in the room, and Michael regretted that he had not brought along his tin of peppermints.

Donally took coffee from the servant. Michael waited for brandy.

"You've investigated me. Why?" Donally asked.

"Prudence."

The servant returned with a snifter of brandy.

"And what did your prudence unearth?"

Michael peered at Donally over the lip of his glass. Brianna's brother had earned himself more than a reputation as a hard-nosed administrator. "You're an excellent civil engineer. Egypt's illustrious khedive practically created the Department of Public Works just to give you a place in his ministry."

Michael hadn't been surprised that someone with Donally's aptitude for disagreeing with public policy had managed to antagonize most of his European neighbors, but he had been surprised to learn how revered he was among the local fellaheen. If Michael didn't know anything else about the man, that alone gave him cause to respect the Irishman. As well as trust him.

"Your wife is an honorary professor in archeology and is currently authoring a book documenting the Coptic history in Egypt."

Donally raised a brow and listened patiently as Michael detailed other aspects of his life.

"You came to Egypt to escape the clutches of your powerful father-in-law and the scandal that ensued after you married his daughter."

"Aristocracy is overrated."

Michael braced an elbow on the mantel. A gilded framed mirror hung above the fireplace. "A sentiment your sister shares."

"My sister is a fervent devotee to social reform."

"It must run in the family."

Donally didn't reply. After a moment, he drank his coffee. "I hope I've been removed from your list of suspects?"

Michael could see the adjoining parlor reflected in the mirror. From someplace in the low din of noise surrounding him, he registered a familiar voice. "You have been." He turned toward the parlor.

Lady Bess was greeting a couple across the hall. As he watched, Michael was vaguely aware that Donally had struck up a conversation with the two men who'd been playing chess and had now joined him at the fireplace. But Michael wasn't listening. Everything inside him had come to a standstill.

Brianna Donally stood with her back to him. He was so accustomed to her in voluminous robes, the shock to his system of seeing her in a form-fitting gown jolted him. Her dark upswept hair had been only half tamed beneath a pert hat with a feather that swept her chin. His gaze easing down the formidable length of pearl buttons at her spine, he knew in that moment why her name had become a topic among the men who gathered in salons over their brandy and cigars. Her cerulean skirts accentuating the deep curve of her waist flared at the hips, and he was aware of a keen sense of anticipation as she turned. The cup she'd raised to her lips froze as her gaze slammed into his—the contact so powerful it was like a physical force against him.

Her eyes dropped down the length of him. Khaki breeches and a tailored uniform jacket topped off his uniform, his leather knee boots giving him more height. Yet, for all of his civilized appearance, beneath his formal facade there was nothing civil inside him as his gaze went over her face, her breasts, her stomach, traveling lower as he remembered the itch of his fingers to touch the wet heat between her thighs. She radiated warmth and fairly vibrated with sexual appeal.

It was there in the feminine curves of her body, the animation that gave her garments life, the tilt of her full lips. Sipping from his glass, his mouth curved into an appreciative grin as she boldly let him look his fill, only the slight tremble in her hand hinting that it was no accident that she'd found him here.

He admired that about her. Her determination. Her willingness to pursue what she wanted. He'd been pleased by her recovery from the ordeal she'd suffered. Except, she was out of her element with him—even if she didn't know it, he did. She had no idea the hole she was digging for herself, and he wasn't a saint who would deny himself forever.

Then her provocative gaze casually touched the man standing next to him, who Michael now realized was taking in more than her presence. And as if seeing her brother for the first time, she choked on the tea.

Nearly spewing into the cup, she whirled back to her companion, who had been talking to her about one of the oil paintings on the wall. A faint smile cornered Michael's lips—until Donally turned to look at him, his blue eyes like chips of ice.

The two men who had joined him earlier were gone. He'd not only been oblivious to their departure, but had been caught flagrantly undressing this man's sister. His mind contained carnal thoughts, and Donally had read it in his eyes, as well as the lack of apology in his stance. Brianna was a big girl. If she wanted to play with the big boys, who was he to play Saint Michael?

"If you will excuse me, Major Fallon," Donally said.

With no change in his expression, Michael turned to the mirror, a quiet oath on his lips. Finishing off the brandy, he watched the Irishman make a straight line toward his sister.

"Would you care for more coffee?" Charles Cross asked.

Brianna automatically handed him her empty cup. Her shoulders had tensed. She turned to the watercolor he had been admiring, breathing evenly, knowing Christopher was on his way toward her.

How could she have been so blind as not to see her own brother standing next to Major Fallon? She gritted her teeth. "You know a lot about lighting and colors," she commented inanely, observing the mist-shrouded spires that dotted the landscape as if it were a Monet. Leaning closer, she saw that she was looking at a temple, and realized why Mr. Cross was so intent on the watercolor.

"It's a Coptic temple," he said. "I wanted you to see it. As I told you, I've an interest in research myself. I would very much like to go with you the next time you do a camera shoot."

Brianna looked at him. Charles Cross had been considerate to her all morning. He'd not deserved her inattentiveness. She turned to tell him as much, but he was looking over her shoulder, a subtle shift of light in his eyes. Then a commotion on the stairway caught her attention.

The consul general had conveniently waylaid Christopher at the bottom of the stairway. The visiting dignitary, the khedive's cousin, ablaze with jewels, stood beside them, sufficiently bored in a circle of men who seemed to vie for his attention. Yet, as if sensing her interest, he shifted his gaze and found her in the crowd. This man had filed the complaint against Major Fallon. A chill went down her spine.

Brianna promptly turned her back to him.

"I assume that you'll be going home with your brother?" Mr. Cross handed her cup back to a footman.

She sensed Christopher nearby. Poor Mr. Cross wilted. Used to the reaction, she was annoyed that her whole family seemed intent on destroying her social life. "We'll talk on Thursday," she said to him. "I'm looking forward to reading the research books."

"I will have them ready." He bowed over her gloved hand. "Sir Christopher," he said, nervously greeting her brother.

Together she and Christopher observed Charles Cross's departure before turning to face each other. "I have a meeting to attend," he said.

Her brother had never referred to the time she'd spent beneath the blanket with Major Fallon during the sandstorm. But she knew he'd seen it, and it was between them now. Brianna's chin lifted. She was sick to death of being made to feel shame when she hadn't even done anything.

Yet.

"I won't be long," he said. "I'll see you home afterward."

With that edict, her mouth flattened. She watched him walk up the stairs, and waited until he was out of sight before crossing the corridor into the other room.

The place was empty.

Her hand went to her hip. Unlike the other rooms in the consulate, this one was darkly paneled and filled with oil paintings. The place smelled of tobacco. How could she have missed Major Fallon's departure?

It didn't help that she was acutely aware of her boorish behavior when it came to this man. "Bloody hell."

"Such language for a lady."

Brianna spun around toward the masculine voice. Major Fallon leaned with deceptive laziness, his strong arms crossed, almost behind the door. She'd passed him coming into the room. It was also clear that he'd been waiting for her.

"Miss Donally." He inclined his head.

She straightened her shoulders, and felt the pull of her fitted jacket against her breasts. "Major."

The air fairly crackled with electricity.

She couldn't be near him without experiencing a whole range of agitated emotions. His eyes told her she was foolhardy for coming in here. They told her other things as well. Things no true gentleman would ever allow a lady to see.

A nervous laugh escaped her. "I wanted to see you. I mean, I'd heard that you'd tried to shoot a sheikh in the head and thought to lend you my support." She set her hands on the back of a chair. "That kind of discussion probably occurs a lot in your line of business."

The corners of his mouth lifted a fraction. "I usually don't waste energy on discussion first. But sometimes I find it necessary to engage an opponent's intentions."

"You left without saying good-bye," she said quietly.

"I thought the understanding we'd reached said more than enough."

I never play for anything halfway, Miss Donally.

"Maybe you didn't say enough," she said.

She felt his attention on her. "Are you sure that you really want to go there, Brianna?"

She looked past his sensuous mouth to his silver eyes. Brianna knew she was dancing a perilous waltz, as if she'd danced to this music all of her life. She was caught by the novelty that he wasn't the least intimidated by her. His eyes still on her, he deliberately shut the door, his gaze instantly enclosing her in a familiar sense of intimacy. The challenge, though unspoken, was there as he approached. He was the only man she'd ever met who shared the same aptitude as her for social disobedience.

Confident that she had given him the opening he needed, she was conscious of the warm sense of being in his presence. He looked well. "How have you been, Major Fallon? Busy, I'm sure."

"Only somewhat less bored than you. Would you like me to give you an accounting of your daily itinerary these past weeks? Ending with your ride over here today with the young, quixotic Mr. Cross?"

She took offense that he might think her dull. "Mr. Cross isn't quixotic. He's merely kind. Harmless."

"No man is harmless," he scoffed.

"Are you referring to yourself?"

"I'm not one of your beaux, Brianna." His voice was almost gentle. "And what you have on your mind is a very bad idea."

"Maybe I'm not looking for a beau."

She hated that his gaze caught the subtle shift of her hands as she pressed one over the other to keep them from trembling.

His silvery eyes lifted to hers. His features could have been hewn from granite. "There's not a whole lot in my future that would interest an indelible romantic. But don't think I'm not tempted." He lowered his voice. "If I thought you knew what the *hell* you were doing."

Her mouth opened. Right before her eyes her prince had turned back into an obstinate toad, and she couldn't think of a single adequate word that would refute his comment. She'd finally gotten the nerve to throw herself into the fire, and he was leaving her to burn.

"You are *such* a hypocrite, Major Fallon," she whispered.

"Am I?" His teeth flashed predatory white.

"Maybe you're the true flirt here."

"You're dangerous, Miss Donally." He took a deliberate step around the chair, then pressed his hands to each edge, trapping her. "If you come near me again, it won't be conversation we'll be having against a chair. Or a wall, or maybe even the floor."

He was absolutely crass, and she laughed, taking care not to avoid his eyes, intending once and for all to banish any thought from his mind that she was a child. "Maybe I'm no more interested in conversation than you are, Major." She'd forced the breathless words to sound casual. But there was nothing casual about her intent.

Their gazes tangled, locked, and turned hot. Her lungs felt restrained by her corset, unable to inhale. She forgot where they were. Forgot that her brother was upstairs and that someone could step into the room at any moment. His hands remained on the chair's edge at her back, his fingers long and tanned, his broad shoulders blocking the window. Neither moved as his gaze lowered to her mouth, and the whole world faded to the desire that stormed his eyes, that imprinted itself on her lips, to the one possibility that he would kiss her.

"So you think you want to be my lover?" His tone was deceptively casual.

Her heart raced in panic. Or was she caught by that secret thrill of discovery that someone would enter the room? She felt six years old again when she'd stood dressed in a chemise at the pond out back of her house and let Frankie Carre, the seven-year-old son of a neighbor, see her. Her mother had caught her and sent her to her room without dinner. But it had not removed the wicked thrill of doing something forbidden.

What did it mean to be a man's lover?

"Are you afraid, Major?" The words were a question, but her tone was a dare. No less the challenge that he'd once thrown at her.

He seemed to contemplate her with a steely-eyed glance, as if to assess not only her, but himself in her eyes. One would think it was commonplace for a woman to throw herself at him, and she didn't understand his hesitation. Any more than she understand her own motivation to do what she shouldn't even be thinking about doing.

"I'm not afraid," he mused, "but you should be. Nothing stays secret in Cairo for long, *amîri*."

He'd just put a step between them when a feminine voice hailed from the doorway. "Major Fallon?" It was the consul general's wife.

Brianna felt the surge of blood rush through her veins.

"There you are," Lady Bess said when he turned to politely greet her. "I thought that I saw you earlier." Trussed in copper-colored taffeta that matched the color of her hair, she extended her hand to him. "We've seen so little of you since your return."

Grateful for the interruption, Brianna walked to the window behind her, hoping the effort would allow her a moment to compose herself, to cool her flushed face. Others entered the room.

Or maybe they'd been there the whole time and she'd not noticed. The thought made her realize how careless she was.

"I wanted to tell you that you received a letter from England," Lady Bess said. "I don't know why it was sent to the consulate. I forwarded it to your office this morning."

"Thank you."

"Will you be attending the picnic next week at the palace?"

"If I'm back in town."

His deep words fell over Brianna. She turned to look at him.

"Of course," Lady Bess said. "I had forgotten. You're escorting our dear Mrs. Pritchards to Alexandria tomorrow. Such a terrible tragedy." Lady Bess's blue eyes fell on Brianna with discreet curiosity. "Miss Donally," she said. "I see that Mr. Cross left."

"He had to get back to the museum."

Lady Bess smiled up at Major Fallon. "If you wish to find anything in Cairo, ask Mr. Cross. He and my husband share a passion for antiquities and good wine. You will of course come to the function," she said, attempting to bring Major Fallon back into the conversation. "It should be nice for a change to relax and enjoy the company of the young ladies here. Don't you agree?"

"I imagine the possibilities are endless this time of year." Seemingly amused, his gaze met Brianna's over Lady Bess's head. "If you'll both excuse me, I need to prepare for my trip to Alexandria in the morn. Miss Donally . . ." His eyes touched hers with promise. "Lady Bess . . ."

After Major Fallon left, Lady Bess chatted a little longer before excusing herself and returning to the parlor. Brianna walked to the long window overlooking the drive and pulled back the heavy velvet draperies. Major Fallon had just mounted a spirited bay. Gripping the reins with a gloved hand, he swung the horse around and raised his gaze to the long window where she stood—as if he'd known that she'd be there—the small turn of his mouth his only concession to her presence. Brianna stared back, making no outward show that her pulse raced and that they had just agreed to become lovers.

Fallon was arrogant and annoying, and positively the most exciting man she'd ever met. Not that she hadn't met enough men in her life.

But there was something about him that drew her into his flame. Heaven help her, when she stepped into his smoky gaze, she burned.

Michael slammed the door to his apartment and walked past the front room into his private chambers, where he pulled at the buttons on his uniform. Outside the window overlooking the narrow streets—similar to a thousand others that meandered through Cairo—noise rumbled through the walls. He pulled out the makings for a cigarette from a drawer, dipped beneath the arched doorway into his office and opened the glass doors in the back. Still working his hands around the tobacco, he leaned a hip against the iron rail. Donally's marble palace—as he termed the luxury—sat across the narrow lake. Michael had spent every day at dawn the past few weeks watching the sun rise over that house. Sitting amidst a garden paradise on a jut of well-protected land, the residence once belonged to a powerful Mogul bey.

Michael had been astonished that Donally had come to his defense against Omar, which rendered his current circumstances a sudden dilemma. He was unused to facing his conscience, or waging war on his lust. Both were usually manageable. The problem now was that he liked the entire family, down to the retinue of loyal servants. There was something refreshing and intriguing about a family willing to defy the mores of the time and stand outside the protected club and sport society that made up Cairo's elite. Nor had he ever met anyone who embodied romantic fantasy with courage and a complete disregard for prudence as Brianna Donally managed to do with a single glance of her tilted-blue eyes.

He wanted to press her against the wall and bury himself in all that life force that seemed to glow around her like sunlight.

"Aye." He attempted to rub the fatigue of the past few days from his eyes. He *was* insane if he let her wrap him in her romantic fantasy. What she wanted from him had nothing to do with love.

So why did he balk?

Turning back into his office, Michael walked to the bedroom. He sat on the edge of the bed, his uniform jacket hanging open as he leaned forward to find a match from the drawer in the nightstand.

He'd never noticed how neatly partitioned and tidy his private space was. Unlike the boxed clutter of his office, which contained floor to ceiling files of his work, his bedroom was nondescript, bare of memorabilia, bare of extravagances, and empty of his presence. He kept little of his life or his work in his living space. The walls were limestone pale, the furniture inexpensive, and today the noise from outside on the streets was intrusive.

Little of who he'd once been had survived the bloody wars in China. Indeed, the man the khedive had labeled El Tazor was not the man who had left England in disgrace twelve years ago.

He remembered a time when he did belong somewhere, when he'd hunted London's clubs and the Season's circuit of marriageable young ladies. As the third son of an old aristocratic family, he'd never been expected to take over the reins of the family fortune. He'd fallen in love and dreamed of all the things an idealistic fool dreamed when he was twenty and naive. Before his father taught him that societal comportment and appearance were thicker than blood. Thicker than a son's heart, and more important than the world he'd tried to build for himself.

In the end, Michael had learned that the only person he could truly count on in this life was himself, and with his emancipation came the satisfaction of a job well done. Some would say that he'd excelled in the art of violence. In the twelve years that he'd walked away from hearth and heritage, he would argue that it was survival.

And now, for the first time in all of those years, he was suddenly looking across a lake at a family that didn't belong to him, and wanting something more than he had.

With an oath, Michael slammed the drawer shut.

He dropped the unlit cigarette on the nightstand and plowed his fingers through his hair. Fifteen minutes with Brianna Donally and he was driven to smoke, and it was his damn luck there wasn't a match to be had.

Half dressed, he walked through the living room toward the kitchen, when he stopped dead and, every sense alert, turned.

Halid sat on one of the pair of chairs that made up the furniture in the living area. With his legs crossed at the ankles, he watched Michael frown.

"By the grace of Allah, it has only taken thee thirty minutes to see me." He clicked shut the silver watch fob. "Fortunately, I am under no one's payroll but yours." His teeth flashed white.

An indulgent spark of humor lifted a corner of Michael's mouth. The last time he had seen Halid was at Donally's desert camp. Halid still wore the blue robes and turban of his tribe. "Remind me to put a chair beneath the door latch in the office."

As if that would truly hold anyone at bay, but at least he'd have noticed the broken glass. The French-designed door had been his one concession to frivolity in his quarters.

Halid walked to the table and tossed down a leather packet. "Your secretary gave me this. He said that you had requested a routing survey of the telegraph Donally Pasha is constructing. And this." Halid held out the letter that Lady Bess had forwarded to his office.

Michael hesitated. He would recognize his sister-in-law's flowery script anywhere. He tore it in half. Caroline had no business writing him, as if she were the sole arbitrator of his family's sins.

Or his.

Halid eyed him curiously. If he thought Michael's behavior odd, he wisely didn't comment. "It is fortunate you have been busy because I found nothing in my quest, except that my parents want me to marry and populate the earth with their grandchildren."

Michael eyed his friend with amusement. "They still like you, then, if they think you're worthy of carrying on the line."

"You would make yourself worthy if you saw my future bride." Halid crossed his arms and leaned against the table. "I have been thinking that it is time, perhaps. There is too much death not to celebrate life when it is within thy grasp to do so."

Michael set the papers in his hand down. "Then congratulations are in order." Halid's comment touched him more than he wanted. For the first time in years, he was beginning to see how vast and void of simple pleasures his life had become. "If you drank, I would toast your health."

"A strange English custom, this drinking for health." He pushed away from the table and they clasped hands in another British custom Halid didn't understand. "For thirty minutes today you had me worried, *Englishman*. I am told that you will be going to Alexandria."

"Unfinished business, Halid. I'll be there a few days. I've had someone watching the Donallys' estate since their return to Cairo. I want you to take over the sentry on Miss Donally."

"Only the younger one?"

Michael turned into the hovel that served as his kitchen and withdrew a flask of brandy, the morning's bread that he'd purchased from the market, and a bottle of jam from the pantry. "Other than her brother, she's the only one who leaves the house."

He'd learned a lot about Little-Miss-Spoiled-For-Life-With-One-Kiss, who wanted to have an affair with him.

Brianna worshipped the sunrise. With coffee in his hands, he'd stood on his balcony at the dawn of every day and watched her at the edge of the lake photographing the sailing dhows that populated the causeway. Every third day, she visited the American mission, where he'd learned that she read to the children in the mornings. On Tuesdays and Thursdays she did Lady Alexandra's bookkeeping at the Bulaq Museum, and every other day she bathed at the women's public bathhouse. Nothing was out of her confines, including the suks, an occasional coffeehouse, and the public fountain where she'd taken photographs. Brianna Donally, if she was anything at all, was as unconventional as a purple leprechaun.

And he was surprised by how much he enjoyed sparring with her.

With the exception of the bathhouse, his men had safeguarded her every day since her return.

Michael didn't tell Halid that his life, whether it went north or south after today, was about to become more colorful. He sloshed brandy into a glass. "To much needed good fortune, Halid."

"My fortune or yours, *essalâmu 'a leikum*, friend?"

Diverted by the comely face and alluring body that possessed his thoughts, Michael raised the glass. "Your fortune, Halid."

It wasn't going to take expensive brandy to add to his.

Chapter 6

❝**I**s there anything written in English?" Brianna asked as Mr. Cross set another pair of books on the desk. Wiping a dusty sleeve across her brow, she glared at the various manuscripts and tomes procured for her research as if she were the next Champollion of her time.

"There will be when Lady Alex completes this project." Mr. Cross looked down at her, his expression staid. "French is all we have."

Brianna was sure she'd insulted him. Especially after all the effort he'd gone through to secure the research material. "I'm a classics sort of student." And a reader of Brontë and Dickens, both of which had been in her personal trunks when the marauders attacked the caravan. The thought lowered her gaze. "You definitely don't want to donate these books to the children's mission book program." She quietly laughed.

"I will see you at noon," Mr. Cross said, and Brianna frowned as he left the dusty, old room that housed the museum's archived tomes. She'd promised to take her lunch with him today outside on the steps.

Brianna twirled a loose curl around her finger as her gaze lifted to touch the single red rose set in a vase on her desk.

Major Fallon had sent the rose the morning he'd left for Alexandra, the illicit promise of his return captured within the essence of every velvet petal. She touched a finger to the stem. In truth, the past few days working in the dusty crypts of the museum did much to drag her thoughts away from a more uncertain, enigmatic pull that had begun to dog her every waking moment.

Today she was having difficulty concentrating as she flipped through pages, frustrated by her inability to decipher the paragraphs with any speed. Unlike Alex, and a score of scholars who worked at the museum, she'd never grasped anything more foreign than Latin. It didn't help that she'd cheated on all of her tests and never completed her assignments. Now she wished she'd paid more attention.

The door opened. "Miss Donally." Mr. Cross entered. "A visitor is here."

"Please tell whoever it is that her ladyship is not here." Brianna didn't look up from the transcriptions. "I'm busy."

"He didn't ask for her ladyship, Miss Donally. He asked for you."

Brianna lifted her head. Alex's aide made no pretense that he considered any visitor to the realm of holy scholars an intruder, so she wasn't surprised by his stiff tone.

But she *was* surprised to see Major Fallon in the doorway.

Wearing his uniform, he carried his military helmet between his arm and his side. A slow smile spread across his lips, and it bore a strange hint of warmth. He'd removed his gloves and held them in one hand. Light seemed to displace the gloom of the room, and Brianna came to her feet.

"Major," she said, her voice barely a whisper.

"Miss Donally," he replied, his eyes on hers.

"You're back."

"It would appear so."

She stared, unaware that she was doing so until she realized Mr. Cross was watching her. "It's all right," she said, conscious that he didn't seem willing to leave her. "Truly, Mr. Cross. I won't let him touch anything."

Brianna waited for Mr. Cross to leave, then hurried around the cluttered desk and stuck her head out the door to check the passageway. There were others milling about the filing cabinets. She shut the door and leaned with her back against the brass key latch. No key sat in the lock.

Major Fallon was watching her, amused, as he turned to take in the small room before settling the force of his gaze on her. She couldn't look away from him. And she suddenly knew what it was about him that was so different from Stephan. His eyes made no apology for his thoughts.

"I can't touch anything?"

Her slow smile was at once challenging. "What is it you want to touch, Major?"

He took a step in front of her. She had to tilt her head. "What do you think it is I want to touch, *amîri*?"

He was tall and handsome, and she wasn't handling herself with her usual poise and grace, now that she was finally alone with him.

Alone.

With their last conversation hanging between them like a kiss of rare chocolate.

He made the room smaller, the walls narrower.

His gaze shifted to the books she'd been poring over. "What are you doing here?" He walked to the desk.

"Research." Reaching behind her, she untied her dusty apron.

His eyes swept her body. "You've a scientific mind, then?"

"I have a mind." She removed her kerchief. "But it's not the least scientific. I'm trying to learn a little about Coptic history."

"I thought that was Lady Alexandra's job."

Brianna traced a finger over the pages. "This project's success depends on getting photographs of places that are still standing. I don't want Lady Alex to fail because of me."

She'd made the mistake of looking up at him. "But I fear my French is very poor."

Lowering his gaze, he rotated one of the books. She watched his hand flip a page. Her eyes traced the blue veins that disappeared beneath the red cuff of his uniform. She'd always thought he had beautiful, strong hands with perfectly tapered fingers. She had felt their strength and seen their gentleness when he'd tended Alex.

Another page flipped, and she found her gaze had strayed to his profile. "I'll save you some time, then," he said. "This is a manual on Middle Eastern sexual customs."

"It isn't!" She dropped her horrified gaze to the text. He laughed, and she hit the solid muscle of his arm. "I didn't think my French was *that* wretched."

He touched the rogue curl that had fallen from her bun. More often than not, the laughter in Major Fallon's eyes reflected the challenge in her own. "I imagine you didn't pay much attention to your lessons."

"I happen to have been a very unconventional student." She leaned on the desk, her hands pressed behind her. "I am the chameleon queen," she said. "If I can't blend in, I fake it." She brushed a piece of lint from his shoulder, and the mood shifted beyond verbal foreplay. Awareness of him prowled through her senses. "You stayed longer than expected in Alexandria."

"I returned as soon as I could."

She knew that he'd returned last night. "That was a very good and kind thing that you did for Mrs. Pritchards." She wanted to ask how everything had fared. Instead, when he didn't reply, she smiled up at him. "Did you miss me, then?"

His eyes hesitated on her lips before he raised his gaze back to hers. "Every day."

Despite herself, her heart skipped a beat. "You're just saying that. You probably didn't think about me once."

He lowered his mouth to her lips. "Would you like to go with me to lunch?" His breath brushed hers. "I'll prove how wrong you are."

"Lunch?" Brianna's eyes eased open. She knew he meant to do more than casual dining.

"Food? Eat with mouth? I know just the perfect place."

He started to bend toward her again.

"Wait—" She looked around him at the door.

He pulled away, if only a fraction, as if reading her uncertainty with amusement. "Why?"

She'd been dreaming of this moment, imagining his hands all over her body, but the fantasy seemed so childish compared to the reality in his eyes: a reality that was at once inviting and formidable.

"I can't eat lunch with you today. I have plans."

"Cancel them."

Taking his hand, she walked him behind a pair of bookcases out of sight of the door. "I agreed to dine with Mr. Cross in exchange for him signing these books out for me. What about tomorrow?"

Crooking a dark brow, he glanced at the crowded space between the shelves, then settled his eyes on hers. "Tomorrow is out."

"Why?"

"I'm committed elsewhere."

Tomorrow was the Sabbath. "I'm teaching at the mission on Monday," she said in frustration. "Tuesday I'll be here again."

"Then Tuesday it is." She watched him set his pith helmet and gloves on the shelf. "There's nothing like mutual cooperation and mutual goals to accomplish a task." He turned his head to her.

"Major—"

"Michael," he corrected. "Don't you think that if we are going to be lovers then we should be on a first name basis?"

He was being very practical about all of this, she realized as she felt herself brace for the impact of his lips. She wondered if he'd come here today to test her strength of purpose.

He tilted her face. "Shall we give this a try?"

She expelled her breath in a rush. What on earth was the

matter with her? "Lord." Backing up a step, she hit the wall. Granting her no reprieve, he followed her. "I don't know what's wrong with me." Her gaze followed the movement of his hands as they took hers and pressed them to the wall, level with her head. "My corset is too tight."

He caged her with his arms and his body. "I thought you were an expert at kissing." The heat of his words feathered her lips.

"I never said that . . . exactly." Her hands still captured, she felt enclosed by his warmth. "I told you that you wouldn't shock me."

"If it makes you more at ease, I've already seen you naked."

Her voice was breathy with shock. "You have not."

"At the watchtower oasis." His eyes remaining locked on hers, a slow sensual smile curved his lips. "Did you know that you have a mole on the small of your back, *amîri*?" There was an edge to his voice, and against her mouth he whispered, "And one on your thigh?"

She had no chance to breathe a single shocked utterance.

His lips covered hers. She moaned against his mouth.

Peppermint.

The taste had become synonymous with him.

Erotic.

Hot.

Tasting him, she only wanted more, and she pressed against her captivity, against the strength that held her pinned to the wall, her body arching instinctively against his. He dipped his tongue into her mouth, lingering and caressing as her own tongue mirrored his. With a groan, he deepened the kiss. The heat began to grow between them, burn. Brianna felt the flush go over her body and pulse through her veins as it settled in her abdomen. Then her hands were free, and his fingers tilted her head and he tongue-kissed her. She felt the kiss all the way to her toes, rose to the balls of her feet and, matching his hunger, encircled his neck as if she were drowning.

Maybe she was.

She couldn't breathe.

They both pulled back, sucking in air, their gazes holding almost in stark surprise. Silver eyes burned into hers, their expression primitive. Murmuring incoherently, her arms wrapped around his neck, she pulled him back to her mouth. She didn't know what she was doing, except whatever *he* was doing to her felt wonderful. She wanted more.

Michael returned his mouth to hers, and they both danced another heated round against the wall. He hadn't remembered feeling this out of control in a long time. This hungry. And thirsty. He had not anticipated many things. Especially his reaction to her.

She made a whimpering sound in the back of her throat. The kiss turned hotter. Tracing the curvature of her corseted waist, he paused, then cupped her bottom and pressed her fully against him. He groaned his pleasure, the sound muffled by her mouth.

He wasn't thinking.

Hadn't even tried to think since the moment he shaved this morning and found himself on his way to see her.

His hands kneaded her bottom through her skirts, retraced their descent on her back and tangled in the heavy mass of hair coiled at her nape. The essence of English roses touched his senses.

Roses . . . like the scent on the veil he'd pulled from the hot desert floor all those weeks ago.

The silky cool texture of her sable hair spilled around his hands. He fisted his hand in its mass, tilting her head back, moved his other palm up her ribs to claim her breast.

Her breathing finally fractured.

One perfect breast filled his palm. A grumble sounded in his throat. "Do you want to quit yet?" His ragged breath traced the slim length of her neck until he was looking down into her upturned face. His erection strained his trousers. "Are you still game?"

He wondered who was playing whom.

Awakened from the depths of arousal, Brianna slowly opened her eyes and smiled. "You don't frighten me."

"No?" His words were hoarse. "Not even a little?"

The challenge in his eyes guided her hands lower over the hardened contours of his waist, down the cool brass buttons on his uniform.

Her gaze on his, Brianna slid her hands beneath his jacket, over his waistband, and came into full contact with him straining against the cloth. Her blue eyes sparkled, as if daring *him* to challenge *her*.

He should have known that nothing scared her for long, and he had to admit that he wasn't interested in trying anymore.

His eyes closed. Empowered by his response, she dipped her hands to his crotch, pressing the heavy length beneath the cloth against her palms. "I've never touched a man like this." With something akin to wonder, she intensified her exploration. He was hard and full, long and alive for her. She started to unfasten his trousers.

"Christ." He grabbed her wrists. "Enough." His jaw tight, he opened his eyes. "I've decided this is a bad idea in my uniform."

His hands went to her waist and edged her away. Kiss-swollen and heavy lidded, she lifted her gaze. "Is this the end of my lesson?" she queried in mock disappointment, knowing it was and clearly pleased with herself.

"You're very bad, *amîri*." He rubbed a thumb along her bottom lip. "One look at you and anyone will guess what we've been doing in here. I've kissed the dust off your face."

Her blue eyes flashed with warmth. "Then I won't have to clean up for lunch, will I?"

Michael plucked his hat from the shelf and walked back around the shelves. His head nearly brushed the low ceiling.

Standing beside the door, he watched Brianna slide her arms into a yellow jacket. Her refreshing lack of modesty, her sensual curiosity, and her innocence had made a mockery of his self-control. Still, he couldn't remove his eyes from her.

She finished the tiny buttons on her jacket, saw that he was staring, and smiled. "Did you really think of me when you were away?"

He looked into her face. "Once before breakfast, sometimes before supper, and always before bed."

Saying it, he realized that he had thought of her a lot.

He also realized that it irked the hell out of him that she was going to lunch with another man, even if it was the fastidious Charles Cross.

"Whatever are ye doin', mum?" Gracie's voice snapped Brianna upright.

Standing naked with her back to the long wardrobe glass, she practically dropped the mirror in her hand. It wasn't as if Gracie hadn't seen her naked from the time she was born, but it was embarrassing that her maid would catch her ogling the tiny, minuscule mole on her backside: a mole someone would have to have a magnifying glass to see.

"Gracie, I do wish you would knock." Brianna dropped a pink nightrail over her head, only because Gracie suffered from a paroxysm every time she found her sleeping in the nude. She was still damp from her bath. "You're liable to give me heart failure one of these days."

"Pah." Gracie gathered up discarded garments off the floor. "You've got that look in your eye, mum."

"What look?"

"The one what eventually lands ye in trouble with your family. That's what look." She wagged a finger.

Brianna resisted the urge to snap at Gracie, who knew her better than most. Instead, she picked up a pearl-handled comb and sat on the bench in front of her dresser to pick the tangles out of her hair.

Gracie left a quarter later, after cleaning up the water tins and straightening the room for bed. The moment the door shut, Brianna set down her comb, pulled out a shiny tin box hidden in the bottom drawer and set it in front of her. Carefully, she wedged off the lid.

A reckless energy came over her when she touched its forbidden contents. How many times this past year had she stolen a glance inside this box as if it were Pandora's original namesake? Lamplight reflected off the lid as she touched the thin rubber sheaths within. French *lettres*, they were called because they tied at the open end with a ribbon. Used to prevent conception, it snugly fit a man's private extremities like a glove—so she'd been told. The savvy young woman who had given her this tin last year had been a nineteen-year-old street bawd that Brianna had met after a suffrage march had landed her in a paddy wagon with twenty other women of questionable character. Brianna had been at the march to photograph the event, and ended up doing a photographic documentary on London's underlife. It was a book meant to promote social awareness of a wretched problem, and instead had been banned in England, a victim of the establishment's hypocritical morality laws.

Her only support had come from her brother, David, the family priest, and Alexandra, who despite Brianna's faux pas had asked her to take part in the book she'd contracted to do for the British Museum. That's why she was working so hard at the museum to make everything work—why she'd been there today when Major Fallon found her buried in books.

The memory of his kiss closed her eyes, and the carnal energy he'd stirred gave way to sensual anticipation that no voice of social conscience could contain. Yet, for a moment that afternoon, she'd surrendered more than her body to his kiss.

Opening her eyes to her reflection, she looked back at the woman in the glass, her blue eyes bright, her cheeks flushed. She was no stranger to the passion of her emotions.

Only the dangers.

She thought it ironic that the one person she knew the least was the only person who seemed to understand her, and her feelings had little to do with how she felt when he bent his mouth over hers and kissed her to the soles of her feet.

He'd not run from her unconventional quirks as if she was a leper. Brianna was suddenly restless to know what Major Fallon was doing tomorrow that he was too engaged to be with her.

She put away the tin and went downstairs. A full moon hung in the sky over the ancient city, and she slipped outside into the garden. Her mind opened to the late night air. The garden was in bloom with many of her familiar favorites— larkspur and jasmine. She walked along the stone path to the edge of the water.

For a long time she stood caught by the breathtaking imagery of the night, the contrast of light and darkness when she looked up and saw him across the waterway.

Brianna took an involuntary step nearer to the water's edge.

Michael Fallon, the man who had agreed to become her lover, who had dared her to kiss him at the museum, who had made the thrill of discovery a defiance of fear—stood on his balcony amid the long row of limestone apartments that butted the shore of the busy channel. He wore a long white robe and *sirwal* pajamas. She might not have seen him at all from that distance, given the show of flowering vines that draped the backside of the apartments. Except she'd glimpsed his movement, and knew the shocking instant that she recognized him. He'd been leaning in the shadows of his balcony, watching her. The cool breeze tempered her flushed cheeks. Wrapped in moonlight with nowhere to move, Brianna remained where she stood. She saw the glow of a cigarette move. Then she saw the pin of light go out as if ground beneath a boot.

She couldn't believe her eyes. All these weeks since her return, he must have been aware of her presence—she'd spent almost every morning and evening with her camera outside—but she'd not seen him at all.

Until tonight.

Brianna returned to her room before a servant came out to find her. She sat on the edge of her bed. Slipping out of her nightrail, she climbed beneath the covers and brought the silken sheets to her chin. She now knew where Major Fallon lived.

Less than a hundred yards of a busy waterway separated them.

The thought was almost as erotic as if he were in this room with her, as intimate as if his head lay on the pillow beside hers.

Almost—Brianna placed her hands beneath her head and smiled into the darkness—but not quite.

The Sabbath came early for Brianna. The chapel on the consulate grounds served the British community, and it was the custom of the Donally family to attend when Lady Alex was with them. But today Christopher and Brianna went to a smaller church in the French section for a more private Catholic service, something they rarely did. Brianna was cordial and sisterly, and at once relieved when they finally returned home. She hurried upstairs and changed. With the pretense that she was going to take pictures, she brought her camera down with her. More than anything, Major Fallon's itinerary today had aroused her curiosity.

Christopher was awaiting her downstairs in the entryway. Brianna's hopes of escape fell. She slowed on the stairway.

"I thought perhaps I'd go with you today," he mildly suggested, somewhat reminiscent of a blue-eyed Napoleon.

"Truly?" She glanced down at her simple split skirt and blouse and wondered what had made him so suspicious. It was the first time he'd suggested that they do anything alone since she'd arrived in Egypt. "You'll probably be quite bored."

"With you?" He adjusted his jacket and gave her a wicked self-effacing smile. "Alex is napping. What better way to spend the afternoon than with my little sister?"

Brianna fervently desired to go out alone. In the end, forced to take her camera, she decided to tour Cairo in all its ancient glory. Christopher was ever cooperative, and with the passing of the afternoon, she began to relax and enjoy herself.

Despite the daily passage of nightsoil collectors, the streets in Cairo had much to be desired. Twice, they nearly missed being run down by a camel. Fending off beggars and peddlers, Brianna finally left the camera with Abdul in the brougham and walked the busy thoroughfare filled with tourists.

Small shops selling goods from food to carpets lined the colorful alleylike streets. Peddlers of sweetmeats wended through the crowd. The air smelled of curry, deep-frying oil, and fish that overlaid the musk of slaked dust and sweat so cloying that it seemed to have been embedded into the very walls.

"Alex and I used to do this every Sunday," Christopher said.

Brianna loved the energy that surrounded her. "People here enjoy their bazaars, don't they?" She laughed with lighthearted ambience as she took her brother's arm and merged into the colorful drove.

Christopher shopped for Alex, while Brianna shopped for herself. She bought henna for her hair and solid glass bangles, as fragile and beautiful as delicate seashells. Within a couple of hours she'd filled Christopher's arms with packages and beauty products that claimed to make hair shinier and teeth whiter. A few moments later Christopher dipped his tall frame through a narrow doorway of a Turkish tobacco shop, while Brianna stopped at a stall that sold jewelry and beautiful bolts of silk. She held an amulet in her palm. A love charm.

The sensation came slowly, and she felt it first between her shoulder blades—someone watching her. The feeling grew so powerful and frightened her so that Brianna turned to where her brother had entered the shop. The alley was crowded. She looked left then right.

That was when her gaze passed over Major Fallon. If it had not been for his height, she wouldn't have seen him in the crowded aisle a block away. Looking much as he did the first time she'd ever seen him in his snowy robes and Bedouin headdress, he stood in front of a fruit stall haggling with a vendor. What felled the smile on Brianna's face was the demure woman at his side. She was veiled, with only her dark kohl-rimmed eyes showing above the silk—and he looked anything but English standing so tall beside her. The woman carried a child. A child that he took from her arms and gave a wedge of fruit.

Brianna dropped her gaze. Noise receded.

The shock of her emotions struck her with dreadful force. Brianna had never considered that he might have a child.

This is what he did on Sundays. Gracie had oft spoken about the time he spent in the Old Quarter.

"You might wish to remove your gloves." Christopher startled her.

She saw that her hand had not moved from the cloth. "Do babies wear red silk?" Her attempt to inflect humor into her voice failed.

Her brother's long eyelashes gave his blue eyes a dark penetrating look, and as if following the invisible trail of her thoughts, he turned to glance over her head.

"What do you think of this one?" She held up a thick square of cerulean silk, hoping to distract him, forcing herself to stand there and moon over a few yards of irrelevant cloth to prove that she could.

"It is very beautiful, yes," the Arab vendor replied, eager to make a sale and spreading it over his arm. Without even haggling, Brianna paid full price. Moving like someone in a trance past Christopher down the stalls, she continued shopping. Major Fallon had a way of making her feel young and foolish. By the time she'd reached the grounds where rows of horses milled behind corrals, she'd told herself a hundred times that she didn't care what he did.

She hadn't been attracted to him because he was a pillar of society. He'd never pretended to be anything other than what he was.

But a child?

Nor did she own him—didn't want to own him—and it wasn't as if she cared whether he had his own personal harem, or whether she ever tasted his mouth against hers again.

Or smiled at her with eyes as beautiful as moonlight.

He was a complete nincompoop!

"Slow down, Brea." Christopher grabbed her arm. "Our brougham is this way."

Packages filled his other arm. He didn't tell her that all of Cairo knew about Major Fallon's native mistress. It wasn't a secret that Fallon had even kept from her.

Silence dragged out. "Let's go home, imp," he gently said.

Brianna became less disconsolate as the evening passed, as a dull resignation took the place of the bruise on her heart. There was still her love of photography and her book, which during the next few days swallowed her attention. She and Charles Cross had already begun mapping what they could of the old Coptic sites within the city. He was so eager to help that Brianna didn't have the heart to turn away his expertise. He knew Egypt's history.

Major Fallon dropped by the house twice. Brianna had missed him both times. She smiled to herself as she slipped naked beneath her sheets those nights and hoped he knew that she'd discarded him. He wouldn't find her at the museum either, because she'd moved her work this week to the Geographical Society, and when she wasn't there, she worked at the mission all day. She'd ended up giving her silk purchases to the reverend who ran the school. Tomorrow, she and Mr. Cross were attending the consulate picnic.

Brianna went outside in the gardens to watch the sun set over the lake. Supper had been served earlier, while she was gone, and now she climbed the garden path back to the marble patio that opened to the dining room. To her shock as she stepped through the doors, Major Fallon was there with her brother.

They stood casually braced with their palms on the table where a large map took up much of the polished surface. A vase of flowers had been pushed aside. At her entrance, they both looked up. Brianna was trapped. Hot color rose from her throat to the roots of her hair. Her eyes stayed too long on Major Fallon's amused gaze. He knew bloody well that she'd been avoiding him, and didn't seem the least bit contrite.

"Why, Major. How wonderful to see you." She wouldn't flee now if her life depended on it. To her brother, she said, "I didn't know that you had company."

Recognizing the belligerent challenge in her eyes, Christopher didn't seem too pleased to have her there either. "This is business, Brea—"

"Then I'm sure you won't disturb me." She looked down the end of the long table. "I probably won't even hear you unless you shout."

She smiled prettily at him as she adjusted her skirts on the chair and had the servant bring her supper. Major Fallon's voice flowed over her in a dark, hushed monotone. With sure quick strokes of his capable hands, he was drawing a perimeter on the map, and at once Brianna's interest piqued. His military helm sat beside the vase. His shoulders stretched the red wool of his uniform.

". . . the caravans had all originated from Cairo," he was saying, returning to the map over the table. Brianna heard the pencil scratch. "I'll wager that someone has been following the telegraph, using it to send and receive advance warning of an approaching caravan."

"The guides were hired at random."

"Obviously not so random."

"What about Omar?"

"He has the means to disperse stolen goods, and he's neck deep in slavery. If he were involved, it would be a simple task for him to get his information from the ministry. I've run a check on every man who works in my office." Major Fallon handed over a list. "It's impossible for me to know if there might be more than these people who were privy to Captain Pritchards's shipment."

Christopher, standing in his white colonial garb, remained serious as he held the paper to the lamp. Major Fallon looked across the vase of flowers directly into her eyes. She dropped her gaze abruptly and hastily spooned peas into her mouth.

Abdul entered and salaamed. "There is someone here to see you, Donally Pasha."

"It's my secretary," Christopher said. "I asked him to bring the survey plats when he finally gathered them together."

After Christopher left, the room grew quiet. She squirmed, and resisted looking up.

"The child you saw was not mine."

She wanted to curl into a speck of dust and float away. "Whatever gave you the absurd idea that I care, Major?"

"Michael."

"Major."

Ignoring his presence was like trying to ignore a wart on the end of her nose or a bonfire lit too close to her back. She knew he was looking at her. She finally glanced up from her plate.

"I saw you at the suk," he said.

Brianna's knife scraped the plate as she cut a wedge of fish. "I'm not your keeper, Major."

"If you had looked closer you would have seen a little boy standing at my knee and another behind me."

"That's very comforting to know."

"I would have introduced you to Yasmeen."

Was he insane? "Your *mistress*?"

"People say a lot of things." He'd moved to the end of the table where she sat. "Most are true. Just as often, the gossip is not."

The chokehold on her neck loosened. Despite her best efforts, tears filled her eyes. "Are you saying you don't have a mistress?"

He squatted on his haunches beside the chair so she wouldn't have to look up at him. "Will you come riding with me tomorrow morning?"

"I can't." She shoved around her peas. "The consulate picnic is tomorrow. I already have plans—"

He tipped her chin. "We can talk about my exclusivity and yours. Among other things. It's time you and I finish what we've started."

His words worked their way down to her bones. "Is this why you came here tonight?"

"I really did have business with your brother. But I only intended to give you a little more time before you and I had a serious chat. Don't think I haven't known where you've been every minute of your day this past week."

"Major Fallon . . ." She set down her knife, alarmed by how quickly she'd lost control of this entire situation. "I've reconsidered many things—"

"Come riding with me tomorrow morning."

"No."

"Six o'clock at your stables. Wear something comfortable."

He was standing when Christopher entered.

"Miss Donally," Major Fallon said in farewell.

Brianna watched him go, her mind racing faster than the blood in her veins. This week had only proven that she'd let everything get out of control. She might as well have put a bull's-eye on her chest and asked for an arrow to drill her through the heart.

It was best that she discontinued all involvement with him now. And if her body language didn't announce her intentions, then he would know when she didn't show up at the stables tomorrow morning.

Chapter 7

⟨⟨⟨⟩⟩⟩

"What the hell do you mean she left here before dawn?" Christopher demanded of the groom when Abdul finally found him and brought him to the house. "Alone?"

"No, Donally Pasha." The groom nervously passed his hand across his mouth. "She went with Fallon effendi."

Christopher had been dressed and ready to leave with her for the picnic. "Did she say when she would return?"

"Tonight." The groom squirmed.

"Tonight?" Christopher felt a swell of incredulity.

"Fallon effendi had his own man with him. He told me that my services would not be needed. So, I stayed behind."

How could Brea be so bloody obtuse? Didn't she know that her absence today at the picnic would be noted along with Fallon's? Christopher raised his gaze to the groom. "She's not allowed within fifty yards of the damn stable from now on—"

"You can't do that, Christopher." The calm feminine voice brought him around.

Alex was sitting comfortably ensconced in a fluffy chair. She had been casually reading until Abdul's visit, and continued to hold her finger on one of the pages in her book. "I'll be here. Tell them she's with me." Looking over her wire spectacles at him, she raised her brows. "You can't control your sister. She's a grown woman."

That had been his whole problem since his mother died. He'd never been able to rein in his sister, any more than anyone else in the family could. And David, who was supposed to be a man of the cloth, had done nothing but encourage her rebelliousness by getting her involved in every social cause under the sun. Christopher dismissed Abdul and the groom before turning to his wife.

Sunlight filled his bedroom. A breeze ballooned the sheer white curtains. The room shone white, from the pale carpet on the floor to the eyelet lace and netting that enclosed the massive white iron bedstead.

"That grown woman, as you like to refer to her, is about to ruin herself." He dropped into the chair across from Alex and scraped his hands through his hair. "Where do you propose that we send her next? There *are* no more relatives who live abroad."

Alex set down the book on the stand beside the chair. "Maybe you're not worrying about the right person."

He raised his head. "I know Fallon."

"So do I." She planted her hands on her knees. "And I'd be more worried about him if I were you."

"What are you talking about?"

Sunlight pulled the gold from her hair. "Haven't you seen the way he looks at her when he thinks no one else is looking? Well, I have."

Hell yes, he had.

"She's bright, charming, and beautiful. She's effervescent, like fine champagne. Who *doesn't* eventually fall in love with fine champagne? And who at the consulate hasn't tried to court her? Except they're all afraid of you."

"Me?"

"You're a bully."

He was a man. And knew a man's mind. He'd been

pleased that his sister had found her string of admirers boring. Most were well-bred idlers and idiots who fancied themselves the cat's cream, with their genteel manners and inflated knowledge of Egyptian affairs.

"Your sister is wealthy in her own right, and much too independent to surrender her liberty. Half the eligible men in Cairo have asked to call here at least once since our return. She likes her life the way it is."

His eyebrows came together. "And this is a good thing?"

"As far as I'm concerned, Major Fallon is perfect for her. He's not afraid of *you*, for one thing."

"And the other?"

"He's not afraid of her. He's the only man I've ever seen that she hasn't been able to lead around by the nose." Alex stood and walked over to him. "She doesn't have to live here, Christopher, but she chooses to do so because she loves us both. Why do you think she's been working so many hours at the museum these past weeks? Mr. Cross told me that she's doing Coptic research for me."

"Brea has her nose in a book?"

Tears filled Alex's eyes. "I haven't even had the heart to tell her that I have no desire to finish the project."

Christopher took her down into his lap, wrapping his arms around her as she leaned against his shoulder. Her silken skirts whispered with her movement. "Why not?" he asked her.

"I don't know." She curled against his chest. "I think something is wrong with me. I can't concentrate. I'm irritable."

His hand slid over her abdomen. "You're pregnant." He still couldn't believe that she carried a child.

His child.

Their child.

He realized how much he wanted this baby.

She hadn't wanted to return to the museum or leave the house in a month. His arms tightened around her. The doctor had said that her state was as much indicative of her pregnancy as the trauma she'd suffered.

He didn't know about emotional pendulums. Or understand how someone could be strong and independent one moment and weepy the next. He only knew that he was trying to understand.

"I love you." He pressed his nose into the soft fragrance of her hair. "Sometimes it scares the hell out of me, Alex."

"I'm not so weak, Christopher," she whispered. "I don't want you to worry about me."

He slid his hand around her nape and pulled her mouth to his lips. His kiss was possessive, rough with need and carnal awareness. Her bottom pressed firmly against him. Her cool hands rose to touch his face. The kiss deepened. He bent her over the arm of the chair, sliding his palm to her breasts, which were fuller in his hands.

"I'll be seeing the physician tomorrow," her voice hummed against his lips.

He brought her back to his mouth. "Fock the doctor." He caught the Irishness in his voice, but was past caring that Alex still managed after all of these years to crack that thin veneer of civility he'd built around his life.

Pulling away, she braced her palms on his shoulders. Her mouth was kiss-softened and moist. "Unfortunately, you're going to be late for your date with Charles Cross." She kissed him on the nose. "Someone has to tell the poor chap that Brianna isn't here."

Major Fallon didn't leave the city, as Brianna had anticipated. Instead, after an exhilarating ride along the outskirts of Cairo, he turned and rode through the center of town, at times threading his way past cupboard-sized shops and the narrow mastaba-shaped benches, where merchants sat out front chatting and drinking coffee. He bandied with many in good-humored assurance and knew most by name. The temperature was pleasant. Flocks of white storks covered the minarets. It was still cool enough that clouds of black flies had not yet appeared. Brianna felt like a tourist.

As they rode through historic Cairo, he pointed out that in

place of rickety wooden houses a new residential quarter had grown up around the palace. It was to one of these structures that he brought her. "We'll rejoin Halid later," he said when his hands wrapped around her waist to help her dismount. When she was settled, a little too close in front of him, he raised his brows inquiringly. "You've said very little since our departure."

Despite all of her self-admonitions to stay away from him, she hadn't. Indeed, she'd arrived at the stables ten minutes early, only to find him already waiting for her. "I was thinking about what my brother is going to say when I don't show up this morning to attend the picnic."

"You don't care a whit about the picnic," he said close to her ear. "Or you wouldn't have come with me."

He was right, of course, though she'd have rather died than admit it to him. His overburgeoning confidence in himself annoyed her. He hadn't even batted an eyelash when she'd arrived, looking stunning in a jade green riding habit. He was already waiting at the stables, as if he had no doubt that she'd show up.

In truth, as Brianna looked at the stone structure, she admitted to nervousness. Curiosity had brought her this far. That and her desire to glimpse a part of Major Fallon's other life. If he seemed aware of her unease, he didn't say anything. The door swung open and a little girl flung herself bodily into the major's arms. She spoke in Arabic, but he answered in English; for her benefit, Brianna realized, and was at once grateful for the courtesy.

"I've come to see your papa and mama," he said.

"I know. Everyone has been waiting." The dark curls on her head bounced as she bent and whispered something into his ear.

Major Fallon's silver eyes smiled into Brianna's as he nodded to the words the girl said. "I think so, too."

She giggled. "Did you bring peppermints?"

Fallon winked at Brianna, who could only stare in response to the change in him. "A lady after my own heart."

He grinned and handed the little girl a tin of peppermints from inside his coat.

Beturbaned and wearing a loose-fitting *thwab* made of white cotton, a man wheeled on a chair into the room as Major Fallon edged Brianna over the threshold. "You're late, Major," the newcomer snapped, but he smiled as Fallon closed the door. "You must be Miss Donally." His bushy brows arched as he looked her up and down like a draft horse at auction. "You've become famous."

"I have?"

"You're a survivor, Miss Donally. Something I can relate to." He eyed Fallon devilishly. "She is a pretty one. Just as I'd heard."

Major Fallon moved behind her, so close that her shoulders touched his chest. His arm brushed hers as he reached around her to take the man's hand in a brief shake. "Miss Donally, meet Colonel Sir Evelyn Baker or Baker Pasha as he is known to his peers," he said. The major's hands went to her arms, the heat of his fingers curling into her sleeves. "He is Yasmeen's husband and the father of the little girl you saw. Yasmeen teaches at the mission. You might know her."

Yasmeen stood back from her husband, now holding the girl. A little boy stood at her side, gazing shyly at Brianna. Yasmeen wore pajamas, topped by a blue satin blouse. She was French. Brianna *did* know her, at least by sight. Yasmeen salaamed, and Brianna nodded in response.

"Miss Donally volunteers two days a week at the mission," Major Fallon told Baker.

Brianna wanted to ask how he knew so much, but her hand was taken in a firm grasp and her attention diverted at once to the feisty man in the wheelchair. The house smelled of coffee and almond pastries.

"Colonel Baker was my superior officer serving under the khedive when I arrived in Egypt," Major Fallon said.

"Recently returned from a military mission to annex the Upper Nile and suppress the slave trade. All to be done under the banner of civilization, of course. As you can see, it is a job better suited to younger men. Now, the major keeps me company when he can."

Yasmeen smiled, and in a quiet voice said, "Major Fallon said that you are a photographer."

"Yes," she replied without preamble.

"The girl should have been here for the opening of the Suez last year." Colonel Baker chuckled at his demure wife. "The canal was blessed by Moslem, Greek Orthodox, Coptic, and Roman Catholic priests, every available cannon and gun fired, twenty military bands struck up, and the fireworks dump blew up, nearly demolishing Port Said. With not one photograph to be had of the blessed show."

Brianna laughed. "Did that really happen?"

"That wasn't even the half of it."

Without saying a word, the little boy at his mother's side touched his palm to Brianna's riding skirt. The girl who Major Fallon had been carrying now leaned against Brianna's legs. The room filled with a pungent odor from burning oil rising from a feeble wick.

"Come, all of you." Yasmeen nudged the boy. "We will leave your father to some peace so he can enjoy his guests."

Screaming children scattered into the adjoining room. The room emptied of noise as the door shut behind Yasmeen's slim form.

"I was about to begin my coffee without you, Major," Baker said.

Brianna looked up at Fallon. "You had this planned?"

Pushing Colonel Baker's wheelchair into the next room, where a stove emanated warmth, he bent nearer to Brianna's ear. "Yasmeen makes delicious pastries," he said. "They come out of the oven like clockwork every Saturday morning."

"Don't let him fool you, Miss Donally. While he's in Cairo, this rascal here plays the paladin. He lets me win at chess—"

"Don't believe it."

"—and takes the children to the market. Last week he bought cloth."

The colonel poured coffee for the two of them, then offered Fallon a cigarette from a green tin box, which to Brianna's surprise he declined, opting for his peppermint tin instead. "Ah, I know that old trick." The colonel turned to Brianna and winked. "Once a man grows to enjoy Turkish tobacco, it is very difficult to stop. Fallon effendi does not like to be a slave to his cravings. Have you ever smoked, Miss Donally?" His eyes twinkled.

Smoking was one of the first vices she'd indulged in upon her arrival in Egypt. She didn't see any point in denying it. "I found Turkish tobacco to be positively revolting." She wrinkled her nose.

"I knew just by looking at you"—he wagged his finger at Major Fallon with an I-told-you-so grin—"she's one of those newfangled suffrage types. Mark my word, she'll own your heart then rule the roost before you blink an eye."

Brianna could have choked.

"If women get the vote, there'll be no stopping the lot from trying to wriggle into our exclusive clubs next." Baker winked at Major Fallon. "Then it will be parliament."

"Since when would that be a bad idea?" Major Fallon said over his cup, his voice light with mirth.

Wrapping her hands around the warm coffee cup, Brianna smiled at the major over the rim. He'd won the round today. Hands down.

The conversation turned to other business. As they sat at the table eating almond pastries and drinking coffee, Brianna's restless gaze roamed the cluttered room. Clearly, Colonel Baker abominated Victorian austerity. He was old school to the core. She also suspected that he was very poor.

"I hear that you're having trouble with our old friend Omar." The colonel set his cup down.

Major Fallon sat forward on his elbows. "He's not letting this latest infraction go."

"What does that mean?" Brianna asked.

"Nothing." Major Fallon looked at her. "At the moment, anyway."

"He yanked Omar's beard hard this time. That's what it means," Colonel Baker said.

The muted patter of a hand-cranked sewing machine broke the silence. "Yasmeen is fitting the children with new clothes," the colonel said, changing the topic. "She lines them up like soldiers against the wall and refuses to allow them to escape until they are measured and fitted. But they wanted to meet you."

"Me?"

Major Fallon straightened and his arm touched hers as he leaned forward on the table. "You are like a lucky penny, Miss Donally."

Again she smiled at him over the rim of the coffee cup. No one had ever accused her of being good luck. Her eyes told on her thoughts, but she didn't care if he read her feelings.

The colonel cleared his throat. "You've allowed this old man to talk your ears off, Miss Donally."

"You're not so old," she said.

"I have something for you." Wheeling his chair around, he pulled out the drawer from the breakfront behind him and withdrew a stack of papers. "Yasmeen grew up here. She's mapped out the Coptic section in Cairo and more that may interest you in your research."

Disbelieving, Brianna took the papers. She turned to Major Fallon, her eyes filled with gratitude, and smiled at him.

"He said you were interested," the colonel said. "I told him that I would have something ready today if he wanted to drop by."

Major Fallon moved behind her chair. Brianna clutched the papers to her chest as she stood. "Thank you."

"Most people who come here are interested only in taking something out of this country. Few ever give anything back. I hope that your book is of interest to our scholars."

"Thank you, Colonel." She held out her hand. "Please give my gratitude to your wife as well."

Outside, the sunlight hit Brianna's eyes. Major Fallon

didn't say anything. Hidden from the street, the horses idled beneath a mimosa tree.

"Why?" she asked, holding her packet as she turned to face him.

He set one wrist on the saddle. He wore no head covering, and Brianna smelled the soap he'd used to wash his hair, maybe that morning—before he'd ridden to meet her at the stables. "Because I like your work. I'm impressed with your vision and your perseverance."

"You are?" Most of her family had never told her that much.

"Especially when you don't speak French that well. I admire resolve in a person, and you possess more than any single individual I know."

She liked that he thought so. "What happened to him?" she asked after a moment. "To Colonel Baker?"

The major lowered his head and seemed to contemplate the gloves he held in his hand. When his gaze lifted, his mouth was tight.

"One night two years ago we were on patrol. I'd been here for six months. Near the Baharia oasis, we captured the biggest hashish shipment in history, and broke Omar's supply line. Three days after he returned to Cairo, the colonel was attacked and left for dead. He took a bullet in his back. Omar was the man who'd fired the shot, but he had an alibi that night, and Colonel Baker's accusation was attributed to delirium. Nothing could be proven."

She held his gaze. "I'm sorry."

He looked at a donkey passing on the street. "I was still at the oasis, and didn't learn about the attack for almost a month. The bullet is too close to his spine to ever attempt to operate." He met her gaze. "I've done what I could."

Fallon helped her mount. He adjusted her foot in the stirrup.

"You're a fraud, Major Fallon," she said as he bent over her boot. He raised his face inquiringly. "You work so hard to extol less than a virtuous demeanor. But for all the trouble you go to get yourself disliked, inside you are really soft and fuzzy." She grinned. "Quite likable. Sometimes even charming."

"Is that so?"

"Borderline nice." She pinched his cheek and laughed.

Conscious of his hand still warm on her ankle, she tilted her chin. "Why do you always look at me like you're trying to figure me out?"

"I've never heard anyone laugh the way you do."

She splayed her mouth with a gloved hand. "Am I too loud?"

"Very." A salacious smile tilted his lips. "But in a good way."

They remained smiling amiably at each other in the sunlight, the day still young, and filled with the promise he'd made her last night.

Suddenly mindful that he was aware of the subtle shift of her thoughts, she crossed one hand over the other on the saddle and looked at the small colorful stone house with bougainvillea hanging in clay pots. "Why haven't you denied the gossip about Yasmeen and you?"

"Because the truth makes no difference to people." He mounted and swung his bay gelding around. His hands reined in the high-stepping horse. He looked very good in the saddle as his eyes moved over her with a thoroughness that quickened her stomach. "And I learned a long time ago not to care what people say or think about me."

She wanted to feel that manner of mental liberation. He dressed in native clothing. He'd stuck a gun against the head of one of the most powerful opium underlords in this country, then ridden back into the desert and dared her with his eyes and his lips to lay with him. Christopher didn't intimidate him—for once, her brother's protective presence didn't eclipse her own.

She wondered if he'd ever been in love.

But not enough to break the mood and ask him.

They rode out of the quiet little neighborhood where Colonel Baker lived and into traffic. It was mid-morning, the busiest time of the day. Sunlight gleamed off white walls. The air was still fresh and the city alive with noise. He kept beside her as they rode down the avenue, and Brianna realized that they were headed toward the waterfront.

Michael shut the door and leaned against the portal as Brianna made a slow turn in the room. Her skirts rustled with her movement. She removed her hat and then gloves, one finger at a time. He said nothing, simply watched her languid movements, the expression in her eyes. Dark curls fell in windswept confusion down her slim back.

"This place is beautiful." She ran her a finger along the bamboo mural on the wall.

Dust floated in the pale streamers of light, stirred to life by the invisible current of Brianna's passing. When he'd bought the houseboat some time ago, he had not inquired as to its décor. Nor did he care. But now he was glad for the pleasant surroundings.

He watched Brianna move to the adjoining doorway. Sunlight filtered through the blinds and laid a crisscross pattern on the wooden floor. He could see the corner of the bed and a plush yellow chair from where he stood. He reached behind him and clicked the lock.

The noise drew Brianna around.

If his intent wasn't clear in his eyes, all she needed to do was look lower and find it pressed against his trousers. He'd already unbuttoned the jacket of his uniform.

"This is a *dahabeeyah*," she said as he pushed off the door with a restlessness that was foreign to him. "I hear the crew outside. Are we going to sail?"

Her heart was racing. He could see it in the rise and fall of her breasts, hear it in the waver of her voice.

"I promise to have us back before late afternoon."

"Is this place yours?"

Without touching her, he leaned his palms against the wall and caged her between his arms. "Does it matter?"

"Then I'm not the first woman you've brought here?"

He looked down at the top of her dark head. "My lack of celibacy was never a point of supposition."

"No. I suppose it wasn't."

"I haven't any tea prepared," he said, so close that he could smell her essence. "Though, if you want some—"

She raised her face and met his gaze. "I didn't come here thinking that you were going to serve me tea, Major."

"Michael."

He bent his head and touched his mouth to hers. He wanted to hear his name on her lips.

Just once, he wanted her to say his name.

He was dimly conscious of movement beneath his feet as the *dahabeeyah* cast off from shore. She tasted of fine coffee. Her cool hands rose to cup his jaw, and she deepened the kiss, drawing him into her arms. Her tongue met then thrust against his, seeking, exploring, burning. He might have pulled away to reassert control but he was drawn by the sheer power of her pull. His hands left the wall and tightened against her waist, pulling her hard against him.

He would hold himself back no more.

Slanting his head, he wrapped his arms around her and kissed her to the depths of her soul.

Or maybe it was his own.

She was soft and warm, and vibrantly alive. Little-Miss-Spoiled-For-Life-With-One-Kiss was a damn fine kisser, and he found that he wanted to be inside her.

He pulled away to breathe. Her lashes fluttered open. Her face was flushed, her mouth wet, her crystalline blue gaze bright in the pale light. "When was the last time you had your menses?" he asked.

"What?" she blinked. "I . . ."

He laid his hand beneath her chin and tilted her face. He'd rarely seen her blush and was surprised that she did so now. "There are ways to prevent conception, but nothing is perfect."

"I should start in a few days. I—" She reached her hand

into her skirts. "I've also thought of that." Pulling out a velvet pouch, she walked past him into the saloon—the front room where she'd set her gloves and hat. "I'm unsure how these work. I mean, it was explained, but not entirely. They are worn by the man." Her eyes lifted to his. "By you, on your . . . it prevents conception. So I've been told."

"Indeed."

He watched her nervousness with amusement, amazed. He had an idea what she had in that little bag of hers, and wasn't even going to ask where she'd secured French *lettres*.

Brianna tipped the contents of the bag beside her gloves. When he remained leaning against the wall with his arms crossed, she turned inquiringly.

"Do you think they'll fit?" he asked, as amused by her optimistic outlook of his stamina as he was by her one-size-fits-all reasoning.

He wouldn't be able to fit into one of those. She probably had no idea the affront that she'd just paid him.

She looked back at the pile. "No one said anything about size."

He approached her and turned her into his arms, setting out to relieve her of her clothes. His hands went to the buttons on her demure jacket. It cinched her waist and accentuated her curves. "I have my own." He put his mouth against her neck. "Not as many as you brought, but enough for today."

Her tongue darted out from between her lips. "Major, I—"

"Brianna." He leaned his hands against the bar at her back. "Why won't you call me by my—"

"You taste like peppermint." Rising on her feet, she wrapped her arms around him. "I don't want to talk anymore. I want to be seduced."

He slid his thumb across her bottom lip. Her pull palpable, he was conscious of the primal need to claim her, of his own seduction. His eyes remained on hers. With the callused pads of his fingers, he unbuttoned her blouse and freed her breasts into his hands. Her corset had shoved them high. She was beautifully formed, nature's perfection against his hands. A slight shiver went over her when he touched her.

He watched her slumberous eyes close, felt the raw hunger swell inside, then bent his head and took her mouth. Her body arched against him. His hands kneaded her breasts, stripped away her jacket, spread across her back, to finally fist into her hair. He savored her taste, the small groan she made, the feel of her body in his arms. She was like warm velvet, soft and responsive to his touch. Her nipples, hard and tight, pressed against his chest. She'd scraped his jacket away, and lowering his arms behind him, he let it drop to the floor beside hers. Her blouse followed. He unhooked her stays. She balanced on the balls of her feet, leaning into his body as her mouth returned to his over and over again, seizing more than his senses. He was physically drowning.

The *dahabeeyah* could sink, and he would not know it. Somehow they reached the adjoining door. Her riding skirt and petticoat slid to her feet with a *swoosh*. Followed by her drawers. He stepped over the discarded clothes and they tumbled onto the bed. The ropes groaned. The frame cracked. Her eyes flew open with a helpless gasp and she panted brokenly.

Michael caught himself above her. Braced on his palms, breathless, he looked down into her unfocused gaze—then joined his mouth to hers again, sucking her tongue between his lips. He felt the feather-light touch of her hands against his chest, her palms opening over the powerful, corded muscle that delineated his shoulders and curved into his back. Her nipples ruched against his hand. Then his lips replaced his hand and he suckled her through her chemise before he gathered the cloth in his fist and pulled it over her head, leaving her wearing only her stockings and shoes. The contrast was erotic, and he pulled back to see all of her splendor. Her skin was flawless, her breasts full and high, her nipples flushed.

Their gazes met and held. She'd never been touched the way he was touching her now. It shone in her eyes as she watched his hungry gaze go over her. "Are you frightened?" he quietly asked.

"Of you?" She shook her head—and something touched him, broke free inside him.

Her fearless passion for living, her sensuality, her innocence, was an irresistible lure, a shiny bauble in a pile of ashes that had become his life. She twisted around and entwined her body with his.

Her flesh was warm and soft and malleable beneath his fingers. He slid his hand, dark against the paleness of her stomach, to claim her completely. "Tell me what you want." His breath touched her lips.

"You."

"Show me. Show me what you want."

Her hands went to his, hesitating, before she nudged them lower. "I want to know what it's like to be touched by you."

He moved a finger inside her, intimately stroking. Her body tightened around him. She was wet and hot. He felt her maidenhead. She did not look away from the intensity in his gaze, and he could not look away from her. "Why, Brianna?" His words were strained. "Why me?"

Her eyes drifted closed on a fragmented gasp. His fingers moved over her. "I . . ." She fumbled for words. "Because . . . you're not afraid of anything." The whisper touched his lips. "Because you would."

Her musk mingled with the scent of roses on her skin.

The garters holding up her stockings pressed into the top of his thigh. She watched his eyes drift upward until he'd pinned her with his gaze, and he felt the kick of her heart against her ribs. She'd heard him laugh below his breath, and sensed the dark undercurrent beneath the sound. "It's nice to know I'm wanted for something, *amîri*."

"I . . ."

He knew she was too lost to understand what he'd meant, lost to the magic of his fingers, to the primal force that became him. She became a twist of emotion, a knot of fire. Small sounds emanated from the back of her throat. "Do you like this?" His voice was a harsh rasp against her ear. "Tell me."

"Yes. Yes, I like it a lot."

"Do you want me to stop?"

"No!"

His mouth caught her cries. Instinctively, she arched against him. His kiss continued down the salty curve of her neck. Determined to take what he wanted, he was also determined to give her what she needed—but not yet.

Her breath broke as he pulled away, leaving her stunned and boneless on the rumpled bed, watching the reflection of the water dance on the ceiling. She slowly turned her head when he returned naked and stood in front of the bed.

She pushed up on her elbows, her dark hair spilling around her face. Michael felt the heat of her blue gaze go over him like a painted stroke, and he wanted more of her touch, more of the fire that claimed his senses. When he could bear the weight of her gaze no longer, he touched her chin gently, and she jumped, her gaze leaping to his.

Brianna couldn't breathe.

"It will hurt the first time." His eyes touched hers.

She watched as his long fingers worked the French *lettre* over the thick length of his arousal. The moisture left her mouth.

"Are you frightened yet, *amîri*?"

Her lashes drifted higher. "I want to touch you," she breathed, and feathered her hands over him, touching him as intimately as he'd touched her, watching him close his eyes.

"What is this made from?"

"You don't want to know. But it's better than rubber."

The backs of her knuckles rasped the swirl of dark hair that surrounded his sex—hair the same color that arrowed up his abdomen and sprinkled his chest. "You are not what I imagined," she whispered.

He pulsed with life.

His head fell back on his shoulders. "Why is that, *amîri?*"

She felt awkward and young in his very male presence. She didn't want her inexperience to show, but it did just by looking at him. "You are far more than I dreamed," she said.

"Christ!" He grabbed her hands and placed his knee on the mattress between her thighs. "That's good." His lips brushed hers. "Because I'm going to give you more than you ever dreamed."

Locking his fingers with hers, he kissed her, plunging his tongue between her lips, bringing them both back to the precipice where they'd been earlier. With a sigh—or was that a moan?—she let him kiss her into submission, and no matter the searing tightness in her own body, let him seize from her what she wanted so desperately from him.

"I want to touch you." Her voice was a rasp.

"No." The word trapped between their lips was uncompromising. He took her down with him to the bed, flesh to flesh. "Not like that. Not right now. When I come, it will be inside your body."

He sank lower against her, drawing first one breast then the other into his white-hot mouth, sinking still lower, over her concave stomach. She twisted restlessly beneath him. Pleasure and desire became one. His mouth was thorough, his possession of her body complete. Before she could grasp what he was doing, he put his face between her legs. Dark, silky hair brushed the inside of her thighs.

Then his mouth pressed intimately against her. With a tortured cry, she clamped her hands in his hair, the rush of heat shattering her frail resistance. She mumbled incoherently. And she opened her legs farther, sinking against the thrust of his tongue, surrendering to the wet plundering heat that engulfed her.

When her gaze again came into focus, he was above her, reading her wicked mind with an amused glitter in his eyes.

And the inherent dare that was as much a part of him as the color of his eyes.

He knew her.

He knew her body better than she did. She wanted to know his.

Twining his fingers with hers, he spread her legs. He was not a small man. Not any part of him. Her eyes were fixed on his, and his on hers. She felt him hesitate, then push through her maidenhead. She had heard that the first time would hurt. That a woman would bleed from the invasion. The pressure between her legs increased.

And it did hurt.

When he entered her, her hands fisted against his.

"I'm not in, Brianna."

"Don't . . . stop."

"Relax." His voice was gravelly against her ear.

Her mouth was too dry to allow speech.

He withdrew slightly, then pushed, gaining another few inches.

Without warning he pulled her up, still partially impaled on him. Her bones melted against him. He sat her on his lap, her weight driving him deeper into her body, until he was buried.

"Hug your knees to my waist," his whisper bade. His face taut with primal hunger, he waited for her to adjust to his size, then began to move inside her.

Shameless.

It was the way he made her feel.

Brianna inhaled his carnal scent, his breath; she let him fill her body, her senses.

In the wild rush of her heartbeat, she found her own rhythm and began to move. His breathing turned harsh and ragged, his eye contact broke. He grabbed her hips. Her mind clouded as he lowered his face to the fullness of her breasts and drank of her skin. She arched, pressing her rose-tipped breasts against his hot mouth, her tumble-down hair spilling over his thighs, and soon she was lost to the rocking rhythm of her own body, her labored breathing the single hushed sound between them. With a groan that was her name, he wrapped his arms around her, one palm going to her bottom, the other pressing into the thick waves of her hair. She spiraled upward as her body moved toward the elusive pinpoint of light that seemed to surround her like a misty shroud. Nothing had ever felt like this, and when the spasms fueled her cries, he silenced her outcry with the force of his hand against her nape, crushing her lips to his and kissing her deeply with a possessive urgency as powerful as her own. His breathing fractured against her lips. Swallowing his deep-chested groan, she returned his kiss, finally drinking in the sounds of his release.

When their hearts had quit racing, he pulled back to look into her face, his silver irises dark on hers. She sensed that she'd somehow throw him off balance, and that made her smile.

"Are you mine today, my wild Irish rose," his voice was rough, his gaze tender and searching, "or am I yours?"

"Wild Irish rose?" She wrinkled her nose at him, that he would equate her to a flowering bramble. "I'm insulted."

"Don't be." He twisted her around and took her down to the bed, capturing her hands above her. Her hair fanned out around her like an inky cloud. "It was a compliment."

Then he proceeded to show her how much of a compliment it was, and what it was like to lie in the strong arms of Michael Fallon.

Chapter 8

Lying naked in the twisted bedcovers, Brianna opened her eyes and stretched. Sunlight filtered through the blinds. Her hand went to the pillow beside hers and she twisted around on her elbow. Her body ached, every inch bearing the mark of Major Fallon's complete possession of her. He had outlasted her. She could barely move.

A pitcher of water sloshed on the commode. A towel and rag had been laid out for her convenience. On the dresser, she saw a bottle of wine set beside a platter of fruit and cheese. Someone had gone to a great deal of effort to see that she was made comfortable when she awakened. Pulling the sheet to her chin, Brianna smiled at the play of light and water on the ceiling before finally sitting up.

After washing, she opened the armoire and found a man's robe. Brianna lifted a feminine slipper, turning it over in her hand. A chemise had been neatly folded into a drawer. Thrusting her arms into the robe, she then belted it at the waist. She grabbed the fruit platter and, tucking the flask beneath her arm, edged out of the bedroom, only to find the saloon also empty. Her clothes had been laid over the settee atop a British uniform. Brianna fingered the sun-warmed sleeve of the jacket and, bringing it to her nose, bent to look behind the blinds. A glimpse outside told her that the *dahabeeyah* had turned and was heading back toward Cairo. The sun was now on the other side of the river. She'd been asleep for a couple of hours.

Major Fallon was sitting on deck when she found him. With his long legs stretched out in front of him and propped on the rail, he wore his uniform trousers tucked into his boots. A white military issue shirt stretched across the width of his shoulders as he dropped his gaze to the glass in his hands. All she could do was inhale the sight of him. She must have made some sound, because he turned in his chair, and Brianna felt that stirring essence of protectiveness when he looked at her.

"Hello," she said, remembering herself almost at once and setting the wine and platter of fruit on the table to share with him.

A warm unfathomable smile tugged at the corners of his mouth. "Hello back to you, *amîri*."

For the first time in her life she was struck speechless by an attack of maidenly shyness. He had done things to her body that no Kama Sutra manual could ever have prepared her for. She'd been naive to think that her experience level would ever equal his—in anything.

Brianna set her hands on the back of the chair that faced his across the table. "Who is sailing the boat?" Her gaze stretched across the length of white canvas unfurled to the breeze.

"The crew is on the other side of the cabins."

The cabins blocked the view. Two walkways stretched the length of the houseboat. "Do they live on board year-round?"

"When the *dahabeeyah* is in commission they do. Their quarters are below the foredeck."

"How often is this houseboat in commission?"

He leaned with his elbows against the table, cradling his drink between his hands, and observed her with alacrity.

"When I want it to be." His eyes were smiling. "Halid lives on board when he's in Cairo. There are two other cabins and a kitchen. At one time I'd wanted to sail all the way down to Aswan."

"Why haven't you?"

"I don't know." He looked out across the water, his expression nearly poignant. "After a while everything seems colorless."

She watched a bank of clouds drift over the distant spires outlined against the bright blue horizon. "I think to enjoy this country, this city, one must be at heart a painter." She turned her head and smiled at him. "For there is color in everything if one looks hard enough." Pulling aside the length of her robe, she sat.

From the corner of her eye she saw his hand go to the tin of tobacco at his elbow. She promptly set her palm over his. "Is it necessary to keep temptation so close at hand?" She arched a brow. "I thought you were trying not to smoke that stuff."

He sat there for a moment, an imperturbable expression in his eyes. His gaze rubbing across the opening in her robe, his bedroom smile was slow, and Brianna flushed as she was reminded of every place that his mouth had touched her. "What do you suggest that I do?" he inquired of her. "With this temptation of mine?"

"Throw it overboard."

"Now, there's a thought." He relaxed back in the chair. "But what would prevent me from acquiring more? Temptation is all around me."

"Then smoke." She thrummed her nails, impudently surveying him as he'd done her. "But I don't want to hear that you want to be free of your cravings."

His roguish mouth tilted. "Did you have an unhappy childhood? Is that why you're so cruel?"

"No." She cut a slice of cheese and slipped it between her lips. "Though my mother died when I was young, I had a loving if not strict family. I suppose that comes from being the only girl and the youngest. Still, we are close." She sawed off another slice of cheese. "You should see us when we play croquet. Our family tournaments are very lively. World domination is a serious objective at the Donally homestead."

He continued to observe her over his glass, as if she was a little touched in the head.

Maybe she was, she decided, when she turned her attention to the fruit. She wasn't like other women.

Nor was she that different.

"In my family, my brothers Ryan and Johnny held some legendary burping competitions. Those two were always the most misbehaved. Far worse than I've ever been accused. At least I have manners and, though I'm rebellious and generally an anarchist, those are faults that I have turned into virtues."

"Is there anything that you won't or can't do?"

"I can't pee standing up. I tried when I was five. It's very messy." Brianna bit her lower lip to muffle her laugh. "I suppose *pee* isn't a proper word in the feminine vocabulary."

Shaking his head, he looked away and laughed. "I don't suppose it is," he offered in a voice rich and deep.

"What about your family?"

"Domination is achieved through manipulation and autocratic machinations." He bent forward on his elbow. But this time his smile did not reach his eyes, and Brianna saw something of the dangerous man he was. "Our games are more serious than yours. And if anyone burped, my mother would have seen that we didn't sit for a week. That didn't mean we behaved, though. My brothers and I got into our share of trouble."

"Your brothers?"

He studied the contents of his glass. "I'm the third of three sons." Lifting his gaze, he grinned. His teeth were white against the beginnings of a shadow on his face. "Though if you ever knew my parents, you'd wonder how they managed that many. Virgin birth was a very plausible theory among us. We didn't know there was any other way until well into our teens."

She laughed, and plopping a grape between her lips, stretched her hand across the table to play with his. "They can't have been so bad as that. You turned out well."

"One of my older brothers died of typhoid when I was nineteen." He looked at her hand, turning it over to trace her palm. "He was the reason I stayed in England longer than I should have."

"I'm sorry," she whispered.

"Even aristocracy is not immune to common diseases that obliterate the ranks of the poor. As our own queen can attest."

Her voice hesitated. "Aristocracy?"

He raised his gaze. "My family's ducal title comes from a battle fought during the War of Roses. Somehow we've always managed to be on the right side of every monarchy crisis in the centuries since." His thumb rubbed her wrist. "Two years ago when my grandfather died, the Ravenspur title went to my brother."

His brother was a duke? Brianna swallowed this news like a lump of salt. No wonder Alex felt camaraderie with him. They'd both practically grown up in the same circle of tyrants. "Did you ever know my sister-in-law?" she asked.

"I met her once when we were children. Her father heads the Foreign Services office. Lord Ware is my superior."

Brianna's gaze clung to his face. "Then you are probably aware that he's a bastard, who practically destroyed my brother's life."

Major Fallon sat back in the chair. "No." His mouth tilted. "I must have been away from England for that part of the opera."

Dropping her gaze to her hands, now folded in her lap, she tightened her fingers. She'd sought to impress him, but feared she'd only managed to equate her life with a complete lack of breeding. She possessed a sudden need to defend her family to him. "My family isn't a bunch of uncouth Irish bumpkins, Major. My brothers have worked very hard to reach the pinnacle of success they have in British society. Each of them is very accomplished."

But there was no censure in his eyes. Indeed, they were hooded. She could read nothing. "I don't begrudge you your happy childhood," he said. "Frankly, it's refreshing."

"Fallon isn't your real name. Or people would know who you are."

"The people whom I want to know the truth know who I am."

She realized that he'd wanted her to know. It had been no accident that he'd let the information slip. "What *is* your name?"

A muscle worked in his jaw as he seemed to contemplate her question. "James Michael Fallon Aldbury."

"Aldbury!"

Brianna knew that name. The Aldbury family was a British dynasty. She'd come across that name in more than one march on parliament.

"No wonder you can afford this kind of luxury," she said suddenly, inexplicably disappointed and defeated.

"What I have here wasn't bought with family riches, *amîri.*"

"What would make someone like you leave your life and become a soldier? To risk your life the way you do?"

"Now that is something I'm *not* willing to share."

Suddenly feeling out of her element, she started cleaning up the table. "You don't look like a James."

"My name is Michael."

"And what do your other women call you? You must have one or two hidden around here. I found their clothes in your armoire."

Laughter lurked in his eyes. "Isn't this the place in my confession where you're supposed to fall into my lap and swear undying love?"

He was mocking her. "If you want that kind of adoration, there is a flotilla of debutantes here in Cairo eager to catch a husband with your credentials. I liked you better when you were just a soldier."

He caught up to her in the saloon. "Why?" He spun her to face him.

"Because I thought that I knew you." She shook off his arm. "Because you're the man who saved my life when I would have perished. The man who brought Christopher back to Lady Alexandra, who visits invalid men and takes his children to the market." She crossed her arms over her breasts and felt the hot burn of tears in her eyes. "I respected who you were."

He tilted her chin. "And you don't now?"

"I don't know what I think, Major. I don't know how you can be everything good and still hate the way that you do."

"Say my name, Brianna. Is it so hard to call me something other than major?"

She turned her chin. *Your name is too intimate* she'd wanted to tell him, when he captured her chin and pulled her face around.

Yet, it was more than that, she realized.

It was the only line she'd drawn to separate the reality from the fantasy. From thinking that her relationship with Michael Fallon could ever be more than what it was when she'd had her own dreams to pursue, a whole world to conquer—when falling in love with anyone else in this lifetime would be, by and far, the biggest mistake she could make.

"Can't we go back an hour to the way we were?" she quietly beseeched, her arms creeping up to enclose his neck. "We've digressed from our affair. Don't you think?"

"I'm easy, *amîri*." His thumb slid with tantalizing slowness across her bottom lip. "What man would turn down a roll with you?"

The stunned quickness of her breath came out in a gasp.

But he did turn her down.

Shrugging into his uniform, he turned to face her as he

settled his hands over the brass buttons that ran up the front of the jacket. "Halid will be waiting when the *dahabeeyah* docks."

To Brianna's mortification, hot tears welled up. "I've never known you to behave so insufferably rude, Major Fallon."

"Am I?" He laughed, his gaze dipping to touch the fullness of her mouth before rising to encompass her eyes. "The truth about me would probably astonish you, Brianna."

Clutching her robe in bewildered disbelief, she flinched when the door shut behind him. Later, she stood alone on the deck when the *dahabeeyah* docked. Brianna watched as Major Fallon disembarked. He looked so at ease in his place of authority, as if he did this on a regular basis. After saying something brief to Halid, who held their horses in tow on the dock, Major Fallon returned to her with such lazy good humor, she could hardly believe that he was the same relentless predator who had stalked his way into her heart.

But in the end, it was Halid who took her home.

Chapter 9

"You had a visitor from the consulate while you were gone, effendi."

Michael took the bundle of correspondence from his secretary. "Did he leave his name?"

"No, effendi." The secretary's eyes were large, and Michael always had a feeling that the man was terrified of him. "Only that it was important that he find you."

"It must not be too important if he chose not to leave his name."

Annoyed by the cryptic silence of the visitor, Michael walked past the desk into his office. Late afternoon sunlight bore down on the room filled with cabinets and two dead plants, creating a lifeless menagerie.

As was his habit before he settled down to work, he thumbed through the pile of missives and social invitations, separating anything important before dropping everything else into the garbage receptacle.

He was in a thunderous mood.

Swinging around in his chair, he looked out the window over the vast tree-lined parkway that encircled the ministry offices. Puddles of water darkened portions of the quiet stone walk where the gardeners worked. He disliked the closed confines of the office. He didn't know how Captain Pritchards had stood the monotony of tea parties and endless meetings. He felt stifled by his life here—by the impotence of conducting a massive investigation that was leading nowhere.

Footsteps sounded from down the long tiled corridor. When the steps finally registered, Michael turned, realizing he'd left the door to his office open. Donally stood in the outer office doorway, having halted abruptly upon seeing him. He was dressed as if he'd just come from the consulate function. Faintly amused by the black look on the man's face, Michael suspected Donally wasn't expecting to see him in his office.

He stepped into the room and closed the door, his eyes hard. "I take it that you've returned my sister to the house. Safe and sound?"

Michael recognized an adversary in the dark Irishman, and in truth he possessed no desire to alienate one of his only allies, but he'd let the man's implied warning be hanged when it came to Brianna. "I took her to visit Colonel Baker and his family." He bent forward and lit the lamp on his desk. Donally watched his every movement. "We were there most of the morning. Halid took her home, and I came directly here."

Michael didn't account for the four hours in between, nor would he defend his actions for taking her away that morning. Brianna knew her mind far better than the ordinary citizen. Hell, she knew *his* mind. Had honed in on his weakness, smiled her smile, and he'd been as lost as any other male idiot in Cairo. It was illogical that a perverse surge of possessiveness had chased away the need for caution when it came to his reactions toward her. Illogical and annoying as hell that he wanted Brianna with a ruthless singularity of mind that he had not felt in years. Yet, another instinct held the surge in check.

Caution.

The need to understand what had happened to him this afternoon. Because he knew something had.

Donally leaned against the door and gave him a mild look. "If you haven't noticed by now, my sister is an impulsive romantic."

"And it's your job to protect her from me."

"Does she need protection from you?"

Michael sought to check his irritation, and sat back in his chair. He possessed the uneasy feeling that he'd just slid into an ambush.

"My sister has a natural capacity to enjoy life that is contagious to those she touches," Donally said. "Perhaps you've noticed."

In frigid silence, Michael considered where the conversation was heading.

"She weeps at the sight of abandoned kittens and volunteers her time at the mission. She's fought for women's property rights, divorce law reform, and the right for children to be educated rather than put to work. She has the courage to go to jail for her convictions, and has been brought up once already on charges under Disraeli's indecency laws.

"I quit trying to rein her in years ago, when I found her sneaking out at night to see the son of my solicitor. That betrothal lasted four years longer than I thought it would. He was never a match for her spirit or her temper. So you see, Major, you're not the first man she's put in her winsome crosshairs. But that doesn't mean I'm less protective, or desire to see her hurt. She is not as worldly as she thinks she is."

When Michael didn't reply, Donally stepped forward and dropped a sheaf of papers on the desk. "These are the names of everyone who works in my office. I've known each of them and most of their families for years. Whatever you're looking for, you won't find there."

Michael sat forward and lifted the packet, turning it over

in his hands but saying nothing. Brianna's character and passions didn't surprise him. When she committed herself to a course of action, she did so with every ounce of heart and soul. He also knew that whatever had happened in her betrothal, she'd still been a virgin until today.

"Omar was at the picnic." Donally's steps sounded hollow on the floor as he stepped out of the room and turned. "I understand that he'll not drop the charges against you."

"No." Michael leaned an elbow on the desk. "He will not."

"Then you also understand your days in this office are probably numbered." His hand on the door latch, Donally studied him impassively. "Count yourself lucky that when you go, you won't be leaving your post the same way that Colonel Baker or Pritchards did."

Except Omar knew Michael would be just as finished.

Brianna's hands paused in their cleaning as she listened to the steps approaching her third floor workroom. "You're still awake." Christopher stopped in the doorway.

"I couldn't sleep." Brianna twisted the lid on a glass jar and turned to face him.

Somehow, she'd managed to avoid being alone with her brother since she'd missed the picnic last week. Her photography work had taken up her time, and she'd spent the last three days in the Old Quarter focused on her project.

The tiled ceiling sloped sharply down from the entrance into the small room to the back, where a pair of trapdoors opened onto the roof. Brianna had surmised that the room must have once been a pigeon roost, now cleaned and come to life with the pieces that made up her world. Her trays and chemicals lined the cabinet.

She watched Christopher walk among the many rows of photographs strung wall to wall. "I had no idea that you'd done all of this work. Does Alex know?"

"You don't think I spend my days knitting, do you?" Brianna poured water over a tray she'd set in a bin.

He leaned a hip against the counter. "Do you know how to knit?"

"As a matter of fact, I knit quite well."

Reaching past her, Christopher picked a photograph off the shelf above her. It was a picture of Stephan Williams—one she'd placed there months before. He didn't seem surprised. "Have you heard from Mr. Williams since you've been here?" he asked.

"I don't expect that I will. He's married."

"I didn't know."

She set a jar on the shelf beside others marked COLLODION, used for coating the photography plates. "No one ever asked."

"Brea . . ." He watched her clean.

"Don't." She slapped a jar on the shelf beside others.

"What happened between you and Fallon?"

"Yasmeen is not his mistress" she said, skipping past his question. But then you probably knew that. You probably even know what happened to Colonel Baker."

"I know what Omar is, Brea," he said quietly.

Neither of them spoke. The room smelled of silver nitrate, and Brianna moved to tilt up the blinds and let in the night air. Her hair was tied back with a checkered kerchief. "I know that sometimes appeasing men like Omar is necessary to get the job completed," she said. "Unfortunately, diplomacy allows the worm to prosper. I like Major Fallon's way of dealing with people like him better."

"Major Fallon's way is about to get him court-martialed. You don't know him, Brianna."

Turning, with her palms on the countertop, Brianna faced him.

"Fallon may be an efficient soldier, but he has not come by his reputation without cause, Brea."

Brianna's chin lifted. "Are you telling me to stay away from him?"

Christopher was still leaning against the counter when

Brianna blew out the lamp. What did he know about her heart, anyway? Certainly less than she understood herself.

Brianna stood face-to-face with the Falcon of Horus painted on the glass door leading into Michael's office. She could hear the rumble of voices inside through the transom. She looked left and right and saw that a man had paused at the door down the long hallway. Wooden cabinets lined the paneled walls, muting the sounds of traffic outside the ministry.

She peeked inside the basket she carried as if to reassure herself that she'd not traumatized the tiny cargo. Soft mews escalated as light fell on the blanket. Closing her eyes, Brianna mentally checked her posture. She could do this.

Besides, she had another reason for being here, which had nothing to do with kittens or her desire to see Major Fallon.

The man sitting behind the desk, a red fez perched sideways on his shiny black hair, looked up as she entered. He widened his eyes, and the expression on his face changed to one of bewilderment. Four men dressed in long cotton *thawbs* sat in the waiting room. Her hand went to the top button on her bright blue cotton shirtwaist. Although long-sleeved and collared, it stood open at her neck. She wasn't underdressed, but neither was she buttoned up like a sausage. Her lapis-blue jacket matched her split riding skirt.

"I would like to see Major Fallon," she offered helpfully, and considered lying about an appointment as the man wasted a great deal of time flipping anxiously through the ledger in front of him.

Clearly flustered, he raised his eyes. "I see no appointment."

"Perhaps if you can just tell the major that—"

The door to the inner office opened. Michael stood in the doorway, shrugging into his uniform jacket, his gaze going from his secretary to her. He looked every bit as tall and dashing as he had when he'd taken her on the *dahabeeyah*, stripped her naked, and told her that her French *lettres* wouldn't fit him.

"Major Fallon." Her heart beat a little too loudly in her chest.

His eyes paused on her. "What are you doing here, Brianna?"

"I needed to see you."

A shadow darkened his jaw, contrasting with the silver of his eyes. He was devastatingly handsome and, with his implied lack of civility, dangerous to her mind.

Brianna watched as his gaze shifted to his secretary. "When is my meeting at the consulate?"

"In an hour, effendi."

He said something in Arabic to the men waiting to see him, then turned with a silent invitation for her to follow. Brianna walked into the inner sanctum of his office. There was nothing impressive for her gaze to latch onto as she glanced at the paneled walls. Nothing except the man wearing the British uniform who now sat with his elbows resting on the desk and his hands folded.

Staring into the murky shadows of the room, she swallowed that dirty little lump in her throat. She didn't understand what had happened between them on the houseboat.

She didn't want him sleeping with other women, but neither did she want him controlling her life—as if he had some indelible right by his masculine virtue to claim ownership of her, when men had mistresses all of the time. Her desires were no different than his.

"Come inside, Miss Donally."

Turning to close the door, Brianna didn't need to see his eyes to know that they slid down her body, but when she glanced at him, he'd turned his attention to the papers on his desk, gathering them up into a pile and setting them aside.

She held her tote and the basket next to her. The mewing sound of the kittens seemed louder. "You look fatigued," she told him.

"Thank you, Brianna." He crossed one wrist over the other as she continued to stand. "Would you care to sit?" He motioned to the worn leather chair facing the desk.

"I'll make this brief, Major." Brianna said. "Whatever happened between us the other day meant something to me. I think it did to you as well. Yet, I've not seen you in six days, and you seem quite content with that arrangement. Personally, I think that you're a . . . misogynic charlatan."

"Misogynic?" He raised a brow, and she thought she glimpsed mirth in the subtle shift of his mouth.

"Reclusive, and a closed-minded . . . fraud."

"Is that what you came here to tell me?"

Brianna withdrew the book in her bag and set it before him. It had shown up unexpectedly at the mission yesterday. *"A Tale of Two Cities,"* she clarified, as if he didn't know how to read. And because he was treating her so indifferently. "It's mine."

Michael slid the book across the desk. " 'It was the best of times, it was the worst of times.' "

The opening words of the book caught her. " 'It was the age of wisdom, it was the age of foolishness,' " she answered.

His gaze lifted. " 'It was the season of light, it was the season of darkness, it was the spring of hope, it was the winter of despair.' "

Brianna regarded him in open admiration. He shared the same passion for romantic prose. She sat in the chair. "You read."

"Indeed." A smile curved his lips. "Actually I read quite well."

"I mean—" She cleared her throat. "You know the book."

"My tutor was a literary connoisseur of Charles Dickens. I had the pleasure of hearing him read once." He opened the book and saw her name emblazoned on the cover. "Why did you bring this here?"

"That book was part of the effects that were with me on the caravan." Her hands folded and tightened in her lap. Streamers of light seeped through the tightly cinched blinds behind him and heated the room. "It was part of my possessions that I had in my trunk when the caravan was attacked.

I found the book yesterday at the mission among other books that were donated. Surely whoever donated it would have seen my name inside. Can you trace where it might have come from?" she asked.

Michael shut the cover. His eyes had grown darker. "Usually stolen merchandise has been taken in trade many times over before it finally comes to our attention. Who brought you here today?"

"Christopher's driver. I'm in the brougham," A smile flirted at the corners of her mouth. "I should feel safe with the two men that you have following me at all times. For purely professional reasons. Not at all because you might care about me."

He walked to the front of the desk, where he crossed his arms. His uniform pulled at his shoulders. "Is there anything else, Brianna?"

She stood, her skirts whispering with the movement. "Why haven't you contacted me?"

He didn't answer.

She dropped her gaze to her hands as they traced a gouge on the desk. She stood so close to him that she could smell the sandalwood used to scent his soap. "I think that if you quit now you're missing out on a great opportunity to get to know me, Major."

Glancing into his face, Brianna hadn't realized that tears had welled, and by then it was too late to look away. He'd restructured the boundary between them—widened it with a buffer zone the size of Great Britain. But she felt his respect for her and knew that it wouldn't take the skill of a civil engineer to build a bridge over the gaping chasm that had somehow opened between them. She wanted to be with him enough not to throw everything away on a tantrum.

"Heaven forbid that I ever learn how to whine prettily, so that you might want to offer me your handkerchief."

He dabbed both of her cheeks with his sleeve. "One whiff of my handkerchief, I promise, and you would be cured of whining."

Laughing at his response, she picked a piece of lint out of her mouth. "I didn't come here today to weep." She cast him a sidelong glance. Traffic from outside intruded.

He leaned to look down at the noisy basket on the floor. "Are you planning, then, to invite me to lunch? Though I would impugn your dubious choice of fare."

His rejoinder drew a modicum of relief. "I thought perhaps you might take this basket to Yasmeen and the children." She set the basket beside him with some uncertainty, worried that he'd say no. "The alleys around the museum seemed to be filled with homeless creatures."

Michael leaned back on his palms. Then he shocked her by laughing. She took note of the warmth in his eyes.

"Do you think to find homes for all the strays in Cairo?" he asked.

"It's not right that any living creature should be abandoned."

When Michael didn't reply, Brianna turned her attention to the buttons on his uniform. "Have I told you how nice you look in scarlet?"

"Are you a woman who yearns for a man in uniform?"

"I quite liked you out of uniform, Major. Would you like to know which version of you I prefer?" She looked him in the eyes.

His gaze drifted over her with lazy thoroughness.

Where it touched, she felt only a sweet fever, a raw surge of desire. Then he smiled ruefully and sinfully. Brianna realized that his hands were on her arms, and he pulled her between his legs, trapping her from breast to hips, the illicit memory of their previous mating hot between them.

"I suppose I've kept you too long." Her heart beat faster.

"Perish the thought."

Light color rose in her cheeks. Looking into her face Michael discovered the duplicity inside him, for he wanted her. It shone in his eyes and strained against his trousers as he held her intimately against him.

In a languorous upward arc, she entwined her arms

around his neck, and kissed him. His open lips parted from hers, but she drew him back with her hands in his hair, and heaven help him he found satisfaction in her arms.

He'd never quite tasted lips like hers, and grappling with the reality that he was quickly losing control, he took her kiss, opened her lips and let her tongue inside. He caught it. Sucked on it. And drank in her gasp of surprise. "Have you always been this bold?" he said against her lips, absorbing the luxury of unbridled sensation of her hands on him.

"I like the way you taste."

She captivated him. Her scent. The press of her body against his. "You like control."

"I like feeling alive." She leaned on her toes to kiss him again. "You make me feel that way. That can be the only explanation for thinking of you constantly. I'm dizzy with the desire to go sailing again."

The adeptness that had helped lead him in the past had deserted him. He kissed her parted lips, and there his tongue ravished hers with a tender savagery that had tightened his hand around her nape to deepen his possession.

She groaned when his hand slid up her thigh and touched her intimately. He smiled at her response, the splendor of that sound beating through his senses. Pulling her against the length of him, he noted in some remote part of his mind that all the control was back in his hands. "Do you need me then?" he managed with little inflection in his voice, his hand absorbing the heat of her through her drawers, and he knew that she must feel the restraint in his touch.

"I must," she said. "I do need you. But I dislike being manipulated," she managed breathlessly.

"But you like my touch." He smiled into her heated eyes, feeling as though a little of heaven had opened before him. He could make her come in his arms, he thought.

Her lashes lifted, revealing deep pools of blue. His eyes stared into hers. Then his gaze lifted to the transom, and he put her from him. "This is not a good place to do what I want to do with you at the moment."

"Will you let me know about the book?"

Michael moved to open the door. He had a full schedule of meetings today, and he was about to cancel them all for her. "I'll do what I can."

Her hand hesitating on the latch, she leaned on the door. "I want to go sailing again, soon." Lips curving into a warm grin, she took the sunlight with her when she shut the door.

After she left, Michael stared at the empty walls and the two dead plants that had practically shriveled to dust in his care—and felt something reckless stab at his chest. A muscle in his jaw flexed as he shook his head, and his gaze went to the kittens.

She was a vixen, he thought, who knew exactly what she was doing to him.

"Do you need anything, effendi?" His secretary peered around the door into the room. It irked Michael that the man continued to tiptoe around him like a deranged rabbit.

"Cancel my appointments."

Michael walked behind the desk and flipped up the blinds with one finger to look down on the street. Brianna sat in the brougham. The weight of her hair was smoothly netted at her nape, and as the sunlight painted the horizon gold and dappled the ground with light and shadow, she took that moment to look up. He let his eyes go over her with a possessiveness that showed pleasantly enough in his gaze—when all he wanted at that moment was to take her back to the *dahabeeyah* and continue what they'd started.

She was fearless.

A splash of vivid color in his unvivid brown life.

And he was intrigued by the poetic vision of a woman who gave him a perpetual erection. Until this morning, he'd not realized that he had done a poor job of keeping Miss Brianna Donally out of his head.

"When Halid arrives, tell him that I've gone to the Old Quarter." Watching as Brianna disappeared past the curve in the street, he shifted his gaze across the park, to where his men pulled out onto the street.

Michael finally turned back into the room. He didn't believe that Brianna's book showing up at the mission was some cosmic coincidence. "I'll be out of the office for a few days."

Chapter 10

"You're not interested in reading the rest of the papers?"

With a quiet oath, Michael dropped the packet on the desk. "I've read enough," he said, turning his back to the room, hands on hips. He looked out over the parkway in front of the ministry.

Unshaved and smelling of grit and sweat, he still wore his white turban and a belted long-sleeve tunic that reached his knees. His leather boots encased his calves. He'd arrived back at the ministry office less than an hour ago, barely had time to shake hands with the man who had come all the way from England to find him before dropping his knapsack on the desk and reading the packet. Whatever he'd expected to hear from his family one day, it wasn't this.

Never this.

His jaw flexed with angry tension. "Who else knows about this?"

"Once I arrived in Cairo, I went directly to the consul general to find you. I came by your office last week. It has taken me this long to catch up to you. Obviously you don't read your correspondence."

The man's identity answered the question of his anonymous visitor last week. Lord Chamberlain had been his father's personal secretary. Michael also remembered tearing up Caroline's letter.

In the total stillness surrounding him, the blood hummed against his eardrums with an emotional force that grabbed hold of his chest and wouldn't let go. "What happened to my brother?"

"He was thrown from his horse. A rib punctured a lung. Edward lived for almost a month before he succumbed to pneumonia. The stallion should never have been ridden. But your brother never let that stop him. He was a lot like you . . . in that respect."

Michael turned back into the room. At first he'd been temporarily shell-shocked by the news Chamberlain had given him, but the numbness was quickly fading. "Edward has been dead for *eight* months. It didn't take that long to locate me. Why wasn't I told this sooner?"

"Lady Caroline was expecting."

"I see." His scoff held the hint of something far worse than disgust. He squinted down at the crowded street without seeing anything at all. "And my mother chose not to inform me until after Caroline gave birth. How it must have galled her to contact me at all. So, Caroline did not produce the needed heir to the Ravenspur dynasty."

"The lineage of succession passed to you three months ago. Your grandmother is the one who has finally summoned you home. You are the sole beneficiary to the Duke of Ravenspur, the Marquis of Farrington, and all the Aldbury family holdings, your Grace."

Your Grace. The title was as foreign to him—to his way of life—as the desert was to the ocean, and too many emotions collided for him to make sense of anything.

He only knew that he couldn't leave Cairo.

Michael curbed his anger. "I'm surprised the Dowager Lady Anne hasn't sent the royal marines to drag me back."

"I imagine that will be her next step if you do not return.

She wants an heir, your Grace. And fully expects you will marry someone of standing and fulfill your obligation upon your return."

Michael lifted his gaze and, as if for the first time, his eyes went over the ingratiating bureaucrat wearing the colonial white suit. The man he'd once revered as much as his own self-absorbed father. Sons of the family of Viscount Carlisle had held the rank of Principle Private Secretary to the Aldbury family for a century. His round face was ruddy, no doubt from good living. His once stock gray hair had turned white. Sideburns cupped his jowls where he wiped a handkerchief across his mouth. The last time Michael had seen Lord Chamberlain had been the day his father had given him his walking orders and disinherited him. His father had died shortly afterward.

"How are Caroline and her two daughters?"

"The infant is healthy. They are all living at Aldbury."

And for the first time in years, Michael's memories took him to the scented clover fields of home. How long had it been since he'd seen Caroline?

Twelve years?

"What is past is past, your Grace."

Was it?

Michael sank into his chair behind the desk, the enormity of the situation now taking hold. Enough light filtered through the venetian blinds to reveal the wine-colored dispatch boxes awaiting his attention. Paperwork loomed everywhere. His gaze fell on Brianna's book—and as foreign as his emotions were, the thought of her only added further chaos to his current state of being.

He turned the book over in his hands.

"Despite everything, I still have a responsibility to discharge here," he told Chamberlain. "I'm not prepared at the moment to leave."

"As I understand, your replacement will be here before the end of the month, your Grace. In less than two weeks, to be exact."

"Indeed"—Michael crossed his hands at the wrist, a slow burn taking root in his gut—"you've heard that? Before I've met with the khedive? From whom?"

Chamberlain's ears grew red. "The secretary to the consul general told me, your Grace. It was only a friendly bout of conversation."

"Just a bit of state business to pass away the time over tea?" His gaze suddenly went to the file cabinet across the room, certain now that he'd overlooked an important lead. He'd not thought about interviewing employees at the consulate for a possible leak. There shouldn't have been a free exchange of information from this office to the consulate.

But maybe there was.

"Which secretary?"

"The consul general's personal secretary, your Grace." Realizing his error, Chamberlain mopped his brow. "I don't normally discuss business with strangers. But I'm not unfamiliar with the chap. His father knew mine. We both attended Eton."

"Does the dowager have anything to do with my recall?"

"It doesn't matter, your Grace. The dowager duchess has enough connections at Whitehall that should you prove stubborn . . ."

Michael's jaw tightened. "She has erred in her assumption that I even want the title."

"That is no longer your choice, your Grace. The matter is done."

"Go back to England, Chamberlain." Michael stood and personally invited the man out.

"Of what shall I inform her grace of your return?"

Michael opened the door. Did he honestly want that answer? "She'll know that I've returned when she sees me at Aldbury Park."

"You can't stay here forever, your Grace." Chamberlain stopped at the door. "Eventually you'll have to face them all again."

Michael shut the door and closed his eyes. "Bloody, blazing hell," he said to the walls and to anyone else who cared to listen.

"You are perhaps missing your Major Fallon?" The dark mellifluous voice at Brianna's back startled her.

Standing beneath a weeping mimosa overlooking the consulate grounds, she turned, her white skirts rasping with her movement. Sheikh Omar stood behind her. The sun had set against the trees behind him. "We have not been formally introduced, Miss Donally." He bowed over her hand.

Brianna's fingers closed into her palm as she watched his lips touch her flesh. Disgust welled inside her. He raised his gaze to look at her.

Taller by mere inches, the sheikh wore a black brocade coat *stambouli*. His fez perched slightly sideways on his head, his black beard harmonizing the decorations on his chest. His two bodyguards were not far behind. She had no idea whether hers were anywhere near since she was with Christopher and Alex tonight at the consulate.

"Excellency." She hid her reaction in a curtsy. Her hair was pulled up, and she was suddenly conscious of her bare shoulders.

"You are very beautiful in the moonlight, Miss Donally." He smiled, and all she could think about was what he'd done to Colonel Baker.

Gesturing with his beringed hand, he indicated the gaily dressed people milling on the grounds. "They laugh and talk, and you stand over here looking somber. Did you not enjoy the concert performance?"

"I appreciate Rossini and Verdi."

"Cairo has an opera house. My cousin has created a splendid European capital, has he not?" He clasped his hands behind him and observed her curiously. "Yet, you spend much of your time in the Old Quarter with your camera."

How would he know that about her?

He crooked his arm. "You will walk with me?"

"I'm sorry." She looked around him through the trees,

wishing now that she'd not walked so far, or drank so much champagne. "I'm waiting for my brother," she lied. "He told me he would be out in a moment."

"Ah, then he will not mind if you walk with me." He inclined his head. "We are of the same mind, your brother and I, on matters of diplomacy."

A fog had begun to settle over the grounds. Distant roofs and domes, minarets and spires, swam in the misty light of nightfall. Earlier, she'd set her glass of champagne on the passing tray of a servant and hurried down the stairs of the consulate into the early evening air. She looked past the sheikh.

"Shall we, Miss Donally?" He extended his arm.

Not wishing to commit some diplomatic blunder, Brianna placed a palm atop his sleeve and they strolled along the garden path toward the small lake.

"Is it common in your country that a woman of your class and beauty prefers to labor over menial tasks rather than marry?"

Brianna turned her head to look at him. "There are many who find life outside marriage rewarding."

"And you are one?"

"Yes."

"When I was in England some years ago, I sat for my portrait. It was a long time ago. While my cousin studied in Paris, I studied at your Oxford University. I met an English girl. Her eyes were like the finest amber."

They walked along the path that overlooked the lake. "I have occasioned to visit London a few times since. But I fear I am unable to get used to your cold. Or your British propensity for overdressing for every occasion. Do you agree?"

"There is certain magic found in wearing eastern garments."

"And now my country is filled with Europeans who also do not like the cold but still have a disposition for overdressing." He laughed. "The inclination for foreigners to congregate here has made Cairo into a little Europe, with its own

Season from November to March. Still, some choose to live outside the circle. Your brother for one." He seemed to observe her closely. "Major Fallon for another."

She became guarded. "I wouldn't know."

"Do you not? Usually men such as he takes his mistresses from the general population. Fallon has not been as prudent as he should with you."

Brianna was conscious of an unexpected flood of color. That Omar knew so much about her life violated her to the core. Before she could grasp his intention, he placed his palm over her hand to keep her from pulling away. "I have known Fallon for some time." He continued strolling. "I make it a practice to study my enemies, Miss Donally. Especially their weaknesses."

She was suddenly frightened. His hand on hers kept her from leaving.

She could fight him. But what would she say to anyone who saw her? They were still on open ground. "What do you want?"

"We shall finish our promenade around the gardens. It would be unseemly for anyone to think that you and I are engaged in anything but the most pleasant of talk. Is that not correct?"

There was the hint of steel in his voice. Her gaze fell on his sapphire ring because she didn't know where else to look.

"The gem is the color of your eyes," he said, noting her gaze. "I will have it made into a necklace for you. Would you like that?"

Brianna withdrew her hand. Diplomatic faux pas or not, she was finished with the walk. "Get away from me."

Stepping in front of her, Omar brought her up short. "I find it provocative that you are not veiled." The sheikh's pithy gaze settled on her décolletage, and it took every ounce of her nerve not to cover herself with her hand. "What is it men of your country say?" He waved his other hand casually. "You would make a good fuck."

She tried to step around him, but this time he grabbed her wrist, swinging her around to face him.

"When Fallon leaves, perhaps I will take you for myself."

Brianna yanked away from him. Omar made her feel worse than garbage. But it was a degradation she'd have to keep to herself. She would not allow this man to use her to hurt the people who were important to her. "Go to the devil."

"You can relay that sentiment to Major Fallon, Miss Donally," he called after her, his laughter like a knife in her heart. "He is here."

"I have to ask you again, Excellency." Michael stood with his back to the window, his shoulders tense, an indelible ferocity turning over his stomach. "Did Pritchards make reports to this consulate concerning activities at my office? Does Donally report to you?"

"This consulate is not responsible for leaks that more than likely came from your office alone, Major Fallon."

Like hell he was going to let someone charge him for dereliction of duty. "Did Pritchards or Donally report to this consulate?"

Veresy dropped into the wide leather chair behind his desk, the groan of castings muffled by the carpet. Michael could hear the orchestra warming up as strands of Mozart drifted up from the floor below.

"Donally doesn't report to me."

Michael sensed Veresy's pause.

"But Pritchards did," Veresy added tiredly. "As a matter of professional courtesy. All information was given in the strictest of confidentiality."

"As was my imminent recall back to England?" Michael felt a harsh recklessness crawl up his neck. "Something that I've yet to be told?"

"That was unfortunate." Lord Veresy sat back in the chair. "But neither was the information classified."

A silence fell over the room. In vain, Michael only now comprehended that he had lost the support of Veresy. He knew what that meant to his job, to his reputation, and to his honor—lacking as it was, he valued the principles of the oath he'd sworn to uphold.

"Your recall from this post was my recommendation," Veresy finally said. "I've already been in contact with the Foreign Affairs office in London. When the khedive returns from Paris, I'll brief him on the matter." Veresy's eyes narrowed to slits. "I hold no patience for those who court a personal vendetta over national interests, no matter the moral ground that you stand. We have to find a way to work with Sheikh Omar. Because of his holdings in the south, appeasing the man works in British interests, especially when the French have such a stronghold here. I know how you feel. You must also know I'm as reduced to bloody impotence by politics as you are."

Michael turned to the tall window that looked out over the narrow patch of lawn. "How long do I have left at my post?"

"The *Northern Star* leaves out of Alexandria in ten days. I already put in for your transfer, even before I received a visit from Lord Chamberlain this afternoon. I understand that you would have been leaving us soon. My condolences on the death of your brother."

Laughter sounded from the thinning crowd outside. For a moment the noise didn't penetrate; he heard only the rush of blood in his veins.

Then he caught sight of Brianna as she ran up the steps from the garden, her dress belling out around her, and the whole world receded. Something primitive grabbed at his insides as he lifted his gaze to ascertain the reason for her hurried pace. But he saw nothing. Brianna wore white, trimmed with the slimmest of lace, her hair smoothly netted at her nape. The moonlight wrapped her in light and shadow.

Maybe his discharge from his post didn't matter anymore. Life always had an ironic way of turning vinegar into wine when least expected. As Donally had once told him, at least he was leaving here alive, even if he didn't want to return to England at all.

As he watched Brianna, two young men in uniform stopped her at the top of the stairs. "What is the occasion for celebration tonight?" he asked, his gaze following Brianna until she disappeared inside.

"It's Wednesday." Veresy opened the door with grave courtesy. "Go join the crush, Major. You're entitled."

Michael descended the stairs to the crimson carpeted landing that overlooked the ballroom. Conscious that he was not in full dress, he knew that he was out of place among the glittering sect and ornamented uniforms of his brethren. He stood perhaps ten seconds before shouldering through the press of onlookers to where a young captain was escorting Brianna out for the first waltz. One look at Michael's countenance was sufficient to inform even the meanest of intelligence that Brianna was his intended target.

"Sir—"

"This dance is already taken, Captain." Michael stepped between the stunned man and Brianna, and pulled her out onto the floor, his method of securing this dance as unorthodox as his intent was selfish.

"Are you insane, Major?" Brianna lowered her voice.

Michael whirled her in a graceful arc around the edge of the ballroom. "Oh, I don't know," he said with combative eyes, the tenor of his mood pulled by something he could not explain. "Maybe I'm just bloody annoyed at watching every other man look at you." Leaning close, he spoke in a low seductive voice. "Have I told you how beautiful you look?"

Blue eyes lifted to touch his, and he wondered if she'd been crying. "I'd heard that you were with Lord Veresy," she said quietly. "Are you going to face a court-martial?"

"There will be no court-martial."

"I would stand as a witness to your character if it ever came to that," she said. "You know that, don't you?"

"Are you all right?" he asked.

She rolled her eyes. "Goodness, how unsophisticated do I sound?"

But her arms tightened around him, and Michael experienced that same curious feeling of protectiveness he'd felt upstairs. "Do me a favor, Miss Donally." He pressed his mouth to the soft scented fragrance of her hair. "I want only one thing tonight. And she's currently ensconced in my arms."

"Surely a man who sweeps me off my feet in front of the whole European community can grace me with a more provocative endearment, less common than Miss Donally."

Their gazes met. Michael took a turn with her out the glass doors onto the terrace, and together they slowed to a breathless stop. He didn't understand the strange undercurrent beneath his mood or the tension that gripped him. "I believe that there's nothing the least common about you," he replied in a soft tone.

"Only compared to social rank perhaps." She took his much larger hand and turned it over in hers. "I prefer to think of myself as bold."

Michael pulled her fingers to his lips. "Bold enough to sneak out of a bedroom window to visit your true love?" He peered over her hand into her eyes. "The man who spoiled you for life with just one kiss?"

She frowned and snatched her hand away. "I see Christopher has subjected you to the usual brother-to-other-man chat."

"I fear that is the case," he said, quietly amused.

"Did he also tell you that I've spent time in a gaol?"

Taking her hand again, Michael walked with Brianna past a pair of colonnades away from the illumination of the ballroom. "I believe he mentioned that fact as well."

The blue flash in her eyes told him that she was not pleased with her brother. "Then while we're on the topic of my indiscretion, you may as well know the other sordid details of my past."

Gravel crunched beneath his boots. A couple strolling past them in the gardens nodded their heads. "That's not necessary, Brianna."

"Truly, I think it is," she said. "Did he tell you that I shared my captivity in a cell full of bawds?

"Bawds?" He hadn't heard that term in ages.

"Prostitutes," she succinctly clarified.

"Hell, Brianna. I know what a bawd is."

"I won't go into the mundane details of why I was arrested with them in the first place." Her voice remained confrontational. "I went on to document their lives in an attempt to bring awareness to their plight and the plight of others on the street."

"What happened?" He'd stopped beneath a tree near the pagoda.

"My work was considered pornographic and banned in England."

"Did you really publish a book?"

"I did." She raised her chin.

Their gazes held; then she looked at his gloved hand entwined with hers. "Stephan and I were together for four years," she said after a moment. "The man I snuck out the window to see. I thought the sun rose and fell with his smile. I was seventeen when I fell in love with him." She leaned against the tree. "One doesn't just fall in and out of love overnight, if you can understand? And it's never taken lightly with me."

He'd entwined his gaze with their fingers but now looked into her face. "Maybe I understand more than I should, Brianna."

"What I haven't told my family, or anyone else for that matter, is that he walked away for someone else. A simple, sweet English girl more fitting of his station. It was a matter of pride that my family not know." She paused as if to consider her next words.

"Not that my family doesn't have good reason for their doubts about me," she said. "I blamed Stephan for being a stupid dolt, yet, I have the unfortunate ability to understand his reasons for what he did. Now, I'm in Egypt . . . and once again it seems that I find myself drawn to the forbidden."

"In that we are both the same, *amîri*."

Michael was not prepared for her effect on him. He was unused to dealing with the fallible human side of his being. He'd been too long in the desert. Too long a soldier who wasn't allowed to have feelings or to show emotion. His existence hadn't lent itself to doubt or dishonor in the day-to-day ritual of survival. He'd served his queen with dubious distinction, but he'd served with honor. Now, as England emerged on the horizon like a vast green morass of uncertainty, for the first time in his life he found the road ahead fogged with no clear path.

"I think the forbidden excites us." She traced a finger along the epaulette edging his shoulder. "Would you like to know my theory why?"

He leaned his palm against the tree at her back, took in her scent and the heat of her body, which imprinted itself on the length of his. "I've never known you to be tongue-tied, so I expect you'll tell me."

"We are both the youngest in a family of tyrants, subjected to all manner of oppression. And oppression breeds rebellion against authority. Of course, I feel sorrier for your circumstance. I can understand why you became a soldier and ran away."

More than anything else, she had the power to make him laugh, and he did so now.

"Was it any harder then than it is now?" she asked.

"Is *what* harder?" He pulled back to look down into her face.

"You said once that you served with Gordon in China. How did you survive the change?"

"One doesn't survive China in a state of distraction. Especially someone who didn't own a single blister on his hands when he left."

Turning his hand over in hers, she raised it to her cheek, and he was lost to her tenderness. "Did you find out anything about my Dickens book?" she asked after a moment.

"It didn't make the rounds of any shops. Whoever delivered it to the mission did so through one of the children there. The book was sentimental to you. Maybe someone wanted you to have it back. Do you have any more admirers that I should know about?"

"Do tell, Major." Her rebuke was weighted with gentleness. Then she wrapped her arms around him and rested her head on the solid muscle of his shoulder. "I've missed you, too."

He slid his hand beneath her hair. "Have you?"

They were in public, and the trees made a poor shield. A reckless more dangerous part of him knew the sordid ugliness that came with gossip, and how quickly a way of life could end. He didn't want Brianna to suffer that castigation.

Holding her face between his palms, he pulled away and looked into her eyes. Bloody hell, he thought, if he wasn't about to do something honorable. Then she wrapped her arms around his neck—and Michael knew a moment when he was lost. Maybe it was some forgotten memory of cool sunny days and blue skies, he decided, that had stamped his psyche forever. No matter its origin, he couldn't stop himself from covering her mouth with his.

He'd meant only to taste her, but as soon as his mouth touched hers, his arms tightened and he pulled her closer.

"Leave with me," he said against her hair, her mouth, as he kissed her again. "I'll have you back at your house before this soiree ends."

Her hand came up between them. "I can't," she whispered. "I came here with my family. I'm sure Christopher has already gotten word of my unorthodox departure from the ballroom."

"Dammit, Brianna." With a thick sound of frustration, the fury that had been seething just below the surface made itself heard in a quiet oath as he set her away. "Our time together seems to be at cross purposes."

"Truly you can be unreasonable about the oddest things."

The absurdity of his irritation caught at him. But Brianna didn't know him as well as she thought, and *unreasonable* didn't nearly touch the raw edge of his emotions.

"Go," he said quietly, paying no heed to her wounded look. "If you stay here, you're going to find yourself flat on your back."

A frown bracketed the corners of her mouth, but she did as he told her. Michael walked up the steps of the pagoda. Leaning in the archway, he watched the sway of her skirts, and knew a hunger deep in his loins. She hadn't walked far when she turned.

"Will you consider lunch on Friday?" She stood on the flagstone path between the shrubberies. "Alex hasn't seen you since we've been back. Two o'clock," she coaxed him, not waiting for him to answer. "Plus or minus an hour depending on her ladyship's appetite."

Michael watched her go. Somewhere beyond the high walls of the consulate, a mandolin played. He rolled a cigarette and looked out across the lake as he struck a match, then laid the flame to its tip. He turned and peered through the smoke as Brianna disappeared inside the ballroom. He couldn't do the family proviso with her. He didn't know how, and it was too late to begin.

Hell, he hadn't even told her he was leaving Cairo.

He'd told her nothing at all.

Then he looked past the blue smoke and saw Omar on the drive. His hand, holding the cigarette, froze in midair. A bevy of dainty women in their tulle veils and ample dresses of saffron silk surrounded him. He watched as they boarded their European carriage in seclusion. Omar mounted a horse and, followed by his dark guardians on horseback, thundered away from the consulate with all the fanfare of a mighty ruler. In disgust, Michael ground out his cigarette.

He didn't even know the bastard was present tonight. Looking back at the ballroom, he grew still. Charles Cross stood at the edge of the veranda, his blond hair nearly burnished gold by a paper lantern that marked the path into the gardens. He, too, had been watching Omar's exit.

As if sensing Michael's stare, he turned his head, the glow of light on his face. Michael remained unmoving in the shadow, unseen from the ballroom. Then Cross turned away and the moment passed.

As Michael's gaze followed the empty drive where Omar had vanished, he wondered at the glimpse of hatred he'd seen on Cross's face.

The streets were crowded and wet as Brianna made her way to the museum the next morning. After handing her horse over to her groom, she unlaced her saddlebags, her fingers slowing as she quickly turned. She'd felt on edge all morning, and knew her confrontation with Omar last night was partly to blame. As well as her emotions about Michael. The terrible feeling was reminiscent of that day in the suk when she'd seen Michael with Yasmeen.

Brianna raised her gaze to the sky. Pewter clouds hung low over the city. Carrying a satchel holding her photographs in one hand and a rare bottle of Italian wine in the other, she hurried up the stairs. Knowing Mr. Cross's expertise on such things, she knew of no other way to thank him for all the help he'd given her.

As she watched him spread her photographs over his desk, going over each one for flaws, Brianna paced the room, finally coming to a halt behind him. He smelled faintly of carbolic acid, as if he'd washed his hands and clothes in disinfectant. She hadn't been able to talk to him much last night, and he left the consulate just after Michael had.

She'd been poor company, she realized.

"Well?" She was impatient for some comment. Anything but this silence. "Will they work for Lady Alexandra's research?"

Without answering, he flipped through two more, discarding one, then another. He did this for another five minutes until Brianna wanted to scream. His was the only expertise she'd sought. She'd had to make sure of her work before she presented everything to Alex. Thunder grumbled outside and the room grew darker.

"These are excellent, Miss Donally," Mr. Cross finally

said, his light brown eyes intent behind his spectacles, and Brianna almost clasped her hands in a prayer of gratitude.

"Thank you, Mr. Cross." She kissed him on the cheek. "I could not have finished this without your help. I plan on presenting them to my sister-in-law tonight."

Mr. Cross surprised her by opening the bottle of wine. He removed two glasses from a cabinet at his back. "If you had been anyone else in your family, Miss Donally," he handed her a glass, "I wouldn't have lifted a finger to help you."

His animosity struck her. "You don't like Lady Alexandra?"

He leaned around her and opened the window to the sound of rain. "I don't like your brother."

Brianna's mouth formed a silent O. The novelty of that sentiment wasn't new, but the tone of Cross's voice was uncomfortable to her. His eyes watched her as he drank. "My mother would have liked you," he said.

She glanced out the window, down on the rubble that littered the landscape, suddenly conscious of his nearness. Two pigeons cooed on the stone turret outside. "Do you have family in England?"

"I have a younger brother." Turning his attention back to the desk, he set down his glass. "May I?" He lifted the other photographs in her collection. She noted that he seemed more casual with her than usual. "You've captured the expressions of the people." He flipped through the pictures. "You should think about compiling these into your own book."

"Do you think so?"

His hands stopped on the photograph of the young man she'd taken in the caravan. "Yes, I do," he said.

Brianna leaned over his arm and eased the photographs from his hands. There were still events in her life that she was not prepared to discuss nor had any desire to remember. "I've been thinking that I'd like to do something more with my work."

"As have I." His voice lifted her gaze. "In matter of fact, I've been investing these past few years. I have no desire to remain in Egypt. I'm preparing to leave quite soon."

"But whatever would you do? You've spent years training to reach this pinnacle in your career."

"I've decided that it's time to move on. Marry, perhaps."

Brianna laughed. Mr. Cross could be so grim at times that she'd oft wondered if he knew how to live life at all. He looked different this afternoon for some reason. Taller. "Don't tell me that you're in love?"

But as she said the words, Brianna was at once regretful. Turning his back to her, he retrieved his wineglass and walked to the window. He'd not deserved the jest. Especially since it appeared by the stiffness in his spine that *she* could possibly be the focus of his heart. Brianna had no desire to be unkind. At the same time, she didn't wish to encourage him in a direction that she had no interest in pursuing. Her goals would eventually take her from Egypt. Nor did she have a desire to return to England.

"Do you like to travel, Miss Donally?"

"Yes. Very much." Brianna glanced at the rubble across the street, aware of how ugly the morning had turned. "Mr. Cross—"

" 'The blossom is blighted, the leaf is withered, the god of day goes down upon the dreary scene.' " Charles turned his head to look at her. "It's offensive that so much of this city lies in ruin. Don't you think?"

"You're quoting Dickens?" She stared at him in disbelief. "I can't believe you're quoting Dickens."

He perused her in surprise, as if she'd just exceeded some indiscernible bar of intelligence. "No one ever guessed before."

Tinkering with the small metal tab on her satchel, Brianna returned the photographs to the bag. She supposed many people read Dickens. Michael did. She turned to face him. "Mr. Cross, I didn't mean to make light of your heart. The young ladies who are here in Cairo for the Season do so for one reason," she reassured him. "And that's to secure a husband. You would make a wonderful catch."

"Even for someone who is seeing another man?"

Brianna's mouth opened. "She is hardly *seeing* another man."

"I'm glad to hear that." Charles sat at his desk and folded his hands. "Especially since Major Fallon will be leaving Egypt before the end of the month. Possibly sooner."

"What are you talking about?"

"He's been recalled by the government. Though, it won't matter. He'll be selling back his commission anyway."

"Why?" A feeling of coldness settled deep inside her.

"He's to marry when he returns to England. He just inherited the Ravenspur dynasty."

Chapter 11

❦❦❦

"**I**s it true?" Brianna said in a quick breathless voice. Her hair wet from the rainstorm, she stood beneath the doorway of Michael's office. "Are you returning to England?"

Palms flat, he leaned over his desk. A single lamp lit the maps spread out on his desk. The rest of the room was dark. He carefully set down his pencil. "Brianna . . ." Behind him, the venetian blinds banged with the wind. "What are you doing riding here in a storm?"

She didn't understand why she'd come here, why she was so frantic. But an hour ago it had somehow seemed imperative to get here. Imperative that she learn the truth.

As if for the first time, Brianna recognized that he wasn't alone. Her bewildered gaze went around the room. Two men in turbans and robes sat in chairs around the desk. Halid stood near the window, to Michael's left. Her riding outfit soaked through, Brianna clutched her satchel of photographs to her chest.

Thunder shook the windows.

"I'm—" She made a futile attempt to contain her emotions. "I didn't know that you were in a meeting." Her eyes continued to hold Michael's stark gaze from across the room. And then she realized—

He knew!

He'd known last night that he was leaving Egypt. He'd known as she rambled on about tyrants and aristocrats, and said nothing!

She wanted to hit him. The same place that she hurt.

In the stomach.

"Brianna—"

"Don't!" Whatever he was about to say, she didn't want to hear.

She spun away, her wet skirts flapping with her hastened dash to the door in the outer office.

She was angry. Angry that she seemed constantly to allow a barrage of attacks on her heart. Angry with Michael for not telling her that he was leaving Egypt. More than anything, she was furious with herself for being caught off her guard, unprepared for what she knew would one day be the inevitable end in their short relationship, for rushing to the ministry and making a fool of herself when she should have just gone home.

"Brianna!"

Michael's voice froze her hand on the door that would take her out into the corridor and down the long stairway to the street. He stood in the doorway of his office. "I'm sure that whatever you bloody heard isn't nearly enough," he said.

"Trust me, it was enough."

"While we're on the subject of my failure to communicate, why didn't you tell me that Omar accosted you at the consulate function last night?"

Brianna's mouth cinched in disbelief that he would know that.

"Halid told me. He was there last night. I missed you at the house this morning. Where the hell have you been? My men lost you in the city."

"Don't you dare turn this around to me."

"You?" He was incredulous. "How do you expect me to protect you if I don't even know what is happening in your life? Do you have a death wish, because if you do, I need to know right now."

"You are a bastard, Michael Fallon," she whispered. "I thought that we had something between us. I really did. But you are such a liar. Such a . . . *man*." It was the worst insult she could think to pay him.

"Dammit, Brianna. If you haven't noticed, I'm a little busy to be carrying on this ludicrous conversation with you."

"Naturally." Her hand went to the door latch. "Except you weren't so busy last night to attempt a liaison with me in the middle of a consulate function. But then what you do well with your mouth has nothing to do with *informative* dialogue, does it?"

His reaction was as volatile as hers. Brianna flung open the door before he could grab her, and collided with the secretary. The force of her momentum knocked his shoulder against the doorway, and the wicker tray he'd been carrying crashed to the floor, shattering the porcelain coffeepot and cups. She would have fallen if not for the strong hands that caught her. Her satchel flipped out of her grasp, and she watched in horror as her photographs spilled over the wet floor.

All of her photographs.

She could only stare at the catastrophe on the floor. Michael snapped in Arabic to his secretary, then gathered up the ruined photos, before pulling her into the room across the hallway. Releasing her, he kicked the door shut with the heel of his boot. His eyes, clearly expressing more than fury, did not move from her face.

"I'm sorry." He held the ruined photographs out to her.

Brianna just stared at his hand. She couldn't bring herself to touch the pictures. Finally, she sank into the nearest chair.

This was her fault. She'd behaved irrationally and this was what came of it. An unequivocal brain rupture.

God was punishing her for behaving like a complete idiot.

Rain sheeted against the window. The room was small, filled with bookcases and shadows—and Michael.

"Forget it," she said. "It was my fault."

"I don't want to forget it."

"I said this was my fault."

"Are we having an honest to God argument over my apology now?"

Brianna finally snatched away her ruined photographs, if only to be done with it so he would leave. The photographs were clumped together and reeked of coffee. She peeled off the top photo and winced as the image remained embedded atop the second picture.

"Can the photographs be repaired?" he asked, his voice softer.

"No." She finally just dropped them on the floor and lifted her gaze. "You can go back to your meeting. I didn't mean to intrude."

"Come here." He pulled her off the chair.

"Go away and let me brood in peace." She held one hand against his chest. "I don't want you to be nice. I just want you to leave."

Michael wrapped his fingers around her wrist and pulled her into his arms. She winced at the touch. He held her wrist out to the light and noted the bruises Omar had left on her wrist. She could almost feel the fury fill him as he looked at them. "Why didn't you tell me that Omar accosted you last night?"

"Because he threatened you, not me. He said terrible things about you. I don't want you to use me as an excuse to go after him again."

A knuckle alongside her chin turned her face, and his expression softened. "I don't need to use you as an excuse."

"I'm all right. Nothing happened. I swear, Michael."

His fingers scraped into her hair. "Michael is it now?"

She opened her mouth, prepared to say something sarcastic, but he silenced her with his finger on her lips.

"I should have told you last night about the news I'd received yesterday, but I couldn't." Abruptly, there was a hint of a smile in his voice. "No one has ever stormed a meeting of mine before. You made quite a spectacle of yourself, and frightened my men away from European women forever. One would think that you cared for me."

"You mock me," she whispered.

"I couldn't talk to you last night because, frankly, I wasn't ready to discuss anything." He leaned his forehead against hers. "In addition to the fact that Veresy recommended that I be called back to London—"

"He shouldn't have done that."

"I learned that my brother has been dead almost a year."

"I'm sorry, Michael." She was appalled.

Why would someone wait a year to tell him? Despite his earlier indifference toward his family, she knew that he'd been hurt. And she was sorry that he'd elected to go through this alone. "What happens now?"

The contempt in his eyes was almost self-condemnation. "The laws of primogeniture have found me an unwelcome recipient of an inheritance I was never expecting."

Brianna slowly untangled herself from his arms. Mr. Cross had been telling her the truth about everything. Michael would be required to marry some bluestocking bride. He'd become a peer, a peculiar insular sect of individuals that lived behind the grand walls of their estates—a man most people would never see again in his original form. At least, not the man he was now. The thought pierced her.

"You have a lot of gifts, Michael. I think you will make a fine duke."

"Listen to me." He rasped his thumbs across her cheeks. "I'm not leaving tomorrow."

He might as well be leaving in the next hour as far as she was concerned. She pushed his hands away. "You're a wonderful man, Michael." He *was* wonderful. Really, really wonderful, with beautiful eyes, a roguish tilt to his mouth, and she liked him a lot, maybe even fantasized about falling in love with him once too often. "But there's nothing else between us."

"Really?" He laughed at her, which made her eyes narrow.

"It would take me about thirty seconds to prove you wrong on that score."

"Aren't you the confident one, *your Grace*?"

She looked down at the ruined photographs on the floor and blindly knelt to pick them up. She stood and held them to her chest. "And I'm sure that any of a thousand women would be happy to help fulfill your obligations."

"A thousand." It was a statement fraught with amusement.

"There must be a pool of eager damsels for your choosing."

"Brianna—"

"Maybe you'll even remember me the next time I march on parliament. Put a good word in for me if I get thrown into the gaol."

He observed her with infuriating calm. "From the moment you realized I was leaving Cairo you've been completely sure only about one thing: that there *is* something worth exploring between us. There has been from the moment you slept with me. Maybe I've felt it, too, Brianna."

Maybe he just didn't understand what he was doing to her.

A knock sounded on the door. Michael backed a step and opened it. With relief, Brianna recognized the secretary's voice.

"The corridor is clean," Michael said to her, and handed her the satchel. It stank of coffee and wet horse. "Halid will take you home."

"That's not necessary. The Public Works building is on the next block. I'll send my horse home with the groom and leave with Christopher." She stepped past him.

Michael's hand went to the door frame and blocked her exit. The muscles in his arm pushed against the sleeve of his uniform. "Then Halid will take you to your brother."

Brianna was too fatigued and cold to argue,

"If that's what you want."

His thumb slid along the line of her jaw, the intensity in his eyes stunning her. "That's partly what I want," he said, and kissed her.

Warm and impossibly near, he slipped the tip of his

tongue between her lips, opening his mouth over hers; then he sifted his fingers through her hair to pull her against him, and her senses were swallowed by the taste, touch, and scent of him. She didn't even brace herself, only tangled her free hand in his thick hair, stood on her toes and let him tongue-kiss her.

"Thirty seconds, *amîri*." His uneven breath hot against her lips, he smiled down at her, turned and walked away.

She narrowed her eyes at his back.

The only consolation to her bruised stamina was that it seemed he had lasted no longer than she did. But what started out as a scathing castigation of her weakness against him had cooled by the time Brianna reached her brother's office. All she had left to cling to, she thought as she sat in the anteroom, were her ruined photographs.

She tried not to get physically ill as she unglued the top few. She might be able to salvage some. Filled with disgust, she stuffed them back in her satchel so Christopher couldn't see.

Thankfully, the gargoyle that had taken over her body earlier had reclaimed its perch on some nether ledge in her brain. She didn't want to think about Michael. He would be out of her life forever, and she would still be here to pick up the pieces of their affair, which hadn't gone at all as she'd expected. Michael had controlled everything from the beginning, even inadvertently down to the timing of his departure.

Yet, as she remembered her confrontation with Omar, Brianna was glad for the forces that would take Michael away from this place. Take him away before he met the same fate as Colonel Baker or Captain Pritchards. Hadn't she already witnessed how quickly people could perish?

Gradually, she became aware of the leather cushion at her back, the sound of rain on glass. The stares of others. She imagined that she looked like a drowned cat. Smiling inanely at their rudeness, she fluffed her wrinkled skirt. "I forgot my parasol," she primly informed them.

Where was Christopher anyway? She had no intention of waiting until he saw everyone present. Brianna stood, she walked to the wall and, clasping her hands behind her, casually studied the photographic images. She smiled when she saw some of her own. Then her eyes widened as she realized that the wall was covered with her work. Much of it she'd taken in England: Cremorne Gardens, pictures of parliament from the Victoria embankment, Soho, and even Spittlefields.

She'd never been in Christopher's office before. She had no idea that he had so many of her photographs.

There were others as well. A picture of the khedive's palace in Cairo. Her heart kicked unpleasantly against her ribs when she recognized Omar standing next to the khedive, his hand extended to Christopher in a gesture of friendship. Leaning nearer, her gaze focused on the youthful face of the young man standing beside Omar. Everything inside her froze.

Brianna looked at the date emblazoned in brass beneath the mounted photograph. Two years ago.

She returned to her satchel and, prying the photographs apart, sought the one of Selim. Her hands trembled. Black and gray streaks from a stone tower smeared his image. She no longer had the plate. The sandstorm on the way back to Cairo had destroyed everything that survived the attack on the caravan.

"Brianna?"

Christopher's voice spun her around. His dark eyebrows raised, he looked at her over the spectacles on his nose, his gaze taking in her state of disrepair. "I was just told that you were here."

"Who is that young man?" She pointed to the photograph on the wall.

Christopher regarded the photograph impassively before removing his glasses and sliding them into his pocket. "Omar's youngest son."

"He was on the caravan, Christopher," she whispered,

aware that the room had grown silent. "I swear that is Selim."

"Brianna"—her brother took her arm and escorted her out of the anteroom—"you couldn't have seen him."

"But I did."

"He's been at school in England for the past two years. He's attending Oxford." She heard her brother's statement as if from a distance, and looked up to see that he'd brought her into his office and had shut the door. "The caravan attacks began last year, Brea. Whoever you saw can't have been him."

She rubbed her temple. Maybe she was mistaken, she silently conceded. The photograph on the wall wasn't completely in focus.

"You can't just make an accusation like that without solid proof, Brea. Even *with* solid proof, you'd have to be damn sure of your facts."

"I know. I know." She scraped her fingers through her tangled hair. She should just lie down in traffic. Get everything over with now. "I've had a really bad day, Christopher." She pulled back her shoulders. "Do you think we can go home?"

"What are you doing here anyway?"

"I was escorted here by the minister of war's henchman."

Christopher's brow arched in amusement. "There is no minister of war, Brea." He returned to his desk and, reapplying his spectacles, returned to the document on the desk. "I won't be that much longer."

"Did you know Major Fallon is leaving Egypt?"

Christopher raised his gaze. "I know. He told me this morning."

"Truly, Christopher." Brianna crossed her arms and laughed. The stylish room had curved cast-iron window frames and a white-marble chimney piece in the Egyptian flavor, designed by the office's previous occupant to celebrate Nelson's victory in the Battle of the Nile. It was a silly room, Brianna thought as her mind desperately sought a distraction. "I suppose everyone in Cairo knows about his inheritance?"

Even Charles Cross, who worked at the museum.

Charles Cross, who'd quoted Dickens and, until today, had never made her feel uneasy.

"You had a visitor today, Sitt."

Abdul met Brianna with a handful of invitations and mail the next evening as she walked into the house, carrying a small package that she'd picked up at the apothecary that afternoon.

Brianna had started up the staircase before she realized Abdul had spoken. "Who?"

"Major Fallon, Sitt. He said that you had invited him to lunch."

Brianna looked past Abdul to the tall clock. "I completely forgot."

No she hadn't. He'd specifically implied that he wasn't interested in dining with her family.

"He stayed most of the afternoon. He and Lady Alexandra had a pleasant chat. He left shortly before Mr. Cross arrived."

Brianna retraced her steps down the stairs. "Mr. Cross?"

"Her ladyship was most gracious, Sitt," Abdul called after her.

Brianna found Alex in the parlor installed on a red velvet Roman chaise lounge, a blanket wrapped around her lap. She wore an emerald dressing gown. A pair of ornate brass lamps cast light over the photographs in her hand. "Brea . . ." She looked up as Brianna stepped in the doorway. Her sun-streaked hair had been tightly wound in a coronet around her head and her color had returned. She looked beautiful. "Won't you sit down?"

Brianna's gaze fell on the photographs strewn about the thick Persian carpet, clearly laid out by category, including those that had been ruined yesterday. "I found these in your bedroom," Alex said. "Why didn't you tell me that you had all of these? They're wonderful."

"They're ruined." Brianna walked to the edge of the chaise lounge.

"Not all, Brea." Alex flipped through the dozen in her hand. "These are perfect. Mr. Cross was right. He said that you had done a quality job. He'd wanted to see more of your pictures. Imagine my surprise when I had no idea what he was talking about."

Alarmed, Brianna looked past Alex into the corridor. "Did you take him into my laboratory?"

Alex laid the photographs on her lap. "I went to your chambers after he left. May I please keep these?"

"Do you really like them?"

"What do you think I'm trying to tell you?" She laughed. "You've helped me decide that if I don't at least attempt to finish this project, I will have done us both a grave disservice. Besides, I have to do something with my time or I shall go mad alone here all day."

"My lady?"

Alex folded her arms over the photographs and looked up. "Did everything go all right today?"

Her expression softened. "Major Fallon wished for me to tell you that he will be leaving Cairo next Saturday for Alexandria."

Brianna looked away. "I suppose you also know who he is."

"I do now." Alex sighed. "You've been through a lot these past months. It's understandable that you would feel something for him, Brea."

"He doesn't deserve to leave here in disgrace," Brianna whispered.

"I know."

All Brianna could do was nod as she set her packet beside the lamp. "I brought you tea," she said. "It should help with your nausea."

Her skirts whispered as she climbed the curved stairway.

Reaching her room, Brianna shut the door. Gracie had already lit the lamps. She walked across her room and opened the glass doors. The cacophony of birdsong had faded with the last of the daylight.

Nothing had been the same since she'd returned from the desert. Having an affair had not been anything like she'd thought it would be. Moving onto the balcony, she searched for a light in Michael's apartment.

"Mum." Gracie was suddenly beside her, testing her forehead. "You look flushed."

"I'm fine, Gracie." Brianna's voice was tired.

"A fever is quick to come upon a body in this clime, mum."

With the instincts of one who had been a nurse her whole life, Gracie set to the task of putting Brianna to bed.

Suddenly she didn't care. Her maid fed her warm milk with her dinner and a miracle elixir that cured everything from toothaches to rheumatism. Then she found herself tucked in bed, buried in covers as she watched Gracie turned out the lamps. "Thank you, Gracie," Brianna quietly said. "At least I'm assured that you've cured me of any ailment before I'm felled."

"The chlorodyne drops will help you sleep, dear." The last lamp beside the door went out, descending the room into darkness. "I'll see that no one disturbs you. Good night, mum."

Chlorodyne drops!

Gracie and all of her medicines. The last thing she wanted to do was fall asleep. She flung back the covers and locked the door. She'd saved the clothes Michael had given her in the desert, and stepped into the tunic and trousers. Adjusting the turban on her head, she walked onto her balcony and looked at the fifteen-foot drop before leaning forward to pull herself onto the nearest tree limb.

Michael heard the scrape of footsteps in the stone enclave above him. The moon was a white face in the sky and lay a patchwork of shadow and light up into the stairwell. Music and laughter drifted from the coffee shop down the street, nearly concealing the faint rasp on stonework as someone moved. He stepped into the shadows, his hand easing his revolver from the holster at his hip.

A slim white figure appeared at the top of the stairs, and Brianna stepped into the moonlight. An oath on his lips, Michael relaxed his grip on the revolver. He could have shot her. And how the hell did she get to his quarters in the first place?

"How long have you been here?"

"What happened to you?"

They'd both spoken at the same time.

"I've been here since eleven o'clock." Brianna watched him ascend. "I didn't know if you would be here. I'd hoped that you were alone. I mean"—she stretched to look around him as he stopped on the stair below her—"I don't know what it is you do at nights when you aren't out roaming the vast wastelands saving people."

Her gaze dropped to the rag that wrapped his knuckles. She lifted her eyes in question. He'd not moved. Then he ascended the last step and stood before her. "I'm alone," he said, and drew a key out of his pocket.

Opening the door, Michael stood aside and waited for her to pass. She stepped past him, her gaze on his as she entered. Once inside, he removed his holster and walked through his bedroom, then to his office. He peered out the blinds at the lake, then turned to face the nemesis in his dreams.

"You've been hurt," she said.

He looked down at his jacket hanging open, the buttons torn from their moorings, probably lost in the alley where he and his men had been ambushed that night. "I'll be all right, Brianna."

"And you don't wish to tell me about it?"

He hadn't moved, but he did so now as he set the gun on the desk. "I don't mean to be evasive, but I've been at the infirmary for the last two hours. Two of my men are there. It really is the last topic I want to discuss at this moment."

"Did you know there are crocodiles in that lake?"

He paused in the act of lighting the lamp. The tunic she wore molded to her slender body. "The lake is part of the Nile waterway." Peering at her, he blew out the match. "It would be to my utmost relief if you told me that you didn't swim the channel over here."

"I borrowed a boat and rowed across the lake. It isn't far if one can take advantage of the current." She shoved the ragged length of the turban over her shoulder. "Do you hurt?"

A grin touched the corners of his mouth. It was the first hint of emotion he'd felt in the last two hours. "Not in the places that count."

Her left brow hitched. "That's good to hear . . . Michael." She looked around her, and in her typical feminine inquisitiveness, asked, "Have you ever had a woman in this apartment? Nevermind. Don't answer."

He didn't.

She turned into the archway, and Michael watched her gaze go over his bedroom. There were no decorations on the walls, no memorabilia that revealed any other existence outside the one he'd lived for the past few years. Even that was limited to one ceremonial spear he'd brought back from the Sudan, given to him as a gift from a tribal chief. His eyes held to her profile before dipping lower. Her arms remained folded over her torso. She'd rolled the length of her baggy trousers, and looked like something ethereal out of *A Thousand and One Nights*.

They were like night and day, shadow and light. Yet, in some abstract way, he thought her the most beautiful thing he'd ever seen.

"The place is nearly empty. You've started to pack, I suppose."

"Why are you here, Brianna?"

When she turned back into the room, her blue eyes

seemed to radiate into his. Lamplight wavered over her slight form, displacing the shadows. And Michael was suddenly unsure of the tenacity of his restraint, of his emotions. It seemed as if for too many years his life had been nothing but shadows and death. He'd lived in the wake of both for so long that he hardly recognized the force that drew him forward. He was wary of his current turmoil. Wary of a heart that he'd allowed to escape from his grasp. Most of all he was wary of himself.

For more years than he could remember, he wanted to make love to a woman almost more than he wanted to breathe.

"I'm sorry that I missed lunch this afternoon." She approached until she stood in front of him. "Had you been more specific in your acceptance, I would have been less forgetful in my attendance." Eyeing the revolver on the desk, she ran her finger over the rag on his hand. "Are you angry?"

"Do you mean could I have accidentally shot you?" His eyes continued to burn into hers for another fraction before he placed the gun on a shelf above his head. "I didn't."

"I'm relieved. I've been told that I have a habit of doing a thing," her voice warmed with her eyes, "then asking afterward."

"That's a very bad trait, Miss Donally." He slipped his fingers beneath the cloth wound around her head and leaned toward her. "I happen to know firsthand that such a characteristic can get one removed from one's post in Egypt." His lips brushed hers, not quite a kiss. "What are you going to do if someone finds you here?"

Brianna rose on the balls of her feet and, caught in that familiar miasmic aura that hovered around her senses whenever Michael touched her, loitered in the warming mist. She knew she was drunk on the affects of the chlorodyne drops and warm milk. "You don't think me too forward for coming here tonight?"

"You're the most forward woman I've ever known." His lips lingered possessively over hers.

"I know this is risky, Michael. But I had to see you."

"Why?" he whispered.

She only knew that she didn't want to be just another woman that he'd forget when he left. She'd always preferred to be fractious and unmanageable rather than insignificant.

Insignificant terrified her. She tried to kiss him.

"Why, Brianna?"

"I want every woman you meet to come up lacking because you've had me." Her eyes glittered with the unexpected tears of her jest. "Because thirty seconds yesterday wasn't nearly enough time to ravish you."

"Christ." His mouth smiled against hers. "You make me ache."

Totally conscious of the heat between them, Brianna no longer held her breath as his lips seized hers. The headache that had plagued her for the past few hours faded as his hands moved over her slim shoulders, pushing past her barrier of doubt whether he would welcome her tonight. She knew so little of his heart, and the control she imagined she'd possessed never materialized. His presence swallowed hers. Walking her backward, he slid his arm around her waist then curved both hands over her bottom. Her breasts ached to be touched. She placed her hands on each side of his face, his jaw rough against her palms, and kissed him as he kissed her.

A deep groan sounded from within his chest. His hand went to her breast, her collarbone, then reached for the cloth wrapped around her head. A tug sent it unraveling to the floor. His mouth closed again over hers, and their tongues danced then melded, tasting and loving.

"Raise your arms." His hand fisted in the tunic and pulled the cloth over her head. Her hair tumbled over her shoulders to her waist. The tunic whispered to the floor beside the turban.

Brianna's fingers slid beneath his jacket and pushed it off his shoulders. It fell to the floor, unnoticed by either of them.

He reached behind him and pulled the thin shirt over his head.

Her back hit a wall.

So did his palms. Gasping for air, they stared at each other, silver eyes locked on blue, his dark hair disheveled. She opened her hands over the light spattering of hair on his chest. He smelled faintly of sandalwood and sweat. He was fully aroused against her. "Tell me, *amîri*"—his hands crushed the loose cloth of her waistband and slid her trousers far enough down to finish the descent with his boot—"tell me I'm not a fool for wanting you as much as I do."

His lips slid down her throat over her collarbone to the full slope of her breast. With feverish impatience, his hand was intent on unbuttoning the clasps on his trousers. A groan trapped in her throat, she dropped her head back against the wall. His mouth pulled first one nipple, then the other. Then he was lifting her easily, his other hand wrapped around his erection as he bent and guided himself inside her, filling her. Alive and hot, different than he'd felt when he'd worn the French *lettre*. Somewhere, a part of her brain rebelled that she wasn't protected. The danger whispered, but Brianna reached to kiss his mouth in unthinking greed.

With the throbbing tempo of her heart, he began to move in a slow rocking rhythm, forcing her weight upward and against the wall. "Tell me, Brianna." His uneven words rasped against her ear, while his body continued in measured rhythm. "Tell me I'm not a fool."

Her palms gripped the corded muscles of his arms. *She'd* been the fool to come here thinking that she would be the one to seduce *him*. She had never controlled anything about this relationship. But she wanted him inside her. She felt protected in his arms, safe in his strength, and too far gone to think whether this union could result in a child. All of her well-planned precautions had combusted.

She clung to his shoulders. "I want you, too, Michael."

"That's good to know, *amîri*." His breathing almost urgent, he returned his lips to hers. "Because I want to be deeper inside you."

He pushed her thighs farther apart. The wall braced her

back. Brianna sought to embrace the subtle violence beneath his emotions. She only knew that he took faster than she could give in return, that he'd barreled through her control and the remnants of her defenses.

She was no longer the simple romantic she'd once been, she realized in some hazy, detached portion of her brain that looked upon her complete submission to him with profound alarm.

There was a darkness about Michael that frightened her; a life she knew little about, except that he had left a world he'd once known and never looked back. What kind of man could do that to his heart?

Except perhaps a man who had left that heart in England.

His arms crushed her against him, sliding her body to meet his thrusts. Her hair draped his shoulders. With a cry, she arched in his arms. Then he caught the back of her head in his palms so he could look into her face, and helplessly she slipped into climax.

Michael watched her through smoldering eyes as she watched him, until her lids were too heavy to remain open, until he took her body to shattering completion and drank in her choked cry. And neither noticed when he finally sank to his knees.

It was a long time later before he opened his eyes. Brianna was draped around him. He scraped the hair off her face and found her smiling. "You said that we have until the sunrise," he said.

"Yes." She locked her ankles around his hips. "So you may get undressed and take me to your bed."

Michael cocked a wondering brow before he took her mouth in a deep, lingering kiss and finished his descent to the floor. He could feel himself sinking into the deep fire of her body. Yielding to her intimacy. She was sweet delicious torture, and he suspected that they wouldn't make it to the bed for some time yet.

Chapter 12

Michael leaned a shoulder into the archway of the bedroom and raised a cup of coffee to his lips as he observed Brianna sleeping in his bed. He'd not shaved. Wearing a loose-fitting caftan open to his chest, and black trousers, he didn't know how long he'd been standing there since he'd risen and dressed. He'd been unable to sleep.

Daylight had begun to displace the shadows, bringing color to the murky gray of his room. Brianna's dark, perfumed hair lay in waves over his pillow. A white sheet wrapped the long curves of her body, the rest of his bedcovers lying on the floor, her serenity contrasting with the wanton in his arms last night. A tremor passed through him that he was unused to feeling except when he was watching her climax beneath him. More and more these past weeks he'd found his mind drifting to her when he should have been working. Found his thoughts pulled by the primal realization that she belonged to him. She made him feel things he'd thought gone forever.

Michael was a man without illusions about his character. He'd spent too many years of his life possessing no heart at all to believe in love. But he felt bloody damn sure that what he and Brianna shared was far better, and more potent, than love. It was more than most people started out with in a marriage— a marriage of his choosing—and now that he'd had the night to reflect on an uncertain future and the possibility of a child between them, he found that he wanted Brianna beside him. He liked the idea. They suited each other.

She wasn't tainted by the elitist circle of his past. She had courage and beauty, and strength of purpose enough to make a duchess. To stand at his side. Like solid eastern philosophy, their differing facets complimented and contrasted each other, yin and yang—the source of light, heat, and darkness that fit perfectly in one circle to make a whole. She'd been a virgin when she came to him, and whether he agreed with the idolatry of maidenhood or not, that act had had a profound affect on him.

The thought of another man in her life, even one as benign as Cross, drove like a stake through his gut. He didn't understand his need to possess her, and now that she could be carrying his child, he only knew that he couldn't leave her in Cairo.

His gaze went to the glass doors overlooking the lake. Sunlight began to turn the steel-gray sky gold, and in the amber mists of a new dawn, Michael watched the sun rise.

"You look like a brigand." The voice came from the bed and arrested Michael's hand as he was about to drink his coffee.

Brianna had turned her head and found him standing in the doorway. He peered at her with eyes that were filled with both tenderness and desire. "And you look like a well-pleasured houri slave girl."

Brianna rolled onto her stomach. Her hair fell in a tangled mass over her shoulders. "Am I part of your harem, m'lord brigand?"

"Would you want to share me, then?"

Brianna leaned forward on her elbow.

She still felt the sluggish effects of the chlorodyne drops

Gracie had given her as she watched Michael set down his cup. "Never."

"That's good. Because I wouldn't want to share you either."

But even as she sensed the tempo of Michael's mood change, Brianna became aware of the sunlight on his hair, on the floor and walls. Her eyes returned with shock to the window. "You should have awakened me."

She swung her legs over the side of the bed and, dragging the sheet along behind her like a Nile queen, swept past him. She frantically searched for her clothes, snatching them off the floor. "This is Gracie's whist morning at the consulate." Brianna slipped the tunic over her head. "She thought I was ill last night and wouldn't have tried to wake me. I still might be able to get back. Why didn't you wake me?"

Michael had moved to the doorway in his office. Beneath the loose-fitting caftan he seemed taller, less civil, as much by what his clothing revealed as what it did not. He was a man who appeared to have staked a claim, not only to the doorway, but to her.

"I'll take you home."

Brianna stumbled in place as she bent to slip on a sandal. And the awful thought struck that he'd allowed her purposely to sleep past dawn. Except she wouldn't believe that he'd put her in that kind of dilemma. Christopher would never forgive her for this indiscretion. "That would be very unwise, Michael."

His arm blocked her passage. "Brianna." He tilted her chin. "You and I need to talk."

"No." She knew what he was going to say. Knew where this conversation was heading. More than the realization struck that she'd had completely unprotected sexual congress with him last night. Numerous times.

"Chrissakes, Brianna. I'm asking if you've considered the consequences of what we did last night?"

"Yes." She glared at the ceiling before meeting his gaze. "I considered it briefly." She poked a finger at his chest, horrified that he might attempt something honorable, and blurted out the first thing that entered her mind. "And if I'd wanted to wed anyone, I'd have wed Stephan Williams years ago. At least I would have been assured of a normal life."

Her voice died as a pair of piercing eyes locked onto hers. "Is that right?"

"I apologize, Michael. I shouldn't have said that." Her burst of panic gave way to misery. "But I don't want some magnanimous sacrifice from you. I am not a brainless twit who can't take care of herself!"

"Your enormous wisdom in this matter is quite apparent, Brianna. I applaud your insight and perception with a standing ovation."

Despite herself, she felt a surge of fury. She felt betrayed by his mockery. She thought that he knew her. That they had reached a mutual understanding. She'd learned the veracity with which reality could tear everything away. Nothing was sacred and nothing lasted. She'd sworn never to fall victim to helplessness again. Never to expose herself to vulnerability.

"In a few days you'll be walking out of my life forever." She dropped to her knees and looked beneath the bed for her other sandal. "I can live with that better than knowing that you sacrificed yourself because of some antiquated notion of principle and gentlemanly honor concerning your responsibility toward me." Snatching her sandal, Brianna stood and looked around the room. She swept past Michael. "Where is my turban? Why can't I find—"

In a daze, she felt the steel pull of his fingers wrapped around her wrist. Her eyes snapped up. His grip was not brutal but she knew she'd not be able to pull away until he chose to release her. "Why are you really angry?" He touched his mouth to her temple. It was hot and burned a knowing path down her throat. "What exactly are you afraid of? Me?"

"Yes!" She'd wanted to rail at him, but the word came out in a barely audible rasp.

Even if he did have the right to plan the rest of her life, had he considered how she'd survive married to an aristocrat? "I can never be a duchess. You must know that. No amount of pride can overcome our class difference. You would only find a reason to dislike me after a while."

"Is that what all of this is about?" He laughed, pulling her tighter within the circle of his arms. She glared at him. It wasn't fair that she couldn't resist him, and had already proven herself exceptionally easy. "Do you know what the third son of an earl is? A commoner, Brianna."

"How can you not understand?" No matter what Michael called himself, he'd still grown up with the Aldbury name. "I grew up fighting the entire caste system your name represents. Lady Alexandra's father nearly ruined our family. I'm Irish, Michael."

"None of which stopped you from coming over here last night."

"The possibility of a child between us must surely be remote. It's not worth ruining both of our lives, Michael. Wait if you must."

Someone pounded on the door, and Brianna nearly jumped out of her sandals. Michael eyed the intrusion with malice.

The pounding came again. "Major Fallon?" They heard a heavily accented voice through the thick door. "We must speak with you."

"Who is it?" Brianna whispered.

Michael walked with long strides to the bedroom window and peered through the blinds. Two men wearing the special uniform of the khedive stood on the street below, holding the reins of a half-dozen horses. Brianna leaned around him. "Are those Omar's men?"

Struggling with the leather strap on her sandal, she hopped behind him into the office and watched as he pulled his gun off the shelf where he'd placed it last night. "What exactly happened to you last night?" she asked.

"I tried to see Omar." He spun the cylinder on the revolver. "Afterward, my men and I were attacked."

"You couldn't tell me this last night?"

"And ruin the whole mood of your seduction? Trust me, you were a far more pleasing weight on my mind. Stay out of sight."

Brianna grabbed his forearm. "Why don't *you* stay out of sight, and I'll answer the door? I can tell them they are at the wrong apartment."

Reaching behind him, he tucked the gun in his waistband, and grinned. The pounding on the door became more insistent. "That's why we get along, Brianna. You have a sense of humor that defies logic."

"Oh!" She snatched her hand away. He caught her wrist and yanked her against him, her furious breath leaving her in a rasp. "You're bloody impossible, Michael Fallon. How could you not tell me that someone attacked you?"

He grabbed a gentle fistful of her hair and pulled her head back to look into her eyes. "Would you miss me if I were gone?"

She tried to look away. Michael tightened his hand on her nape, and her eyes snapped to his. His gaze burned with white-hot intensity. Pressed to the hardened length of his body as she was, she didn't even try to break his grip on her wrist. They stared at each other, suspended in light and sound; then haltingly he lowered his lips.

"You and I are not finished with our conversation, *amîri.*"

The last person Michael expected to see on his porch when he opened the door was Christopher Donally, his hands shoved in his pockets, pacing the narrow enclave. Michael shifted his gaze to the man who had been pounding on his door. Wearing the green and scarlet uniform of the palace guard, the captain was braced with his hands behind his back. Halid leaned against the stone wall that divided the stairs. Michael noted that he was unarmed.

Donally spoke first. "You're a difficult man to find."

"Are you here to protect me?" Michael asked pointedly. "Or to see me arrested?"

"Omar's dead," Donally said, straight to the point.

"Dead." The word was a statement, an undigested response. Incredulity. The captain shifted, putting an end to any illusion that he was there on anything other than state business. "Since when do they send the Public Works minister to act as constable?" Michael asked.

"Sir Christopher was with me when the captain arrived at the ministry office this morning, Fallon effendi," Halid said.

"I'm here because my wife has a great deal of fondness for you, Major," Donally explained, "and understands the justice system as well as you and I. Halid seems to be the only man in Cairo who knows where you live, and he thought it prudent to cooperate."

Michael shifted his unblinking eyes to the captain. Making a decision, he reached behind him and carefully withdrew his pistol. He handed it grip first to the captain. "Tell thy men to stand down," he said in the vernacular, moving to allow Donally and Halid to pass through the doorway.

The captain hesitated, but he dismissed his men before entering Michael's quarters. Folding his arms, Michael leaned with his back against the door and took all three men into his gaze. "Couldn't this interview have waited until I came into the ministry this morning?"

"You were at Omar's residence last night," Donally said.

"Omar wouldn't see me."

"And you could not break into his residence and hold a gun to his head this time?" the captain queried. "Do you recognize this weapon, effendi?" He unrolled a thick cloth. A blood-smeared knife thunked to the table. "Omar was found early this morning stabbed to the heart. The last time he was seen alive was last night at eleven o'clock. Where were you?"

Shaking his head, Michael looked away in disgust. The authorities were going to pin the murder on him. Christ . . . Omar was dead. It wasn't the first time he was innocent of something of which he'd been accused. He focused his next statement on Donally. "Do I seem like an idiot who would leave a murder weapon in my victim?"

Leaning his hip against the table, Donally folded his arms, his eyes stark in the shadows. "I'd hoped that you were not."

"You were attacked last night," the captain said, seizing the conversation again. "You must have been very angry. Angry enough to seek revenge."

Disgusted with the captain's peremptory tactic, Michael cocked a brow. "What makes you think that Omar was responsible for the attack on my men when he is supposedly innocent of such deeds?"

The man's dark eyes faltered. "I only assumed—"

"That he would try to kill me?"

"I assumed that you would presume it was he, effendi."

"Last night I was too concerned about getting my men to an infirmary. I didn't notice my knife missing. Yes, I'd been to see him before that, but as witnesses can attest, he was alive when I left."

The captain's spine notched. "Can you prove where you were last night at eleven?"

Michael was growing increasingly annoyed, and when he set his fists on his hips, he looked intimately deadly to anyone who knew him. He hadn't gotten to his apartment until nearly midnight.

"It's a legitimate question, Fallon," Donally said.

"I wasn't alone," Michael finally replied.

"No one assumed you were," Donally said.

The man didn't know the half of it.

Shit!

He squeezed his eyes shut and pinched the bridge of his nose.

Movement behind Donally lifted his gaze. Brianna stood in the doorway to his bedroom. She'd found the turban and had managed to wrap her hair. But there was no mistaking the curves on her body, no mistaking that she was a woman. Long, sooty lashes, clearly a Donally trademark, framed her huge eyes. They'd frozen him with their intensity.

After today, every bloody person in Cairo would know she'd spent the night.

The captain turned abruptly, as did Halid, who had sat down at the table.

The captain, clearly startled, moved forward. Donally's arm slapped out. "No," he rasped.

"Major Fallon was here all night," she said, chin high.

"Jaysus, Brianna," Donally whispered.

"I got here before eleven." Her chest rose on a sudden inhulation, and the construction in Michael's gut lightened. "I would have preferred that you didn't find out this way, Christopher. I'm sorry."

"You are Donally Pasha's sister?" the captain asked. Even he had the intelligence to back down a step.

Her eyes touched his. "I couldn't let them take you away."

Then, before Michael could think of something relevant to say, Donally turned with a growl, "You son of a bitch!" A fist swung directly into Michael's jaw—a glancing blow because Michael had seen the move coming and reacted instinctively. Christ, the man hit like a bloody rock. Michael figured he owed the brother one requisite, lucky, son of a bitch hit. After all, it was no less than what he'd have done had the circumstances been reversed. But Donally wasn't finished.

"Stop it!" Brianna shouted as Michael's legs hit the back of a chair and he stumbled flat on his ass, legs spread. Brianna knelt down beside him. "That's enough, Christopher," she furiously admonished. "I wasn't dragged here. I came of my own free will. On my own. Uninvited."

"Spare me the details, Brea."

"He's not going to fight you. Are you, Michael?"

Rising to his elbow, Michael pressed the heel of his hand against his bloodied lip. He could barely see straight. "You hit like a bloody Irish crag, Donally." For a man who spent too much time behind a desk, he wasn't the least bit soft.

"Welcome to the family, Fallon." Donally stood braced,

feet spread like some avenging archangel. "And I don't care who you think you are."

"Oh bother, Christopher." Brianna got to her feet. "Spare me your masculine indignity. We've already discussed the matter. I'll tell you the same as I told him. I'll make my own decisions about my life."

"You have no focking idea about your life, Brea—"

"You have no room to preach morality to me," she said, wagging a violent finger at her brother. "No room at all! I'm past the age of majority. You cannot tell me what to do. I will be the *only* one who says whether I shall wed. As of right now, both of you can go to the devil."

Peering through one eye, Michael rested an elbow on a knee and dabbed at his lip. Fireworks still danced behind his eyelids. He was resilient, but the better part of valor was prudence, and he knew when to keep his mouth shut.

Donally turned to the unfortunate captain, who had yet to move. "Do you have any more bloody questions for my sister?"

"No, Donally Pasha."

Donally swung open the door, fully expecting his sister to precede his exit. "I expect that I'll see you sometime today, Fallon?"

Casually, Michael saluted in affirmation. "I expect I'll be meeting your solicitor?"

Brianna glared fire at her brother, then turned her head, her expression direct. "I won't be there," she said flatly.

He let his gaze travel over her slim form. Michael knew her well enough to know that she'd meant what she said. Hell, he could almost believe she'd added murder to her list of his sins.

"I think you have made a most wise choice, effendi." The captain chuckled as if he alone were responsible for laying Michael on his backside. If the bastard were two steps nearer, Michael would have kicked his feet out from under him. "She is preferable to a cold cot in detention, yes?"

"Do you have any other suspects in Omar's death?"

"He is no longer your problem, yes?"

Hell, the look in Brianna's eyes told him differently. "Why don't you let me decide that?"

The captain moved to the door. "The man who killed him knew the private quarters of the palace. I suspect now that it was one of his own, which would account for your knife. Omar dealt only one way with those who failed him. The attack on you failed. Perhaps someone did not wish to die so easily this time. They did our khedive a favor, I think. And thanks to the beautiful houri in your bed, you are no longer suspected of the crime." The door shut behind him.

In the silence, Halid walked over and handed Michael a handkerchief for his mouth. "That went very well, do you not think, Englishman? She is a woman in love if I have ever seen one."

Michael snatched the cloth. "Do you think?" He remained on the floor, testing the injury on his tongue. "What was Donally doing in the office this morning?"

"His men found two abandoned camps in the desert. Omar's death suggests the possibility that perhaps we are witnessing a fight from within. He was an evil man, effendi. It is over for you now."

Michael didn't answer, and only looked up as Halid opened the door and chuckled. "If I were to ever ask an Englishman for counsel about women, it would not be thee, effendi."

Michael didn't waste his breath on a caustic response, merely threw away the handkerchief in disgust, welcoming the silence that followed Halid's facetious departure.

Without changing, Michael washed his face and poured a glass of bourbon. He stood in the doorway of his room and looked at the bed. Omar's murder afforded him no sense of triumph, and he felt muddled by the turn of circumstances. It seemed that, without even knowing how it happened, one part of his life had abruptly ended just as the other was about to begin. Halid was correct on both accounts.

His job was over.

And he didn't know a hill of beans about women—except he wanted this one. Whether he'd planned it this way or not, he only knew that Brianna's days of climbing out of balcony windows were over.

Chapter 13

⟨୨⊙୨⟩

Brianna's life as she'd known it was over.

Her character lay in tatters, the pall like a shadow weighing down her shoulders. Hearing raised voices outside, she slipped into a wrapper and, still damp from her bath, she walked to the open doors to her balcony. The argument was coming from Christopher and Alexandra's bedroom across the terrace.

"Maybe I should go down there," she said.

"And maybe you best be stayin' out of sight, mum." Gracie waddled about the bedroom, picking up Brianna's clothes. "The whole household went into hiding since your brother brought ye home. 'Tis a shame, it is."

Brianna tied the wrapper at her waist. "I can take care of us, Gracie."

"And maybe I'm not thinking about myself, mum. Even if I won't be receivin' another invitation to the consulate."

Brianna turned back into her room, walked to her dresser and found a comb.

"You've a kind heart, mum. Most of the time. When you're not on one of your tangents." Gracie wagged the sandal in her hand. "But there's no accountin' for the truth that

191

you're young and have a lot to learn in life. No one is going to be forgiving of you this time."

"Don't you think I'm aware of that?"

She was to blame for the discord between Alex and Christopher, having publicly embarrassed her brother and Lady Alexandra. Brianna knew enough about the machinations of society to recognize that she was in trouble.

"Oh, my poor wee dove." Gracie seemed to sense her distress, and took Brianna into her arms. "What a fix you've gotten yourself into now. Major Fallon will do the right deed by ye, mum. He'll not leave you to be picked clean by the vultures. Your brother will see to that."

"Really, Gracie," Brianna attempted to dissuade her faithful servant from killing her with such an optimistic outlook of her future. "I swear, I'm going to perish just considering his goodwill."

It had taken an insufferably long time to get from Michael's apartment to the house this morning. The silence between her and Christopher had been the worst to endure. He'd barely spoken, except to confirm that Omar was truly dead, stabbed through the heart with Michael's knife. He'd not questioned whether she lied about being Michael's alibi, and Brianna had not divulged it. When they got to the house, Christopher had sent for his solicitor. Brianna didn't have to ask him why.

She knew she hadn't been thinking rationally that morning when she stepped forward and gave Michael an alibi. Terrified for his safety, she'd acted impulsively, the thought that he might be guilty never occurring to her. Christopher hadn't seen what Omar had done to Colonel Baker. Hadn't seen the devastation to the caravan or listened to the screams of people dying. She only knew that Michael was not like Omar.

By now, Michael had no doubt rethought his proposal to her. If it could be called that. Wisdom would force him to see that he was a peer of the realm, for goodness sakes. What could she ever bring to a marriage like that? It seemed that fate surely had a haughty laugh at her expense.

Brianna padded up a set of narrow stairs that led to her darkroom. This was her sanctuary, her livelihood, and she breathed in the familiar scent of collodion and silver nitrate that clung to the air. No photographs hung from the string draped laterally across the room. But she would change that. She needed to replenish her plates and magnesium flares. She wasn't helpless or dependent on anyone to make her happy. She could take responsibility for her own actions.

She'd been the one to compromise herself, completely and utterly without Michael's help. Had she not arrived at his quarters in the first place, she would not be in this position. Nor would he.

Yet, had she not been with him last night, Michael would most likely have been arrested. It was strange how fate always seemed to play out between them. Her own conduct showed that she trusted him.

Brianna's gaze fell on Stephan's picture. She lifted the frame off the shelf and sat in the chair that backed against the only table in the room.

It hurt just to breathe. She'd once been captivated by the fairy tale of romance and happy endings. She'd believed in forever, believed that someone could love her quirks and her dreams. Could love her.

Perhaps she'd been too absorbed in her own life, her own mission to save the world because she'd been so inept at managing hers. Maybe she'd just wanted to make her path the same way her brothers had. At one time, she'd been content with her goals and her dreams. Content with the erroneous belief that she had the wisdom to manage her own destiny.

At least until she'd met Michael.

Major Michael Fallon, who didn't know the meaning of playing fair, who was as domineering as any of her arrogant brothers.

Indignant, she thought of Michael's own scapegrace tribute to morality. Why would a woman ever consider marrying? She would take a man's name and, in return, he would control her life, forever. He could take her children, have a mistress, and vote—all in one day if he chose. If she behaved properly, he would toss her that rare bone on which she could blissfully gnaw.

Brianna knew she held very little that was truly hers, but her heart was hers alone to give away.

A noise in the doorway turned her head.

Carrying his pith helmet, Michael had stopped on the threshold of her personal, private sanctuary. "May I come in?" he asked.

Longing and uncertainty twisted itself into a tight knot in her stomach as he gazed at her. Wearing his uniform, he looked too bloody desirable, when she had knotty hair and swollen eyes. "How did you find me?"

He dipped beneath the doorway. "Your maid directed me."

"If Christopher discovers that you're—"

Michael shut the door and clicked the lock. "I'm not interested in anything your family has to say. Will you let me talk to you?"

"I'm surprised that you feel the need to ask, Major."

He scraped a chair around the table and sat down in front of her, his knees spread, his elbows resting on his thighs. "I thought it a prudent way to begin, after this morning." Amusement touched the words, but only as far as his opening salvo. "I didn't kill Omar."

Brianna's gaze moved to his face. "It doesn't matter—"

"It does to me." Michael tried to gauge her thoughts and could not. Brianna put weight into words. He knew that whatever he said now would be taken as his measure forever. "I've been a bloody proficient soldier for twelve years, Brianna." He studied his hands. "As you can see, I've not shown myself to be as fine a diplomat, not in any area of my life. But I didn't kill Omar. It's important to me that you believe that."

For an instant Brianna held him with the force of her gaze, her eyes wide. "I believe you, Michael," she said.

He was suddenly aware that he'd needed her belief in him. That he'd come here today with every intention of forcing her hand any way he could. He was not a gentle person, but as he sat in front of her, he felt only an urgency to grapple with her fear. Without a doubt, a future with her had completely seized his thoughts, and the knowledge that she possessed the ability to tear him up inside offered no measure of ｉｌｌ ｆｏｒ ｈｉｓ ｓｔａｔｅ ｏｆ ｍｉｎｄ. Ｉｔ ｗａｓ ａ ｎｏｖｅｌｔｙ ｔｏ ｈｉｓ ａｎｏｒｍｏｕｓ psyche, for the man that he had become since leaving England did not suffer incertitude.

Aside from the fact that he knew damn well the reasons for her discontent with matrimony, in this arena he was resolved that she would lose. Brianna was bright, independent, and adept at keeping men in their places. She was also as beautiful as moonlight, generous to those she loved, and passionate. The glimpses of that passion proved more powerful than her sweetly curving body. She'd given him herself. And instilled in him a belief that there could be something more inside him than what he had. He didn't want to force her hand. He didn't want a martyr in his bed. He needed a responsive woman willing to stand at his side.

"Are you all right?" he asked her.

She answered him with a nod. Already she was recovering from that morning.

"You know why I'm here," he said. "I'm asking that you not come to me by force, Brianna."

She didn't reply. But neither was she ignoring him. His gaze dropped to the small portraiture in her hand, which she made no effort to conceal. Michael slipped it from her hands.

The subject of the photograph was a man he'd not seen before. Instinctively, he knew who it was.

"Why did you leave England?" she asked.

Michael drew in his breath, sat back in the chair, and knew he probably looked as disgusted as he felt. Brianna had a right to know. But how did one tell his future wife the filthy details of life? When the past was gone and irrelevant? When it didn't matter to him anymore?

He was not one to allow himself to feel vulnerable, and after today he would never discuss the matter again, but he felt safe in doing so now. Her presence was a powerful compulsion to bear his soul.

"My father disinherited me," he said flatly.

Sitting forward, he turned his hands over. A white scar ran the length of his knuckle to his wrist. His father who made sure that he would never return to England. "I was twenty, and a fool in love with a woman I couldn't have. At least that was part of the problem." He looked at Brianna. "I caused one of the biggest scandals in history. If your family had been part of the ton twelve years ago, your brother would not be so eager to see you married off to me."

"Because you were in love and behaved foolishly?"

"Yes."

"Who was she?"

The pale light made her blue eyes nearly liquid. Being the obvious romantic that she was, she clearly empathized, and he might have played on that sympathy if he'd been innocent. He wasn't. He'd deserved some if not all the blame that had been leveled against him.

"Caroline and I grew up together. Her properties bordered my family's. She followed me everywhere, and eventually she became part of the coterie, so to speak—the gang, being my brothers and hers. I fell in love with her when I was twelve. When I was eighteen, I'd decided I was going to marry her. Unfortunately, my brother had his own plans. Two years later, while I was at Eton, Caroline's father, the Duke of Bedford, announced her betrothal to Edward. I went to my father, never realizing how cold-blooded he was until he'd twisted my dreams to his own political advantage. He wanted Caroline's dowry for the family coffers and Bedford's powerful alliance in parliament. It was as simple as that. She was to marry Edward. I was to accept the decision for the good of all."

"But you didn't."

"I never forgave my brother for going behind my back to have her. A week before the wedding, I met Caroline at the summerhouse on my property. When my brother discovered us, he called me out. I nearly killed him. Afterward, my father disinherited me, and I left England to join Gordon in China. That is my sordid past."

"Are you still in love with her?"

He set the photograph in his hands on the table. "Are you still in love with Stephan Williams?"

She shook her head, finally turning the photograph face-down on the table. "No," she whispered, and dragged in her breath. "Is the investigation over?"

"It is for me." He pulled her into his lap, holding her close as he smoothed the damp hair off her face. "My career would have ended anyway. You were the one real thing to come out of all of this, Brianna."

She turned her head away. "What do you know about me, Michael?"

His long fingers came alongside her jaw and turned her face to his, and his gaze seized hers with a reality of all they had yet to share, yet knew intimately. "I know that you like the sunrise and the way the air smells in the morning. You love roses, and miss the rain." He'd repeated the same words she once told him, long ago in the desert, before he kissed her for the first time. Before he'd taken her to the *dahabeeyah*, and everything about that day changed the center in his life. "You've marched with ladies of suffrage. Most recently, you've had a publication banned in England and found yourself exiled to Egypt. And you think that I have the most beautiful eyes you've ever seen." He finished by saying. "They're not quite blue. They're—"

"Gray, ashen, stormy?" she whispered. "At least you still have all of your teeth." She gently touched where her brother had smashed him in the jaw that morning. Her chest rose in an exhalation.

"What about love, Michael?"

Tilting her face, he pulled back to look into the deep blue of her troubled eyes, and knew without a doubt that what they'd shared was better than love. "You could be carrying my child, Brianna. I'd be gone before you knew for sure."

"What if I'm not?"

"Then there's the matter of your innocence to consider."

"Please don't, Michael."

"You're still compromised beyond all hope." He said the words against her lips, only the amusement in his eyes betraying his tone. "You have proven beyond a doubt that no good deed goes unpunished."

"Oh!" She tried to sit, but he held her easily. "I *should* have kept silent today and let them cart you off in chains for all the reward my nobility has bequeathed me."

"And there's this, Brianna." His mouth covered hers.

He sensed hesitation in her response, parted her lips under his and let his hands slide over the sumptuous silk of her robe, molding her softness to his harder frame. Their tongues tangled, and he drank in the unraveling sigh that touched his lips as her fingers sank into his hair.

The kiss deepened, and he spread his hand over her wrapper, spanning the back of her rib cage, berating himself for allowing the wave of desire to flood him. This time when he pulled back to meet her smoky, luminous gaze, something far more carnal filled his eyes as he held her in his arms and remembered what it was like to fill her.

"You don't fight fair, Michael."

"I never claimed I did, *amîri.*"

No one could ever accuse Brianna Donally of cowardice, she told herself hours later as Gracie finished the final touches on her hair. Excited servants had filled her room, but Brianna sent them all away, confused by the strange flutter in her stomach.

"This is a very happy day for us all, mum." Gracie slipped a pin beneath the waterfall of curls. "You'll be leavin' for Alexandria in a few days to catch the packet to England. That will give us enough time to pack your belongings and have a gown or two made for the English clime. January in London is cold, mum. This year is worse than normal."

A knock sounded on the door behind her.

Brianna turned her head when Christopher entered. He stopped as he surveyed her sitting at the dressing table. With a nod, he dismissed Gracie. He was a formidable figure dressed in black, with a white shirt and a neatly turned cravat.

Her fingers interlaced in her lap, Brianna turned away from the door and stared through her veil at the faintly tilted blue eyes so unlike hers that it seemed as if a stranger looked back at her. She'd dressed in a gown of pale blue watermark taffeta that she'd once worn at a festive Mayday celebration.

"The contracts are signed, Brea." Christopher set down the papers in his hand. "It is done."

The words sounded so final. Her hand spread them in front of her. She looked at each page, seeing nothing but the bold signature at the bottom of each below Christopher's, and finally below hers on the last page. Her heart beat a strange tattoo in her chest.

Though she'd glimpsed a portion of Michael's tenderness these past weeks, Brianna didn't know the other man beneath the name, the image of the man embodied by the bold scrawl—the aristocrat, James Michael Fallon Aldbury, the tenth Duke of Ravenspur.

With him, she knew that there would never be any holding back for the sake of self-preservation. She sat still, her breathing even, conjoined to her thoughts. Her heart in chaotic flutter.

All day, she'd endured growing trepidation, aware of the melodrama of her feelings, yet, unable to quell the escalating uncertainty. First, that Michael would recognize his mistake and abandon her. Now when she realized that he'd not deserted her, that he truly meant to marry her, uncertainty grew into something visceral. After tonight she'd be his wife in truth, with all that it entailed.

How could she ever be equal to that?

"Does he know he's wedding an heiress?"

"He doesn't want your shares of D and B."

She lifted her veil and looked at her brother's reflection in the mirror.

"Maybe he recognizes your need for autonomy in some matters, Brea."

The elation that she'd expected to feel didn't materialize. Maybe her autonomy rested on her ability to bring something into this marriage.

Christopher sat beside her on the bench, his shoulder touching hers, his back to the mirror. He braced his elbows on his knees. She folded her hands. For a moment neither spoke.

"I've wired Ryan and Johnny to expect your arrival in a few weeks." He seemed to study his hands. "Alex will be going back to England with you. Fallon and I are in accord with getting both of you out of Cairo."

She turned her head. Her brother's gaze gentled over her face. "As for me," he added, "I'll get to England before my son is born if I have to swim."

"Your son?" She laughed quietly. Men were so arrogant.

Yet, she knew he'd have to be afraid to do something as drastic as sending Alex away. Nor had she considered the possibility that Michael might still be in danger. Or that the danger could extend to her and Alex. But someone had attacked Michael last night, then framed him for Omar's murder. And those questions remained unanswered.

"I don't want you going downstairs thinking that you're alone, Brea. You haven't asked me to give you away. Not that I blame you—"

She wrapped her arms around her brother's solid form and clung to him—the oldest and the youngest in the Donally clan. Fourteen years divided them. She loved him with her whole heart. "And deny you this moment?" She laughed through her tears. "You've been waiting for this moment since I was twelve, I'm sure."

His low chuckle rumbling in her ear, he embraced her, the beat of his heart heavy against his chest. "Fallon is lucky to have you." Awkwardly, he adjusted the veil over her head, his eyes touching hers through the pale gossamer. "Our mother would be proud of you, Brea. You're just like her."

Brianna remembered very little about her mother. She looked down at her dress. Christopher stood and held out his hand to her. "I think we've kept Fallon waiting long enough."

The butterflies that fluttered in her belly did so now out of alarm. She let Christopher lead her out of the room, turning just once to look back before she straightened her shoulders and moved forward.

Brianna descended the stairs, but slowed at the sound of voices. "Brianna." Alex swept out of the parlor. "You are beautiful." Looking radiant in saffron silk, Alex took her hands. "The minister is here."

Brianna knew a priest would marry them later.

Abdul was suddenly standing before her. Brianna looked into his brown crinkled face. She would probably never see him again. She took both his hands. "This is for each of your wives, Abdul." She rose on her toes to kiss his cheeks. "I have enjoyed our acquaintance."

"As have I, Sitt Donally." He salaamed and stood aside.

Gracie handed her flowers of white jasmine and, with tears in her brown eyes, told her that she looked beautiful. Brianna was suddenly feeling very much like a bride. The few servants gathered in the corridor belonged to Christopher's household staff. They made a path for them as her brother walked her toward the parlor. Caught by the charged hush that began to fall over the room, Brianna stopped in the doorway.

Her breath caught. Dressed in full mess uniform, Michael stood beside the minister near the veranda doors. Through the gossamer whiteness of her veil, she looked directly into his silver eyes, more blue than gray in the sunlight. More day than night. Like the mists over the lake of dawn that bound her to the promise of a future that seemed as vast and unfamiliar as it was frightening.

They spoke their vows outside on the veranda beneath an ancient Cyprus tree, standing in warm squares of sunlight, surrounded by the smells and scents of an exotic world. Then Michael was lifting her veil and she was raising her face to meet his kiss. Her fingertips whispered across his muscled shoulders where the sun had warmed his back. She was conscious of the taste of peppermint, the pulse of his heart and the beat of hers. He pulled back and her eyes opened to the intensity of his silver gaze. The man who had been her lover was now her husband.

Chapter 14

"**M**ay I get you more coffee, your Grace?"

Michael lifted his gaze. The wind sent a salty spray over the lower deck of the *Northern Star*. He sat with his long legs stretched out in front of him, his pith helmet lying low over his eyes as he watched his wife tend to her mare. An empty mug sat in the space next to him at the table. Even his great coat could not keep the icy wind at bay. Lady Alexandra and Gracie had retired an hour ago. Michael had promised Donally that he would see his wife safely home to England. It was not a pact that he took lightly, no matter how angry her ladyship had been at the arrangement her husband had made.

"Black, if you will," Michael said, leaning to look around the steward as Brianna removed her cumbersome cloak and set it on a table. A length of her dark hair had fallen from the bun at her nape.

The ship swayed and the royal-blue-clad steward caught his balance. Coffee sloshed from the pot onto the table. "I'll return with a new cup, your Grace," he said.

The deck had emptied in the last hour as the seas strengthened. Brianna rode the awkward sway of the ship as she made her way to the rail. He'd been watching her the last hour, and awaited her surrender to the inevitable. His wife was simply incapable of losing a battle. Any battle.

Barely visible in the mist above him, the great funnel, one of two that stretched the length of the deck, sent a plume of smoke into the sky. "Is there anything else you need, your Grace?" the steward asked Michael over the noise, handing him the steaming coffee.

"That will be all."

The steward mopped up the spilled brew on the table. "The seas are rough and most of the passengers are sick in their cabins. Supper in the dining saloon will be served cold tonight."

"I imagine that's typical fare for this time of the year."

"Yes, your Grace." He placed the rag on the tray. "If I can be of further assistance, please let me know. I'm in charge of your suite."

Michael's gaze followed the man's departure. Beyond the makeshift stalls, a pair of young military officers wearing regimental uniforms had gathered to play shuffleboard. He'd seen their open glances at his wife. Sliding the helmet lower over his eyes, Michael leaned back in the chair and crossed his ankles, content to remain where he was.

He didn't see Brianna look up as he stirred his coffee, or know that not for one moment had he been dismissed from her thoughts, any more than he'd dismissed her from his. She knew that he watched her from beneath the rim of his helmet with eyes that were anything but lazy. Even after three weeks, he still made her heart beat faster than it should.

She was unused to feeling like someone's chattel. She'd always been adept at fending for herself and making her own decisions. Yet, in the course of the last few months, she'd managed to lose her virginity, common sense, and her liberty. Some men just had the natural ability to bring out the worst in a woman.

Gripping the rail, Brianna began to regret her stubbornness to come topside. Her bonnet had fallen off and now clung to her neck by its ribbons. The deck heaved and sank away again, and the drenching salt spray stung her face. Within sixty seconds she was beyond caring whether she was cold or might be sick on the deck. A hand fell over both of hers, which were clinging to the rail. "Come, amîri." Michael turned her into his arms and wrapped her cloak around her shoulders. "It's time to go below."

Lifting her easily, he swung her around in his arms and walked with her across the swaying deck. It wasn't fair.

"I'll secure the mare for the night," he said.

She leaned her head against the solid strength of his shoulder. "Thank you," she murmured matter-of-factly. "I suddenly find that I can't walk." The churning of the paddle box blocked out the sound of her voice as he passed beneath the doorway and down the stairs.

"I imagine this service is included in my duties as your husband."

She knew that he'd been annoyed that she had not sent a steward topside to feed the mare, that she'd insisted on taking care of the horse herself.

The drawing room off their sleeping quarters was furnished with plush armchairs and tables topped with Italian Brocatelli marble. It was disconcerting as he sat her in a chair and removed her stockings and shoes that he should appear so capable.

"G-Gracie and Alex haven't been well either." Brianna's hand splayed the muscled curves of his shoulder as he knelt beside the chair. "I've been told the sea is rough this time of year."

"This is the Atlantic in January, Brianna." He pulled her to her bare feet. "It's bloody rough. And ass-freezing cold."

The faint hint of rebuke in his voice was more than her pride could endure. "I owe you," she said.

"Do tell, love." He tipped her chin. "Put it on my bill along with everything else that you claim to owe me."

"You know how I feel—"

"When this trip is over, I'll send you a goddamn bill, Brianna. Would that make you happy?"

"Yes."

How dared he be so obstinate about something that was important to her.

The ship rode a swell and threw her against him. "Are you finished?" Michael gently burrowed his hand into her hair.

Through a haze of misery, she eyed his perfect coloring with hostility. "Actually, I w-would have preferred that *you* were s-sick."

"I know."

"The malady would make you . . ." She flitted a hand in the air. "What is the word I'm s-seeking?"

"Manageable?" Michael carried her into their sleeping quarters. "Helpless?"

"Normal." She stumbled against him as he lowered her feet. "The Irish favor their curses about the devil and Brits, your Gr-Grace. But I would never wish anyone to feel helpless or at another person's mercy. *That* would be unkind of m-me."

"Indeed." A corner of his mouth tilted.

He used his hands on her shoulders to turn her around. He touched his mouth to within a sigh of her ear. His body was a solid wall at her back. "I've noticed that about you, *amîri*." He made quick work of her gown. Her teeth had started to chatter in earnest. "While other debutantes hold court over their flock of admirers, you like to beat the hell out of yours. You've a man's thirst for blood."

"Very amusing, Michael." She'd wanted to take offense at the backhanded insult, but she rather liked the analogy, or would have if she hadn't felt so ill.

"Fortunately, for me, your rifle was empty that day at the oasis," he said. "To think that you could have spared yourself this trouble."

"What a terrible thing to say."

"Then you are content with your life, Lady Ravenspur?"

Outside, sleet began to pound the port window. Finally, her chemise followed the way of her stays and she stood in front of her husband naked as the day she was born. She opened her eyes and stared into the handsome face so close above her own. The invisible walls that had been her security since Stephan had walked away from her no longer separated her from her heart. She had never loved with her soul. But Brianna felt the dangerous flutter of wings in her heart and knew the strangest urge to fly. Not away into the clouds, but toward the sun.

She could not answer that question except to look away. His very nature demanded her dependence on him. She could not be strong and be in his presence.

A soft down comforter went around her shoulders, and the hint of sandalwood rippled against her senses. "Do you think the physician made it to Alex and Gracie's quarters?" she asked.

Michael wrapped her snugly and sat her on the edge of the bed. He poured two snifters of brandy and thrust one into her hand. "Drink."

She watched him toss back the glass, then studying her own glass, did the same, but with far different results. Fire burned down her throat and exploded in her belly. She coughed and sputtered. For all of her progressive drive for equality, she was excruciatingly aware that she drank like a novice, and that Michael noticed.

But after a moment her limbs grew warm and languid, and she plopped on her pillow like a log. Her eyes became dreamy. "How many people have you nursed, to be so capable, your Grace?"

Michael slipped the glass from her fingers and remained looking down at her profile. She was already asleep. The life of a public official in Egypt called for forbearance when dealing with the unanticipated. He'd repaired broken bones, dealt with dysentery, and delivered babies. "Treating one stubborn bride with a glass of brandy hardly takes the skill of a surgeon," he said quietly, adding another comforter to the bed.

Outside, the weather had worsened. Michael made sure the stove had ample fuel. He returned to the deck and found that he wasn't the only fool outside. Another man stood in the darkness by the rail. Michael slid his hand into his coat and retrieved his tin of mints. He snapped open the lid and slipped one between his lips as he peered toward the man's back, but the icy spray climbed beneath his collar, and he lowered his chin to make his way through the darkness toward the berth where Brianna's mare was stabled.

He could hear the upper half of the stall door banging against the bulkhead. None of the horses had been tended, and as the storm beat down on the deck, Michael secured the mare, shut and bolted the latch on the door; then he did the same for the two bay geldings on either side.

He'd allowed Brianna to bring the mare with her to England. It had seemed important to her, and he'd practically moved mountains to see it done in the short time they'd had before leaving Cairo.

She'd not petitioned anything else from him, when it had been her right to do so. While he'd been preoccupied at the consulate that last week, she managed to put together a winter wardrobe for herself and her maid, and to have a heavy coat made for him. She'd settled her own accounts before leaving. A part of him knew that it was important to Brianna to come together with him as an equal. If only because in some things, she could. But attempting to pay her way in this marriage only proved there was no wisdom to stubbornness.

The ship rode a swell and Michael caught himself against the rail. He reached the passageway to find the door locked against him.

He turned to look behind him. The man who had been standing at the rail was gone. With an oath, Michael struggled to make his way up the stairs to another entrance, barely avoiding the dangerous wash of waves. He was wet and furious by the time he found his way inside. He walked down the corridor to check the door, but found it unlocked. A vague smell of something medicinal filled the passageway. He retraced his steps and checked his cabin door to make sure it was locked. Hesitating a moment, he removed his helmet and knocked at the cabin next to his.

The door eased open. Lady Alexandra raised her gaze to meet his in surprise. "Major Fallon. You're looking somewhat dampened." Her red silk dressing gown whispered as she stood aside to let him enter.

"You haven't opened your door recently?" he asked as she closed it behind him. "The corridor smells like a restorative retreat."

Lady Alexandra held up a damp rag. "My maid and I are caring for Gracie. I fear she's quite ill. A steward just brought me a new supply of rags. Thank you for sending up the physician this afternoon."

"Brianna was concerned. I should have made her see the physician as well."

"Would you care for tea, your Grace? Or do you still prefer 'Major'?"

Michael walked to the port window. Bracing a hand against the wall, he peered out into the darkness. "You're my sister-in-law. Michael would be a more acceptable moniker to me in private." He took the cup from Lady Alexandra's hands. Wearing his military boots, he towered over her. "As for the other? My military duty will officially end upon my return." Turning a leafy mint sprig over in his hand, he dropped it back in the tea. "Is this a miraculous antidote against vomiting?"

She regarded him with warmth. "Mint helps to calm one's stomach."

He drank, his gaze going to the door that opened into Gracie's room. Alex touched his arm. "My servants will be with Gracie tonight."

"My wife and Gracie have known each other a long time?"

"Gracie helped deliver Brianna into this world. She was with her when her mother passed away. The death was very hard on Brianna. Twenty-two years can forge a bond as strong as one forges with family."

Michael leaned a hand against the wall and stared outside the window toward England, somewhere on the unseen horizon. He was no longer thinking about the weather or the strange scent in the corridor. He wondered if he'd ever been truly close to anyone in his entire life.

"How long since you've been home?" Alex asked.

"Too long. Not long enough. Twelve years. I'm under no delusions as to my homecoming." Turning back into the room, he peered at her over the rim of his cup. "Already, England is as cold as I remember."

"Where will you be going once you get there?"

"My family has a London residence," he said. "We'll go there first, until I can get my affairs in order." He would need more than the one suit of clothes he had. "Brianna will need time to adjust."

"You underestimate her." Alex merely smiled. "Brea kept me alive for three days in the desert. She protected me with her life by sheer force of will because she is stubborn and she loves me. She loves me enough to suffer through research and poor French to help me finish a book no one but a handful of scholars might read. Because she has a need to protect me from my peers," Alex said, turning her head and her gaze to him. "She's already loyal to you. And you're not even Irish."

Michael lifted a faintly ironic brow. "Neither are you."

"True." She leaned against the window, her eyes also looking toward home. "Christopher and I left England shortly after our marriage," she said. "We did not leave on the best of terms with his family. I'll be surprised if anyone shows to take me home."

He set the cup down near a lamp at his hip. "Your husband wired his family before we left Alexandria. They'll be waiting when we arrive. I'll wager my inheritance on it. You're part of their family. One of them."

She laughed. "I suppose you can refer to the Donallys as *them*. They are a very tight-knit, earthy family. Protective of their own." She leaned against the window. "Cairo in April is no place to be when this baby comes. But it doesn't make me feel any better to leave." Touching her abdomen, she looked up to find Michael watching her. "Forgive my immodesty. I fear that marrying a Donally has corrupted all sense of propriety."

Michael remembered a particular photograph caught by a particularly talented photographer of Lady Alexandra wearing only gauzy veils and a seductive smile. At the time, he'd been intrigued that she had somehow escaped the confines of her life. Now, he realized that it had been more. It was that he'd envied.

"I like impropriety, my lady."

Brianna stopped just inside the grand salon, her gaze scanning the few people present. A small orchestra played music to an empty floor. Yule decorations remained scattered over the tables and draped across doorways, remnants of the celebration held here last week. Michael sat at the back of the salon, bent over a chessboard. She wondered what he thought about when he was alone.

He'd not been in the room when she finally crawled out of bed late that afternoon. She'd eaten with him at breakfast only because he'd forced her to eat; then she promptly fell back to sleep. Later, when she felt human again, she'd visited Alex and Gracie. Out on deck, one of the stewards told her that Michael had already fed the mare that evening.

"He's sitting in front of the window, Lady Ravenspur," the steward said as he pushed a food cart behind her.

She still wasn't used to that name. As Brianna approached, Michael lifted his head. She wore a rose-colored gown. Her hair lay in glossy waves over her bare shoulders and down her back. Behind him, the gunmetal-gray clouds of yesterday had surrendered to the fading glow of a sunset. "I hope you haven't eaten supper," she said.

Brianna directed the steward to leave the cart. He stopped in front of Michael. "Is there anything else you need, your Grace?"

"That will be all."

Still unused to being invisible by virtue of Michael's presence in any room she shared with him, Brianna remained where she stood as the man walked past her. People talked to Michael in crowds. Acknowledged his presence with deference. Respected him.

His gaze made a slow pass over her. "The kitchens are closed. Did you coerce the cook to do your bidding? Or was it merely your smile?"

"Neither. I promised that you would write a glowing report of his culinary prowess to the captain. It seems he's looking to advance his position to head chef, and the recommendation of a duke in his portfolio of endorsements is worth a bribe in gold."

He ran his thumb over the queen in his hand. "Is that right?"

Brianna caught herself watching his hands. Behind her a quiet waltz played. Michael had removed his uniform jacket and seemed more vulnerable—as if he'd eliminated the protective outer layer that always surrounded him. Now, as she pondered her next words, she felt other things as well. Guilt. Regret.

Relief.

Like clockwork, she'd started her menses that afternoon. Her body never failed her in that regard. She would have to tell him. As much as she trusted that Michael had done the right thing by her, the tiny seed of doubt inside grew. Now that the real reason for the marriage was no longer an issue, he could be free of his responsibility to her. Or not.

"How are you feeling?" he asked.

"Alive." She swept around into the chair. "Thank you for taking care of my mare. And checking on Gracie last night. That was very kind."

His gaze followed her. "I'm a kind person."

"No you're not. I mean you are about some things. You can be charming when you choose. And you look nice. Your uniforms are always clean and no one but you sees that it is. It's true that we have differing expectations of marriage."

"You've made me aware of that."

Brianna brushed her skirt. There was so much that she didn't understand about herself when she was with him. "I wanted you to know that there will be no baby." She'd tried to make her voice sound level.

Brianna had half expected anger, disappointment, some recriminating comment that he'd ruined his life for naught. "I started my menses today. In case you were not polite to ask how I'd know."

"I'm not that polite, Brianna. I assumed that to be the case."

Despite herself, she felt her face grow hot. "We'll be in England in a week. I'll agree to an annulment. You can go your way, I'll go mine."

"Where is it that you want to go, Brianna?"

Daunted by his words but comforted by the authority he seemed to take over this matter, she dropped her gaze to the sleeve on the chair. She didn't really want to go anywhere, but said the first place on her mind. "India," Christopher had once been there, "the Himalayas."

Michael was watching her, his expression unchanged, yet his eyes seemed less stark. "Don't you think it's insulting? We've been married three weeks and you want to leave me for the Himalayas?"

Despite herself, she almost laughed. "I'd think that you'd be glad to find yourself free to marry whomever your family wanted you to marry."

"You don't need to explain your feelings."

"I do." She cast her gaze to the wall. Deep sapphire watered silk draped the windows that overlooked the sea. The room was no longer gray with the passing day, but filled with a soft, luminous brilliance that came with candlelight and seemed to pick the silver from Michael's eyes. "I don't want an annulment." She finally voiced the words she'd come here to say tonight. "But neither do I want to find myself relegated to a shelf in your life. I want to know you. I want you to know me. It seems that we started out backward, upside down. Literally, on our backs."

Michael continued to watch her over steepled fingers.

Even now, his presence consumed her. The novelty of passion, the intensity of her emotions, had proven to be an intoxicating paradox for her. She craved their physical intimacy, yet, she also needed the simple comfort of camaraderie that could last into the daylight hours. She needed to be in control of her emotions again.

"What we do in bed is very nice. More than nice. I like it a lot. But I want a chance to . . ." She wanted to know that she was important in other areas of his life. "I want what we have in bed out of bed as well." She clasped her hands in her lap. "I want more."

"Meaning . . . ?"

"I'm asking that we go through the process of getting to know each other. Perhaps start from the beginning. The real beginning."

"Then what? You'll tell me if I pass your test?"

"This isn't a test."

She sat across from him as if the heat and intensity in his eyes didn't burn her to an ember. She was illogical to the point of contrary.

Yet, sometime during the last few weeks, Michael had ceased to question what kind of woman he'd married. He knew what kind warmed his bed at night.

The kind that could sit between his knees and make him come with her mouth. An enchanting houri girl with eyes like heaven and laughter like moonlight that halted any thought remotely wholesome in or out of her presence.

For on an entirely higher level, he and Brianna were like two lions circling one another, equally matched in fight and spirit. There was passion beneath her pride.

Passion that had touched him when she'd stood up to the authorities and cleared him of murder, no matter the cost to

her future. Passion when she'd looked into his eyes with the
fortitude to speak her vows for the sake of a child they might
have made. Willing to take a chance on an uncertain future
ahead of them. He wanted that woman beneath the fervor of
her emotions that fueled the heart of her. Who could face
down brigands in the desert—including him.

Who was unafraid to confront anything or anyone—
except herself.

Which left him precariously balanced on new ground,
aware that she'd twisted him into a pretzel without knowing
how she'd managed it.

Instinctively, Michael knew if he did not grant her
request, she would never ask anything else from him again.

"Do you play chess?" he finally asked.

Brianna blinked, unable to comprehend why he would ask
her that.

"Maybe you'd care to wager for your position?"

She clearly didn't trust the challenge in his eyes, but she
wasn't going to back away. "I wouldn't wish to humiliate
you, your Grace."

"I'm glad to know that we are still of a like mind on something."

She was beautiful, her hair lying in waves across her
shoulders. She gazed at him with the realization that they
shared a like mind on many aspects of daily life and behavior. None of that had really changed.

"What is it that you are playing for?" she asked.

Picking two pieces off the board, Michael leaned an
elbow on the table and held out his closed hands. "You. In
my life. No annulment. One week, I'll court you."

Her shining gaze rose to his. "Four."

"One. And I can still touch you anywhere."

"Two weeks." Her voice was sounding oddly breathy. "We
live in separate quarters."

"One," he said. "Separate quarters only when we reach
England and only for the allotted time. But the rooms have
to connect."

"Did you really let Colonel Baker win at chess?"

He arched a brow. "You'll have to play me to find out."

Tension coiled between them. Brianna tapped his left hand. He turned his palm over. She'd picked her own color. No matter what anyone said, she would always think it better to go first.

"Have you played chess long?" Michael asked conversationally.

"Since I was ten. Ryan taught me." She opened the game by moving a pawn. "Then I promptly beat him, and afterward he wouldn't play me anymore."

"Ryan is?" Michael rebutted her move with a like move.

"The youngest of my brothers. And you?"

He followed her next move with his bishop. "Chess and whist are the pastime of naval officers. I come from a family of admirals."

She arched a brow. "Yet, you went into the army." She seemed to study him with that thought in mind. Then she lowered her gaze. For a long time she merely stared at the pieces before moving her bishop. "Would you have married me if you weren't returning to England?"

Michael moved his queen, and hesitated.

It took her a moment to register the action. He'd put her in checkmate. Just that fast. Queen, bishop, three.

They faced each other across the small table. She was waiting for an answer to her question. An answer that he didn't know how to give, except the truth for what it was. Brianna would never believe anything less. His inheritance had changed everything.

But Brianna had changed even that.

"Never mind." She folded her hands. "I know the answer to that question. We would have waited the three weeks or however long it took for my menses. Eventually you would have returned to the desert, and I would have met someone else. On some other continent, of course."

She was wrong on so many accounts that he didn't know where to begin. "There is one truth you should know, *amîri*."

He rose. She came to her feet as he walked around the table. "I let you oversleep that morning your brother came to my quarters. I knew that after that night I couldn't leave you in Cairo. There was no nobility in that need. No honor in my actions. My intent was simply to keep you." His voice was oddly chilled compared to the heat inside. "So look at me closely, Brianna." He slid his palm around her nape. "And tell me again that I would allow you to take another man in my place while I yet walk this earth."

At first she just returned his stare. Then he saw the radiance in her eyes. "Do you know when I first thought of you in less than wholesome terms?"

They were suddenly in each other's arms dancing to the quiet music. No one else was on the floor.

"When?" His voice was whisper soft.

"When I saw you undressed, shaving for the first time by the pond. When we were in Baharia. Everything about you was a shock to me," she added with a careful smile. "It's the only way I can explain my insane attraction to you, and everything that I did afterward." She turned her face away and blinked back moisture. "Do you know when I realized how beautiful you are? Truly beautiful?"

Michael brushed the hair off her face. "When?" He spoke quietly in deference to her tender admission.

"Last night."

He absorbed the simplicity of her declaration, unable to take his eyes from hers. She was deeply familiar in ways that left him searching his own heart for the depth of his feelings. He realized that it had been too long since he'd let anyone into this part of his life as completely as he'd allowed her. As a man who was accustomed to giving orders and having authority, he found the vulnerability unpleasant, his demons alive.

She pulled him down to her lips and in the softest of whispers said, "Maybe some deeds committed are worth the consequences after all."

He pulled away to look into her eyes, and all the light in the room settled in that brilliant blue gaze.

"How did you beat me in three moves?" she asked.

Moving one hand to her waist, he teased her bottom lip, if only to hide the tilt of his mouth. He'd beaten her because, as dark as the night, he'd cheated.

Chapter 15

Not yet dawn, the sky was still flecked with a smattering of stars as Brianna pulled Alex and Gracie through the throng of passengers to squeeze into a place at the rail. People frowned at her alacrity, but she didn't care. The decks on the *Northern Star* were crowded with those gathered to disembark. Brianna felt the planks vibrate beneath her feet. The engines churned the water, as the huge wheel seemed to reverse in power.

They were home.

The last time Brianna had seen these shores, she'd been leaving her life. Now she was returning a duchess. Nothing had gone as she'd planned, yet every incident had been a step toward this very moment in time. If any event had not occurred as it had, if she'd never met Stephan, she would never have met Michael.

As she watched the sky turn amber, her heart raced in anticipation. "Do you see them, my lady?"

Alex was dressed in a white fur cloak. Her breath hung in the frosty January air. "The docks are too crowded." The hood of her cloak framed her face as she searched the shore. "I can't tell."

Christopher had wired Ryan and Johnny before their departure. Surely, her family would be here to take Alex home. Surely, old feuds had been forgiven in the wake of Christopher's absence for the past four years. She would never forgive her family if they snubbed Alex.

Never!

"Wait." Alex stood on her toes. "Yes," she whispered. "They're here. I see them, Brea! At the end of the docks standing near that carriage." Her hand went to her mouth and she laughed. "They came."

Suddenly Brianna couldn't bear to waste a moment of this new day. Looking around her, she searched for Michael. When she returned to the cabin, she found her luggage already moved. She pressed through the crowded corridor as she hurried along the length of the ship toward where her mare was berthed, and stopped at the rail to search the lower deck.

Two men were preparing to move her horse. Michael stood to the side, overseeing the proceedings. He wore black trousers and a burgundy silk paisley waistcoat, his sunbronzed strength tamed beneath a heavy overcoat. A hand rested on his hip. She'd seen him brushing out the suit of clothes that morning. Now, as her gaze went over the tall unmistakable length of him, she marveled at the change, his ability to transform so easily. His dark hair curled at his nape and blended with the coat he wore over his jacket.

The engines quit rumbling and, in the abrupt silence, the steamer drifted into the dock. As Michael turned to look toward the shore, Brianna's hand paused at the rail.

How did one feel returning home after so long? Except for the one time in Cairo, Michael never talked about his family. It was impossible to think that they could not love him or would not be waiting to see him. Almost as if sensing her, he turned his head and saw her standing on the upper deck.

He slid his hands into his pockets. His sleeves rode up to

his wrists. There was something in the way his gaze could grab onto hers and pull. He knew it, too, and smiled.

Brianna smiled back. Yes, indeed, she decided. It was a fine thing that today would begin their courtship.

"Ryan and Johnny are here," she said when Michael met her at the bottom of the stairs.

"And Lady Alexandra was worried no one would show."

Standing on the bottom step, Brianna could easily see into his face. "My family is hardly that vindictive." She absently brushed at her skirts, restraining her hands from wandering beneath his coat. "Temperamental and rowdy, yes, but after today I can strike vindictive off my list of familial faults. Will you be here much longer?"

A shout behind him drew Michael around. Her mare was about to be removed from the stall. "Will she be all right?" Brianna asked.

"I need to arrange for her dispatch to Aldbury Park."

"Lord Ravenspur." A ship's officer approached, a thick fellow with a red beard and Scot's accent. He was winded. "The captain, he will see you now. He is apologetic that he missed you earlier, your Grace."

"I had a slight mishap the other night," Michael said, answering the question in her eyes.

"Nearly got hisself washed overboard, when the door latch stuck," the officer said. "Wouldn't do no good if we lost ourselves a duke."

Michael's gaze when he met the officer's was less conciliatory than in his words to her. "Go join your family, Brianna."

"I'll go with you, Michael."

He smiled down at her worried expression. "I'm a big boy, *amîri*." His hand went to button up his jacket. "I'll find you later."

"Jaysus, Brea." Ryan sat back in his chair. His riding boots squeaked as he laid one ankle across his knee. "Do you think you might have let me buy you out of the company before you'd wed?"

Breakfast platters sat on the elaborate sideboard against the wall. They had arrived at the inn over an hour ago. "Even if I'd wanted to exercise that option, it was hardly possible," Brianna said, passing the butter to Johnny, on her left.

Ryan leaned forward. "Did Chris finally put his foot down and make someone do the honorable deed by ye, Brea?"

Buttering a biscuit, she looked up to see the young serving girl blushing over her brother as she poured him coffee, and practically rolled her eyes. "It's just like you to be crass, Ryan."

The most uncompromising of her brothers and the sibling most responsible for seeing her sent off to Egypt, Ryan had confined his dark hair in a queue. Women gawked at him. Brianna didn't understand the attraction. In her opinion, his only redeeming quality, other than the fact that he was one of the top civil engineers in the world, was his affection for his little girl. He'd lost his wife a year ago, and now Mary Elizabeth was everything in his life.

Johnny turned to Brianna. "He's been like this since he received word of your marriage." His voice lowered. "He has no trust for the aristocracy. No offense, my lady," he said to Alex. His mouth crooked boyishly. "But then I never took offense with ye."

Alex returned Johnny's grin with warmth. "Thank you. And Ryan," she added, taking them both into her all too innocent gaze. "I've never doubted your heart-felt generosity either. Not for a moment."

Ryan folded his arms as he observed Alex with a spark of humor. "It is difficult not to feel generous when one is threatened with castr—When one is warned to behave." He grinned. "Still, it would be nice if we departed Southampton knowing that we're leaving our precious sister in the hands of a man she won't be apologizing for at family gatherings."

"Major Fallon was involved in trying to shut down the opium and slave trade in Egypt." Alex stirred sugar into her tea. "I warrant she won't be apologizing to anyone for his grace."

Ryan sipped his coffee, considering Brianna with an amused smile resting lightly on his lips. "So how did the two of you meet?"

"They met in the desert," Alex said.

"Actually . . ." Brianna smiled in good cheer. "Lady Alexandra smashed him over the head with the butt of her rifle. Then he tried to kill me. It was quite romantic, really. Love at first sight."

Ryan sat forward. "Then you're in love with him, and he with you. I'm relieved to know that it was not the butt of Chris's fist that convinced him to make an honest woman of ye, Brea."

He'd said the words in brotherly jest, but inadvertently or not, Ryan had touched her most tender spot. Perhaps if he had not nailed down events with such precision, the banter would not have hurt.

"He was the one who brought you both out of the desert," Johnny said. "The story made the papers here. Chris wasn't specific with details in his letters. Except that Lord Ware contacted him recently."

"Lord Ware heads the Foreign Service." Brianna turned to Alex. "Why would your father contact Christopher?"

"There is a theory that the attacks that were occurring in Egypt are connected to the trafficking of antiquities in London," Johnny explained when Alex didn't answer. "It's big business and big news."

"Maybe you should talk to your husband, Brea," Alex said.

"Maybe we should just finish breakfast," Ryan suggested, and the topic at the table quietly slipped into news from home.

A fire crackled in the marble hearth. Brianna didn't know what had happened to Michael. She left the dining room to check the hotel registrar, and discovered that their luggage had been delivered to the room an hour before. Gracie had not seen him.

The Westgate Inn proved to be a palatial three-story brick mansion with a colonnaded entrance and surrounding veranda that overlooked a garden. She was thankful now that Ryan had secured the private dining room. Her brother's gaze gentled considerably on her when she returned. "We packed all of Mam's porcelain and lace," he said as the breakfast dishes were cleared away. "Christopher told us to make sure your dowry was ready to be delivered when you were ready."

Brianna looked between her brothers. She didn't want her family to feel sorry for her. They were thinking that she'd married some boorish oaf who'd wed her only because Christopher had beat him to a pulp. To show disappointment in Michael's absence would be a further criticism to him. Instead, she smiled her thanks. "I'll send for everything when I'm settled. Are you in London?"

"We've moved most of our operations north to Carlisle—" Ryan's gaze suddenly went to a point over her shoulder. Brianna's heart began to pound. "He's here, Brea," Ryan said, and she turned in her chair.

Michael stood in the doorway.

Tall and dark, in that silent dangerous way that gave people cause to notice him, he was handing his coat to the host before his gaze found hers. The clouds shifted and sunlight spilled into the room from the window behind him. It was all so perfectly melodramatic and timely that Brianna knew a sudden lightness of being.

"I apologize for my tardiness," he said to everyone, but most specifically to her. "But I had a mare to dispatch to Aldbury." Then introductions were made and Michael shook hands with Ryan and Johnny.

Fit to his clothes, Michael looked every inch a peer. And if Brianna had been worried that her husband couldn't take care of himself with her family, he quickly proved himself charming and self-assured, his arm resting across the back of her chair, one ankle on his knee as he casually conversed as if he weren't two hours late.

Brianna could only stare as Ryan, who had verbally incinerated the aristocracy, carried on a conversation with Michael in a way he'd never done with her. And she found herself reassured that Michael was not a man who needed anyone to apologize for him—least of all her.

Brianna wept only a little when she finally said good-bye to Alex. "I'll see you in April, before the baby is born."

"I'm staying at the country estate near Epping," Alex said. "We aren't so far from one another that we can't visit."

They hugged and held onto one another while Ryan waited on his horse and Johnny stood outside the carriage, shivering in the cold. Finally, Brianna stepped off the drive and watched her family ride away. Michael remained leaning against the wall on the veranda, leaving her alone. It was strange, but she didn't want to be alone. She turned and walked up the steps to where he stood, his collar raised against the cold. She braced her hands against the rail at her back, six feet separating them.

"Ryan and Johnny behaved themselves," she said.

"Did you think they wouldn't?" he asked, his voice gently amused. "They were respectful of me because of you, Brianna."

The simple words and what they meant hit Brianna as nothing else had that day. Or perhaps because of everything, the sentiment weighed that much more. She looked down the road, now empty of her family's presence, and for the first time in her life, they were no longer a rallying force around her. She was no longer a Donally. Her world as she'd known it was truly gone, and all of her uncertainty, her need to understand her life, her husband, and her heart meant nothing compared to the reality that Michael was her future. And she was already afraid of losing him.

Courting him suddenly seemed incongruous in the mix of

her feelings, when all she wanted to do at that moment was crawl inside of him. He had not made love to her since she'd lost to him in chess.

Brianna folded her arms beneath her cloak. "Why would Lord Ware contact Christopher?" she asked after a moment. "Alex implied that it had something to do with you."

Michael's brows pulled together. "If I knew my business half as well as everyone else in this godforsaken world, I'd need a secretary to keep track of my bloody life."

Brianna waited for his answer. Michael was not pleased to give one.

"My integrity and that of my office was brought into question," he finally said. "Some at the consulate went so far as to suggest that I should be investigated for any links that I might have had to the caravan attacks."

"Who would say that?" Brianna was incensed.

"I wasn't privy to that information." Michael walked to where Brianna stood, pleased that she could go no farther than the rail at her back. "My office had prior knowledge about every caravan detail that was attacked. I was conveniently absent when Pritchards took my place on the caravan that held the payroll shipment. I conveniently appeared in the same place you had run. And Omar's death conveniently coincided with my departure from Cairo." Michael lifted a dark curl from Brianna's shoulder. "In reality, the few brains in government have *conveniently* misplaced the facts. Captain Pritchards reported regularly to the consulate. There have been no other attacks since his death."

She retrieved her hair from his fingers. "Which implies that the leak came from the consulate."

"The implications thrown at me are whitewash to cover that disgrace. Lord Ware isn't an idiot. He'll see that." He leaned his palms on the rail, bracketing her between his arms.

"What is your theory?" The words sounded breathy.

"That someone got very rich on the sale of stolen goods and artifacts and retired on the payroll shipment."

"And framed you for murder." He felt her gaze touch his lips. "I'm glad that you are no longer in Cairo," she said.

"You are so fierce in your protection, *amîri*," he whispered against her hair. "For someone who wants to throw me out of her bed."

She untangled herself from his arms. "I have been worried about you this day, and you walk into that dining room two hours late, God's curse to stubborn Irishmen. Were you really nearly washed overboard? What did the captain say about the door latch?"

Michael tipped her chin and gazed at her soft, full mouth. "That it had a tendency to freeze during storms. Like my good sense. Since I was out there that night because of your damn horse. But alas, you are not a widow yet. You have cursed me, I think."

She stepped around him. "I am the one cursed to listen to your boorish humor."

He caught her arm. "Why are you so angry?"

"Because I won't be the cause of your demise."

Pulling his mint tin from his pocket, he watched her swing open the door. "Are you engaged for the next week?" he asked.

"Are you asking if I'm available, your Grace?"

He slid a mint between his lips, his gaze going over her before he found himself looking in her eyes, wondering what the hell he was doing acting like some green sixteen-year-old in the throes of his first crush. "I'm asking." His voice held a dark edge.

"In that case"—she leaned against the door—"yes, I'm available."

That evening, Michael and Brianna stayed in Winchester. They visited the only operating theater in winter, an old hurdy-gurdy show that no gentleman would take his wife to see. They were the only souls foolish enough to walk outside on an icy January eve, but Brianna didn't care. On the carriage ride to London, they played cards as he displayed another side of himself she'd never seen. Lifting his gaze, he caught her watching him over the rim of her cards. His gray eyes changed with the light and his moods. He looked at her now, his dark hair longer, his teeth when he smiled as white as the shirt he wore tucked into black trousers.

"Your bid," he prompted.

She suspected that she would lose this game just as she had the last three. "When did you say I'd be meeting your family?" she asked offhandedly.

She'd discovered their first day on the road that he didn't like talking about his family. "I didn't."

"Do you intend to let anyone know that you're in London?"

"Not for as long as I can help it."

Brianna narrowed her eyes over the tops of her cards. He'd been very good at manipulating the conversation around that topic. With a casual deliberate movement, she shifted seats and sat in his lap. "What did you say beats four queens?"

When she turned to look over her shoulder, there was laughter in his eyes, and something much hotter. "Four kings?" He fanned out his cards on the seat, thus shaving off another day of their courtship.

She knew that he was cheating at cards. Two could play that game, she thought, and wriggled her bottom against his crotch. "You can't hide your life from me forever, Michael."

Impassively, he let her wriggle, but his eyes were sizzling on hers and sent a sensual thrill through her veins. The thought of him inside her made her heartbeat quicken and, just as fast, she decided to return to her seat.

Two days later Michael and Brianna checked into the grandest hotel in London. Guests could travel to the upper floors in an ascending room, a hydraulically operated lift that thrilled Brianna as she clutched the cage and looked six floors below her. She rode the contraption twice before Michael finally pulled her off and led her, laughing, all the way down the corridor to her room. He unlocked her door.

"I will see you tonight." His voice all silky and hot, he edged her into the room.

Before Brianna could feel disappointed that he'd not come in, he shut the door, leaving her to stare at the oaken panels.

It was the scent of roses that finally made her turn around. The fragrance pervaded the chamber and filled her senses. Her jaw dropped open. The room was like something out of Arabian tales. Sheer hangings the color of a desert sunset draped the windows and the huge four poster bed. Rose petals littered the floor.

She untied the laces on her cloak, dropped it on the bed and walked into an adjoining chamber, where she heard Gracie talking. Nile-green tiles covered the walls and floor, depicting a mosaic landscape filled with palm trees. A porcelain tub on four clawed feet dominated the room. Red petals seemed to float on the steam still rising from the water.

"Mum." A young girl dressed in a black dress and white mobcap curtsied. "Your bath is ready. Your towels are heated." She pointed to a low cabinet against the wall, a pull rope on the wall, and scented oils.

Candles danced and shimmered in the cooling draft as Brianna skimmed a finger through the water. "Thank you," she whispered, and the girl left.

It was the first real bath she would have since leaving Cairo. That Michael would do this for her warmed her heart. He'd sent a rider on ahead from their last rest stop outside London, and now she knew why. He'd been ever so polite since leaving Southampton, playing his side of the bargain as he played everything else. Succinctly and with sleight of hand.

"Oh, Gracie." Brianna lifted her hair. "Undo me, please."

Brianna climbed into the bath and sank into the luxurious froth of scented bubbles. She splashed them on her face, shoulders, and breasts. She lathered and soaped. When she came up for air, she lifted her feet out of the water and wiggled her toes. This was contentment, she thought, feeling like a warm cat. Movement to the side caught her attention and she turned her head.

Michael was leaning with his arms crossed in the doorway. He wore a black robe belted at the waist, his chest visible through the open V at his neck. His gray eyes held hers pinned until her cheeks flushed hot. He'd been watching her for a long time.

"I take it you approve?" he asked.

She leaned against the tub's rim. "Pray tell, your Grace, are you trying to win extra favors?"

"To the very best of my ability, Brianna."

Michael continued leaning against the door, and Brianna was conscious of more than her racing heart, for what was in his eyes must surely be reflected in hers. She felt wanton and flushed, surrounded in bubbles—a woman well-loved.

Or she feared a woman falling in love.

She pulled her knees to her chest and wrapped her arms against her legs. Her hair shiny black in the candlelight fell over her shoulders and framed her face.

"This is cheating," she said when he approached.

Michael knelt beside the tub. "I know."

His intentions always started out honorable with Brianna, yet when it came to his actions, he found himself doing things he never intended to do. He'd never intended to have an affair with her, or to go back to her after their time on the *dahabeeyah*. He had never intended to betray her trust, but after she had come to him that night in the apartment, he knew he could not let her go.

He'd taken away her choices, her independence, probably even her dreams. Now he set out to conquer her heart, body, and soul, and intended to use whatever means at his disposal.

If the fires were not already running rampant through her, they were burning him enough for them both.

"How did you arrange this so quickly?" she asked.

"I sent someone ahead," he said without taking his eyes from hers. "The rest of the details were left to me."

"What details?" Ink-dark lashes framed her eyes.

"This." He buried his fingers in the damp thickness of her hair and looked so deeply into her eyes that he believed she could surely read his soul. "And this." His mouth covered hers. And it seemed hours before he finally dragged his lips from hers.

Hours where her hands had crept up to the collar of his robe and gripped it tightly.

She was so incredibly beautiful, he thought, that one conviction was immediately brought into certainty as he felt his eyes slide closed. His complete surrender had come so subtly that the moment of reckoning was over before he'd so much as realized that it had even arrived.

Brianna lifted her gaze to his in an unconscious request for another kiss. The moment she did, his mouth seized hers again and the kiss turned explosive. He stood, bringing her up with him. Seemingly suctioned to him from head to toe, she surrendered to a groan. Then she surrendered to him.

Hot and fervent, her body fanned the flames. Her arms slipped around his neck. He stepped into the tub, following her down into the frothy bubbles. Against the silky heat of her flesh, he could feel the hard arousal of his sex. "You are going to smell like the sweetest of flowers for days, your Grace."

"I've smelled worse."

"What about our courtship?" she asked.

"I was going to play out the courtship," he said, both tender and determined. "We still can." He shifted, settling her thighs over his, the taut curve of her stomach cradling his erection. "You wanted more. But in the end, I can give you no more than I am, Brianna. Tell me now if you want me to stop."

Michael felt her silence for what it represented. But if he thought that she could not commit to him, he was wrong.

She moved over him, onto him. His name a breathless whisper on her lips. Her name an answering rasp.

Hunger seared him. He filled her. She leaned her head against his and shut her eyes.

Water sloshed over the rim of the tub.

Her hands slipped across his chest. He felt the heavy thumping of his heart, the warmth of her flesh against her fingers. She pulled back to look into his face, his other hand bracing her bottom, they moved in slow harmony, giving then taking, back and forth, a long slow glide that sharpened his hunger, made it agony—and ecstasy. She licked his tongue with a flickering caress, deeper still, her mouth covering his, capturing his lips, if only to draw breath from him. "Jesu . . ." he rasped against her lips. She escalated his senses to higher levels. To the moment when all barriers fell away. To the moment when it was only him. Only her. And the words whispered in passion between them. There was power in her presence, the force of her movement against her, driving him to lose control, but he took her with him when he did, and when she climaxed, she kissed his mouth as thoroughly and intimately as she'd taken his body, stamping an impression of her forever on his lips.

"The ring is of the first quality, your Grace."

Brianna held the crafted piece to the light, reading the inscription inside the band.

"Your diagram was specific," the jeweler added, clearly nervous since she had yet to respond. "Onyx inlaid in a serpentine gold band. Not too pretentious and not too dull. As you said."

"It's perfect." Laying the ring on the black velvet cloth atop the display case, she shifted her gaze to the balding jeweler and smiled. "Mr. Smith, you've done a superb job in such a short time."

Brianna had found the jeweler three days ago during Michael's fitting at the tailor. The band was to be a surprise. She'd had the date of their wedding engraved next to the

Latin word *aeternus*: eternal. She had been in a romantic mood that day, and optimistically inclined to hope that eternal meant blissfully happy.

As Mr. Smith wrapped the small box, she opened her reticule and removed the draft she'd drawn from her funds in the Bank of England.

She felt a prickle on the back of her neck. Not the first that day.

A large plate-glass window covered the front of the shop. The viewing salon was open to the busy street.

Brianna walked to the window. Glancing up and down the crowded thoroughfare, she saw that the Aldbury carriage, the rising swan crest visible on the door, had arrived. She'd sent Gracie that morning with the luggage to Kensington and had taken a cab to the jeweler on Bond Street with instructions that the carriage come there.

That morning, Michael had put on his uniform for the last time. His meeting with Lord Ware would be over at noon, and she wanted to greet him with her surprise. She did not intend him to walk this path alone.

A breeze stirred the tendrils of her hair and diverted her attention from the window. Mr. Smith stood beside her, holding out the box. "It has been a pleasure doing business with you, Lady Ravenspur. I hope your husband is pleased with his gift, and that you will return."

Brianna ran her gaze over the quaint shop. Her first day here, he'd proudly shown her his finely crafted pieces. Whenever she'd sat across the street at the tailor, she had never seen anyone enter the store.

"Have you any timepieces, Mr. Smith?" she asked offhandedly. "My husband could use just such an accessory for his new wardrobe."

Brianna purchased a silver watch with diamond inlaid numerals, and also a beautiful amethyst swan clasp, perhaps as a gift to his mother.

"My nephew designed these." Mr. Smith held the swan to the lamp.

Brianna studied the piece. "You must give him my compliments."

"Perhaps when you see your brother again, you can give him my greetings. . . . Sir Christopher," he clarified. "We had cause to work together four years ago. He needed my expertise on a piece of stolen jewelry. A piece similar to the one in your hand."

"Truly?" She couldn't hide her thrill of surprise.

"How are your brother and his wife, mum?"

Brianna informed him that Lady Alexandra was back in England. After a few minutes of idle talk, she tucked her cache in her reticule, pleased with her find and that she'd met someone who knew Christopher.

Once across the busy street, she put her attention to setting the watch. Grabbing the ends of her leather-encased fingers with her teeth, she pulled off one glove, then glanced down the street for one of the fancy lamppost clocks that stood at each end of the street.

She'd scarcely taken a dozen steps when she saw that something hung from the door latch of her carriage.

Brianna stepped closer. An icy chill raced down her spine. She lifted the amulet.

Set in a golden scarab, a jewel, with the brilliance of the sky, glittered against her palm.

Her fingers closed over the golden scarab and yanked. The chain snapped.

"Your Grace!" The driver and footman hurried out the door of the building adjacent to the carriage. "Let me get the step."

Ale tainted his breath. "Who has been watching this carriage?" she asked.

"No one is going to steal from the Ravenspur carriage, your Grace."

"Of course someone would steal from this carriage." The man was senile to think otherwise. "Take me to Westminster now."

"Yes, your Grace."

Brianna had never spoken so rudely to any servant. But he worked for the Aldbury family. He had no right to leave his post. No right at all!

The carriage jerked forward. Brianna opened her palm and held the amulet to the light. She'd seen nearly this same amulet in the *suks* of Cairo.

Cheap trinkets, love charms meant to symbolize an eternal bond into the afterlife; but here in London she felt only a sense of depravity as she realized someone was trying to play a cruel prank on Michael. Someone had obviously been reading the papers and knew who Michael was.

But why leave a trinket? Something about the stone bothered her.

Her hands trembling, Brianna held the amulet to the light. She had seen this stone once before, or one exactly like it in shape and size. In Cairo. On a ring that Omar once wore. She wrapped the scarab in the black cloth that had held the watch, and shoved it beneath the warming blocks under her seat, as if the act would rid her of its presence.

Omar was dead. But she was suddenly afraid for her husband.

He was waiting for her in the marble plaza outside the ministry office. The wind battered her cloak as she stepped out of the coach. Tenting a hand over her eyes, she fought to affect some semblance of ease in her expression as he saw her and dropped a cigarette to the ground beneath his boot. She hadn't seen him smoke in over a month.

She hurried up the stairs. "I'm late. Have you been waiting long?"

"No you're not." Michael passed her, then waited as she joined him at the bottom of the steps. "I'm early."

The mall where they stood was crowded.

"Are you officially a civilian?" she quietly asked.

He saw that her hand trembled, and took her palm into his, turning it toward him. "What's wrong?" he asked, tipping her face.

Smiling up at him, she brought his hand to her lips. "I

maintain my original stance about your name. You don't look like a James."

He tucked her hand against him. "My name evolves from the Latin name 'Iacobus,' or Jacob," he said. "Did you know I actually had an Uncle Iacobus? Everyone called him Ick."

"Uncle Ick?" Laughing, she reached the carriage.

"He was given that name for a reason, I assure you."

Listening to Brianna talk, watching her smile, Michael removed his pith helmet, standing aside as the driver set out the step. She held his hand to her cheek, the hood of her cloak framing her face. Her touch soothed him to the very core of his being. She had come to be with him, and all the anger that had filled him this day vanished in her eyes.

"Major Fallon?" a perfectly cultured male voice queried.

With Brianna in his arms Michael turned.

He registered the derringer pointed at his head. Even as he heard Brianna scream, a part of his mind had already seen, too late, the flash of gunpowder. He felt his head explode.

Then he felt nothing at all.

Chapter 16

"I'll cut his fucking heart out!" Michael's arm shot out and caught the doctor by the throat. "Where is she?"

"Keep him still, damn you!" The physician fought to fill a syringe. A bowl crashed to the floor, spilling bloody water. Michael fought the two footmen who struggled to pry his fingers from the physician's throat. "I said hold him, God blast you!"

Shoved aside in the wild rush of panic, Brianna slammed against a chair as two footmen pushed past her to hold Michael down on the bed. Her knuckles pressed against her mouth, she trembled at the virulent force in him, watching helplessly as the tableau unfolded. Someone screamed.

"Hold him, for Christ's sake!"

"Stop it!" Brianna pushed to reach the bed. "You're killing him!"

But someone grabbed her by the waist and dragged her away, fighting.

"We've got to finish stitching his head before he bloody bleeds to death!" The physician jammed the syringe in Michael's hip. "Get her out of here." The physician fell away from Michael's grip.

Brianna found herself in the corridor, the door shut in her face, her breath coming in gasps. The locked door was an immovable object against her shoulder. She pounded furiously.

Outside Michael's room, servants had gathered in the hall. Someone in the corridor was shouting. They'd brought Michael to his residence in Kensington. It had taken three men to carry him upstairs. He'd been fighting since he regained consciousness. He wasn't in his right mind.

He hadn't known her. He hadn't known anyone.

Someone wrapped a blanket around her, but Brianna wasn't aware of it. Footsteps sounded up and down the corridor. Michael's arrival had ruthlessly thrown the household into chaos. Her numb gaze fell to the carpet at her feet. She had not noticed the blood on her skirts. And on her hands. She had not noticed anything.

"You mustn't worry, mum," a kindly voice said. "He is in the best of hands. It will be all right."

But it wouldn't be all right. Didn't anyone understand that?

Nothing would ever be right again.

The salon where the kind woman took Brianna was paneled in cherry wood. Lemon oil scented the air. A parlor maid worked on lighting a fire. Brianna saw all of this as if she were detached. She stood unmoving.

"Head injuries are unpredictable, your Grace," someone in the room was saying. The man wore the uniform of a constable. "We won't know the extent of damage. It could be possible he'll have no memory of any of this. Or himself," he said to the elderly woman on the settee.

The woman's hands gripped the sterling head of a cane. "How could this have happened to my grandson in broad daylight? In public?"

"We believe it was a robbery attempt, your Grace. The lady's reticule was stolen."

"It was not a robbery," Brianna said in a parched whisper.

Could he be any denser? Were they all idiots?

The room had grown silent as all eyes turned to her.

"Your Grace," the constable bowed his head in her direction. "You said the assailant had a tattoo on his wrist. Do you remember anything more?"

Scraping the dark hair from her face, Brianna found her gaze impaled on a pair of sharp gray eyes. "No," she whispered.

"Leave us. All of you." With an impatient wave of her gloved hand, the woman dismissed the people standing in attendance. "Except you, Chamberlain," she snapped. "I want you to shut the door. And be quick about it."

Brianna could see the resemblance Michael bore to this woman. It was there in her silver-blue eyes and in her bearing. She had caught glimpses of this side of her husband, and hadn't liked it.

"Come forward, child. There is nothing more you can do at the moment in that sickroom for my grandson." The dowager wore a heavy black crepe de chine gown gathered sternly at her wrists, and it rasped with the movement. "Come. Let me see you."

Her gown stained with Michael's blood, Brianna made no effort to move. The woman's gaze made another assessing pass. "Who is your father? You are not familiar to me, child."

Brianna closed her hands in her skirt. Her throat ached, and for all of her effort to remain brave, it took standing in this room to achieve that task. "You wouldn't know him. His name was Brian Donally. He was an alchemist and inventor." She didn't add that the international corporation her Irish father had founded probably employed twenty thousand people in a good year, because she knew it wouldn't matter.

"There is a Sir Christopher Donally who is the Public Works minister in Egypt." Chamberlain cleared his throat. "It's very possible that your grandson did wed her," he allowed. "She is one of the two women he brought out of the desert after the caravan they were riding in was attacked and everyone lost. Sir Christopher's wife was the second—"

"Yes, I'm aware of that." A hand waved him to silence. "I

read the broadsheets, too. Was the account true?" the dowager inquired.

"Yes, your Grace," Brianna said. "Now, may I beg your leave?"

"And are you always this fresh with your elders?" Her eyebrows curved into a perfect arc of displeasure.

"No, your Grace." Brianna pressed her fingernails into her palms. "Only to those who treat me with the disrespect that you have shown me. My husband is lying in another room, while his grandmother is interrogating me as if I were a criminal. It is out of respect for him that I have not yet dumped the contents of that teapot on your head and left your presence."

"Dear heavens!" The lorgnette hanging around the dowager's neck went to her eye. "I should have known." The monocle performed one more reprimanding pass, but her eyes had gentled. "James always did attract the wild ones. That's why he was forever in trouble." The dowager's gaze moved away before returning to Brianna. For a long time it seemed as if she couldn't speak. "He won't die, Brianna."

The words, so unexpected in the stilted formality that surrounded her, tore a sob out of Brianna. Her hand went to her mouth as if that act alone could hold everything inside.

"I came here when I received word from Aldbury Park that my grandson had arrived in London," the dowager said, her chin lifting. "He is my grandson, you see. And he has not come all this way to perish by some thug's deed." She held out her hand, and for the first time Brianna saw that it trembled. "Now, come here and sit beside me for a moment."

Brianna swallowed the aching lump in her throat. Horrified by the damning break, she took a step backward. "I'm sorry," she said. "I'm so sorry." If she cried now, she would never stop.

She would die.

Turning to run from the room, she was brought up short as a footman stepped in front of the door.

"Your maid has been instructed to take you to your room,

Brianna," the dowager said. "You need to bathe and eat. It will do my grandson no good to find that I have allowed you to neglect yourself. We must carry on as an example to everyone else. Do you understand that?"

No, she didn't understand.

She understood nothing!

"Come, mum," Gracie said from beside her. Hands went to her shoulders to stop her from running. "I've a bath drawn and waiting. We need to clean you up."

Brianna stood staring at the dressing room walls as Gracie unlaced her soiled gown, then helped her into the tub. She sat unmoving in the bath as Gracie washed her hands and her face, until the bath turned cold and Gracie returned to wrap her in a warm robe. A tray of food waited for her. "You must eat something, mum," Gracie said, carefully drying Brianna's hands. Her knuckles were raw as if she'd scraped them on gravel. "You need to keep up your strength."

Brianna walked to the window seat and sat. "I will, Gracie."

"You must trust that the physician can do his job, mum."

But Brianna trusted in no one and nothing.

Leaning her cheek against the frosty glass, she stared out at a dead brown world, finally bringing her knees to her chest and wrapping her arms tightly about her legs. The tears started to fall.

She couldn't stop them.

And it seemed with every breath, the tears grew heavier and heavier, until the pain had pulled her under and exploded. Until she'd begun to cry with huge sobbing gulps.

Brianna wept because she was terrible and selfish, because she was alive when so many other people had died, because she was afraid that she'd failed Michael and he would die because of her.

If she had not distracted him, if she had paid more attention, cared more, loved more. If she had done anything but what she had done.

Dimly, she was aware of the door shutting behind her, of the descending darkness. The world of nightmares where there was no escape.

Of terror that came suddenly and completely.

The way the ground seemed to shudder and build beneath her feet. Of memories she'd buried. Of gunshots and screams. Darkly clad riders swarming over the sand, an image that had burned into her head, her memories, and her life.

Omar's clawed hand reached out of the darkness to touch her.

The stone is the color of your eyes. I will have it made into a necklace for you.

Brianna came awake with a start. Had she screamed?

Heart pounding, she looked around her.

She was sitting up in bed. Someone had moved her and covered her with a feather comforter. Outside, the sun had dipped below the horizon, leaving a blazing sky to consume the clouds. She'd been asleep for hours.

She donned a simple gown of lavender muslin and plaited her hair. Kneeling in front of one of her trunks, she opened the lid. Her fingers wrapped around the revolver Michael had once given her at the oasis. She checked the load and shoved the gun in her pocket. While Michael yet breathed, she would never go anywhere without it again. Dragging her cloak off the bed, she left her room.

The corridors were empty. The house silent.

She walked down the stairs and out of the house. Her flat-heeled slippers left tracks in the snow outside. She entered the carriage house, her breath hanging suspended in the air. In the half darkness, Brianna made her way to the carriage she'd been riding in that morning. Something skittered in the shadows. A rodent perhaps. Her hand hesitated before she opened the door. Dark stains covered the seats and floor.

Crawling inside, her hands trembling, she withdrew the amulet that she'd shoved beneath the seat. Carefully, fearfully, she unwrapped the black velvet, its presence burning into her thoughts.

Ice-blue facets glittered in the cooler shades of light that sifted through the eaves and laid a crisscross pattern on the floor.

Brianna had not seen the face of the shooter. He had worn a hood. Even the tattoo was not distinguishable. But she had this. She had to find out what it meant. For deep inside, she recognized that the amulet had somehow been meant for her.

Someone had used her to lead the assassin directly from the jewelers to Michael.

The amulet had been meant for her.

"Your Grace?" Light spilled through the carriage house entryway. "Are you in here?"

Brianna tucked the amulet beneath her cloak. Wiping the tears from her face with the heel of her gloved hand, she stepped away from the carriage. One of the coachmen stood at the doorway carrying a lantern.

"Are you all right, mum?" he asked.

They were all worried about her state of mind.

Brianna could see it in the glances the servants exchanged as she entered the house. Skirts clutched in her hands, she ran up the stairs past them all. Michael's door was open when she reached his room.

Hesitating on the threshold, she neither moved nor breathed. A fire burned in the stone hearth, the smell of peat mixing with the scent of carbolic acid. The draperies had been drawn over the frost-laden glass. Shadows danced on the floors and walls.

Brianna walked to the bed, afraid of what she would see. Tears welled in her eyes. Michael lay unmoving beneath the huge canopy. A bandage, lighter gray in the darkness, marred his dark profile. His face was turned away from her, his features thrown into sharp relief by the rusty glow of the fire, and she stood watching him with an aching, possessive need that seemed to crush her chest.

Someone had undressed him, the white sheet against his body, a pale contrast to the man he was that morning. There were dark circles under his closed eyes. She stretched a palm over his chest and felt the slow beat of his heart.

"I'm sorry, Michael," she whispered.

"He should remain asleep until tomorrow," someone said from the shadows behind her. The physician sat in a chair near the hearth. A book in his hands, he regarded her over his spectacles. "He has a possible fracture in his right clavicle from where he hit the pavement. Certainly shoulder damage. We won't know much more until he awakens." He'd closed the book. "I'm sorry that we had to remove you earlier, your Grace."

Brianna turned back to her husband. "Will he . . . live?"

She didn't ask if he would regain consciousness or if it were possible that he could wake up and have no memory of his life. Those were issues too terrible to consider. She only want to know that he would live.

"He must be kept immobile, your Grace. But he's strong."

Brianna stayed the rest of the night and for two nights afterward.

She remained in a chair beside his bed, feeding him soup, milk, and tea, anything that he could ingest for strength. She held vigil until exhaustion consumed her.

She'd been assured that Michael was strong. But he had proven vulnerable. She had no knowledge of head injuries, no true nursing skills. Only the will to see him live.

She took his hand and pressed her cheek to the warmth.

Blue veins protruded against the pale flesh. His knuckles were callused and scarred, his fingers long and tapered.

His were capable, dependable hands. They'd touched her with passion and gentleness. They'd touched her with so much more.

She didn't know how long she lay with her face pressed against his hand, the hot tears running onto the sheets, and she didn't see Michael turn his head, only felt his hand open over her cheek. She lifted her face and saw that his eyes were open. Dawn was peering through the draperies. There was a slight frown between his brows, his handsome countenance dark with stubble.

"Why are you crying, *amîri*?" His voice was barely a whisper, and she wouldn't have heard him at all if she'd not pushed back her hair and stared in shock. It was the first lucid sentence he'd spoken in days.

Blood had stained the bandage above his ear.

"Is that water?" His voice was raw-edged as he looked behind her.

Brianna twisted to reach the nightstand. She brought the glass to Michael's lips and helped him drink. She could feel the steady pounding of his heart, the hardness and strength of him beneath his skin. When he finished, he lay back on the pillows, his eyes on hers. Unmoving.

"You're lying in bed at your London residence." Brianna laid a hand on his cheek to check for fever. "Your driver brought you here."

"How long?"

"I . . . three days," she whispered, a break in her voice.

"Come here." The bandage heightened his dark, unshaven features, thrown into the shadows by the glow of the fire.

"I can't. I'll hurt you."

"You'll hurt me more if you struggle," he rasped in weakness, but there was strength in his sinewy forearm as he pulled her wrist. "I want all three of you in bed with me. Christ . . . I'm seeing in triplicate."

She laughed through her tears, and her tattered emotions were no barrier against Michael's will or her need to touch him. She eased her cheek into the crook of his uninjured shoulder.

"I love you," he breathed before she could raise her head and wonder at what he'd said. For a moment the world quit spinning.

Then his eyes closed and the sights that would haunt her for as long as she lived briefly faded in the wake of his warmth and the soft rasp of his breath on her hair. She wanted to believe, if only she could.

He was dead.

As sure as God made angels, He'd created hell for men like him. Hell was lying paralyzed, dazed and stupid, unsure of his own name. Michael awoke to a splitting headache, a bandaged shoulder, and a sense of urgency driving him into wakefulness.

The canopy on the bed was opened. A fire crackled. Someone moved, and his gaze focused with determination on the figure of a man, his black coat opened to a vest and white collar.

The pungent scents of carbolic acid and peppermint tainted the air, and no longer came from the wall of his dreams. In his dazed and drowsy state, he stared at the man working his hands on a syringe and tried to comprehend why he seemed so familiar. Gradually his vision cleared. The man straightened and was preparing to give him a shot of morphine. It took Michael some moments to realize that he was lying in bed, the previous gaps in his memory closing like a door.

He reached out and, with incredible strength, grabbed the hand that held the syringe. "I swear on my life if you stick me with that again, I'll snap your bloody wrist." His mouth was sore from a cut that his teeth had made when he'd fallen, and he thought he might have slurred the words. "Drop it."

"I believe my grandson has made his point clear, Blanchard." The familiar voice drew Michael's gaze to the chair on the opposite side of the bed. The dowager sat in a large wing-backed chair situated like a throne next to his bed, a lonely formal figure, dressed in black. "Leave us," his grandmother directed the physician.

"But your Grace—"

"I think I am safe enough from my own grandson."

Michael raised himself on his elbow. He wore no shirt and the sheet fell to his hips. He struggled to recall why his grandmother was here, briefly questioning whether he was hallucinating.

"I see that you're still as temperamental and unpredictable as you ever were, James," she sniffed. "You've tried to kill Blanchard twice. No wonder everyone is scared half out of their wits of you."

Michael narrowed his eyes. Clearly, she was no hallucination—or he was indeed suffering in hell and had only imagined that he'd ever left England. The sense of urgency increased. Recognizing the room now, he sought to understand the circumstances that put him here.

"You've had a severe injury to your head. Blanchard said you may not remember everything that happened."

Michael refocused on his grandmother as if seeing her for the first time. She held a white cane in one hand, her palm absently clutching its ivory head as she endured his cynical assessment. Her hair had silvered completely since the years that he'd seen her last. He wasn't annoyed by the diamond hardness in her eyes, only by the headache that grew and throbbed in his temples as he realized he wasn't as unaffected by her presence as he thought he'd be.

Or wanted to be.

He murmured an oath, and pulled his legs over the side of the bed. "Where is my wife?"

"Surely, you're not going to get out of that bed. James," his grandmother gasped, "you're *not* wearing any breeches."

Michael hesitated long enough to see that she spoke the truth. The room spun. He'd moved too quickly, and his bandaged arm and shoulder made it difficult to move with any modesty. He wouldn't have cared who'd seen him bareassed naked, but as it was, he was incapable of walking.

"Where is Brianna?"

His grandmother pushed to her feet, and he followed the awkward whisper of her gown as she halted in front of him. "She is a stubborn and determined chit, with not one obedient bone in her body." A hand rose and yanked the bell cord beside the bed. "She's been by your side since you were brought here. She is asleep in the next room only because Dr. Blanchard gave her a sleeping potion."

Michael lay back on the pillows and peered up at his grandmother. There was an inkling of softness beneath her starchy exterior. She thrummed her fingers on the head of her cane. "The constable has been here twice, as well as a detective inspector from Scotland Yard. Your wife would not allow anyone near you. Protective chit that she is." His grandmother sniffed dismissively. "I should have known that you would bring back a bride." Her eyes twinkled. "Your mother was quite positive that you would never deign to return at all."

"But you had every confidence that I would." Michael gingerly rubbed his temple. "If I'd thought that you played a hand in nearly seeing me court-martialed—"

"Pah, you needed no help for that, James. Even after all of these years, it's clear to me that you're as obstinate as ever."

He saw that his grandmother had difficulty standing without her cane. He brought his gaze up to look into eyes the same color as his. The heavy velvet curtains were open to the dreary winter light. A lifetime of memories surrounded this home and Aldbury Park, not all of them bad—and seemed to domino through barriers that fell like hollow oaks in his weakened state. His grandmother's presence made him think of warm cider, the yule season, and a family that he would never know again.

"You changed your name," she said, as if reading the momentary stillness and pouncing on the weakness she erroneously thought she saw there. "You may not like who you are, but you'll take your rightful place at the head of this family with a duchess who will do the same." The old dowager step-tapped to the door. "And since you brought one home for us already, I'll assume that she understands her responsibilities. Your brother gave me my first great-grandchild within nine months."

"Grandmother?"

Leaning on the cane, she turned to face her grandson.

His hair was black in the firelight, his sun-bronzed shoulders broader than when he'd left England. Long ago, she'd thought him soft. There was nothing left of that young man now.

"I dislike having my life meddled with."

"I know." She remained unmoved; then a sly smile touched her mouth as if she were privy to something he wasn't. "But I never did think that Caroline was suited to you, James."

Chapter 17

Brianna stood in the doorway of Michael's room, unob-served by the occupants inside as she listened to her husband speak to the inspector from Scotland Yard. Sleet had dampened her cloak. She scraped the hair from her face, every muscle sore. The movement drew Michael's gaze and she froze, poised in the trap of his misty-gray eyes. The lamplight had colored his hair black against the bandage on his head. After a few moments the inspector rose.

"I'll be in touch, your Grace."

Michael sat with his back braced against a stack of pil-lows. He wore a pair of black baggy pajama bottoms that clung low on his hips. A lamp burned on the table beside him. She folded her fingers into her skirt. More than once she'd looked down at her hands and caught them trembling for no reason at all. She had never considered herself a cow-ard, so was having difficulty coming to terms with her fears, with the nightmares that had already awakened her twice this week.

Setting aside the papers, Michael carefully peered at her. Outside, the snow that had been falling for most of that day had turned to sleet and tapped against the windows. "Where have you been this morning?" he quietly asked.

"I went to see Lady Alexandra." She bent her attention to her gloves. "Are you hungry?"

"Sit beside me."

Unfastening her cloak, Brianna moved into the room and laid it over a chair. All week, Michael's mood had been like the weather, unpredictable and stormy.

Today she'd taken the amulet to Mr. Smith, if only to get it out of the house. Smith had once worked for Christopher and she trusted him. She didn't care how much it cost her to trace its origins, if that was even possible. She intended to know what the talisman meant. She intended to see the people who did this to Michael hang.

"You saw Lady Alexandra a few days ago," Michael said.

"I was worried about her," she said evasively. "Ryan and Johnny aren't in London. I really don't wish to discuss this, Michael. I'm very tired, and you need your rest despite what you keep telling Blanchard."

"The authorities found your reticule," he said.

With a start, Brianna turned and saw that the contents had been laid out on the table near the hearth. She approached and stared down at the objects. But could not bring herself to touch the watch or the swan.

"Everything but the ring was inside," he said.

Her handkerchief was missing as well. Maybe more. She didn't know.

"It seems strange since the ring is the only item that can be traced back to you."

And the only item that had meant anything to her.

Brianna had told Michael about the ring a few days ago. Straightening her spine, she reminded herself again that she was made of sterner stuff.

"Yesterday, you went to the gaols with the constable." His voice drew her attention. "Tell me about the tattoo."

Heart racing, she dropped her gaze to the papers he was

reading. "You're not exactly in any condition to conduct this investigation, Michael. Besides, such mutilations are not unique enough to raise too many eyebrows. No one seemed impressed. Tattoos are common here."

"Stay out of the gaols."

Someone had brought a pitcher of water and shaving soap into the room, setting both on the nightstand. Brianna snatched up the towel and sat on the edge of the bed, her hair unbound to her waist, in no temperament to defend her actions to him.

She lifted a razor from the nightstand. Close to two weeks' growth of stubble blurred the outline of his jaw. "You need a shave."

He took the razor from her hand and set it down. "I can shave myself, Brianna."

"Now you're being difficult." She would not lose her temper.

"Brianna . . ." He took her chin in his hands and made her look at him. Hard. "Whatever happened to me, I'll deal with the people responsible when I'm capable of putting one and one together."

"Deal with? As Omar was dealt with?"

"Omar got off easy, *amîri.*"

She moved to pick up the hot water pitcher and found her wrist captured. Her gaze snapped to Michael's. His intensity and purpose of revenge frightened her. Then he was taking her down to his massive bed, turning so that she lay on her back and he was above her. Her palms splayed the hard muscles of his chest. He would injure himself.

"What are you doing, Michael?"

"I've missed you, *amîri.*"

His mouth opened over hers, and in a moment everything changed. He caught her breath on a hitch. His tongue swept into her mouth, possessive and all-consuming with the race of her emotions. She didn't want to be afraid. The tip of his tongue touched the pulse at her throat, then moved to her ear. "I know what it's like to see things that you'll never forget, Brianna. Right now, you're suffering from shock." He caught her chin so she could not pull away. "So for once in your life, understand that your days roaming the countryside are over. You'll not leave this house anymore."

"You can't stop me from getting involved. I'm already involved."

"You can't even sleep at night. Your hands shake."

That he would know appalled her. "Get off me!"

The more she struggled, the more she realized that Michael's strength overwhelmed her with little effort. It should have been impossible to be so injured and so strong at once. There shouldn't have been enough space in his body for two such opposing forces.

"You'll heed me on this, Brianna—"

"Sir." The butler knocked on the open door. "There is a Lord Bedford here to see you at your request."

"Bedford?" Brianna stiffened. She recognized the name. "Isn't he the renowned Lady Caroline's father?"

"Brother," a voice said from the doorway. "The current Duke of Bedford. Have I interrupted a marital tiff?" Bedford casually inquired.

Michael moved his body slightly and she shot out of bed, but his reflexes were still quicker than hers. He caught her wrist, bringing her up short as he came to his feet. "Do you understand, Brianna?"

Her jaw clamped shut.

She despised his bullishness. Resented that he thought himself impervious to death. He hadn't been the one to suffer fear or weep tears. He hadn't been the one to watch himself shot down. Brianna only knew that she never wanted to feel that kind of helplessness again.

For she would surely die.

"I understand that if this is how you behaved with your family, it's no wonder they threw you out of England, your Grace." Lifting the edge of her skirt, Brianna swept around Michael to leave the room.

Bedford stepped in front of her, and for the second time in

as many minutes, a man brought her up short. "Caroline told me that you'd written to her from Southampton, Ravenspur," Bedford said to Michael, though his eyes were on hers. "But you didn't tell her how lovely your wife was."

Michael had written to Caroline from Southampton? Bedford lifted Brianna's hand to his lips, yanking her gaze from Michael's. But not before she saw the deadly look go over her husband's face. She snatched her fingers away. Blond-haired and brown-eyed, the man clearly possessed an exceptional opinion of himself.

"Excuse me, both of you."

Brianna swept past Bedford, and as Michael was left holding the other man's gaze, he fought that familiar wave of antipathy—and a hint of something far more primal.

"You look like bloody hell, Ravenspur." Bedford folded his arms and leaned against the desk. "The physician said there wasn't much but your skull between that bullet and your brain."

"My wife is off limits, Bedford." Michael eased his arms into a black robe. "She's having difficulty enough without putting her in the middle of our sordid little family history."

"My sister wanted to be here, especially when the newspapers splashed this story across the front pages," Bedford said. "A memorable homecoming, Ravenspur. It's not every day that a peer of the realm is shot down on the street. You always did know how to impress the ton."

Michael looped the belt at his waist. He and Bedford had once been the best of friends, hell-raising, hard-drinking aristocrats, reckless in their actions, arrogant to think that the world was theirs to command. Twelve years had passed since they'd last seen each other across a dueling field. Bedford had been Edward's second that day Michael had nearly killed his brother. But antagonism aside, his old friend also served in the Foreign Services department, and it was in that capacity that Michael had specifically requested his help.

"Did you obtain the passenger manifest from the *Northern Star*?" Michael walked to his desk and dropped into the chair. "I need to know who was on that ship."

Bedford crossed one ankle over the other. "I have a man on it. You are sure that someone followed you from Cairo?"

"As sure as I am of anything else." The incident on the ship, the man he'd seen against the rail, the wedged door—all of it was detailed in a deposition Michael had given yesterday. "With Donally still in Cairo, I suggest that someone be sent to Lady Alexandra's residence."

"Already been done. Though I don't see the danger to her. She and your wife both survived the caravan massacre—yet when the shooter could have killed your wife at the plaza, he did not, which leads to the conclusion that this was a robbery, as the constable believes, or you are the only one targeted. Since we don't believe the attack on you was robbery motivated, that leaves the latter. Perhaps the official wigging our government gave you over that Omar affair wasn't enough for someone. Frankly, I'm surprised you've survived as long as you have."

"Thank you. I'll take that as your formal welcome home."

Bedford brushed at his jacket sleeve. "Edward forgave you long ago. You should have at least kept in touch with the family."

Michael eyed the brandy flask on the desk, his jaw tight. "I did what I did." He sat back in the chair. "What do you want me to say?"

"Did you ever think about Caro at all?"

"Aye, I thought of her." And there must have been something in his voice because Bedford raised his head.

He had thought of Caroline every night for three bloody years. He'd thought of her in Edward's bed, bearing Edward's children. He'd thought of her laughter. But there was nothing left of the young lord who had pledged his heart and his life to her forever. His callused hands were washed with the blood of a decade of campaigns. He'd survived because he learned to fight his battles, and had known little tenderness these past years. Except that given by a young courageous Irish woman who had managed in some elemental way to scrape away the layers from his soul and invite him to live again.

He wanted only to protect her from the digressions of his past.

"I remember that she pledged herself to my brother," Michael said. "I remember that she sent a message to meet me at the hunter's cottage. Then stood silent when my brother accused me of cuckolding him."

"She thought if Edward believed that you two were lovers, he'd call off the wedding."

"Because she couldn't stand up to your father? Her lack of logic was astonishing. I almost killed Edward over her. Where would her great plan have taken us both then?"

"She knows that now."

"And has made you her sage emissary, I see."

"She wants closure, Ravenspur. Before Edward died they'd both agreed to name you his daughter's guardian," Bedford said after a moment. "That should say enough about the accord Caro and your brother reached in their marriage. I believe my sister even grew to love Edward very much."

Michael folded his hands on the desk. "I feel no animosity or need to extract revenge on her, if that's what worries you both," he said. "Nor did I come home to rehash old rivalries."

The crackling fire in the hearth seemed louder in the silence. "Nor do I wish to rehash old rivalries," Bedford rejoined after a long moment.

Finally, withdrawing an envelope from inside his jacket, Bedford set it on the desk. "The office has confirmed that there is a connection to the attacks that have been occurring in Egypt to the trafficking of Egyptian antiquities in London, and to the recent murder of a customs inspector. If that's true, then the suspect who shot you may be our only link. Can you tell me anything more than what we already have?"

Michael withdrew a pen and paper from a drawer. "I don't know if the tattoo my wife saw on the man's forearm is the same as those found on the arms of three men involved in the caravan massacres." He dipped the nib in ink and scratched out the image in his head. Even with his arm immobilized, he could draw better than he could do anything else at present. "But if it is, you have your connection."

Bedford held the paper to the light. "What is it?"

"A scarab," Michael said. "A beetle of sorts. Unpleasant creatures. A thousand years ago the pharaohs used to bury dissenters alive with these. It would take four weeks to strip a man's bones clean."

"No bloody ballocks, Ravenspur?" Bedford said, ever the skeptic. "I've read about vengeance killings, also." He folded the paper, careful not to smear the ink. "I suggest that you and your new bride get out of London until you recover. Let this office handle the inquiry."

Cloaked in the semidarkness of his library, Michael poured himself another snifter of brandy and walked to the window. One arm tightly wrapped in a sling, he·worked to sort through images in his head.

There were holes in his memory from that day on the mall, but something had been bothering him since Bedford left that afternoon.

Michael had lived in Egypt long enough to know the signs of vendetta killings. Someone had tried to frame him for Omar's murder. If that person was the man he'd seen that night on the *Northern Star*, the attack on him could not have been motivated by vengeance, for the man would know that he'd had no hand in the sheikh's murder.

"Excuse me, your Grace." Brianna's footman stood uneasily in the doorway. "I was told that you wanted to see me."

The tall clock at the far end of the corridor began to chime the hour. Michael knew that clocks all over the residence did the same, a legacy of his grandmother's collection of timepieces, as if there wasn't already a reminder of his mortality—and here he sat troubled about his wife, with the same apprehension he'd felt since Bedford left.

He hadn't gone to her. He went to the library instead, to nurse his restraint, celebrating his first night in two weeks without laudanum. Only to find himself slowly getting drunk.

"Where did my wife go today?" Michael asked without turning from the window.

"To a jeweler on Bond Street, your Grace."

"The same one she visited two days ago?" Michael asked, and the man nodded. "She didn't visit Lady Alexandra?"

"No, your Grace."

Michael knew about the ring that Brianna had the jeweler make for him. So, why had she lied about something as simple as that?

"Did she meet anyone?"

"Only the jeweler, your Grace."

"That will be all."

Michael could see the dull glow of lamplight on the wet street. It had been too long since he'd had control over anything in his life. Too long since he'd cared about anyone else. He was troubled that Brianna could so easily lie to him.

Setting down the brandy glass, he walked upstairs. Brianna lay in her bed, surrounded by velvet hangings. She faced the hearth, her hands folded beneath her cheek.

His shadow fell across her. Her lashes lifted.

And all he had to do was look into her eyes to know her vulnerability. All he had to do was look into his heart to know his.

He should have told her that he'd written Caroline to tell her that he was coming home. He'd sent the missive with the men he'd hired to dispatch the mare to Aldbury. Caro had had a right to know.

But there was more on his mind tonight then revisiting a chapter of his life that he now realized had been closed for a long time.

"Tomorrow, we're leaving for Aldbury, Brianna."

Chapter 18

Brianna scarcely noticed the lack of dialogue in the carriage as they passed beneath an imposing wrought-iron arch that opened into broad, rolling, seemingly endless expanse of parkland, punctuated by towering oaks and maples. The Aldbury cavalcade had traveled several hours, stopping for lunch and continuing again into dusk. She had not seen but two cottages for an hour among the maples and oaks, and now both stood tucked away on one side of the road. Lights glowed behind the windows. Flower boxes lined the sills. Down one sloping ridge she saw the lake bathed gold by the dipping sun on the western horizon. She scraped frost off the glass in an effort to see more, enthralled by the charm of the passing countryside.

"We've been on Aldbury land for the last hour," Brianna heard Lord Chamberlain say. He sat beside her on the tufted velvet seat.

She turned from the window and noticed that everyone was watching her. The dowager sat on the opposite seat, and Michael lounged against the window, no longer asleep. She realized he'd been watching her for some time.

"It's beautiful," she said quietly.

For indeed everything around her was. She had never seen the size and scope of such a manicured park, an encapsulated fairyland of ice and sunlight. The road dipped downward and was sheltered now by tall trees.

"The estate sits on forty thousand acres, half granted by King Henry VII after a Yorkist rout for the crown failed in 1487." Chamberlain narrated Aldbury history as if he were obligated. Brianna had learned that he was Michael's private secretary, bequeathed to him as heir to the Ravenspur dynasty. She was to be his pupil in all things Aldbury. "Keep looking out the window, your Grace," he said.

They breasted another steep rise and she saw the magnificent house in the valley below. She pressed against the glass, her jaw gaping.

Bathed in amber mist, set in an Arcadian landscape of terraced gardens, the palatial three-story apparition covered some four acres, with huge corner towers of Doric columns, steep rooftops dotted with chimneys, and sunlight glistening off hundreds of mullioned windows. Ten minutes later, as the carriage clattered across a Palladian bridge and rounded another corner, Brianna was struck by the preeminence of Aldbury Park. In the growing darkness, she could see candlelight showing from every window. Heart racing like a child's, she raised her gaze to Michael's, but unexpectedly felt any comment inadequate within the scope of her dismay, wishing now that she hadn't allowed him to be so reticent concerning his life. She couldn't believe that this place was his home—that he'd grown up in this glass and golden fairy-tale world. She had only guessed at his past, and her interpretation had fallen far short of reality. His life suddenly seemed surreal, belonging to someone other than her desert warrior. Her own family was wealthy and held lands, but nothing of this magnitude. The idea that people actually lived this way was beyond her scope.

"It's overwhelming at first, Brianna," Michael replied to

the silence, as if understanding her growing trepidation, and that he had been less than candid about many things.

Nor did the magnitude of her feelings change as the evening progressed. The line of servants that greeted the carriage led all the way up the long manicured walk, the steps, and into the enormous foyer. The women were dressed in black dresses, the men in tailcoats, wearing a white shirt and scarlet waistcoat beneath with black trousers and buckled pumps. All had come out to meet Michael.

Brianna had not expected the show, or the subtle display of affection shown Michael as he greeted each one. He knew many by name.

Standing beside the dowager, Brianna watched as he walked up the granite stairs, knowing that the long ride had drained him of strength. His steps were slow and precise, the laudanum he'd consumed earlier having taken its toll, but he worked his way through the line of servants as protocol demanded. Despite everything between them, Brianna felt an enormous swell of pride for him. His great coat fluttered in the icy gusts. His arm, still pressed to his body, remained insulated beneath the woolen warmth.

She saw him look back at her once, as she followed her personal entourage up a huge seventeenth-century carved staircase to her chambers. She turned away.

Her bedroom was magnificent, filled with three centuries of historical treasures from the Genoa velvet bed hangings and the white marble fireplace to the ivory inlaid tables. She quietly explored the length of her dressing rooms and her private salon in the adjoining rooms, but ventured no further for fear of losing herself in this house. She hadn't asked where Michael's rooms were.

Brianna reached inside her pocket and withdrew a silver-plated derringer, and set it in her nightstand. Mr. Smith had given her the weapon in place of the revolver.

She would go nowhere without it. Walking to the window, she stared out over the vast emptiness of the world where she would now live.

At least out here, isolated within Aldbury's forty thousand acres, she didn't have to worry about Michael's safety. His physical limitations would prevent him from returning to London for a while. Brianna laid her cheek against the cool glass, finally turning into her dimly lit room. She would not allow herself to be afraid. She would not allow herself to hate this place. And, right now, she would not allow herself to think about Michael.

Gracie entered.

Brianna saw the hot tray of food she carried. "Dinner from now on is at seven, mum," she said. "Her Grace thought you would want to know."

Brianna took the tray and set it on the window bench. "Do I have you to thank for supper?"

"She told me to take you this tray. You have to eat something, mum."

Stiff upper lip and all that, Brianna surmised, drawing in her breath as she looked at the long silver box delivered on the tray.

"Is there anything else that you need, mum?"

"What is this box?"

"I don't know. But his grace put it on the tray for you."

Carefully, Brianna removed the lid.

A single red rose lay within.

Brianna nearly collided with Dr. Blanchard the next morning at the top of the grand staircase. "His grace is not in his quarters," he informed her when she asked where he was. "He left this morning after he dined with the dowager at breakfast. Mark my words, he'll be back with a fever. It's only been two weeks since he was injured."

"Where did he go?"

"He had some matters to attend to in the village. Ask Chamberlain if you want an up-to-date report. I'm only the physician."

A servant stood beside the door where Brianna had stopped. "The dowager is waiting inside for you, your Grace."

Remembering why she was here, she nodded politely and entered a private drawing room. The dowager sat in a large wing-backed chair facing the window, her ever-present cane in her hand.

"You're late," the woman snorted without turning to see who had entered the room. A blanket covered her thick skirts. "Do sit down."

On this, her first morning at Aldbury Park, Brianna had overslept. She was awakened when Gracie entered her bedroom with a hasty edict to rise. After dressing in a warm woolen morning gown, she left her quarters and was brought here. She stood in front of the dowager and curtsied.

"Good morning, your Grace." Her long hair was tied back with a yellow ribbon. Brianna felt as young as she knew she probably looked.

"Good morning indeed." The dowager's shrewd gray eyes shifted from the window. "You've slept it away." She peered at Brianna through her lorgnette. "Do sit down, child. You're putting a crick in my neck."

Brianna spread her skirts on the window bench and lifted her gaze as a servant approached with a tray.

"Are your quarters acceptable?"

"They are quite . . . formal, your Grace."

"Those suites have traditionally been the lady's rooms in this house. Every Ravenspur duchess has slept there for centuries. Have you any idea what you're in for here?"

"In for?" Brianna queried. "As in what crime did I commit to find myself a prisoner?" She folded her hands. "I wed the Ravenspur heir."

"Indeed." The dowager harrumphed, not fooled by her briskness. "A blind man can see my grandson is smitten with you."

Brianna's interest stirred but her expression remained neutral. She wasn't entirely confident how Michael felt about anything.

"Would you care for some tea?"

Brianna preferred white java but accepted tea. When it

was served, she blew at the wafting steam. The dowager drank hers heaped with cream and sugar, so Brianna elected to suffer the same. They sat in polite silence until the maid curtsied and left. Brianna did want to develop a relationship with the woman. She was Michael's grandmother, after all, and seemed to hold some sway over her grandson, whether he admitted to it or not.

"James was always impertinent," the dowager sniffed. "In and out of trouble, Defiant, even as a nipper. It's no wonder he brought you home rather than a house, A bride any of us found for him. Are you perchance with child?" The hopeful tenor of her voice matched her eyes.

Brianna blushed to the roots of her hair. "No, your Grace."

"No matter. The Irish always did know how to procreate with a passion we Brits lack. I expect that my grandson knows how to perform his duty by you."

Without managing to choke, Brianna set down her tea. "What is it that you wished to see me about, your Grace?"

"Fifty years ago I sat where you're sitting now." Turning her head, the dowager looked out over the brown fields of Aldbury Park. "I was seventeen. The only difference is, I didn't have me sitting in this chair giving advice." She chuckled, clearly favoring her advice above all else. "I was filled with a zest for living, even if I didn't know quite where to put all that ebullience. I soon learned that pride in these lands goes back centuries and that I was now a part of it all."

Brianna looked out over the placid landscape, impressed by its scope if not by the serene beauty. Yet, there was a sense of desolation in the brown fields that surrounded this estate.

"The crops have failed for years," the dowager said, following Brianna's gaze. A sigh fell over her expression. "I fear Edward was as incapable as his father when it came to managing these lands." Her gray eyes focused on Brianna. "My grandson will not have an easy time. His days will be filled with the endless routine of making this estate whole again. He is gone now because he is needed someplace. Even he feels responsibility to his heritage, though he's not prepared to admit as much. He can't be worrying about you."

"Perhaps it is I who worries about him, your Grace."

The answer had not been what the dowager had expected. Her whole expression gradually shifted. "Do you know the grand advice my mother-in-law gave me?" The dowager's cane thumped the carpet. "Men will stray, she told me. It's the lot of the wife to bear the burden of her gender. Which was the biggest mash of poppycock I ever heard. The only thing I ever bore were my children."

"Then she was wrong about your husband?"

The dowager's mouth pursed. "If he ever found interest elsewhere, I never knew, nor did I want to know. But I was married for forty-seven years because I became someone *I* could respect separate from my husband's enormous shadow. For it did become enormous, both at home and in the governing body of this country. Who you become is up to you. How you become that person will shape your future and James's."

A knock on the door sounded and the majordomo entered, followed by Lord Chamberlain. "Your carriage is waiting, your Grace."

"You're leaving?" Brianna stood as the duchess edged to her feet.

"Alas, my home is near Wendover. The drive is not long. Just unpleasantly bumpy." The cane wobbled, and Brianna reached out to touch the elder's elbow in an effort to steady her, only to be stopped. "One must maintain appearances." The dowager patted her hand fondly. "I will have no one think me feeble. Least of all myself." Her voice lowered. "But I don't mind if you take my arm, dear."

Brianna walked beside the dowager and her retinue of personal servants past the grand staircase, with its massive crystal chandelier lit to brilliance high above them. Even with the cane, the dowager's energy abounded in every muscle of her sixty-seven-year-old frame. "Make my grandson happy, Brianna."

It was an order, albeit affectionately given with the addendum that the dowager liked her grandson's choice of bride, but an order nonetheless. Brianna's uncertainty had no place in the patent scheme of things. Chamberlain agreed as he politely handed the dowager into her carriage, leaning nearer for a little chin-wag about the preparations he was making to ready the Ravenspur duchess for public consumption. As if she had nothing important of herself to offer her new position.

But though she resented the constipated pomposity of the man talking around her as if she didn't exist, she wanted to believe that he could help her through this transition. "You'll meet me in the second floor salon at three o'clock for a new wardrobe fitting," Chamberlain said as the carriage pulled out onto the drive. He'd already turned, expecting her to follow. "I've arranged for music and dance lessons."

Michael still hadn't returned by the time she suffered through lunch with Chamberlain. Left alone in her chambers, Brianna wrote letters. In her fervor, she wrote to various members of her family, one to Lady Alexandra and another to Mr. Smith, letting him know where she could be found when he learned something about the amulet. She rearranged her bedroom, scooting her desk in front of the window. Michael had returned by the time she finished with her wardrobe appointment, but Blanchard's opium concoction had knocked him out.

"His fever is back, as I warned," Blanchard said when she arrived in Michael's room.

Brianna reached her palm out to touch her husband's brow. "How the mighty do forget they are human."

A hand wrapped around her wrist, bringing her to full alertness and a sudden trip-hammer pounding in her chest. The light of the flickering fire revealed Michael watching her. "I haven't forgotten, *amîri*."

"You've been busy today," she said, touching his fevered brow.

"I swear I'm going to strangle Blanchard." Michael's eyes drifted close. "For . . . his bloody . . . potions."

"You need your sleep, Michael." Unimpressed with his bullishness, Brianna waited until she was sure her husband was breathing evenly before she stood. "You have my permission to see that he stays in bed," she said to Blanchard.

The next morning, Michael was still asleep when Brianna had dressed and decided to explore her new surroundings. She fastened her cloak. Then, on her way out, she shoved the silver derringer in her pocket. Gracie was still unpacking.

"If Lord Chamberlain should appear, tell him that you don't know where I am," Brianna said.

Behind the house lay the stables, barns, and coach houses, which together with the greenhouse formed a small working village of its own. Brianna rode her mare past the stables. The buffeting wind snatched at her hat and cloak. She did not use a sidesaddle. When she reached the edge of the lake, she turned and looked back at the massive house. Sunlight checkered the serrated rooftop, a dozen smoking chimneys, and turned the mullioned panes of glass to gold. The sight remained extraordinary for a novice duchess and only confirmed her first impression of the size of everything at Aldbury Park.

Later, Brianna found a two-story Tudor cottage in the woods. Tying her horse to a branch, she was as surprised by its sudden appearance rising out in the brambles and thickets as she was to find the door unlocked. This was once an old Elizabethan hunting lodge.

Upstairs, paintings lined the wall or stood on easels, some covered, some unfinished. Someone at the house was an excellent artist. She realized this lodge would make a perfect photography studio.

A voice outside the long window pulled Brianna into an alcove, and wrapping her cloak tighter, she leaned into the glass. A little girl of about eleven sat cross-legged on a fallen tree, tormenting a kitten, watching as it chased its tail. She wore no wrap against the cold, and was soon called to task for her neglect. A woman wrapped in a heavy cloak and carrying another approached. The two had come from an opposite path to the one Brianna had ridden. As if sensing they were being watched, both turned to look up at the window. The cool light fell on the woman's lower face before she yanked the girl around and walked back toward the main house.

The whole incident had lasted less than a minute, and Brianna, sole proprietor of the scene, wanted to know who they were. Wrapping the cloak around her slim shoulders, she retraced her steps, only to find that her mare was gone.

Untied and let loose, more like it, she realized as she looked down and saw smaller shoe prints encased in the mud at her feet. The little brat tormenting that cat had sent her horse off.

"Is she a servant's daughter?" Brianna stood at the sideboard an hour later and saw only porridge for breakfast. For all the glorious architecture of Aldbury Park, the food was terrible.

"That would be Lady Amber Catherine, your Grace," an older man said. "Edward's eldest daughter."

"I see." Brianna sat at the table, adjusting her skirts. She'd trekked across the field and managed to suffer a blister on her heel. "Will her mother be in attendance at this meal?"

"Lady Caroline rarely takes her morning meal anywhere but in the nursery with the children."

She suspected Michael would be asleep all day. At least she hoped he would be. He needed his rest. "Then I assume I'm alone this morning?"

"Lord Chamberlain is in the library at this time. And Countess Aldbury dines in her room—"

"Countess Aldbury?"

"Your husband's mother, your Grace. She lives in the east wing. You might have seen her with Amber Catherine. They take their morning constitutional together. Sometimes to the lodge, where her ladyship used to dabble with paints. She hasn't been inside the place since Edward passed away. I imagine it is quite untidy."

"Has Michael . . . has his grace seen her since his return home?"

"No, mum."

"But why ever not?"

"I wouldn't presume to know the answer to that."

But they all did. She could tell in that brief glimpse, that every servant present knew the history in this family.

Brianna fidgeted with the corner of the napkin. Finally, she stood. "Where is the nursery?" she asked.

"Up the stairs and to the left corridor." He cleared his throat. "You will probably hear the little nipper. She hasn't been feeling well."

"Has Dr. Blanchard seen the child?"

"I don't believe so, your Grace. Should I send for him?" He seemed eager to do so, and Brianna could see that he cared for the child.

"Tell him that I said so. I fear he feels his current services are being wasted and this will give him something of importance to do."

Brianna didn't hear the baby, so it took her longer to find the rooms in the blaring silence of endless corridors. She was beginning to wonder if there were any signs of life in this house at all when she'd reached the end of the hallway and heard muffled voices behind the last door. The door opened and a servant stepped out.

"Your Grace." She hastily dipped and nearly dropped the foul smelling bundle she carried in her arms. "I didn't see you."

"Is Lady Caroline inside?"

"Yes, your Grace."

Brianna stepped into the room and was at once struck by the bright yellow and lavender wallpaper that covered the walls. Purple draperies had been drawn and sunlight found its way everywhere into the room. A woman sat on the floor, gently cooing over a wriggling child. She looked up as Brianna entered. Her face warmed into a smile.

Instinctively, Brianna knew that this was Lady Caroline and not some nanny or caregiver. "Don't get up, please," Brianna said.

"Please join me, then. You must be Brianna." The woman held out a hand. "The new Lady Ravenspur. I'm sorry that I didn't get to see you downstairs the night you arrived. She's teething, and when she fell asleep, I fear that I did as well."

Lady Caroline had fine blond hair rolled in a bun at her nape. Her eyes were the color green of a rare piece of jade. She was neither exotic nor breathtakingly beautiful, but she possessed something far more attractive than looks. With her freckled nose and cheerful deportment, she was like a daisy in a bed of roses—something Brianna would find appealing in a friend. Her smile was genuine, if not reserved, as she invited her to sit on the floor.

Was this Michael's Caroline, then? The woman who had sent him oceans away? The woman he'd written to from Southampton?

"You have another daughter?" Brianna asked.

"Yes, Amber Catherine," Lady Caroline said.

Brianna sat on the floor. "I saw her playing with a kitten outside the lodge beside the lake. There was a woman with her."

Caroline's face lifted from her baby. "That would be Countess Aldbury." Her voice hesitated. "Did she see you?"

"A glimpse perhaps."

"You'll have to get used to her. She doted on my husband. I fear she's been a recluse since Edward died. You've met the dowager?"

"She left yesterday."

"Don't let that gruff exterior worry you. It broke her heart when James left England." She traced a finger over the baby's nose. "It took us three years to learn that he no longer went by the name of Aldbury. Did you know that Michael was the name borne by the archangel closest to God? There is irony in that, I think."

"Why is that?" The masculine inquiry came from the doorway.

Michael leaned with his good shoulder against the frame, clearly measuring the situation as Brianna tried to ignore the escalating beat of her heart. He was dressed in knee-high boots and casual attire, his arm in a sling. He'd not shaved and looked as if he had just awakened.

"Because you were the least saintly person I ever knew, James Michael Aldbury." Caroline climbed to her feet. Her hands brushed at her skirts almost self-consciously. "You were terribly wicked. If there was trouble to be had, you found it, and the rest of us would not be able to sit for a week after the thrashings we received because of you."

Michael had not taken his eyes from Brianna.

"He always led a terribly dangerous and exciting life compared to the rest of us," Caroline said, drawing Michael's gaze, a dull recognition growing inside Brianna that these two had a long history. "I envied you your freedom."

"I saw two campaigns, Caro. Freedom was a luxury I *didn't* have."

"I heard what happened in London."

"A moment of inattention that won't happen again."

Michael walked past Caroline and dropped to his haunches beside Brianna. She was aware of his crystalline eyes focusing completely on her. "You've been busy, *amîri*. My apologies for missing supper with you last night."

"Not at all," she said, unashamed that she'd ordered Blanchard to knock him out. "I was glad to provide you with the opportunity to sleep."

"Remind me to thank you properly."

Brianna's confident smirk faltered. The infant cooed prettily and Michael dropped his attention to the baby, leaving Brianna to ponder the promise of his words. "Have you been practicing holding her?" he asked, with such smug certitude that a hot flush of color burned her cheeks.

"Her name is Edwina." Caroline hovered as any anxious mother would around a one-armed uncle. "She and Amber Catherine both have the Aldbury eyes. Aldbury children are famous for the trademark."

As the Ravenspur bride expected to produce one of those, Brianna squirmed. The certainty that the current owner of those translucent silver eyes would do his duty by her in that regard leaped to the forefront of her mind, especially when that thoroughly gray gaze slowly raked her. He was so close she could smell the clean scent of his soap.

Suddenly she had to escape from this room.

"She's my angel." Caroline lifted her child, looking oddly at Brianna and Michael. "Have you been to see your mother yet?"

"No," Brianna heard Michael say.

The air had chilled. The mood changed, and Michael stood.

"For the record, I thought that you should have been summoned home sooner," Caroline said. "It wasn't my idea to wait."

"What do you want me to say, Caroline?" Michael helped Brianna to her feet. He was not going to let her flee. "That I wished everything could have been different? Trust me. I do."

"Dammit, Brianna, I didn't bring you in here to bleed me—"

"Don't move." She bent Michael's head to the side and clipped the second stitch above his ear. "How could you not see your own mother?"

Brianna stood caged between Michael's legs as he sat on the corner of his bed. A pair of scissors and tweezers, one in each hand, she faced him like an army field surgeon. He lifted a dubious brow. "Are you sure you know what you're doing?"

"I would be worried, too, if I were looking at me with scissors in my hand. Especially after I'd just left the room of my husband's former true love. Do you think she's still pretty?"

Michael caught her wrist. "You have a temper, *amîri*." He removed the scissors from her grip, his dancing eyes passing over hers. "I'll wait for Blanchard to finish the job, before you drain me of more blood."

"I'm trying to discuss something important, Michael."

"So am I." In one fluid motion, he pulled her down onto the feather mattress and turned her squirming beneath him. She realized then that she'd forgotten to take the derringer from her pocket. That it was still loaded from when she'd taken it on her ride that morning. "Maybe I should have Blanchard feed you the same potion he's giving me," he said.

"I'm sorry if you were upset about that."

"Upset?" he scoffed. "I need my senses about me more than I need a few extra hours of sleep. Don't do that again. Unless you care to test my stamina." The subtle threat sent a dangerous thrill through her veins, for he had kept his distance from her. Or she from him. She didn't know.

No matter, her hands surged to his chest. "You are highhanded with your attentions, Michael. You always end an argument like this."

His mouth paid intimate homage to the pale mounds of flesh that pushed above her bodice. "Are we arguing?"

The confusion and hunger eating at her tightened her stomach. He so easily manipulated her, and his injuries made it that much easier for him to get his way because she worried about him. Indeed, she'd spent too many days and weeks worrying about him. "I won't lie down with you because you snap your fingers, Michael." She gave him her cheek. "I won't."

He put the side of his thumb to her face and turned her toward him. "Did you hear my fingers snap?"

His mouth covered hers.

A long intimate exploration surpassed her gasp and her intent to deny him. He'd taken his arm from his sling, and his fingers extended into her hair as he deepened the kiss, his body making any verbal comments superfluous; then she forgot to think at all.

A part of her wanted to lie trapped against his heat. To accept her duty, bend to convention, and rally behind motherhood. She tasted him, felt her body respond. Panic infused her limbs.

She thought she knew him, but she did not.

"Michael." She desperately breathed against his mouth. The derringer pulsed her hip. "Stop."

Suddenly they were both staring at each other. She was breathing hard with her exertion; he was barely breathing at all, and to her reeling mind, stood in dire need of comeuppance. She would not relent.

"Do you want me to throw Caroline out?" he drawled calmly. "I can send her back to her brother. Or to a remote cabin in Siberia perhaps."

"Ask sweetly, and I will allow her to stay." She lay with her hair spread beneath her, looking up into his face. She would never ask that he send her away. He was her children's guardian.

Besides, this was about more than her jealousy, and he knew it, could read it in her eyes. She had a perfectly legitimate reason to be furious with him, beginning with his lack of information concerning his whole gilded life. Nor did she understand his family. This icy disdain among members of the same family was simply foreign to her. With her kin, at least one understood where one stood and did battle accordingly.

"Go to your mother, Michael." She took a fortifying breath. "You're fortunate to have one. Mine died when I was very young. She died before I even understood that she was ill. I never even said good-bye."

"My mother is a loon, Brianna."

"That's a horrible thing to say."

"Hell, Brianna. Enough already." Michael turned on his back and she shoved out of bed. The comforter fell like a ruby waterfall to the floor in her wake. "You've made your discontent with me on the topic clear." He winced when he set his arm back in the sling and met her gaze. "But I'm not asking for bloody approval."

"Truly, Michael." Brianna shakily adjusted her skirts and straightened her bodice to some semblance of decorum. "How could I approve or disapprove of something I don't understand?" Interested only in escaping, she went as far as the door. "Do not worry about me—"

His hand came over her shoulder and shut the door in her face.

"And you can demand that I not breathe, for all the good it will do." His other arm remained in a sling, but no less a barrier at her back. She squeezed her eyes shut, the scent of him filling her every pore. "You ask about my family," he said against her hair. "I have never been privy to my mother's thoughts or her heart. Stiff upper lip and all that. Unlike the Irish, we Brits find any display of emotions coarse." He tilted a finger against her chin, turning her in his arms.

"My father was a tyrant who would have sold his children if it could have bought him political favors—who did sell off a son who fell far short of his expectations. He was master in his kingdom. One bowed first and last to the ever-present status quo. Men of Chamberlain's rank stand at the gates of this dynasty like Peter guarding heaven. Despite what you may think, I'm an outsider here as well."

A knock sounded on the door. Lord Chamberlain spoke from the other side, reminding Michael of an appointment. Annoyed, he lifted his gaze from Brianna's. "I'll be down in a moment," he said through the door.

"You could let Chamberlain handle the estate management."

"But I won't." He brushed his thumb over her lips. "Right now people don't trust me," he said, his words focused on her, "but they will."

"Yes, they will, Michael." She was insulted for him, infuriated that people could dislike him. "You were born to rule."

Their faces only inches apart, he abruptly pulled back.

"You have all the traits," she reassured him.

"You are content, then, to be here?"

"Naturally," she said quietly, sensing his interest as she weighed the subtle change of topic. "Who wouldn't be struck with awe?"

Opening the door, he looked back at her standing in his room. Then it occurred to her that she might be overplaying her hand, considering their conversation in London. She wondered if his talk about trust had been more than rhetorical and especially aimed at her.

"Thank you for the rose." She could think of nothing else when he looked at her in that way.

"You're welcome, Brianna."

Watching his tall form disappear down the corridor, Brianna folded her arms and leaned into the doorway. He was being completely agreeable for once. So why did it strike her that she should be worried?

Chapter 19

"**I** believe I have several matters of import to discuss with you, your Grace." Chamberlain stood in front of the desk in Michael's library. He'd been three weeks in residence and little had changed from their last conversation.

A pile of papers sat on the desk, awaiting his ducal signature. Tenants, bankers, and solicitors all sought his time. For weeks his days had been filled with an endless amount of exhaustive meetings, account reviews, and estate tours. He'd barely finished paying off the third set of death taxes in less than eight years on the Aldbury holdings when Chamberlain presented him with a full accounting of the estate.

Distracted, Michael dropped the paper in his hand. "Do you want to tell me what my brother did with the income from this estate for the last three years?" He waited for Blanchard to stop probing his shoulder before he grabbed another memo and glared at Chamberlain.

His hands clasped behind his back, the man rocked back on his heels. "He built an infirmary in Aylesbury."

"That was Caroline's doing. And we're obligated a fortune to complete the construction. I have to go there this afternoon."

"He collected some of the finest racing horses in England."

"Which clearly assisted him to his demise. Every horse will be sold, and it still won't pay off his markers in London alone."

"I was not the keeper of your brother's conscience, your Grace."

"Only the executer of his funds. Ouch . . . Christ—" He winced as Blanchard rotated his arm to shoulder level. "Do you want to warn me before you do that?"

Blanchard merely looked over the bridge of his nose. "Your patience is still required to heal completely, your Grace."

"My patience?" Michael snatched up his shirt and shrugged into the sleeves. "I'm a living example of patience." He eased the shirt into his trousers. "Hell, most would consider me a bloody saint for my exemplary patience. But my arm needs my shoulder to work."

"I recommend exercises. But it could still be weeks before you have full use of both your arm and shoulder, your Grace."

"Would you care for some brandy, your Grace?" a servant inquired from the doorway.

Michael's fingers worked the jet-black buttons on his burgundy vest. His trousers were black with a thin gray strip running down the crease. His jacket remained off. "Yes." He waved the man in as Blanchard packed his leather bag.

Michael slapped the cravat around his collar and worked the cloth into a knot at his throat as he sat. He stared at the papers on his desk. His expertise was not in finance or farming, but even he recognized a poorly managed estate and the shocking hemorrhage of operable funds that seemed magnified because of three consecutive crop failures and a multitude of poor business investments.

Somewhere in the corridor a vase shattered.

"It is she!" Blanchard stepped back into the room, his face pale. "Someone will have to fetch her governess."

"Fetch her mother, more like it," Chamberlain snorted. "Lock the bloody door before she comes in here."

"You can use the veranda door," the butler suggested, his expression plaintive.

Michael looked in disbelief at them all. "Send someone to clean up the mess, Blanchard. And shut the door on your way out." He added, "How the hell is it that someone can't manage a bloody eleven-year-old?"

"One doesn't *manage* Lady Amber, your Grace," the butler said.

"Doesn't she have any friends?" But he knew before Chamberlain said anything that their only suitable neighbors lived an hour away and had no children. Even if they did, Michael was convinced they'd have locked them away from his niece. His brother's eldest child was what one genteel servant generously described as a rambunctious little shaver. Michael was considerably less optimistic. His niece was a spoiled brat. People ran when she entered a room.

He took the snifter from the silver tray the servant offered. Noting the letters on the lace doily next to his brandy, he lifted them from the tray. They were addressed to Brianna, and at once he felt the tightness slide away.

"I can take those upstairs, your Grace," the butler said.

Michael set down the glass of brandy. One letter was from Lady Alexandra, two from others who bore the Donally name, but the fourth was from a Mr. Smith on Bond Street. Michael edged a thumb over the sharp corner of the letter. "Is this name familiar to you?"

"Yes, your Grace. Your Grace?" The butler's voice lifted Michael's head. The man's gaze pointed to the letters in his hand. "Should I tell her, then, that you have intercepted her mail?" The gray-haired butler shifted his gaze over Michael's shoulder. "I mean, she'll ask about the letters when she goes to her chambers, your Grace. I always put her mail on her desk."

"Does she always receive this much mail?"

"She has a large family, and they seem to be very passionate in their correspondence." He cleared his throat and flushed. "She told me, your Grace."

"And in her discourse, did she also share with you what she does along the way when she goes to Wendover to visit my grandmother, or to Aldbury for that matter?"

"No, your Grace."

"Is my wife back from the stables yet?"

"Yes, your Grace. I expect that she went to the lake again."

Michael walked to the glass doors that overlooked the distant lake. He wouldn't see Brianna until later.

"Your wife discharged her music instructor, your Grace," Chamberlain said, "or she would be in the conservatory at this time."

From Gracie, he'd learned that Brianna kept herself occupied with projects and seemed determined to make her way without Chamberlain's help and without his. But in the evenings, he knew he could always find her in the library. On that score at least, Michael had earned her sincerest gratitude. Aldbury had a magnificent library, and he'd given her the freedom to explore every tome. But too often he'd found himself watching her rather than working, not understanding this insane fellowship of disjointed emotions.

He thought of her constantly.

He had allowed her space only because he'd been handicapped with his injuries. But he realized it was more than that. He wanted her to come to him.

"Your carriage will be brought around in fifteen minutes, your Grace," his butler informed him. "Shall I fetch your coat? It looks like snow on the way."

Which would probably force an overnight stay someplace.

Movement in the doorway stopped the conversation in the room. The butler turned. Chamberlain, sensing the ominous silence, looked over his shoulder. "Countess Aldbury." He snapped to attention as if caught by Napoleon sloughing off while on the front lines. "My lady."

The countess acknowledged Lord Chamberlain with a small nod, but she looked at Michael, standing by the glass doors. "James." Opening her fingers, she smoothed out the bunched material on her black skirt, followed by a moment of awkwardness as she seemed flustered by the attention of so many.

Michael didn't move, except to nod his dismissal to those present.

Easing the letters into his pocket, he was curious what monumental occasion finally drove the countess from her quarters to seek him out. As always, she was flawlessly neat, adorned in black, though Edward had been dead for over a year.

Brown eyes looked from him to the library shelves filled with leather-bound tomes. His brother had never been a connoisseur of literature, but every year since he was in the schoolroom, she'd purchased books for Edward. Michael, however, had been the one to read them all.

"Since you have chosen to ignore my presence these past weeks, I thought it time to find you," she finally said when the door shut. "You are the only person who can exercise any control in this matter."

Michael's brow arched. "I don't know how far-reaching my control is." It certainly hadn't seemed like much lately.

"It concerns your wife. The servants are talking, James. It's never good when the servants talk."

He just watched her. "What about my wife?"

"She has taken . . . she has *stolen* my summer cottage and made it into a . . . a lodging to take photographs."

Michael resisted pinching the bridge of his nose. Twelve years without a spoken or written word between them and his mother's first dictum demanded that he throw his wife out of the cottage she'd been working so hard to repair these past weeks. "She develops photographs there, Mother. The cottage wasn't being used. It was falling down."

"I paint there in the summer months. The cottage is mine."

"Would it be so difficult to share? Have you talked to her?"

"I'll not share. The idea is preposterous. And I'm talking to you. It's time that we speak. Don't you think?"

Michael's hands went to his hips. His shoulder stitched, and he welcomed the pain as he looked away. He didn't bother to ask her where she'd been when he'd spent four days of his first week at Aldbury in bed with a fever. Nor did he point out that in all the years he'd been exiled from this family, not once had she ever written a single word to him.

Ever.

"She has painted the rooms, James. She had no right." Agitation brought fire to her eyes. "Tell her that she doesn't belong there."

"I'll see what I can do, Mother."

"Edward . . . he would have known what to do," she whispered.

"Edward isn't here. I am."

The room grew silent. A log snapped in the fireplace. Seeing her so confused created an unexpected surge of compassion in him. "I know that you are not Edward," she said, her gaze going to where his hair had grown out over the scar on his scalp. "But he would know what to do."

After his mother left, the butler returned with Michael's coat. He shrugged into it and walked out onto the terrace. With his chin down against the stiff chill, he looked at the horizon. The clouds were darkening into what looked to be an approaching late winter snowstorm.

"Uncle James?"

Amber Catherine stood at his side, looking up at him, her blond curly hair like a wild nimbus around her head. He'd noticed that she always followed him, and more than once he'd nearly stepped on her. She held an orange kitten in her arms. Decked out in little red bows, it peered up at him through glassy eyes begging to be put out of its misery. "Do you think your cat enjoys being dressed like a doll, Amber?" he asked.

"His name is Sam." Her arms defiantly wrapped the kitten tighter.

"Return inside, Amber. It's cold out here."

Her expression fell, and something about the crestfallen mien stabbed at Michael. He suddenly felt sorry that she was eleven years old with no friends or father, and had lived with her grandmother's crap every day of her life. He pulled the collar up on his coat. "Only because it's cold, Amber, and you're wearing no cloak."

"Papa used to come out here after he talked to Grandmama, too," Amber said. "He would smoke. Sometimes he drank. Lots of times he swore. Grandmama didn't like him to swear. She said he would go to hell like you. Are you going to hell, Uncle James?"

Despite himself, Michael grinned. "Not any time soon. And Amber . . ." he said as she started to turn away. Her big eyes rose to his. "I like the name of your cat."

Brianna was standing on a spindle-back chair, cleaning the windows in what would be her sanctuary, when she glimpsed Michael coming into the yard. Her hand automatically went to the red kerchief over her braided hair. Bending nearer to the glass, she watched as he stopped and talked to one of the lads hauling out a bucket of dirty water. Wearing his heavy military-style cloak, the collar snuggling his neck, Michael looked very British Foreign Service. Christopher had been an intelligence officer long ago, and Brianna always considered it a romantic profession.

These last weeks with Michael had been both confusing and difficult. While he'd been recovering from his wounds, he'd begun to court her as he'd never done, and in the evenings, she spent her time with him in the library while he worked. She would stare at him bathed in the lamplight, and sometimes he would catch her watching. She knew uncertainty beneath the weight of her heart.

Already his household staff had informed him that she had rearranged the Green Room, where she slept; sacrilege, to be sure, in quarters that had not had a single piece of furniture moved in a hundred years. And he'd said nothing when she'd changed the daily menu last week.

Seeing that he was also on his way inside the cottage to see her, Brianna leaped from the chair, her feet thumping on the floorboards, wondering what had finally brought him to her. Servants had carried every movable object outside, since sanding and varnishing the floor had begun that morning. She'd carefully stored the beautiful watercolors and paintings out of the way in what would eventually become her darkroom.

Hearing Michael's voice, she rolled down her sleeves and hurried out. She'd been in a closet earlier, an old burlap apron tied around her dress and now noticed that her bodice was covered in cobwebs. She was still brushing at her apron when she met Michael at the bottom of the stairs.

She looked into his deep silvery eyes, surrounded by dark lashes that rose slowly with his brows as he surveyed her with a slow smile.

"I've never had carnal thoughts about a servant before."

"You aren't supposed to come here until this lodge is finished," she chastised him. "You promised."

He smoothed a stray lock of her hair. "I have to talk to you."

"Lady Ravenspur." A young girl came up behind Michael. "Where do you want the blue paint?"

"In the room above this one."

"How many people do you have working on this project?" Michael asked, looking around.

"Twelve, not including myself."

"From my staff?"

"Good Lord, no," Brianna laughed. "They're from the village. She's Mr. Freeman's granddaughter. Freeman is your stablemaster."

"You just walked into the village and hired twelve people to come out here to work?"

"And a carpenter." Brianna was especially proud of the carpenter. She turned and ran her palm over the new banister. "I want you to hire him. I noticed the greenhouse is in need of cabinets."

"This estate already has a carpenter."

"With a deplorable manner no staff member should possess. How could your family have allowed this place to die such an ignoble death?"

"Brianna . . ." He shook his head. "It's only an old house."

"Filled with your history. You should see the artifacts I've found. They belong in a museum. How could you not be proud of your heritage?"

"I didn't realize that you had something like this in mind. How did you get anyone from the village to come up here?"

Standing on the stair above his, her eyes were level with his mouth. "I asked."

The shadow on his jaw darkened his eyes. "You never sleep, Michael."

"Is that an invitation?"

"I wasn't under the impression that you cared for such civil formalities."

"Maybe, I've changed."

"Your Grace," a footman said from the open doorway. "The carriage is waiting outside. We're set to leave."

Brianna met her husband's gaze. "Who else is with you?"

"I'm taking Caroline to Aylesbury for a hospital benefit. Her benefit. She's staying the night with friends." He seemed so casual about it all. Brianna dropped her arms. "I brought you these." He handed her some letters. She hadn't seen them in his hands until now, and took the moment to study them rather than look in his face.

His finger tilted her chin, and he bent slightly to look into her face. "I just found out about the benefit last night. I'm unable to ride a horse, Brianna. Since we're headed in the same direction, I see no reason why I can't drop her off. This isn't a conspiracy to exclude you."

Contentiously, Brianna flipped through the letters. When she saw Mr. Smith's missive, she decided it was just as well that Michael was leaving. "Thank you for bringing me these." She dropped the letters into her apron pocket. "Why did you come down here? To say good-bye?"

He pulled her against him, his hands on her waist, hot through the thin cloth of her dress. Then he was moving his mouth over her throat, and she could feel his hunger surge through her body. "Who's Mr. Smith?" he asked.

"My jeweler," she said without hesitation, knowing that he was bound to ask and grateful that he hadn't opened the letter. "He's the one who designed your ring. His shop is on Bond Street."

Nothing was a lie. He could look into her eyes and see only the truth of her words. But he didn't look into her eyes. She almost wished he would so she could see what he was thinking. Except his mouth was doing shivery things to her throat, and her head melted back against her shoulders. She would have slipped her arms around his neck just to feel him hard against her, if not for the other people in the house.

"It looks like snow," Brianna said, glancing behind him at the pewter-lined sky and willing the topic to change. "Just promise that you won't get trapped in a blizzard with her."

He raised his gaze from her mouth to her eyes, then stepped away. "Stay out of trouble, Brianna."

Why would he say that?

A skein of alarm snapped her straight out of her idyllic haze, but his long purposeful strides had already taken him out the door. The wind whipped his dark woolen cloak around his legs, giving her a scant glimpse of his boots as he paused to look back at her just before he climbed into the carriage. She remained in the doorway of the lodge watching her husband ride off with his former true love.

Chapter 20

 ~~~⟡~~~

Brianna clutched her wrap against a frigid gust of wind that stirred up snow and blinded her as she raced across the street. It was only mid-afternoon, and she'd planned to be back by nightfall, but the weather could vastly change her plans. Snow had begun to fall. Quickening her pace, she walked past a group of men huddled around a fire they'd set in a drum, their mood anything but harmonious.

Shoving open a heavy oaken door, Brianna stepped into the common room of the traveler's way-station. The inn sat a block from the London-bound train depot. Weeks ago she'd passed this depot on her way to Aldbury Park, but the stop had only encountered a patron or two. Now the place was packed. The acrid odor of smoke lingered thick in the air, pressing against her senses with the sound of laughter and clinking glasses of ale. A barmaid disappeared into an adjoining room.

Brianna walked beneath the large wooden stairway into a dining room where the smell of roasting meat had pervaded into the walls. Bent over a trencher, Mr. Smith sat at a corner table in the back. She knew he was intending to catch the six o'clock train to London, and her time was sorely depleted as it was. Brianna pushed through the crowd, and he looked up as she approached.

"Your Grace . . ." Choking, he stood abruptly. "I thought the weather would keep you away. I ordered dinner."

Brianna looked at the behemoth of a man who had also come to his feet at her approach. "This is Mr. Finley," Smith said, introducing him before wiping his mouth with a napkin. "He and I have on occasion worked together. One could say that he is a friend of your brother's."

The big Irishman grinned. His front tooth was chipped. "You might even say we're sparring partners when he's in town."

"Christopher boxes with you?"

"I've tried to add character to his pretty mug, but he refuses to cooperate."

Brianna sat across from Mr. Smith. "I think my brother must have led a secret life."

"It's because of him that Mr. Finley decided to help," Smith explained. "I didn't know if you'd get my delivery in time today."

"What have you found out?"

Finley withdrew something from his pocket. Setting it on the table, he unwrapped the cotton cloth. Light flashed off the sapphire stone as he slid the amulet in front of her. "To say that this is very valuable and illegal for ye to have is an understatement, colleen."

She refused to touch the amulet. "How do you know this?"

Finley and Smith exchanged glances. "We went to an expert. Mind ye, we didn't tell her who our client was, and she didn't suspect."

Brianna didn't need a high degree of intelligence to consider their source. There was only one famed lady Egyptologist currently living in London. Lady Alexandra had been distraught upon hearing of the attack on Michael, and it had taken all of Brianna's persuasive skills to keep her sister-in-law out of this muddle.

"If Lady Alexandra suspected for one moment who gave this to you, I would know. Why did she trust you?"

"It's a long story, that goes back to your brother," Smith replied. "Suffice to say, she knows I'm a jeweler, and would accept that I might have come across this. She also said that if I believed in curses, I would not wish to hold onto this. Frankly, I believe I'm in more danger of being mugged, which is why Finley is with me."

Brianna's studied the amulet. "What did she say?"

"This is a mate to others." He pointed to a strange symbol below the sapphire. "It's worn as a pledge to an eternal brotherhood."

"You mean a sort of secret society?"

"Thousands of years ago the pharaohs in Egypt would put those individuals who they believed disagreed with them into a tomb filled with these bugs." Smith cleared his throat and looked distinctly uncomfortable. "Scarabs, she called them. You can only guess that the victims would never be seen again. Eventually, the families of the victims gathered and became a secret brotherhood of blood. In retaliation, they would attack caravans that belonged to the pharaoh. It looks as if you've been invited into the brotherhood."

"That's utterly . . . absurd!" Brianna stared at them both as if they'd been conjoined at the head. "What do the other symbols mean?"

"The sapphire represents the Seeing Eye of Re. Nothing escapes Re." Smith looked at Finley for confirmation. "This Re chap seems to be one of those all-powerful gods that know everything. According to her ladyship, this amulet was unearthed two years ago. She thought it was in Cairo."

"What is the curse?" she asked quietly.

"It promises dire consequences if I don't return this to its owner." He slid the amulet back to her side of the table. "Which is you."

Finley shrugged. "The Irish are a superstitious lot, colleen."

His dark eyes bore self-effacing humor. "Ye know how we take our curses."

"You're not Irish," she accused Smith, itching to give back the amulet. Someone could see the huge sapphire. How would she be safe then?

"Lady Alexandra mentioned the name of an antiquities dealer just arrived from Cairo. Appears they'd worked together in Egypt. He contacted her to tell her he was in town. A Mr. Charles Cross."

"Charles Cross?" Her voice was a whisper. Brianna had forgotten that he said he was returning to London.

"He's letting the widow Solomon's old estate near Green Park in London." He chuckled. "People stay away from the house."

"Why?"

Smith tore off a chunk of bread with his teeth. "They say the widow was as beautiful as a golden angel," he said over the bite. "Killed herself by jumpin' off the roof ten years ago. People claim the house is haunted."

Brianna had had her fill of superstition. "When did you say that Mr. Cross arrived in London?"

"Less than two weeks ago. Maybe if the amulet is as valuable as her ladyship says, he'll offer to purchase it for a substantial sum."

"But it's illegal. Mr. Cross would never do that."

"It's a popular trade, your Grace. The market is huge among the upper class. Cross will most likely make a fortune."

Brianna's temples had begun to throb. "Do you have the other item I requested?"

Finley withdrew a packet from inside his coat, hanging on the back of his chair. It was the *Northern Star* passenger list, and it had cost her a bundle to attain. Brianna ran her finger down the three columns of names, two hundred passengers until she reached the Cs. Charles's name wasn't listed. She pursed her lips. The hood she wore covered her profile as she bent nearer to the candle on the table. Mr. Cross had told her he was leaving Cairo even before he knew that she and Michael had wed.

"What about my husband's shooter?"

"I can assure you that whoever attempted to kill your husband isn't from here. Something like that would have been bragged about in every stew in London. Nor has your stolen ring shown up anywhere. Your Grace, there were no other ships that arrived in England from Cairo between the time your ship arrived and the day your husband was shot."

Again her gaze dropped to the passenger list. "Someone followed us back from Cairo, didn't they?" Her voice was flat, raw against her throat as she stared outside. "Someone who arrived on the *Northern Star*."

Everything somehow connected to the amulet. But why had she been singled out?

Her mind whirled, her thoughts caught by currents of apprehension. She was one of two who had ever survived a caravan massacre. But Alex had not received a similar amulet. If someone had wanted her dead, Michael's shooter could have completed the task himself. That someone wanted Michael dead.

"Your Grace," Finley said, "perhaps it's time that you talk to your husband. Seein' as how you'll be carrying that amulet, we'll have to see ye safely to your home anyway."

"He won't understand. . . ." She was suddenly afraid for not having told him what she was doing. Her gaze went out the window over Finley's shoulder. A cold draft seeped through the panes. Snow had piled on the casement. What if she couldn't get home tonight? How on earth would she explain that to him? Michael had told her to behave today.

Why had he said that anyway?

Almost as if the words had been a warning—

Brianna's head lifted. Turning in the chair, she twisted around to let her gaze wander the dining room, touching each face as a sudden surge of alarm filled her.

He'd read Smith's letter.

He'd known where she was going today.

Her heart skipped a beat, then thundered. She froze. Michael leaned casually against the back hearth, his boots crossed at the ankles, a galling study in British self-control. His heavy cloak seemed to give his shoulders unneeded width, and in his hand was an empty glass of what had likely been ale. He'd been watching her a long time, and Brianna now met the cold steel of his gaze.

Neither moved.

Being smart with an instinct for survival, she would gladly have fled were she confident of reaching the door before he could catch her. Then again, there was the welfare of her two companions to consider. A log fell with a shower of sparks in the hearth.

Michael pushed away from the wall, the dark woolen coat blending with his hair in the dull light. There was something about the predatory cadence of his walk that matched the look in his eyes.

"Should we stay or leave, yer Ladyship?" Finley calmly asked, clearly accustomed to facing men with murder in their eyes.

"It doesn't matter."

For suddenly Michael was at the table.

"Brianna . . ." Snow had melted in his dark hair and left it damp. He smelled like rain and smoke from the common room, and the combination was strangely reassuring.

He remained standing as she made the introductions, his tall form blocking the rest of the room from her vision. "They are doing work for me," she said, suddenly tongue-tied for an explanation that justified why she was in the company of someone who looked like he could be a crime boss from London. "I hired Mr. Smith while in London."

"This would be yours, your Grace." Smith handed Michael the *Northern Star* passenger manifest. "You may want to look at that."

Michael dropped into the seat beside Brianna and his knee touched hers beneath the table. Watching him remove his gloves, she reminded herself that there were more important matters at stake than mounting a case to defend herself. Or that his very presence now seemed to relegate her to the irrelevant. But at the moment she couldn't think of one.

Michael unfolded the papers. Brianna felt a growing heat building around him. She saw the vague hint of surprise crease his dark brows, and watched as he lifted his gaze. Finley's silence made no secret of the illegal means by which the original was acquired and copied.

His gaze again pinned Finley's. "And you said you were from where?"

"I didn't." Finley's mouth eased into a battle grin. "But I'm sure ye won't be having any acquaintance with the London borough from which I hail. I'm here because of her tie to Mister Donally."

"I asked Finley to join us," Smith hastened in an effort to cut through the tension. "Her Grace came to me about a piece of jewelry."

Then Michael's gaze fell on the amulet half hidden beneath her folded hands. His expression no longer frozen, Michael took the piece and held it to the candlelight. A breeze fluttered the flame.

His head turned, and she suddenly found herself in his gaze. Ever since Michael had left Cairo, he'd disappeared into the civil veneer of his new station, but the man who looked at her now was the man she'd seen that night at the watchtower oasis. Dangerous.

Unrelenting.

Furious.

"Where, Brianna?"

"I received it the day you were shot. Before I met you at the plaza. Someone had latched it to the carriage door."

"Do you know what it is?" Smith asked.

"Why didn't you say anything about this?" Michael asked her.

She wanted to tell him that he'd been in no condition to chase demons. He still wasn't. But the argument seemed illogical now, with him sitting beside her. In truth, she'd been protecting him because she'd been the one who was terrified.

"It belongs to an ancient blood cult in Egypt," he told Smith without taking his eyes from her. "This is no reproduction," Michael finished in a soft-spoken tone. "You're in a lot of trouble, *amîri*."

She glared up at him. "You opened my mail. Violated my privacy. I can't *believe* you did that," she whispered.

"Isn't that rather hypocritical of you?" he returned in a harsh rasp. "Where were your bloody Joan of Arc principles this afternoon? You lied to me." His tone held disbelief and something else, far worse.

"I didn't lie." She toyed fitfully with her velvet riding skirt. "Mr. Smith did design your wedding ring."

Both Finley and Smith were listening with apt interest. Smith's gaze was apologetic. "Maybe he has a point, your Grace."

Michael shifted his gaze to Finley, who sat with his big hands around a tankard of ale, amusement in his eyes. "Do you know anything about a scarab tattoo?" Michael asked. "It looks like a spider to anyone who doesn't know what it is."

"A spider? Like this?" The big Irishman slapped a bulky forearm on the table. Thick fingers nimbly rolled up a heavy woolen sleeve to display a black widow, engraved in his muscled forearm. "I have more if you want to see." His teeth were white. "No one notices tattoos here."

"I'm relieved that you're a man without fear." Michael leaned both elbows on the table. "Because the people who brought this to London make your street toughs look like model citizens. They took out a whole group of British soldiers, women, and children in the caravan with which my wife was traveling. They have no qualms about slaughtering men like animals."

"Fin," Smith whispered, nudging the other man with his elbow. "Listen to what he's sayin'. Think about what happened last week." He looked at Michael. "There were two murders on the docks," the jeweler explained. "Not that killings are a strange occurrence on the docks, but these were different."

"The two men were slit from aft to stern with a knife like none of us ever seen," Finley said carefully.

"The victims weren't from around here," Smith said.

Her eyes on Michael's profile, Brianna felt her stomach churn. Did he think the deaths relevant? Smith's eyes shifted nervously to hers. "Do you want that I should approach the dealer and sell the amulet?"

"I don't care what you do with it. Throw it into the Thames."

Michael pulled her from the chair. "As of now, my wife is no longer in charge of this little investigation. In fact," he gathered up the passenger list and the amulet and shoved both into his pocket, "I'll speak with you shortly. But at the moment, I need to get her home."

"How dare you treat me in this way!" Brianna tried to pull away.

"Provoke me now, wife, and I'll bloody welcome the fight."

Michael escorted her from the dining room as if she were a recalcitrant child. She could feel the hard muscles of his arm beneath her fingertips. His body thrummed with fury. "Do you understand the chance you took coming here?" he demanded, his voice harsh in her ear.

The common room had grown rowdy and smoky. Pulling Brianna into the protective custody of his presence, he pressed his way toward the door. A barmaid called to him and asked if he wanted ale to warm him, but he brushed off the woman with a lighthearted promise of another time. People shifted as he passed and, as many had started to recognize him, a slow sense of reverence began to ripple over the crowd. These people knew Michael because they worked and lived in the surrounding boroughs.

Never more than at that moment was Brianna aware of his

station, the importance of his image, and her lack of judgment in coming here. Lowering her head, letting the hood of her cloak swallow her, she felt a heavy weight descending upon her shoulders. On top of everything else, she'd disgraced Michael. She had hurt him, the way she always managed to hurt everyone she cared about.

The door opened, blowing in a man on a gust of snow. The Ravenspur carriage sat across the street, the drivers and footmen bundled in heavy woolen cloaks, hats, and gloves. Six fine blacks stomped and snorted restlessly. Someone had secured Brianna's mare from the livery.

"Will this carriage make it back to Aldbury Park?" Michael called over the wind to the driver.

"I wouldn't chance it until the snow dies down. But it does look like the worst is passing."

"The London train leaves in an hour. You'll be taking my wife back to Aldbury without me."

Brianna clutched the edges of her cloak, unaware as Michael took her arm and brought her back inside. He managed to let a room from the owner of the establishment. "It ain't much, but it's a bloomin' sight more than most people downstairs have," the tavern maid said, grinning up at Michael with mute interest as she set down the water pitcher on a narrow dresser. "Will ye be wantin' something else, guv'nor?"

Michael looked over her pert blond head at Brianna, who stood by the window, glaring at him. "Whatever is being served for dinner will be fine."

The door shut behind her, and Michael whirled a chair, tipping it against the latch.

"That girl liked you. Why don't you just go with her?"

"Don't tempt me." He walked to the window, next to Brianna, and edged aside the curtain to look outside. "For all the tender affection we share, I have no doubt the company will be warmer."

"You're insufferable, Michael."

"And you are the very soul of a gentle and loving wife, who holds no qualm in lying to her husband."

"You knew what I was when you married me."

"Which is why you are not accompanying me to London, sweet."

He eased out of his coat and laid it on the table. Then, fighting for control, he dropped the amulet atop the sleeve before turning to face his wife. He held the passenger manifest in his hand. Unbelievably she had secured the list.

At first she just returned his stare. Then he saw the sparkling brilliance of her eyes beneath her hood before she turned away from him. She knew damn well, what the amulet meant. He wanted to shake her, press her skull between his hands and force sense into her brain. "You should not have been going through this alone."

"You'll need to telegraph Christopher," she instructed him.

"I know what I have to do. Your brother didn't send his wife back without arranging some security at his estate." He couldn't believe that she would dictate to him his bloody responsibility.

"You opened my mail. Why didn't you just confront me?"

"I tried, and listened to you babble about Smith being your jeweler. Even if you were going to meet him in a secret assignation to pick up another ring, I didn't believe that you would be foolish enough to ride here alone. But I should have known you better than that." He dropped the list on the table. "Do you really believe Finley is an acquaintance of your brother?"

"My brother didn't always lead such a sterling life. There are things in his past that he'll never tell anyone, not even Alex. Trust me, if Finley wanted to get rich, he could have just taken the amulet. It's probably worth more than he could get for me or you, at least until the summer revenues start refilling the family coffers."

Her knowledge of Aldbury finances surprised him. But he wasn't in the mood to be impressed with his young wife.

Hell, he was cold, and set about lighting the stove. The coals caught and began to heat.

"You're going back with Finley and Smith, aren't you?" She'd sat down on the bed and burrowed into her cloak. "You want to know more about that warehouse."

"I have four men accompanying you back to Aldbury Park."

"And the amulet?"

"Belongs in the hands of the authorities."

"To authorities who presumed you were guilty of that which you'd been charged in Cairo. When were they in defense of you against Omar?" Her voice became passionate. "Where were your precious authorities when I watched you get shot down in broad daylight? When you were alone fighting for your life? You already suspect someone followed us back from Cairo. The amulet is evil. And it's mine to destroy."

"Tell me, Brianna," he knelt on one knee, so close beside her he could smell the roses in her hair, "that is, if you are capable of honesty in this matter. Do you really believe getting rid of the amulet will make this problem go away?"

"I don't know." She dropped her head into her hands. "If you had known about the amulet that afternoon, would it have made a difference?"

Michael sat next to her, his thigh touching hers. He was bothered that he possessed no memory of the actual event. He remembered nothing until he'd awakened to find his grandmother sitting next to the bed. Maybe had he known about the amulet, he would have seen the threat before he'd allowed the danger to come so close. "It doesn't matter." He stared down at his hands. "Your feelings and mine at this point are irrelevant."

"What *are* your feelings, Michael?"

He looked at his wife, surrounded by shadows, and felt as if someone had hit him in the gut. Then as if drawn by a will stronger than his own, he pulled her into his lap. "I'm not accustomed to others managing my affairs and problems,

Brianna." He tipped her chin, forcing her to look up at him. What had begun that morning in Cairo when he'd let her oversleep had now opened a gaping chasm in his feelings. He hadn't understood himself around her then any more than he understood his actions now. Tonight had proven his vulnerability, and had scared him.

She hadn't seen the atrocities done to Pritchards and the others on that caravan. Nor had anyone ever found the women and children who had disappeared, or the hundreds more who vanished forever in the desert.

He tried to think sanely, while the different factions of his heart warred inside him. He was angry that she'd come out here by herself. That she undertook an investigation that was too bloody dangerous and out of her realm of experience, risking her life.

"It was never my intent to lie to you, Michael."

"Yet, you had so little respect for my name that you decided to appear here alone regardless of the physical danger to you. Regardless of social impropriety? What consequence is a lie on top of that, Brianna?"

"Oh!" She wriggled in his lap, to get free, but he held her tight. "Do not take the moral high ground with me, Ravenspur! Mr. Don't-Bother-Me-With-Rules, who waggled a gun at a sheikh and incited an international incident. For your information, since I've been at Aldbury I've been poked and prodded by a dozen modistes, endured etiquette lessons, frogs in my shoes, frogs in my bath, rude servants, all in the name of Aldbury honor. Were I a man, you would welcome my aid as a course of loyalty and friendship."

Her voice was filled with hurt, and he was truly sorry about the frogs, but there was little he could do about any of that. "Except you are not a man. You're my wife. I'm not willing to see you die, certainly not in defense of me." Tipping her chin, he forced her to look at him. "And furthermore, if you ever engage in the manner of folly you have today, I'll lock you in your room to rusticate until your hair grows gray."

"You can't lock me in my room. That's . . . illegal!"

"Not if I'm in there with you."

Brianna weighed the warning in his eyes, not because she feared acting on her passions, but because she knew instinctively that he would do exactly as he promised. "You are such a bastard, Michael."

"You knew what I was when you climbed over your balcony and decided to pay me a visit in the middle of the night. Though I may be guilty of influencing the outcome that day, you, sweet, were guilty of executing the sin. I'd say that we both made our proverbial bed.

They stared at each other, suspended in time, the wind whipping against the window. His fingers at her nape held her.

He was aware of her nails digging into his coat. Then slowly, haltingly, Michael lowered his lips to hers.

He kissed her. Each thrust of his tongue, seeking hers, deepened his foray inside the hot shelter of her mouth.

He felt her bottom pressed against him, tasted the texture of her mouth, felt the pattern of her fingers clinging to his arms, and inhaled the scent of her presence. She was his air to breathe, and as he kissed her, he sought fervently for what he wanted to find inside her, finally pulling from her sweet lips the soft sound of his name.

Without breaking the kiss, Michael reached up to dim the lamp, returning his hand to cup the fullness of her breast, bounty in his palm. She turned her head, but he followed, capturing her lips, and offering no apology for his behavior, brought her down on the mattress.

They were fully clothed, though he'd deftly managed to unlace her bodice and the corset beneath. Her cloak fell away and she suddenly came up for breath, pressing both hands against his chest as if suffocating. Her startled eyes were wide. "There are those," she gasped, still entangled within his arms, "who take their newfound power too much to heart. I would not let your station rule your lust."

"Ah, my fey wife speaks." His mouth burned a knowing path to her throat. "A moment ago I was sure that your tongue was incapable of such mundane work as framing words." He observed her, unmistakable heat in his eyes. "We can survive the next few hours in some manner of conjugal harmony or you can resent me and freeze. It's up to you."

"Why are you behaving like this?"

Holding himself up on his elbow, he stilled her fight with his arm. Tension charged the air between them. He sensed the battle inside her, no less fierce than the one he waged with himself and, watching her turn her face away, he recognized a helplessness he'd not felt before.

Yet, he was glad she was distraught, for she had shown so little fear and emotion earlier, she'd become a danger to herself. "You fight for everyone else, Brianna. With no thought to yourself."

Her dark hair fanned the mattress. "You don't understand—"

"I do understand. More than anyone in this world, I understand. You have to trust me to finish this. Do you trust me?"

His hands moved to caress her. She grabbed his fingers.

"Then you still defiantly hope to carry the day. You seek . . . what, Brianna?

She tried to turn her face away from his probing gaze and Michael felt a slow burning fury—or frustration to reach her. He had her pulled flush against him. He could feel the wild pounding of her heart.

"If it's your pride that taunts you, then count this coup lost by force."

Again he lowered his mouth to hers. He held her and kissed her. Her lips trembled, but her fingers relaxed. He was aware of the supple contrast of her body to each sinew and tendon of his, of the smell of peat, the scent of roses, his own lust. Her plaintive sigh touched her ears. He caught her lips and his hunger coiled low in his abdomen to knot with his need. The heat gathered in his groin and between her legs where he'd set his hand.

Let her be angry with him. He reached between them and

freed himself. At least it was passion equal to his. He slid one finger into the depth of her, parting her, exploring the musky clefts and shallow dips. Touching her was like touching fire. He groaned into her mouth. Her palms slid upward into his hair. For a moment his own limbs seemed weighted as she responded, taking from him the fight he waged. She pressed her forehead against his, then looked down at her limbs entwined with his, bringing his gaze to hers. "You are so beautiful," she said.

Even in the dimness her gaze was a startling blue. Dil anna's eyes held his and did not turn away. The rhythm of her movements escalated his, and she cradled his face between her hands, and kissed his mouth. He had thought it impossible to feel more than he did. Then the power surrounding them took him, rushed over him until he couldn't breathe within the roaring tempest, and, shoving his fingers into her hair, at last he groaned and poured himself into her.

Brianna opened her eyes. Her clothes still in disarray, she lay on her side beneath a blanket, her arm tucked beneath her head. Michael sat on a chair beside the bed. Already dressed, he was wearing his heavy coat, and leaning with his elbows on his knees as he watched her sleep.

Her cheeks flushed, she felt the corners of her mouth tilt. "What are you thinking?" she asked.

A shadow cooled the line of his jaw and contrasted with his eyes. She was reminded of the first time she'd ever seen him—tall and dangerous, in his long hooded robe as she'd met the soft glitter of those silver eyes. "I'm thinking that you and I are finished with separate chambers," he said. "It's time that you occupied yourself with your duty to me as my wife."

Brianna sat up in bed. After a moment of struggling with her stays, she startled as he moved her hands aside and performed the feminine task with annoying familiarity and speed.

"If I can undo them, the least I can do is repair the damage before I go on my way."

Brianna slapped his hands away and stumbled out of bed. "You are so cavalier," she said in absolute confusion. "How can I even feel anything for you at the moment?"

He caught her hand and pulled her into his arms. She dared not meet the diamond sharpness of his gaze, but he tipped her chin and she was left wondering if she did not love him completely. Then he turned her around and finished hooking her gown. "Will you miss me then?"

"Probably not."

He set her cloak on her shoulders and gently tended to the clasps. "That's good because I won't miss you either." His arms flexed against the fine wool of his coat as he bent and gave her a kiss that curled her toes.

Later, huddled in her cloak, Brianna listened to Michael's voice outside the carriage as he spoke to the driver. The sun had set and the wind had died. Then the coach jerked forward in a clamor of chains and harnesses and she caught herself. Michael remained a lone figure in the street. Pressing against the window, she watched the gently falling snow swallow her husband's dark form.

Chapter 21

As she had every morning for the past two weeks, Brianna awakened to the dreary sound of rain on her window and the undaunted patter of Gracie moving around in her dressing room. Only this morning a scream rent the air and Brianna shot straight up in bed. A tray crashed to the floor. Heart slamming against her ribs, wearing a diaphanous gown worthy of Aphrodite, Brianna raced through her dressing room into the salon before she'd remembered to grab her derringer. Gracie stood over the contents of a shattered teapot, steam still rising from the floor, and a lone frog calmly hopping its way toward the door.

"It touched my shoe, mum," Gracie fretted, twining her fingers. "Startled the life out of me."

A sigh of relief escaped from Brianna's mouth. After rescuing the newspaper from the floor, she went to the wall and rang the bell, but a footman had already reached her door. Winded, he straightened to present himself.

She calmly handed the frog to him. "Please return him to the greenhouse."

"Be grateful it isn't summer or you'd have had worse,

305

mum," he said. "Lady Amber 'as gone through a dozen governesses with what she finds in that place."

Coupled with the prickly pinecones placed in Brianna's bed a week ago, the poor frog hardly merited the drama. But Gracie was old, and Brianna had to take into account the possibility of heart failure should these incidents continue.

"And please send up someone to clean this mess." Brianna shut the door.

"You shouldn't have taken her ball, mum," Gracie fretted.

"She was throwing it against my bedroom window."

Lady Caroline had withdrawn to London after her hospital benefit and would not be back for another week. Though the baby had gone with her mother, Amber Catherine had not, as attested to the incident that morning and the feline that curled around Brianna's feet.

Smiling to herself, Brianna picked up the cat and scratched behind its ears. He was a friendly orange tom with huge rolling purrs. They'd become close friends, mostly owing to a healthy stash of catnip Brianna carried around with her these days. She'd made sure that Amber's cat followed her everywhere.

Walking to her desk, Brianna spread out the paper. Every day she scoured the various London dailies for any news of possible interest. She'd waited for letters. But Michael hadn't written.

Alex had scribed numerous posts and mentioned that he'd been to see her and had spoken with Charles Cross. Caroline had written to Amber. Brianna noted that she was staying at her brother's Grosvenor Square residence. But from Michael, she'd heard nothing.

The man who had taken such wicked delight in tormenting her in Cairo, who had encouraged her independence, defied her brother, and welcomed her boldness, now didn't even seem to remember that he had a wife. She wanted to hate him at that moment. She wanted to hate him for taking away her independence, for his warmth, and for all the ways he'd insinuated himself into her heart. She wondered why she tortured herself over him at all.

Brianna dressed and went downstairs. The library was the one place in the house that she'd found refuge since living at Aldbury Park. The books she'd been reading ranged from law to various legal cases ultimately presided over by the House of Lords. Because Michael would soon be taking his seat in parliament, she'd found such works fascinating.

But that morning after breakfast, Brianna merely propped her chin in her hand and stared out the large glass windows. As usual, she'd been the only one in attendance at her meal. An entire sennight of mornings had dawned cold, the skies bleak, the very air she breathed a chilly gray. Or at least it seemed that way as she stirred her tea and mentally went over her plans for the day. She was too busy to miss Michael.

It wasn't until she'd read the society column two days later and saw the Duke of Ravenspur mentioned prominently as a guest at Lord and Lady Bedford's spring soiree that Brianna decided not to read the paper anymore. Steeling herself, she closed the *Times* and left the room.

"My apologies, your Grace. But his grace's orders were very explicit." The stable master wiped his hands on a rag before hanging it on the stall door. He wore mucking boots that went to his knees.

Brianna laid her gloved hand on the mare's long nose. She wore a simple blue muslin gown beneath her cloak. "I didn't come here to ride, Mr. Freeman. Do not worry. I have no doubt the price of your disobedience to my husband's royal edict."

Once, that morning, she'd been prepared to fly to London. She wanted to ride to him wherever he was. For what? She wondered why she tortured herself at all. If Michael had wanted her there, he'd have brought her.

Drawing in a breath, Brianna lowered her hand from the mare. "Your granddaughter didn't show up this morning at the lodge. Is she all right?"

"Don't you know? The countess told everyone yesterday that if anyone returned to the lodge, she would have them all arrested for trespassing. I'm sorry, your Grace. I thought you knew."

"No, I didn't."

Once back at the house, Brianna handed off her cloak and gloves to the footman and, holding her skirts, swept up the stairs. She had once cherished the hope that she and her mother-in-law could be close, but that had ended her first week at Aldbury.

Dr. Blanchard was leaving the countess's suite as Brianna reached the rooms. "Good morning, your Grace."

Brianna stopped him. "Is she ill?"

"Ill enough to discharge me, your Grace," he said indignantly.

"You are not discharged," Brianna said flatly.

"Thank you, your Grace." He looked over her shoulder at the door. "She is in bed with her usual headache. You go in at your own risk."

Brianna stepped into the rooms. With a quiet swish of her skirts she moved into the bedchamber. The heavy velvet curtains were drawn against the light. A lone lamp on a dresser beside the bed cast light on the occupant lying in bed with a rag over her eyes. Chamberlain sat beside the bed, his elbows braced on his knees. The two were talking.

"Is she all right?" Brianna asked.

The countess removed the rag over her eyes long enough to view her intruder with a groan and lie back on her pillows. "Did I not tell you that she would be up here," the countess murmured. "Tell her I am ill and dying and wish not to be disturbed."

Brianna arched her brow. "Tell the countess that I am standing in the room and she can tell me herself, for I am not leaving."

"Tell her that she is insolent."

"I'm still not leaving."

With a sharp gasp, the countess struggled up on one

elbow. Fully dressed and bound like a sausage, it was no wonder she thought she was dying. Michael's mother, with her classical facial structure, high cheekbones, and wide mouth, still held a hint of her past beauty, even as she glared at Brianna. "The lodge is mine," she said flatly.

"His Grace agreed to handle the problem," Chamberlain hastened to say. "Clearly, he chose not to do so. She paints at the lodge in the summer months." His voice lowered. "The place is her refuge, your Grace."

"Do not whisper around me, Chamberlain, as if I require a hearing tube. It is not a refuge. I only go there to escape here so I can paint in peace."

Unfortunately, Brianna understood. The lodge's very popularity through the Aldbury generations was evidenced by toys and other artifacts she found there. "Then you're the artist?" Brianna had admired the woman's talent so much that she'd hired the carpenter to frame the pieces she'd found. "There is a whole trunk of wonderful work in the cellar—"

"You did not find my work in a trunk."

Brianna looked around the room and saw similar drawings hanging in frames on her wall. "The work belongs to his grace," Chamberlain said. "From when he was younger."

"James was forever doodling." His mother lay back on the bed. "Drawing Spanish galleons and pirates. Such a fanciful boy. Gentle. His father disliked that immensely."

Fanciful? Gentle? That the man known in Egypt as El Tazor had ever picked up a paintbrush shocked her. "What happened to him?" She straightened her shoulders. "I mean . . . you must have been very proud of his talent."

A visible inhalation from the countess preceded a sigh. "If there is anything to be proud of, it is that he has survived his life this long."

Brianna looked at the miniature galleon on the wall. "Why didn't he join the Royal Navy?" She couldn't help asking.

"Because his father expected him to join the navy." The

countess removed the rag from her eyes. "Why did you say you are here?"

"What about you? What did you want him to do?"

"I was only his mother. One does not tell James to do anything." She glared at Chamberlain. "One does *not* tell him that a bride would be chosen for him upon his return to England."

Brianna found it unfortunate that the countess had lost the ability to laugh or smile—like everyone in this house—for otherwise she might have found humor in her own thoughts. As for Michael's reason for marrying her in the first place, Brianna had already suspected the worst, and found it a moot fact.

After a moment she decided that what she had learned here today far outweighed her current work at the lodge. She would let that rest for now. "My maid is very good with herbs and can help you with your headaches." Brianna didn't know if the countess had heard the quiet words. "I'll send her in here."

Nodding to Chamberlain, Brianna turned to leave.

"You'll be disappointed here," the countess said, stopping Brianna at the door. "It takes more than a new wardrobe and etiquette lessons to make a duchess. Isn't that what you told me, Lord Chamberlain?"

Brianna met the man's gaze, and he suddenly became engrossed by some defect on his sleeve. As for the countess, she wasn't going to get off the maternal hook so easily. Brianna knew that if she possessed one talent in life, it was that she could scale walls. At least if they weren't too high. "Then perhaps it is time that you and I begin enjoying afternoon tea together," she graciously offered. "And you can help me learn."

Later, Brianna found herself in Michael's room, her mood greatly dissipated and fragile as she stood over his bed. One would have expected a former artist to exist in ordered chaos. Unlike her room, cluttered with every monument and testament to her life from photographs to lacy doilies that had once belonged to her grandmother, nothing of himself lined the walls or shelves—no piece of furniture had been moved. Her arms wrapped against her torso.

The curtains were open to the stars, and it seemed to Brianna as she leaned a shoulder against the window that she should not be missing Michael, or feeling remotely sympathetic about his upbringing or sorry for his mother, for it seemed that the countess could have displayed more backbone in defense of her son. But the past few months had taken its toll on her body and made her weak—so she did miss him.

Staring at the moon, she only remembered feeling this trampled once—when she'd fallen off the roof with her friend Rachel. But it was impossible to tell which made her feel worse.

Missing Michael. His family. Or two broken ribs.

"There's someone here to see you, your Grace."

Brandy in hand, Michael turned from his place at the window before he realized that he was not the one being addressed. Bedford's butler had stepped into the smoky parlor and pulled Lord Bedford from a game of whist. With typical British impassivity, Michael returned his attention to the window. His reflection stared back at him like a shadow on ice, his shirt white beneath his waistcoat and jacket, pulling color from the glass. He could see over his shoulder as Lord Ware entered the room where a dozen of Bedford's associates waited for him that evening.

Michael found the moon had again captured his gaze for no apparent reason, as it seemed wont to hide behind the clouds. He'd been in London over two weeks.

A sweep of the docks had begun three days ago near the point where Finley discovered the two dead men. The bodies had been exhumed from a pauper's grave at Potter's Field and reexamined after a scarab tattoo was located on the wrist of one.

"A spot of congratulations to you, your Grace." Lord

Ware's undersecretary stood eagerly beside him, smelling overwhelmingly of ale and not the least bit disinclined to complain that he'd lost a fortune to Bedford in whist.

The man's eagerness faded when Michael turned. "In what way?"

"Your name was mentioned prominently at Lord Ware's office today. It seems you have provided the first break in a case that has kept the government of two countries at heel for two years."

Without reply, Michael drank from the brandy snifter. He'd done little but follow up on Finley's information, a source that he owed to his wife. The real break in the case had come from the most unlikely of sources.

"Mr. Cross is here, your Grace." The undersecretary stood aside, and Michael's eyes locked on Cross standing beside Ware, handing his coat over to the butler.

Michael set down his brandy with the same aversion he'd felt when he discovered Cross in London. Not only did the man work for the Foreign Ministry; he was the chief adviser in Egyptian antiquities. He'd taken charge of the amulet Michael had given him.

"My source is meeting me tomorrow morning," Cross told the gathering crowd of men, his light brown eyes nearly gold behind his thick spectacles. "He knows the exact location of the warehouse we're looking for. He wants his money to-night."

Cross went on about the arrangements, briefing those gathered in the plan for tomorrow.

After a while Michael removed himself from the group to retrieve his coat and hat. "You're not satisfied with the arrangement?" Lord Ware approached him. A big man with graying hair and muttonchop whiskers, he was Lady Alexandra's father and a rumored thorn in the side of the entire Donally clan. Michael felt almost disloyal admiring the man. But then, his wife was no longer a Donally.

She belonged to him.

"Has anyone checked the validity of Cross's source?"

Michael asked, shrugging into his coat. "Brought him in for questioning? For the kind of money this government is paying—"

"Mr. Cross believes the man will flee if he gets wind of a double cross," Ware said. "The informant does have what looks to be a scarab tattoo on his forearm. Cross feels he is legitimate and will take us to the others. Perhaps letting one go is the price we pay to get the rest."

"Even if that one may be the leader? Or the bloody bastard who shot me?"

"Some of the items the informant brought in belonged to Captain Pritchards's outfit. Evidence enough to link the smuggling to the caravan attacks. London was the receiving end for what went out of Egypt. With Sheikh Omar dead, I also believe the Cairo connection is severed."

"It's obvious we're close enough to the heart of them," Cross said, his words sounding loud as silence filtered down the ranks of the room. "Someone has clearly decided to exchange the end of a rope for his life."

Michael's gaze settled on Cross. His burnished hair was nearly blond in the lamplight. The man didn't appear as bookish in these surroundings as he had in Cairo. Nor timid. "You're a very good actor, Cross," Michael said quietly, knowing damn well he would offend most of the men in the room, who fancied Cross a hero. "I wouldn't have recognized you from the man I saw at the Bulaq Muscum in Cairo."

"It was a job," Cross said. "One that I obviously performed well."

One that Michael felt he sure as hell should have been informed about.

"Or maybe your pique springs from injured pride," Cross said. "You failed to find these thugs. I have not."

Sliding on his gloves, Michael transferred his gaze to Ware, then Bedford. "I'll be taking my leave."

"Major Fallon," Cross said. "Would you give your wife my regards? Your marriage was sudden even by polite standards. I didn't have a chance to see her before she left Cairo. Perhaps I can call on her."

If Cross wanted to live a long and healthy life, he would stay far away from Aldbury. "If you will all excuse me," he said to Ware.

Bedford caught him as the butler was handing him his hat and cane at the front door. "I've been curious about something ever since I read about your discharge from the army," he said, amused. "The British consul in Cairo was ready to sacrifice you to appease the khedive's loyalists over Sheikh Omar's murder. What happened?"

"I had a credible alibi," Michael responded laconically, aware that he had crossed a line with his mood and would not pretend otherwise.

"A firebrand with blue eyes, no doubt. Maybe the injured pride belongs to Cross. By the looks of it, you took something that he wanted. Will you be at the docks tomorrow?"

Michael's gaze lingered on Cross, who had turned away to receive a drink from a footman. "Who is watching him?"

Bedford observed the subject of Michael's query. "That would be my men."

"I'll be there."

Michael left the house. The night was wet and he pulled up his collar as he approached his carriage. Streetlights blurred in the thickening mist. "Your Grace?" The driver leaped off his perch to reach the door before Michael. "You've company," he whispered to Michael's arched query. "I thought—seein' as how there's folks about—you'd be wantin' to know."

The curtains in the carriage were drawn shut. Caroline sat inside, her face pale beneath a fur blanket. The back of her hand went across her cheeks, and whatever she'd been thinking when he opened the door went behind the mask of her posture. "I needed to talk," she said.

Their eyes met in the gilded shade of light cast around her by the lamp. She'd been stunning as a younger woman. She was no less beautiful now. She was also drunk, he realized. He could smell the bourbon.

"You're impossible to catch alone," she said. "I'll be going back to Aldbury probably before you. I've been away too long from my daughter."

A subtle shake of his head told his driver to remain in the drive. He climbed inside. "Do you do this often?" He eased a flagon from her hand. "Wander outside in the dead of night? You'll have your brother's servants thinking this house is haunted."

"I've been drunk twice in my life, James Michael Fallon . . . Aldbury. Both times because of you. You have no right to take that bottle from me."

Michael held the flagon out of her reach and set it on the floor. "I have every right."

"I despise domineering men. Hounds and horses—" She leaned against the corner. "Especially horses . . . and domineering men. You think that you are not like him. But you are."

Michael adjusted the collar of his coat and sat back, bracing an arm across the seat. "Is that a perceptive remark from one who knows me?"

"I didn't want you leaving tonight until I could talk to you. Alone." Her green eyes glittered brightly in the lantern light beside her head. "You're Edward's family. My daughters' guardian . . ."

"I know all of this, Caro."

Somewhere outside, a dog barked. "I've never been able to tell you that I was sorry," she said. "I made such a mess of both of our lives. I was young and foolish. And frightened. I should never have allowed you to take all the blame for something that was my fault."

Although the age difference between them was barely a year, she was suddenly that girl he'd tormented with frogs and spiders. "You don't deserve all the censure for poor judgment, Caro. Do you honestly think what happened was the worst incident in my life?"

She peered at him in amused horror. "How can you joke about that?"

A grin turned up his lips. "You live a sheltered life, Caro."

Beneath the blanket, she folded her arms. "Was it hard for you . . . after you left here?"

"Not as hard as coming back and starting over," he said.

"I . . . didn't know if there would ever be a chance for us. . . ."

"I'm in love with my wife, Caro," Michael said softly.

She didn't miss the softening in his expression. "And you will find she is an understanding person . . . to a point." He opened the door and stepped out. "I may be used to facing the ignominy of a tattered reputation, but you're not. Do you want your maid?" He lifted her from the carriage. She wore a gown of soft white silk, ridiculously virginal against her curves. But it wasn't her body Michael felt beneath his hands or her scent that made his heart beat harder in his chest. He felt sorry that she had lost almost everything.

"I can walk, thank you, your Grace." She wobbled with dignity.

"That's good, Caroline. Because if you pass out on the ground, I'll get you a blanket. I'm not taking you to your room."

Nodding to his footman to escort her to the door, Michael waited at the carriage to make sure she would make it back to the house. She turned. "I would be lying if I told you that I did not envy her."

Long after Michael left Bedford's house, long after he realized that the investigation might finally be over, he sat in his carriage, the lingering cadence of his thoughts lulling him to sleep.

He loved Brianna.

The words he'd spoken struck him—not so much because of the discordant observation, but because they were true. At least in part.

He was obsessed with her. There could be no other explanation for his need of her, especially after he'd made love to her that night in London and let her climb inside his soul. He wanted her.

Was utterly consumed by it, and could easily trace the beginnings of his ignoble defeat back to the day he'd found her head scarf beyond the watchtower oasis. To the point when he'd seen her for the first time draped in desert moonlight like an apparition out of his deepest erotic fantasy, never mind the gun she'd pointed directly at his heart or that he walked into her snare like some bloody tenderfoot. Or that he'd been making careless blunders with his life ever since.

He lifted his head and saw a distant flash of lightning out the window, as if the storm churning inside him were not enough. For long ago, disabused of wonder, Michael had stopped believing in many things.

Perhaps there was irony that love could find someone like him a willing recipient at all. For indeed it had.

Hell, he could only blame it on the moonlight.

And Brianna's gentle touch.

The door slammed.

A portent of doom to anyone within listening distance of the lodge.

Amber spun around, surprise and horror momentarily stalling her decision to run as her round gray eyes crashed against Brianna standing with her palm braced on the portal. Her rare show of fury had already left the servants at the house exchanging nervous glances. Yet, as she'd made her way to the lodge today, no one had wondered what force had fallen upon her to put her in her current state.

"I wouldn't if I were you," Brianna warned as the girl darted her gaze to the window in the other room.

Her doll clutched in one hand, Amber's small chin hiked like a porcelain martyr ready to face down the forces of death. Brianna might have admired her defiance if the precocious brat hadn't been in need of a thrashing. She could very well have burned down the entire lodge yesterday with her antics in this lab.

"I didn't mean to drop that bottle!" Amber cried. "I don't even like this stinky old room!"

"Oh, please, Lady Amber"—Brianna rolled her eyes at the dramatics—"you honestly don't expect me to buy those tears, do you? For someone who is a holy terror, I expect more courage from you." Brianna clicked the key in the lock, then turned to face her adversary. "No one is going to save you, no matter the screams of pain and agony that they hear."

Amber had backed against the desk, and Brianna tossed the quirt on a wooden chair. "You aren't going to strike me?"

"Why?" Brianna set her fists on her hips. "Would that keep you out of this darkroom? Or save that poor frog in the greenhouse? Is that the attention you want? If I can't make them notice me one way, then I'll do it another." Brianna knew the type. She'd looked at that woman every day in the mirror for twenty-two years. "How old are you?"

"Eleven."

"When I was eleven no one would have captured me." She held out her hand for the doll Amber clutched feebly to her chest. Reluctantly, the girl parted with her precious treasure. "Your uncle James gave you this?"

Brianna examined the frilly ruffles and curls. Michael had given her the doll after one of his trips into the village. "What's her name?"

A shrug of her shoulder told Brianna that she hadn't been named yet. "It usually takes me months to name something, too," Brianna said. "I haven't even named my horse. Names are special."

Implied permanence.

"I named my cat Sam." Amber studied the toe of her slipper. "Sam is the name of the man who clips the grass. He always runs my cat away with a rake. So I named him Sam and dress him up in ribbons."

"That will show him, won't it?" Brianna crossed her arms. "Do you want me to leave Aldbury Park? Is that why you're doing the things that you do?"

Amber wiped the back of her hand across her nose. "Everyone always leaves," she whispered; then her eyes narrowed as if Brianna had tricked her into revealing something about herself she didn't want to share. "And you can't make me be nice to you. I put vinegar into Lord Chamberlain's milk this morning. I'll do the same to you every day."

"I hadn't thought about vinegar." She set the doll on the chair. "Is that the worst you've done?"

"I put ants in my last governess's bed."

Brianna was unimpressed, and it showed.

Amber slanted her a glance. "What about you?"

"I guarantee that whatever you think up, I can think up a lot worse. You do *not* want to go to war with me, Lady Amber. There are spiders and snakes in this world that put our English species to shame. You'll never get another decent night's sleep as long as you live, wondering if you might find something beneath your pillow. Think about that the next time you decide to disobey me."

"What kind of spiders?"

Brianna walked to the desk. She reached into the bottom drawer and pulled out a box. Inviting her young protégé to sit on the floor, she carefully removed the lid. "What I'm about to show you can never leave this room without my permission. These are mine and I will cut off the hands of she who disobeys my edict."

Reluctantly, Amber watched as Brianna laid out her photographs. Her mouth dropped opened. "Yes," Brianna said. "Those are dead people. Mummified after being buried in the desert."

"They're real live dead people?" The girl's voice held awe.

"Real enough. I was in that tomb. Along with this . . ." Brianna showed her a picture of the black scorpion she'd taken. Scorpions weren't really considered spiders, but that was merely a matter of specie semantics at this point. "One hit from that tail and you're gone."

"Vanished?"

"Dead."

"Oh . . ." Amber brought the photograph closer. "Did it suck out all the blood from that mummy person?"

Brianna thought about spinning some tale of bloodsucking spiders, but decided Amber probably didn't need to be that terrified. Besides, the tale paralleled too closely the nightmare in her life. "Mummies always look shriveled. They died thousands of years ago. The desert preserved them. Like pickles in vinegar, except better."

Amber wrinkled her nose and flipped to the next photograph. It was of Christopher and Alex on the back of a camel in front of the giant pyramid in Giza. A solar eclipse framed the pyramid. It seemed an eternity ago that she'd taken that photograph. Six weeks before they'd left on the caravan. She had not yet met the infamous El Tazor or even suspected how much her life was about to change.

And something squeezed her heart.

Now she was living in England, married to a duke, chasing down a precocious eleven-year-old, her hard-fought independence swallowed by Michael's shadow and his world. Certainly, if she were the root of his problems, he was the core of hers. For Brianna was flummoxed that she could be so intimate, so completely in love, with a man who could divorce himself so easily from his family, his affections, and her heart.

Amber started asking questions about the strange clothes in the photograph, what a pyramid was, why someone would build such a thing just to bury a person. Who sat on the camel?

The girl was a natural font of curiosity just begging to find focus. Acutely aware that no one had knocked down her door yet, Brianna leaned over the photograph. "That's my brother and sister-in-law," she quietly said. "Your uncle James wore clothes like that when he was in the desert. You should have seen him."

"Do you think Uncle James likes me?" Amber suddenly asked.

"I think he likes you very much. He didn't give *me* a doll."

"Papa said that Uncle James once loved Mama and that's why he left and never came back." Her lashes lowered over her eyes.

"I think it was a lot more than that, Amber. And it wasn't fair that your father said that."

"I want Uncle James and Mama to be together like a family."

"Don't you think I love your uncle James, too? Don't you think that we could all be a family?"

Amber flipped through two more photographs of veiled women at the central fountains, the crowded suks, a pair of camels, and a family of cats that she'd taken in Christopher's stable. Amber's hands stopped.

"I have a soft heart for cats," Brianna admitted. Except for sentimental value, the picture was artistically worthless.

"I like cats, too." And it seemed with those simple words that something inside Amber smiled. Cat lovers always shared special tics.

"Sam and I are good friends," Brianna said. "Especially when I carry catnip in my pocket."

Amber laughed. It was a beautiful laugh. The girl's bow-shaped lips tilted, her eyes sparkled, and suddenly, capturing a precocious eleven-year-old hadn't been so bad after all. Packing up the photographs, Brianna said, "If you want to do something fun, then I'll teach you how to take pictures and even develop the plates."

"You will?" Amber helped close the box lid. "Like these?"

"But I don't allow children near my camera or in my lab. So, if you decided to do this with me, it would be as a young woman, my assistant."

"Mama doesn't think I'm a woman."

Brianna laughed. "Nonsense. What do mamas know? As your aunt, I say that you can be a young woman if you choose to be. I also say there's a time and place to play. And my closet or my lab isn't either of those."

"Yes, Aunt Brea."

Brianna lifted the box, prepared to return them to the desk, when her gaze froze on a spot over Amber's head.

Michael stood with his shoulder propped in the connecting doorway to the adjoining room. She didn't know how long he'd been standing there listening, his arms folded, a restless silhouette framed by the splendor of Aldbury Park in the window behind him. Her heart raced.

For the last three days the entire front page of every newspaper had been filled with the story about the early morning raid on a dockside warehouse that had netted a coup in priceless antiquities and stolen goods. The operation had been touted a monumental testament to the skills of the government agencies involved.

She had not known when he was coming home.

Michael's gaze moved to Amber. His heavy cloak shifted around his calves. "Your mother will be at the house in about fifteen minutes," he said.

Amber's small face brightened on an exclamation. She'd climbed to her feet and was halfway out of the room when Michael stopped her. His gloved hand went to her chin. "I have something for you," he said, withdrawing a tin of chocolates from his pocket. "But you'll have to keep them a secret from your mother and promise not to eat them all in one sitting."

"Thank you, Uncle James!" Amber grabbed her tin.

When she was gone, Michael turned back into the room, gray eyes laced with the mists that hovered at the cusp of every dawn. His hair was almost blue-black in the daylight surrounding him. Brianna stood unmoving. "Do you have any other surprises in your pocket?"

"I might." His tall form filled the doorway. "What is it your heart desires, Brianna?"

She was gawking at what her heart desired, her emotions

on her sleeve, visible even for a blind man to see. The breeze coming from somewhere downstairs tugged at his long woolen cloak. She supposed that he wore new clothes and boots. While in London, he would have finished his fitting with the tailor. Everything about him had changed, and with that thought, Brianna knew a deep-down fear that his acceptance in the ducal realm would come at a high price to her. But then, she had always known the power of the establishment, the ever-present status quo, as it were. Yet, she wanted him to succeed.

"Brianna . . ."

He took a step toward her before Brianna realized that she'd not moved; then she dropped her box and at once was in his arms. He was kissing her soundly, his lips rasping over hers, his body sending vibrant warmth spilling through her veins. His hands slid into her heavy hair, tilting her face to the provocative warmth of his body.

"Is it true?" she asked shakily when he finally pulled away and her lips and cheeks were flushed.

His parted lips came back down on hers. "That I missed you?"

"Did you?" She searched his silvery eyes.

His hand splayed the small of her back. "Every day."

Brianna laughed. He would have been too busy to notice her absence, but she liked that he said it anyway, and knew a decadent thrill at the words. "You should have given warning of your return, sir. Will you tell me about London?"

He told her a little, briefly sketching the events that led to the warehouse raid. Charles Cross worked with the consul general in Cairo. She'd only known that he was leaving Cairo and that he hadn't been on the *Northern Star*, at least according to the manifest.

"Our government had an arrangement with the khedive to help stop the pilfering of Egypt's national treasures," Michael said. "That was his job in Cairo. In London, he set himself up as an antiquities dealer."

"Then if I had tried to sell him the amulet, he'd have arrested me." Brianna leaned into his chest. "I only want this to be over."

"We'll talk about everything at the house." Michael wrapped his arms around her. The top of her head brushed his chin. "Though I don't agree with your means, I would be remiss if I didn't tell you that this case wouldn't have broken without you." The gentleness in his voice surprising her, she stood iron-locked by her need of him. "You've been busy at this lodge," he said, stepping back to admire her state of dishabille.

She inspected a broken nail rather than meet his assessing stare. "Did you think that I wouldn't be?"

"Bloody hell yes," he laughed, "I forgot to warn you that my mother was on a rampage."

She frowned her displeasure at him. He'd conveniently forgotten to warn her about many things. He seemed to be in surprisingly good spirits despite his offish London experience, and when he asked her to show him around her lab, she did. Later, leaving Mr. Freeman with the cart and horse for Gracie, Brianna started with Michael out of the yard, intending to walk back to the house. A black horse stood outside the picket fence, its reins carelessly lashed to a branch, as if the rider had been in a hurry to dismount. Michael had brought the stallion with him from London.

He lifted her into his arms. "The carriage should be at the house now."

"Your shoulder—"

"You're not that heavy." He held her against the wall of his chest. Her legs draped his arm, her white petticoat feathering around her like a bridal gown. "Indeed, you're somewhat fluffy."

"You rode all the way from London on horseback?" She laughed.

"Only the last mile."

"How did you know I'd be at the lodge?"

"I went to the house first."

He set her on the saddle, then dark gloved hands grabbed the reins and he swung up behind her, setting her half across his lap. The horse pranced sideways. At a nudge from Michael's knees the bay leaped into a gallop, and they were suddenly running across the open field. The wind snatched away the red ribbon in her hair, setting the tresses free, and she was laughing as she leaned back and looked up at the blue sky.

Canary yellow flowers bloomed in the fields, scenting the air with a honeyed sweetness. When Michael had left almost three weeks ago, the trees had still been bare, the roads muddy. Today the air was fresh and pure. Sunlight had turned the fields gold. Like the color of desert sand against the stark blue sky.

Field workers gaped at them as they passed. Up at the house, where she'd set the staff to cleaning soot and dirt from the windows, the servants had turned to watch the horse carrying her and Michael through the field of yellow flowers. He held her against him. She didn't want to see him as the conqueror who'd practically imprisoned her these last few weeks, but he'd chosen his ground with the skill of a soldier, and Brianna burrowed her cheek against the warm woolen collar of his coat.

She wanted to hear more about London. His silence on the subject worried her. Mostly she wanted to hold him like this. "You are fortunate I'm in a generous state of mind, your Grace."

He touched his lips against her hair. "I hope so, because we have guests."

With a gasp, Brianna twisted around to the drive.

"Lord and Lady Bedford," he said. "They rode back with Caro."

The couple stood beside the carriage, watching them. Six fine blacks, harnesses still jangling, pawed the ground. Brianna recognized Caroline's brother. Standing beside him, his wife raised her parasol, a frivolous piece of frippery that brushed the top of her wide-brimmed hat.

"They'll only be here for tonight," he promised.

"Oh . . ." Brianna wriggled from his pawing. "What must they think?"

He reined in the horse, spraying gravel as he came to a halt beside the blacks that stood before the carriage. "That I want to take you upstairs and ravish your naked body"—he kept her trapped against him with his arm, his other hand gripping the reins—"with my mouth."

"And without a doubt you're indecent, your Grace."

But the flash in her eyes had been warm and generous as he eased her from the horse.

"Your Grace." A stable attendant stood waiting to retrieve the horse.

Michael flung a leg over the saddle and slid to the ground, his gaze briefly touching the two men standing next to the carriage. Finley had given him his best. But it was his wife who commanded his attention.

Leaning his forearms on the saddle, Michael watched her hurry toward their guests, the pleasant sway of her skirts redolent of his mood as he admired her shapely derriere beneath the length of her hair, and he knew a sudden contentment to be home.

Chapter 22

"**Y**ou shouldn't sit there, Aunt Brea," Amber stoically informed Brianna. "The grass is wet."

"Wonderful." Brianna stood. The back of her dress was wet. "Donald tried to dump a glass of cider on me."

"Double wonderful." She swiped at the back of her gown. She wore a dress of green silk stripes, and hoped it would hide the stain. "I should probably stand here until my skirts dry."

"You shouldn't let them bully you, Aunt Brea," Amber said with all the awareness of a young adult.

Brianna turned her head. "What makes you think I'm being bullied?"

"Because you're over here hiding with me." She'd lowered her voice to a whisper, and it took Brianna a moment to realize that she'd stepped into the middle of a game of hide and seek. "You're going to give me away, Aunt Brea. I don't want to be *it* again."

"Oh." Brianna stepped away from the tree.

She stood undecided, looking around at the faces of those mingling nearby. She welcomed the breeze. Children played in the grass off to the side of the makeshift polo field where she and Michael had come today to celebrate the spring festivities. Nearby, musicians played for a high-stepping jovial group of young people quite lost to the jaunty tune of pipes and lutes. It was a day for merrymaking and Brianna had walked among the tents selling wares and spice cakes.

She had traveled with Michael to Wendover yesterday to partake in the seasonal celebrations that came with the warmer weather. Almost overnight, the clime had warmed. Flowers bloomed. The trees sprouted green. In the midst of this enormous change, Brianna had begun to feel a strange quickening inside her. Twice this week she had awakened queasy. That morning, Gracie literally dragged her out of bed. Now she didn't feel well, and thought it might be best that Michael take her home. She wanted to go back to Aldbury. To the bed that she shared with him.

She could see her tall husband among the men gathered at the keg. She let her gaze linger on him. He wore a sapphire waistcoat and white shirt. Black trousers shaped his long muscular legs and clung to his taut waistline and hard narrow hips. The dying light of the afternoon revealed the whiteness of his teeth as he laughed at something the man beside him said and lifted the pint of ale to his lips. She realized Michael was watching her over the rim. He smiled at her from behind his glass, a glance she shared, and she felt her mouth answer in kind. He never let her out of his sight for long, she realized.

"There she is," dowager Lady Anne said, and holding out her hand, beckoned Brianna forward to her needlepoint circle.

Brianna dipped into a curtsy. "Your Grace."

"I daresay, let me have a look at James's new bride." The woman on the dowager's left peered over her spectacles at Brianna. They were all dressed in black. "She's a pretty thing," Lady Chalmers reassured the dowager. "Quite frankly, the prettiest gal here. Shy, though."

"There's not a shy bone in my granddaughter's body," the dowager replied, sniffing at the thought.

A cheer went up over the crowd behind Brianna. She turned. The polo match was in full swing. Players, mallets, and panting horses collided noisily.

"Have you watched a game of polo before, Lady Ravenspur?" Lady Chalmers asked.

The thunder of horses rolled down the field as another sharp cry went up in the crowd. "I believe the object is to hit the ball with precise blows through the opposite team's goal," she said.

"You are looking piqued, dear," the dowager observed.

"I'm a little tired," she admitted.

Three lorgnettes rose to pass over her. "Are you perchance with child, my dear?"

An untimely blush covered her entire person. Brianna was aghast as much by the disconcerting question as she was by the possibility. The three older women looking fondly back at her thought it natural to discuss such things in public, as if the virility of the Duke of Ravenspur had been something of a wager between them. Squirming in her slippers, Brianna resented the unspoken notion that he might have done his manly duty by her. The knowing glances of others felt almost voyeuristic.

"I am . . . not with child, your Grace," Brianna said, prepared to flee the cheeky threesome. She was nursing a splitting headache.

"Did your husband tell you that we're all old friends here?" Lady Bedford asked Brianna. She sat in the circle of ladies behind her, and Brianna turned.

"Some better than others." Lady Halsford smiled judiciously at Brianna. She wore a wide straw hat tied at the chin with a red bow. "Your husband acquired more than his share of feminine interest. Some"—she took half the woman present into her gaze—"who must now be kicking themselves for letting him get away."

"You all have known each other a long time?"

"We're a lot older now, with children the same age we were when we used to swim in that pond across the field.

The same rivalries," a younger woman said, glaring at Lady Bedford, with her perfectly manicured hands and tightly nipped waist. Bold stripes accentuated her elegance.

"And thank goodness for Caroline and James, without whom this family would be terribly boring and scandal free," Lady Bedford simpered behind a colorful fan of Chinese art. "She is still chasing after him."

"It's about time you found your way over here, you young whelp," the dowager said to someone behind her. "You have been neglecting your bride."

"Not so, Grandmother." Michael wrapped an arm around Brianna's waist. His chin pressed against her temple. "You'll have to watch out for her sharp tongue, *amîri*," he said to her. "She's been known to flay a flounder."

"I've been known to flay bigger fish than that." The dowager grinned wickedly. "Just let them swim in my way."

"Will you sit awhile and talk, James," the diminutive gray-haired woman next to the dowager requested. "Tell us how someone like you snagged such a comely bride as this. You don't deserve her, young man."

"Why, Lady Chalmers, I see that I have to work to win your affections all over again."

Brianna had expected Michael to leave the dowager's side. Instead, he spent the next half hour with her hand tucked beneath his arm, talking to his grandmother. Others meandered over, and soon people sought him out. Brianna watched him. But not as others did. The notion had dawned on her in slow degrees, that there was little left of the man he'd been in Cairo. Her desert warrior had turned into an aristocrat.

Standing beside him, Brianna knew only that she was in love.

When Bedford arrived the conversation changed from the weather to the major arrests in London a few weeks ago.

"I was so worried when I'd found out that my husband was in charge of that entire investigation." Lady Bedford threaded her arm around her husband's. "I was certain he would be killed. I vow, I still have nightmares over the whole incident."

"It is all over and done with," a woman consoled her. "The culprits were caught, and those who survived will hang. We are all quite safe."

"Cross has resigned from his post," Lord Bedford said, drawing her gaze from Michael.

"Really?" Michael said. "Isn't that abrupt?"

"He even turned down the accommodation offered for his services rendered to the crown these past few years. A knighthood. He doesn't feel it is right that he receive the honor for merely doing his job well."

Bedford turned to Brianna. She was unaware that she'd moved within the circle of Michael's arms. "Cross said that he'd hoped he could visit you during the time he had left in London. Something about collating your work for a book."

"Did Cross say where he was going?" Michael asked.

"He wants to travel," Brianna said. "He told me in Cairo that he wanted to retire. At the time, I thought he meant he was retiring from the museum not the Foreign Service department. I imagine he thought my response completely unsophisticated." She looked at Michael. "He was the one who told me that you were leaving Egypt. Now, I understand why he had that information."

"It's rumored that he purchased a wedding trousseau for some young woman," Bedford said. "I assume that he is returning to Cairo to marry, since she didn't come back with him."

Nearby, the roaming musicians struck up a tune.

Cross wanted to marry, she thought. It was very logical that he found someone else in Cairo. But that didn't change her uneasiness.

"You don't appear to be enjoying the event," Michael said against her ear, leaning nearer to put a glass of cider in her hands.

Brianna looked out over the countryside, where an array of colorfully striped tents dotted the landscape. Pennants flapped in the breeze. The Ravenspur carriage sat across the polo field among others.

"It's very beautiful here."

Another roar went up over the crowd. Horses thundered past. "A game of maharajas and khans, devised by gentlemen and played by thugs," Michael said with a smile as he watched the horses collide.

"Maybe next year you should play," she suggested prettily.

And everything caught her then, how Aldbury had become her home.

Amber joined them. Pulling Michael away, she walked him to the edge of the polo field, where the game had ended and the horses were being led away. Amber had been politicking for a pony these past weeks. Caroline joined them, and together they talked to one of the field attendants.

"Alas, it's always the wife who is the last to know," Lady Bedford lamented behind Brianna. "Just look a little closer," she said when Brianna turned on her, ready to do battle. "Look at Amber. Have you ever wondered why she looks the image of your husband?"

Michael arrived home late from Wendover. "Is my wife here?" He handed his cloak to the sleepy-eyed butler.

"Yes, your Grace. She is upstairs."

Michael slowed to light a cheroot, striking a match to bring it to the tip as his gaze went up the stairs. He was restless and moody. Furious. He hadn't even known that Brianna had left the grounds until he looked up and saw the carriage gone. He took the stairs and started to turn toward his chambers when he caught sight of the lone figure standing at the end of the gallery. A wall sconce bathed her in shadows. But Michael recognized her pale silhouette.

As if sensing his presence, Brianna turned her head. As they each stood at one end of the gallery, neither moved.

He drew deeply on his cheroot before grinding it out in a dish beside the window, then closed the space between them.

Without turning toward him, she said, "You would make a poor assassin."

When he didn't answer, she sought him in the shadows behind her. Wearing a pale wrapper, she'd left her hair to hang freely over her shoulders.

"I'm sorry for embarrassing you, Michael. I shouldn't have left."

"I'm not Amber's father," he said quietly, watching her shoulders let go of some of her tension. "A physical impossibility, as Caro and I never engaged in the kind of activity that would produce a child."

"I know that. Amber is the image of her father."

Michael looked up at the portrait in front of them. A thick wave of hair framed his brother's face, while his eyes were gray and gleamed with humor, as if he'd found the entire lordly impression painful. It was an image of his brother that he'd forgotten.

"Nor did I have an affair with Caroline in London," he quietly said, in an effort to allay the rest of her doubts.

"I know that, too." Tears welled in her eyes. "You would never do that."

He slipped out of his jacket and laid it over her shoulders. "I refuse to be responsible for your catching a chill."

She laughed aloud. "It would serve me right."

"I'm sorry that you had a rough time today," he said.

She leaned into him. "I didn't have a rough time." Her voice was muffled against his shirt. "I like your grandmother."

"Brianna . . ." He finally pulled her back to look into her face, then wiped the tears from it with the heel of her hands. "Then what is the matter?"

"Oh, Michael." She buried her face in her hands and wept. "I'm going to have a baby."

The words, so contrary to anything he'd expected to hear, took a moment to settle. His eyebrows lifting in mild astonishment, Michael looked down at the dark head of hair pressed so tenderly against his heart. He could only stare at her in disbelief. His beautiful, young, independent wife was going to have a baby—one of those squirming, helpless, pink-skinned, noisy creatures that only a parent could adore.

Suddenly, he laughed.

Brianna was simplicity and innocence. She was as complicated as a maze. He wanted to shake her for scaring the life out of him.

"It's not funny," she said. "Don't you dare be so smug."

His hand went possessively to her abdomen. "You mean that I'm going to watch you grow huge and waddle around here like a duck?"

"Oh!" She slapped away his hand, but he pulled her struggling into his arms and sat in the chair behind him. "You joke."

"Because I am happy, Brianna."

"I will not be displayed like some mounted animal his grace has brought back from the savage interior of North Africa."

He tilted her chin. "I guarantee, no one here will mistake you for a mounted beast. Mounted perhaps. But not a beast."

Brianna gasped, and as if for the first time smelled the ale on his breath. "You're . . . intoxicated."

"I can't vouch for my state. But I can for my passions."

Lowering his mouth, he stilled her head with his hand at her nape, and tenderly kissed the soft yielding lips. "Maybe I haven't made it clear how I feel. But my heart beats in my chest for you."

He loved her.

He loved her laughter. Her stubbornness. The melodrama of her emotions. Even with all the complicated facets and flaws of her personality, she'd proven herself tactile as his duchess, in more ways superior to his own adjustment here because she was enduring his family and his friends, her greatest strength her singularity. She tamed wild little girls with the same capacity for love that she gave all things, no matter how blighted. She was like a bright blue flame that he cradled in his palm that gave color to his existence.

And now she was going to have his baby.

"I've been remiss in not fitting you with my ring." He rubbed his thumb over the delicate bones of her fingers. "One that will match the Ravenspur gem you'll receive on our first anniversary." Michael cleared away the screen of dark hair that had fallen over her shoulder. "It's purple . . ." he admitted, wishing it was a sapphire. "Amethyst."

"I've never had a purple wedding ring. Or imagined that there was such a thing."

He smiled into her eyes. "Are you insulting my family's colors?"

"Your family's colors are purple?"

"And black," he declared. "A very indubitable banner at medieval tournaments where the Ravenspur liege spent many an hour trying not to get knocked onto his arse. Legend claims that the realm feared the purple and black, for its representatives never lost a challenge."

"And to think that my ancestors beat yours up with sticks."

He laughed aloud, his response unexpected, even to him. His fingers wandered lightly over her waist and he traced his thumb over her navel, meanwhile looking around him at the walls filled with the faces of his ancestors. How many times as a boy had he walked this corridor in awe of those who looked down at him from the centuries? Now, by some twist of fate, his legacy would be Aldbury's future, and even he had to appreciate the capricious twist of fate handed down to the black sheep of the family. He wanted to be a better man than his father or his brother.

"I love you, *amîri*."

His lips leisurely caressed hers, contrasting to the harsh tempo in his chest. Brianna caught his face in her hands and kissed him fiercely.

He missed very few things from his old life.

But he did miss the moonlight on desert sand, the

jasmine-scented sunlight in Brianna's hair. He only knew that he'd been too long alone in his life, and found that he never wanted to go there again.

"Aye." He chuckled. "Worse has happened to us both."

Chapter 23

Brianna found Chamberlain at breakfast the next morning studying his copy of the *London Times*. He was engaged in an article and didn't hear her enter. Having deliberately sought him out for many reasons this morning, she drew in a deep breath. "Lord Chamberlain?"

"Your Grace." His gaze went over her attire.

She was wearing a bright apple-green gown trimmed with gold cording. The gown was neither shy nor demure. The color and style was simply who she'd always been. Brushing at the velvet on her skirt, she sat across from him and removed her gloves, her face serious.

"Would you care for java, your Grace?" the footman asked.

"Yes, please." Brianna eagerly accepted a cup, noting with surprise that someone had made her favorite white brew. Astonishment lifted her gaze.

"I hope we got it right, your Grace," the uniformed butler standing next to the sideboard replied.

Brianna dropped her nose to the cup. "I haven't had a cup of white java since leaving Cairo." She drank as if it were heaven.

337

"You have a letter, your Grace." A footman interrupted. He bowed over her with a silver tray. "It arrived special courier just now."

Noting at once that the seal belonged to Alex, she quickly opened the letter. Heart racing, she read the hastily written petition. "My sister-in-law has gone into her confinement early. She's sent for me. This is from Lady Alexandra's physician."

Brianna looked outside the glass doors at the rain. Darker clouds sat on the distant horizon.

"Is everything all right, your Grace?" Lord Chamberlain set down his fork.

"I don't know," she whispered, turning the letter over in her hand. Why didn't Alex write her? "I need to get a message to my husband at once," she said after a moment.

"I believe he returned to Wendover, your Grace," Chamberlain said. "He's due back tomorrow. But I'll send a rider."

Michael had left before she'd awakened that morning. They had spent all night in perpetual bliss, making love, alternating moods of teasing and seriousness as they talked. She only knew that no matter what lay between them, they would climb the hills and survive the gullies together.

"Perhaps you can ask that he meet me at Lady Alexandra's home."

"I can do that." He ordered the carriage brought around.

Brianna started to stand, but hesitated. The carriage would not be out front for at least an hour. "I'm aware that I've been stubbornly resistant toward you," she said, her eyes brilliant on him. "Tell me that I need something, and I'll prove that I don't. Truly, it's one of my worst traits. That, and my ability to ostracize myself by my own thoughtless actions. It was the reason my family threw me out of England."

He buttered his toast. "Ah, yes. Something to do with a book on the plight of—" Clearing his throat, he set down the knife. "I believe you know the piece to which I am referring. The dowager told me," he explained, to her horrified look. "She has a copy in her library. Naturally, I consider it disgraceful that you young aristocrats manage to find little else to do with your time than turn your noses up at propriety."

"I'm hardly an aristocrat, my lord," she said, very nearly insulted, yet not so much so that she sniffed in disgust. "I certainly wasn't one when I wrote that book, anyway."

"What is it you wanted my help with, your Grace?"

"I have some mail that I wish to be detained." Brianna folded her hands around the cup. "Or shall I say handled."

"Does this have anything to do with your visits to the village on Thursdays?" He sat forward and observed her with keen eyes. "It seems the roof to the school will be repaired by midsummer. You are a preponderant supporter of education, I see."

A flush stole over Brianna. "I do what I can."

Chamberlain withdrew an envelope from his pocket. "Lord Ravenspur has not insisted on seeing the mail that comes into this house. But I kept this one aside." He slid the envelope across the table. "This estate has had a recent influx of cash from a banking investment."

Brianna knew the letter was from the Bank of England. Flicking the corner of the envelope, she lifted her gaze. Her entire life, she had always wanted to make a difference to those she loved. Perhaps she couldn't on their same scale. Her brothers built worlds. Stephan Williams served to uphold the bastion of democratic ideals. And Michael would soon take his seat in the House of Lords. Her contribution was to motherhood . . . and Aldbury.

"It's my dowry," she said.

"It's more than your dowry. You sold your shares of Donally and Bailey Engineering. He would never have allowed you to do that."

"This estate needs working capital for what my husband wishes to do. Legally, it's his money anyway. Aldbury Park needs it."

"He's not naive, your Grace. He knows that you've been working with the vicar. Eventually he'll learn how you've been funding everything."

"Then let it be a surprise."

Sipping his brew consideringly, Chamberlain regarded her bouncy feathered hat. Clearly, she was a jarring impact to the sterile grandeur of Aldbury. But she liked it here. Michael's world was like a splash of sunlight on a blank canvas, and the possibilities for a finished masterpiece had become endless, if she could just learn how to paint with the correct brush.

Brianna's gaze dropped to the envelope in her hand. "My maid has gout," she stood. "I don't want her trapped in a carriage all day. Besides, the countess has become somewhat dependent on Gracie."

Gracie always did want a patient who appreciated her medicinal potions.

"I will send Louisa with you. She has never been to London. Perhaps she will consider this an adventure."

"And one more thing, my lord." Brianna pressed an impulsive kiss on his whiskered cheek, flustering him with her exuberant display of emotions. "My staff will be returning to the cottage house to finish the job I paid them to do. The countess can learn to share."

Chamberlain's brow lifted in subdued astonishment. "I'm quite positive that will be an education for you both."

She smiled. "On that fact, we can both agree."

He looked out the tall window at the slate gray sky and churning clouds, and mild panic stirred Brianna. It had been raining heavily since early that morning. "If you're going to get to your sister-in-law, you best be leaving soon."

"Please see that his grace gets this message."

Michael closed the missive and looked up at the boy who had delivered it. "How long ago did you get this?"

"It came to the dowager's this afternoon, your grace. We didn't know fer sure where you were. Then her grace, the dowager, said to try the Boar's Inn since ye fancy taking your meals here on occasion when you are out."

Lord Bedford entered the inn and doffed his rain-soaked

jacket and hat. Michael excused the boy and watched as Bedford sat across from him. Water dripped from the man's hair and eyelashes. Michael didn't intend to stay long.

"Why the cloak and dagger routine of a clandestine meeting, Ravenspur?" Bedford demanded.

"I want you to call the wolf off my wife."

"The wolf?" Amused, Bedford flagged the barmaid for ale. "No one has ever referred to my sweet Amy as the wolf."

"No doubt their adjectives are far more descriptive and less fit for mixed company." Michael leaned back in the chair. It creaked in protest to his weight. Long riding boots hugged his calves.

"There have always been rumors surrounding me. Most have no basis in fact and don't even dignify a response. The one about Amber is new and is as low as anyone could get to hurt innocent people, including *your* niece. You were good friends with my brother. What would Edward think about having his daughter's parentage questioned?"

"Amy was always loyal to Edward." Bedford contemplated the ring on his finger. "What can I say? I love her."

Michael paid the barmaid for the ale and ordered coffee. Behind him the sky had darkened, and most of the common room remained lit only by the fire in the hearth. He leaned forward on his elbows. "She's having a difficult time. I'm asking for a reprieve until she can get her feet beneath her."

Bedford's chair creaked as he shifted weight. "All right," he said, and removed an envelope from inside his waistcoat.

"I wasn't able to get into Charles Cross's files," Bedford said.

"Secret?"

"Closed." Bedford sat back in his chair. "You'll have to wait until next week when I can find a clerk who can navigate the basement. Do you want to explain your interest?"

"I don't like him. Is that reason enough?"

Michael accepted coffee from the barmaid and waited until she took the meal away. Turning his attention back to Bedford, he regarded the man over the cup rim. "I have an emergency to attend to in London. While I'm there, I need your office to find someone else for me. Sir Christopher Donally is or was the Public Works minister in Egypt. He resigned his position four weeks ago and hasn't been heard from since—"

"He arrived in Southampton two days ago. Had a deuced tough time getting back this time of year."

Michael's coffee cup clinked in its saucer. "You just happen to know this?"

"The foreign secretary has a vested interest in Donally, considering the man is his son-in-law. They hate each other, but the arrogant bastard is ecstatic that his daughter is well on her way to delivering him a grandchild. She's been living in her father's Denmark Hill residence for the past three weeks completing some book about Coptic temples. Though I prefer *The Plight and Prejudice of London's Poor* a more fascinating read. I understand your wife is the author of that titillating piece."

"Where did you say Lady Alexandra was living?"

"With her father. Somewhere near the university district. Leave it to Ware to be obtuse about his place of residence."

Michael was sure that Brianna had not known that Alexandra was not living at home. Her message had stated that she would be going to Epping. He turned in his chair and looked out the window at the growing green and black sky.

"London is getting pounded," Bedford said, looking out the window. "The approaching night promises to be black as hell."

"Are you sure Lady Alexandra is staying with her father?"

"I just left London." Bedford stood and shrugged into his coat. "He's been leaving Downing Street early every night."

"Because she's ill?"

"Hell no." Bedford finished his ale and shrugged into his coat. "Because she's home."

"The bridge is under water, guv'na." A man hunched in a black slicker shouted over the rain as Michael reached the crossing three hours later. A lantern swayed in the man's hand as he checked the railroad trestle. "No one is getting through to London tonight. Leastways not from this place." Behind him, the train stood huffing in the pouring rain, an occasional blast of steam sounding akin to Michael's black temper.

"I need to get to the High Beach area," he yelled over his shoulder. Still atop his horse, Michael held the reins clutched in his gloved hands. The stallion did an impatient turn. His calves wrapped the barrel of the horse in an unforgiving vise, "How far is the next crossing?"

"There ain't no guarantee the bridge in Watford is in better shape." The railroad conductor raised the lantern. In the hours since the rain had begun, the waters were still rising. "Either way, you ain't getting to London, guv'na. You're better off sitting tight here."

Michael stared at the torrent of rushing water that had breached its banks in an ugly surge of swollen, muddy water. Swinging the bay south, he didn't make it far before the sullen waterway again blocked his path. "You'll have to go to St. Anne's abbey," someone yelled out from the darkness. Michael had been desperate enough to cross.

He slammed his hand against the edge of the saddle and stared in fury at the sky. The rain blinded him. He knew he'd kill his horse if he continued on to find another crossing. Or he'd kill himself in the dark. Though she didn't know it, Finley's men were with her, and he had to trust that they would guard his wife with their lives.

The roads were dark and flooded when Brianna reached the outskirts of London. Turning down the lamp, she raised the curtain in the carriage and looked outside. There was something ominous in the road's emptiness. She heard the driver's whip crack. The carriage picked up speed. Louisa was curled inside her cloak on the opposite seat, asleep.

The carriage had pulled out of a way-station what seemed hours ago. She'd learned the bridge behind her had been closed. The men outside needed to find shelter. Brianna laid her head against the velvet squabs. She thought of Michael, and wondered if it was raining where he was as well. Had he gotten her message?

Or had he already returned to Aldbury?

Something smacked against the roof, and Brianna awakened with a start, looking around her. For a moment she'd forgotten where she was. Sheets of water cascaded down the window. The carriage had stopped.

Brianna pulled aside the curtains, to see trees bent and swayed. They were on Christopher's long drive; her brother's Elizabethan manor house loomed in the shadows, a distant light in the back marking the late hour of her arrival. Across from her, Louisa remained asleep. The driver had not set down the step. How long had she been here?

Pressing her face against the glass, Brianna cupped her hands around her eyes. Tree branches lashed the house in a frenzied tantrum. The wind rocked the carriage.

Suddenly, the front door opened and a man stepped onto the porch. Backlit by the lights that began to blink on in the corridor, she could barely make out his shape, though she couldn't see much beneath the shiny slicker. One of her footmen must have gone to get someone to open the door. At this hour, most of the servants would be retired to their quarters out back of the house.

Anxious to see Alex and to get out of the storm, Brianna didn't wait for the man to make his way out to her. The wind yanked the door from her hand and it slammed against the side of the carriage. Louisa awakened with a gasp.

"Wait here," Brianna yelled over the wind. "Someone will come out and get you." Holding her reticule with one hand, she gripped the hood of her cloak and slammed the door with the other. She turned and ran past the figure approaching her, his head bent against the slashing rain. "Get Louisa," she cried, lifting her skirts and taking the slippery stairs into the house where Barnaby would be awaiting her.

She didn't know who was awake to greet her. Once inside with the door shut, the noise seemed to abate. "Look what I've done. I'm so sorry, Barnaby." Laughing in frustration, she glanced down at her muddied boots and felt like a dog in need of a good shake. Water dripped on Christopher's beautiful polished floor. "Are you the only one awake?"

"No."

The strangely accented voice whirled her around. Brianna raked the hood off her face. Her hand froze.

"Jackals travel in packs, Sitt Donally. Didn't you know?"

"Selim . . . ?" Her voice was a whisper. Her heart frozen in her chest.

And the look on his face turned into a sneer of unspeakable evil. "Where is Major Fallon, Sitt?"

The light in the hall was dim, but not so dim that she didn't recognize the eyes staring at her from the shadows. She'd last seen him alive on the caravan. He'd been the boy in her photographs. He wore no black turban and tagilmust. His black hair was long and dripped in tangles around his face. He was the youth who'd posed with Napoleonic fervor beside a camel and befriended her over a meal of couscous.

The horrible carnage at the caravan came back to strike her.

He was Omar's son.

"Oh, Jaysus—" She started upstairs, only to be blocked. Her brain trailed seconds behind the action. "What have you done to Lady Alexandra?"

"You will not see her again, Sitt. You will not see anyone." He shoved her and she hit the banister. She had a vial of rosewater in her purse and it clunked solidly against the derringer.

The derringer!

The front door opened and the man wearing the black slicker stepped inside ahead of the slashing rain. Sheathing a long knife, he spoke something in Arabic to Selim, sharing a laugh. Louisa had been the only one outside.

The door shut.

Her gaze suddenly caught the mark beneath the man's sleeve. These people had tried to kill Michael.

"The letter from Alex's physician wasn't real," she whispered.

"Fallon is a lot of trouble, Sitt. How do we get him out of hiding? Let me see?" He rubbed his bearded chin in sarcasm. "We have you."

Something inside her broke.

They would not use her to kill Michael.

"To think that I felt sorry that you'd died." Brianna swung her reticule, smashing Selim in the face. The bottle of rosewater shattered in her purse, striking a gash across his cheek. "He'll kill you!"

Brianna made it up the stairs before Selim caught her ankle. Twisting around, she grabbed the spindles on the rail and kicked out with all of her might. Kicking again and again, she smashed Selim's nose. With a piercing shriek, he tumbled down the stairs and crashed into the other man. Brianna's reticule dropped and, grabbing the rail, she watched in horror as it hit the floor below.

Selim had recovered enough to call her a bitch. Brianna didn't wait to see the knife he pulled from his tunic. She ran blindly up the stairs and down the long corridor. She darted into Christopher's room and slammed the door, her hand freezing over the knob. There was no key in the lock. With a choked sob, Brianna scraped a chair across the floor. She braced the knob, then ran into the dressing room and flung open Christopher's old military chest. She knew her guard and driver were probably dead. And what of Alex and Louisa? Alex's staff?

Somewhere down the long corridor, over the raging storm outside, she heard doors slamming. She prayed that Christopher still kept his service revolver inside his chest. Brianna rifled through old uniforms, a haversack, and a holster. Her hands wrapped around the cold metal of the gun. It was an old 1857 Colt firearm. Outside the room, a shoulder slammed against the door. No door barred the dressing room. Dropping to her knees, she searched the bottom of the chest, desperate to find cartridges. Her hand closed over the pack.

With a start, she realized that someone had come into the room.

Her fingers steadily loaded the gun. Early on, she'd felt that split second of blind terror before swinging her reticule. But now she felt more rational, and aware of every sound.

A dark shape began to form out of the shadows just beyond the dressing room. Lightning flashed, illuminating the room.

"Stay away!" The ammunition in her hand rolled to the floor. She'd only loaded one shell. Both hands gripped the handle and she cocked the revolver with her thumbs. "I swear, I'll shoot you."

The quiet that came over her was terrifying. Something banged against the roof of the house, a tree limb perhaps.

"Brianna . . ."

The voice was quietly beckoning and familiar. But Brianna had already pulled the trigger.

Chapter 24

Donally's house, with its high sloping roof and gable windows, sat at the top of a rise delineated by the indigo sky. A wind gust swept the avenue of hornbeam and massive oaks that lined the gravel drive before dying to a tired breath. Detecting a sudden alteration in the manner of his horse, Michael wrapped the reins around his fist and held the horse in check. In the widening silence, he removed his gun. The man on the mule beside him stirred.

Michael had spent a restless night with a hundred others stranded at St. Anne's abbey, huddled against a damp stone wall. By the time he'd reached this house, the day had again yielded to the closing darkness. A few moments ago he'd met Donally's groundskeeper on the road.

"Most of the servants that work here live in the cottages out back," the thick-set man told him, leaning forward in the saddle. "Her ladyship returned from Cairo in January. But she is visiting her pa right now."

Michael gave his full attention to the man. "When was the last time you were here?"

"Before the rain. Day before yesterday."

"And she was gone?"

"For two weeks, your Grace."

Michael slid from the saddle and explored the ground with careful fingers. He found a recent indentation of a horse track.

"Stay here," he said.

Moving toward the darkened house, Michael could make out part of the gazebo silhouetted against the encroaching lake. No recent carriage tracks marred the drive.

Bounded by a low stone wall, a garden terrace ran around the side of the house. Somewhere, a horse snuffled. From the gravel drive, his horse answered, and pulled Michael's attention to the stables. His gun at the ready, he stood in the shadow overhang of the roof, his thumb easing back the hammer of the revolver. A barely audible answering *click* warned him of another person's presence an instant before he swung his pistol around the corner of the house. Distant lightning flared, briefly throwing the face of the man standing before him into sharp relief, barely freezing his finger on the trigger.

"Christ, Donally." Face-to-face with a .44 Smith & Wesson, Michael felt the ungainly slug of his heart against his ribs. His tone was dry and harsh. "How long have you been here?"

Michael knew Donally could see even less of him in the darkness.

"That's a bloody fooking way to get your head blown off, Fallon." Donally pulled back his revolver. "It's the wrong night to be prowling my garden. Where the hell is my wife?"

Lady Alexandra was sitting down with her father when a stir and bustle in the corridor interrupted supper. "I'll announce myself, Alfred," a wonderfully familiar male voice was heard to say in an irrefutable tone, and then Christopher was standing in the doorway.

"What the bloody devil?" Austere in his black dinner coat and cravat, her father rose.

Christopher stepped beneath the archway, and his tall, black-garbed form filled the room. She was suddenly in his arms. Holding him. He carried a rider's quirt. His boots were spattered in mud. He wrapped his arms around her and held her pressed tightly against him. "Lord Ware," he said, acknowledging her father with a curt nod. Then he pulled back and placed a possessive palm on her abdomen. "I've just spent a hellish three weeks on a cargo ship to get here." He kissed her openly in front of her father and wrapping her arms around him, she returned the affection. "It took me that many days to get into this bloody city." His lips curved against hers. "Finding you gone from the house has cost me my temper. So forgive the state of my arrival. Tell me Brianna is with you."

Alexandra opened her eyes and saw Major Fallon standing behind her husband. With the exception of his shirt, his clothes were black—overcoat, trousers, and boots. Shock reeled her back. A growth of beard and stormy eyes that looked as if snatched from the sky added to the menacing impression. For Major Fallon was clearly in a dangerous mood.

"I don't understand," she said to Christopher.

"At your physician's request, Brianna left Aldbury Park yesterday to join you, pending your early confinement. We believe she went to the manor house, unless you've started to wear attar of roses."

"As you can see, I'm quite well." She looked between Michael and her husband. "I authorized no such request. She didn't even know I was here."

"My daughter has been here for two weeks." Ware leaned forward on his cane. "I thought it best . . . with my grandchild so near to term."

"And you didn't bother to bloody inform me?" Michael's voice had lost its customary command. He'd already swung away when Donally called after him.

"We need daylight to check the roads leading toward the estate. Your horse won't make it."

"Standing here doing nothing won't find my wife!"

Donally caught his sleeve. "And running in bloody circles won't get my sister back."

"She is alone out there." His eyes bleak with violence, Michael threw off Donally's grip. "She trusted me to keep her safe."

What sane man could sit and do nothing, for Christ's sake!

Michael rubbed his temple with one hand. Brianna had been lured away. But in the deepest part of his soul, he knew she was still alive. That she wasn't meant to die. Indeed, he suspected that whoever had sent that letter to Brianna expected him to be with her. If he had not gone to see his grandmother yesterday morning, he'd have been at Aldbury when she received the physician's letter.

"A letter was delivered to Aldbury Park by special courier from your physician, my lady. It bore your personal wax seal. Who else would have had access to your stamp?"

"No one." Alex was growing hysterical. "My stamp is here with me."

"Her physician has known her since she was a child," Ware inserted. "He would not betray her or me."

"Maybe she hasn't gotten to the house." Alex desperately clutched her husband's coat. "A carriage just doesn't vanish into thin air."

Except people did vanish. Whole caravans of people vanished forever. "One can, if it's planned." Michael leaned a palm against the window and looked out over the muted glow of gaslights illuminating the sky over the city. All that he loved in the world was somewhere out there in the night. His wife and his child. "I bloody knew everything had fallen into place too easily here in London. I knew it and let myself get talked out of pursuing this investigation!"

"What did we miss?" Ware thundered. "There was no more information to follow after the warehouse raid. No evidence that we had not caught everyone involved."

"Take an accounting of your staff tonight." Michael turned back into the dining room. "Find out who else could have gotten hold of your seal. Do you have any new servants?"

"Her servants came from Donally's staff and have been with the family for years," Ware said. "A young lad delivers her posts from the manor."

"I was only planning to be here for a few weeks," Alex whispered. "My book is due at the publisher the end of the month. Mr. Cross was spending so much of his time traveling back and forth to the manor house. When my father's invitation came, I took it."

"Charles Cross has been here working with you?" Michael asked.

A hush deepened in the room.

"When was the last time you saw him?"

"I received a note from him today telling me that he's ill. Why are you looking at me like I just committed some grievous sin?" Her voice grew strained. Light from the candelabra on the table fluttered as she whirled around. "We've all known Mr. Cross for years. He works with Foreign Services. You would not have broken the investigation if not for him."

"If Cross was Foreign Service, that would explain the consul general's friendship with him," Donally said to Michael, unaware that Michael had already made the connection. Now, with his name coming on the heels of Brianna's disappearance, it seemed ominous and plausible that the two incidents could be connected.

"If he were involved, he would also have been in the position to supply the authorities with information about the warehouse. Especially since it was probably a matter of days before we discovered the cache there ourselves. He was bloody saving his own skin." Michael looked directly at Ware. "Where does he live?"

"We have to approach this with deuced care." Ware leaned both hands on his cane, unhappy with the direction of dialogue.

Alex pressed her fingers to her temples. "He let a house in the Green Park area. The widow Solomon's estate."

"That house hasn't been lived in for ten years," Ware said. "Who did he let the place from?"

"I don't know. I only know that he's worked hard to get to his place. He comes from humble roots and still managed to graduate from Oxford at the top of his class. In Cairo, he was always sending money and packages back to his mother. How can a man who does that be suspected of something so heinous?"

"That's the most illogical nonsense I've heard you speak, Lexie," her father said.

"Alex—" Donally folded her in his arms.

"You don't understand." She tried to shove away. "I introduced Brianna to him. What if I did this to her?" She pressed her fist against her abdomen as if to quell her pain. "What if he could have been using me to get to her? I want to go with you—" Alex broke into tears.

"You're not leaving anywhere." Donally lifted her and turned to Michael, Alex sobbing in his arms. "I'm going to take my wife upstairs."

Michael looked down at Lady Alexandra's softly swollen figure with a sudden fierce ache. Even if she hadn't been nearly nine months gone with child, he wouldn't have allowed her anywhere near Cross tonight.

"Papa," Alex pleaded over Donally's shoulder. "Help us find her."

Michael was left looking at Ware when Donally was finally gone. "Her address book should be in her study," Ware said awkwardly, and left.

Michael dropped into a dining room chair and buried his face in his hands. Everything inside him told him Cross was his man. But it would not make sense for him to take Brianna to the first place anyone would look. He would already be out of the city.

For the first time in days, Michael felt the ebony grasp of Morpheus close around him, a tenuous hold that lasted only minutes. Too often it was the way he'd trained himself. A catnap was often more than he used to get while in the field.

"My daughter's address book, Ravenspur." Ware leaned

over the dining table, a leather-bound notebook spread before him, his eyes sharp as he considered the pages. His brows lifted. "Are you up for a drive?"

"Try stopping me."

Ware ordered his cloak and carriage brought around, his somber gaze grazing Michael as he spoke. "And another cloak for Lord Ravenspur." He checked a watch fob in his pocket. "If we're going to make a late night call to Cross, then you'll need to look more refined than a thief."

The trip through London took little time on streets that were nearly deserted. The rain had washed the garbage from gutters and the coal dust from the air. Street lamps marked the shiny pavement, the *clip-clop* of their horses mixing with the noise of an occasional hansom that was ferreting late night partygoers. Though the Season had yet to begin, most of London's clubs carried a brisk business. Michael saw the towers of a church framed against the sky. Just beyond that, he glimpsed stone turrets of a distant house. Secluded behind a grove of knotty trees and a high iron gate, the medieval roof was all they could see from the street. There was a sleepy stillness to the night.

The carriage rocked to a stop. "This place is high-priced real estate for a man who came from humble beginnings." Michael let his eyes go over the high stone wall that banked the property. The darkness was impenetrable; then the breeze stirred the clouds and laid a breath of gossamer moonlight over the shadows, allowing a glimpse of the house through the trees. Three stories high, the interior of the house was dark as the night. Iron grates covered the windows and doors like some aged fortress. "What happened to the widow who lived here?"

Ware leaned into the window. "They said she was insane. No one knows what happened to her sons. It doesn't look as if anyone is home," he said impatiently when no one appeared at the gate.

Michael checked the chamber on his revolver. "I suggest that if you can't hike to the door, then stay with this carriage.

Make sure the constable who walks this beat knows who you are. He'll probably pass by here in the next half hour."

"Bloody hell, Ravenspur." Ware tapped the top of the carriage and waited for the door to open. "He very well could be ill, like his note said. You're not the bloody cavalry."

Seated on a red velvet wing-back chair, Michael sat forward with his elbows on his knees. He lifted his head when Cross stepped into the room, his steward behind him. Michael unfolded his form from the chair.

"Lord Ware," Cross acknowledged the older man. His eyes wide behind his glasses, he slid an uneasy glance over Michael. "Has something happened to bring you here at this hour? I sent a note—"

"I apologize for intruding," Lord Ware began, "but it was important that we see you."

Cross coughed into a handkerchief. The man looked as if he could barely stand. "If you don't mind, I need to sit. Fever . . . you see."

The steward hastily prepared the pillows on the chair. The old man was of Arab descent. Ware made no secret of the fact that Brianna was missing, and as the former diplomat spoke with quick, authoritative tones, Michael remained silent.

Charles Cross had changed in the month since Michael had seen him in London. His white stock, loose and unkempt at his neck, accentuated the weather-burnt pallor beneath the pale skin. Black lashes shadowed his strange gold eyes, attentive behind his spectacles. But no formality of posture could hide the gravity of his appearance. One look at the man's pallid complexion dispelled any doubt that Cross was seriously ill.

"We've come to inquire about a certain amulet that was given over into your possession some time ago," Michael heard Ware say. "Lord Ravenspur spoke to you about the matter when he was here in London last."

"I have seen that the amulet was returned to the museum in Cairo. Your daughter is aware of this."

"Have you received anything else . . . that you would term illegal?"

Michael had put too much hope in the expectation that Cross would be his man. Brianna wasn't here.

No longer able to contain his restless energy, he stood as Ware spoke inanely. Rich hangings, silken carpets, and exquisite lamps lined the walls and floors. The salon was a throwback to history, an antiquated museum of eastern artifacts and furnishings, from the ivory-inlaid tables to bamboo and Chinese ebony chairs. Photographs shared the walls with a tiger's head and fanged beasts. He stopped in front of a photograph, the kind usually taken at fairs. Two boys sat on each side of a pretty woman, embraced by a palm frond sitting in a vase at her back. She wore a simple dress that was in fashion ten years ago. One boy looked about fifteen, the other ten. Both were leaning into the woman, their hands in their laps. The boy on the left was clearly Charles Cross.

"You have a brother?" Michael asked. Realizing that he had interrupted, he turned. "My apologies, your lordship," he said to Ware.

"He attends Oxford," Cross said behind his handkerchief.

"This is your house?" Michael asked, letting his gaze go around the room. Indeed, for a man of humble beginnings, he had come far.

"This house belonged to my mother. She passed away shortly after that photograph was taken."

Lord Ware stood. "We apologize for disturbing you, Mr. Cross."

"Please convey my apology to Lady Alexandra," Cross said at the door. "As you now understand, I felt it best to stay away from her."

The house was still. Michael glimpsed the unmarked layers of dust and shrouded furniture in the rooms on either side of the entryway. Yet, some subtle atmosphere in the air bothered him. Something more than the hint of disinfectant that surrounded Cross, and the realization that he'd smelled that same scent in the passageway of the steamer the night someone had jammed the door.

"You like fresh flowers?" Michael casually asked. "Not many florists sell roses this time of year."

"Mine does."

This time when the handkerchief came away from Cross's mouth, Michael saw the blood. Slowly, he lifted his gaze. Their eyes met.

Michael knew! Goddamn, he knew!

Cross's expression no longer benign, he dabbed the corner of his mouth. "Do you think it incongruous that I would wish to fill this place with something patently innocent? Look around you, Fallon, and tell me that even a single rose would not add life to this sordid existence?"

Ware's fingers wrapped around Michael's forearm. "We have kept you too long, Mr. Cross," Ware said.

"You should have let me kill him, brother." The words were spoken from the shadows behind Charles Cross.

Charles stood at the long window overlooking the yard. "What have you done with her?" He'd spoken in Arabic without realizing. He despised the crude language and didn't like that he'd slipped. The opium made him careless.

"She did not get out of the room," Selim said.

Charles finally smelled the roses. The scent was coming from Selim. There was still the shattered residue of attar of roses on his clothes. The house probably reeked of the scent. Damn Selim for his stupidity!

Charles dropped the edge of the curtain. He held his arms to his side and let his faithful steward remove his jacket to check the bandage beneath. "You are bleeding. You must return to bed," the older man said. They'd served many years together. "You will die, effendi. . . ."

Selim stepped forward into the light, his youthful countenance no longer recognizable behind the bruises and swelling on his face. "Why do you bother with the girl after what she has done to you? Her presence condemns us all. He will tear down this house looking for her."

Charles lifted his gaze to the ceiling. The hunger he had lived with since she'd left Cairo returned to gnaw at his gut with burning force. Brianna had not understood his devotion to her. She had no idea how he'd protected her. How he still protected her. Selim had wanted to kill her, but then, Selim had always hungered for blood, more so since the girl had blackened his face.

He moved slowly into the entryway, every step agony. He'd recognized the glacial look in Fallon's eyes, and knew that only Brianna's presence had kept them all alive tonight. But maybe it didn't matter anymore. Already his plans had changed.

He gripped the balustrade as he eased up the stairs. The staircase window was high and latticed with stained glass. A chandelier filled the space above the entryway, and as he raised his gaze, he couldn't remember ever having seen the crystalline fixture alive with lights.

"Light them," he told his steward, who had remained behind in the shadows. "Light everything."

"I'm a liability," Ware rasped over his breath. "You should leave me and go for help."

"Stay in the shadows." Without taking his eyes off the gate, Michael had worked the revolver from his waistband. "I should have killed the son of a bitch. . . ." His long coat brushed his calves as he walked with Ware. The driveway was matted with weeds. Moonlight spattered across the ground like broken eggshells.

"It looks like someone beat you to it," Ware asked. "He's coughing up blood. Gunshot?"

"Which explains why he's still in London. He has no intention of leaving that house alive."

"If his mother has been dead for ten years, it's obvious what Cross has been sending back to England. He couldn't have been working alone."

But Michael was no longer listening as he attempted to remove himself as a walking bull's-eye. He could feel the pulse and danger of the night swirling around him. His hands and stomach were cold with fear and rage. But as suddenly as his fury and panic had come upon him, it ebbed into something deadly. This wasn't a walk that he preferred to take, but there was too much at stake. If he broke off now, Ware would be left unprotected. Nor could he charge into the house, any more than he could have dragged Cross outside if he ever wanted to see Brianna alive.

"When we get to the carriage, I want you to find the constable."

Ware slowed. "You're going back alone?"

"He won't be alone." Donally spoke as Michael passed through the gate. "She's my sister, Fallon." Dressed in clothes that blended with the night, the black stubble on his face, the former Public Works minister for the khedive was leaning against the stone wall. The streetlight picked out his blue eyes as he shifted them to Ware. "You've surprised me by breaking the law so blatantly, my lord."

"Don't tell me you came alone?" the man's father-in law scoffed.

Wind breathed across the street and stirred the gnarled tree branches above them. "I'm not as foolish as some."

Michael's gaze lifted. Surrounded by leafy branches, Finley crouched on the weathered stone wall above the street. He smiled like a wolf. "My men are already on the grounds, your fancy lordship."

Tucking his gun away, Michael cocked a brow at Donally, hastily removing his coat. "How is it that you two know one another?"

"We grew up together." Donally lifted himself onto an overhanging branch.

A moment later Michael settled beside him in the tree. He was glad for Donally's friends. Water dropped from the leaves onto his hands. "Your Grace." Finley held out a knife, hilt first. "You'll be needin' this."

"Keep it. I have my own. And don't anyone touch Cross. He's mine."

His focus clear, his footing sure, Michael lowered himself off the ledge and into the night. Then he was sprinting full-out through the trees. Nothing else mattered but finding his wife. And if Cross didn't die first of his wounds, Michael would kill him.

Brianna sat on the edge of the bed. The turnkey had returned. She tried to talk to the dullard who'd refused her food and water. So weak, she'd tried desperately to distract him to get to the window.

"What does the bitch want now?" Selim strolled into the room.

He'd spoken to her guard in Arabic, but Brianna recognized the tone well enough to know what he'd said. His venomous gaze went over her before he backhanded the hapless guard. "*Abît*. Idiot. What is she doing untied?"

Realizing he intended to strike her as well, Brianna leaped off the bed, too frightened to breathe. Dizziness swarmed over her senses. She didn't know where she was. But a gust of wind sent branches scraping the roof above her head and mingled with the creaks and groans of distressed joints. She suspected that she'd been put in the upper reaches of a house. The ceiling sloped to within three feet of the floor.

"All I want is something to eat and drink. Is that so much?" Her voice was hoarse, her throat dry from screaming so long in the gag.

"Do you think you'll live long enough to die of starvation?"

Selim lifted her and tossed her on the bed so hard, she heard the frame snap. Fighting to regain control of her panic, she struck out at him and screamed, only to hear her high-pitched rasp. Her legs entangled in her skirts. He tied her ankles. "We weren't supposed to be here but for you."

"Enough!"

Through a waterfall of her hair, Brianna saw Charles Cross leaning against the door frame, a wine flask held loosely in his hand as if he were drunk. Her friend. Her ally in Cairo. For a moment he struggled to stand, and Brianna, disbelieving, noted his pallid features, the way his hand trembled against the door frame. Until now she hadn't known for sure that he'd been the one she'd shot. Someone had hit her and knocked her unconscious. But now she knew.

"How could you?" She tried to scream at him but couldn't as Selim turned her over on her stomach and bound her hands tightly behind her.

How could he be associated with a murderer like Selim?

"I have no," Charles said to the younger man. "Now!" he said again, when it looked as if Selim would argue. "You are free to go."

"You still have time, my brother," Selim pleaded. "We have avenged our mother. We have won. You don't need to stay. Come with me."

"Go, Selim. Before it is too late for you."

"I cannot!"

"Go. And lock the door."

Glaring at Brianna through tears, the younger man whirled away and stalked from the room. *Mother?* They shared the same mother?

His face hidden in the shadow, Charles seemed to be staring at her. She heard the click of the door, and struggled to sit against the cast-iron headboard. Selim was Omar's youngest son. Brianna remembered what Omar had once said about having an English mistress while he'd attended Oxford. Brianna's gaze rose to Cross's. No sound escaped her.

"With my hair and coloring, my illustrious father thought I could be of more use to him if no one knew the truth, that I could even care the slightest for him after he made a whore of my mother." Charles moved into the dull sphere of light cast by the single candle on the nightstand. She could see the bloodstain spreading outward in a circle on his shirt. "Do you know what he used to do to the young servants in this room? Sometimes he would even bring my mother and me up here to watch."

"You are the one who killed him." She'd exhausted herself in her struggles. "He was never part of those caravan raids."

"Had I been able to convince Fallon that Omar was the one behind the attacks, I could have trusted him just to deal with the bastard. That gold shipment raid had been our last. I'd accomplished what I'd gone to Egypt to do. Ruin Omar. I'd wanted him to know that his bastard sons were better than he was. I could go anywhere in the world and live like royalty with what I took off that caravan."

"I live like royalty. There's better ways to ruin your life."

He chuckled, such a normal sound that they could have been sitting down over tea. Pain creased his features. "You shot me, Brianna."

"I didn't know it was you. How could I?"

The bed dipped as he sat beside her. He smelled of disinfectant and sweat. Brianna turned her face away as he held the flask to her mouth. "You have to drink now, Miss Donally."

"Please . . . don't."

"You are thirsty. And this will help."

She tried to fight. The wine dribbled over her lips and down her chin. Then he shoved a fist into her hair and pulled her head back. "I have no need of poisons, Miss Donally. This will not hurt you."

She was so thirsty, her throat could barely swallow. She breathed it into her lungs and choked. Suddenly, Brianna found new strength. She rolled off the other side of the bed, stumbled and hit the wall.

He seemed startled that she would run from him. Watching her gag, Charles drank from the flask and considered her over the rim. "Fallon has already begun to turn London upside down looking for you."

She wanted her husband. Needed him desperately. She raised her eyes. "How do you know?" Her voice was a pathetic whisper.

"We've just been chatting downstairs. A pleasant chat,

actually. I told him that you belonged to me. Do you know what he did? He left."

Her gaze flew to the window, where he might even now be outside.

"You needn't fear me, Miss Donally. I could have taken you many times." Cross pulled a chain from beneath his shirt and withdrew the amulet. "I came back with you on the steamer. I was in the suk that afternoon you'd gone with your brother. I used to watch you ride. I gave you back your book. I helped you with your research. I wanted you to know that I felt the same about you that you felt for me."

"I should have known. You quoted Dickens."

"I know you were forced to marry Fallon."

Dizziness tried to pull her down. If he'd been the one who returned her book, then . . . "Your job allowed you to get stolen merchandise and rare antiquities out of the country. You knew which caravans carried valuable goods," she whispered, the full scope of his crimes hitting her. "You've murdered British soldiers, women and children. You would have murdered me."

"Not you." He eased around the bed to stand in front of her. "Never you. Don't you understand?" he rasped, as if she should have no qualm comprehending his motives for everything he'd done. "Selim was in that caravan to see that you weren't killed. I knew that Lady Alexandra was seeking the location of that Coptic temple and that she'd planned to stop near there. We'd arranged for Pritchards to be the one to take that caravan out of Cairo."

Tears burned her eyes. She stumbled, then hopped in an effort to maintain her balance.

"Because Major Fallon knew the desert. He would never have depended on the guides," she said.

Brianna had heard of people who had no moral compass. People unable to grasp the difference between right and wrong. He'd murdered his own father, thought nothing of killing Alex and Michael, and possessed no remorse, no inkling of the horror that he'd wreaked on hundreds.

Somewhere in the madness of her thoughts she heard doors slamming as if from far away. Shouts. "You are very wise, Mr. Cross." God, he was insane, and she was trying to reason with him. "We could still go away together." She'd worked one hand loose from the rope.

"I know you're lying, Brianna." His knuckles caressed her cheek. "But that doesn't matter. Soon we'll be together forever."

It was then that she smelled smoke. It seeped from the floor like a slow rolling mist rising from a bog. "The wine will make this painless, Miss Donally. Do you know what *suttee* is?"

In that fatal moment, Brianna realized what he had planned. "You are insane!" He'd sent the house up in flames like some ungodly funeral pyre. "I'd as soon go to hell than spend a second in eternity with you!" She stumbled against the wall, hitting her head when she fell. She lay momentarily stunned.

This couldn't be happening!

"You don't mean that, Miss Donally."

In frustrated rage, Brianna hit the wall with her feet. Pain ricocheted up her deadened calves, but she didn't care, her kid boots absorbed the impact. Soon, plate-size pieces of plaster began to crumble. She screamed for Michael. The wine at least had given her back her voice. Then there was another roar in her ears, as if the sound of the sea crashed through her head. Dizziness pulled her down. She only knew that if she didn't stay conscious, she would die.

"He's set the goddamn house on fire!"

Even as Michael watched, a tapestry in the sitting room went up in flames. Fire licked at the photographs on the wall. Boyish faces melted and blackened. Michael's heart hammered in his chest. He met Donally's desperate gaze across the corridor. "She has to be here!"

Within a half hour, six of Cross's men were stripped of arms and lying facedown on the drive. Panic had erupted into chaos as the first hint of smoke touched the air. But there was no sign of Cross. Michael and Donally had been tearing the house up looking for Brianna.

"The carriage is inside the cottage at the back," Finley gasped as he ducked around the corner into the narrow smoke-filled corridor. "Your wife's trunks are still inside."

Michael's blood ran icy cold. "We've missed a door someplace," he shouted to Donally, rolling his hand to signal that he should go back into the cellar. Michael took the stairs, his eyes on the walls and the floor, looking for someplace that pulled at the tendrils of smoke.

"Here!" Finley yelled, laying a shoulder against the wall, nearly crashing through to the corridor on the other side.

Michael took the long staircase into the darkness. "Listen!"

Above the shouts and gunshots outside, he could hear something banging. He followed the noise down the hall, throwing open doors until he reached one that was locked. "Brianna!"

Michael smashed his boot heel against the metal plate of the door. Brianna was somewhere inside, and then he forgot to care whether there might be more men about as he emptied his gun into the lock and kicked open the door. There was a deadliness about him as he ducked inside the smoke-filled chamber.

"Get Donally out of the basement," he called to Finley. "I've found her."

The vision of Brianna dead would haunt him until he could no longer bear it. Seeing her lying motionless on the ground, her knees bent against the wall, her face turned toward the window, he ran to kneel beside her. Cross sat unmoving against the back of the bed.

Then Michael was sawing at the ropes on her wrists and ankles and pulling her into his arms. Somewhere, he heard shouts, but the only reality was Brianna in arms, his mouth pressed to hers, holding her to his heart as if he feared that she might somehow get away.

"You're late, Ravenspur," he heard her hoarse whisper.

"It's a big house, *amîri*."

He had known little of love his whole life, even less of tenderness, but today he'd learned what it was truly like to lose both, and he never wanted to know that devastation again. He lifted her into his arms. "It was Charles Cross all the time," she murmured.

"I know."

"He's Omar's son," Brianna murmured.

Michael had guessed that much when he recognized the second boy in the photo as Omar's youngest son. Her head lulled against his shoulder. He swung around to get out of the room. Cross moved, and Michael was suddenly looking into his eyes. The man was still alive.

"It won't matter what you do," his voice whispered. "Where we're going, you can't follow."

Michael saw an amulet clutched in his hand.

"The amulet," she whispered. "Get it off me. Now."

He pulled the chain over her neck. "Where you're going, she'll never be—" Michael tossed the amulet at Cross. "You bastard."

Brianna murmured, and Michael knew she was slipping out of consciousness. He turned with her in his arms. The corridor was narrow. Then he was running. Whatever happened to Cross would be in the hands of a far higher power than his. Smoke burned his eyes. He had to get out of the house. Bars covered the windows. Michael broke the glass in the bedroom. He kicked at the bars, but nothing moved. He did the same for both windows. The bars were solid iron. He stopped in the doorway, pushed back by the flames that had already consumed the front of the house. Helped by kerosene, flames caught the draperies and chased up the walls to lick at the ceiling. Light fixtures shattered.

With an oath, Michael turned and ran back up the narrow stairway, encountering smoke rising from the floor below. He could only pray that the stairs led to the roof and that he could get down from there.

Gunshot splintered the wood next to his head. "Burn, Fallon!" Cross stood at the top of the stairs, blocking their escape.

"Can you stand?" Michael asked Brianna, setting her down behind him.

"I would fly if you asked," she murmured with a weak smile.

Tilting her head, he looked into her eyes. Barbiturates. Michael didn't know how much she'd consumed. Cross had fed her the same drug given to widows in India who were burned to death on the funeral pyres of their husbands. Reaching behind him, he pulled the revolver from his belt and checked the load. One *fucking* bullet. Brianna leaned a shoulder against the wall. Another bullet smashed into the doorjamb, then another. His heart pounding slowly, heavily, Michael knew he had no choice but to step into that stairwell. He must take a chance on getting shot. But regardless, he had to take out Cross.

Michael stepped into the stairwell. A bullet creased his sleeve. Cross had panicked and fired too soon. Michael's arm was already raised. He fired and hit Cross between the eyes. Cross fell against the wall.

Michael turned for Brianna and found her eyes wide on his. He pulled her into his arms and ran up the stairs. He found a way to one of the turrets on the roof. Smoke bellowed from the windows below.

"We have to climb," Brianna said, stumbling toward the branches of a tree. Michael grabbed her hand and looked down. A long way down.

Then he was stripping off her skirt to her chemise. He held her by the shoulders and looked into her eyes. They could both die leaping onto those branches, and he had something to tell her, so help him God.

"I know," she said before he could voice the words. "I love you, too, but if we don't get off this roof none of that will matter."

Michael stopped her. He kissed her lips, brushed the hair from her sooty face, and kissed her again. Then he lowered her to the thickest branch about three feet below the turret.

"I'm not watching," he said. "Christ . . ."

But he did watch, helplessly, as she wobbled to the center of the tree and started down, disappearing into the thick smoke. Michael jumped across and soon he'd caught up to her. Donally and Finley waited below, and when they hit the ground, they started running. Behind him the fire burned. The scene was dramatic. People had moved away from the yard.

Michael stood on the drive watching the flames lick at the sky before turning to join Brianna inside the carriage. She was conscious, her hair singed, her face black, and he pulled her into his lap.

"How did you know I was in that house?" she whispered.

The shouts had disappeared, and a pale stretch of light, faintly purple, had begun to change the sky. "English roses," he said against her hair, and he felt the smile on her lips, the welcoming embrace of relief as he held her. "It was the same scent that led me to you before."

In a world far away, a long time ago when he'd found her veil in the desert. Michael tried to explain what he'd meant, but it didn't seem to matter, for she knew. "It took you long enough, Ravenspur."

And he knew that she'd be all right.

Chapter 25

⟨ ⟩

"**C**ross might have gotten away if she hadn't shot him." Michael raised a steaming mug of chocolate to his lips and drank. "Selim has been convicted of three counts of murder and accessory to murder for crimes committed against everyone found in the carriage. The verdict was issued yesterday."

"Thank you Jesus that most of this was left out of the newspaper," Ryan said, stabbing a cigar in an ashtray at his elbow.

The sun had risen hours ago, and the men gathered around the settee and chairs in Christopher Donally's library remained tense, though no one admitted as much. Setting the mug down, Michael leaned forward on his knees. "You owe Ware for keeping this out of the papers," he said, looking at the faces of Brianna's brothers gathered around the chairs.

Michael noticed the cozy picture they made. In contrast, Lord Ware stood outside the circle of camaraderie with his hands clasped behind him. "It seemed that Charles Cross sailed from Alexandria under the name of Solomon." Ware's hand opened and closed over the head of his cane. "It was his legitimate name. From what we could discern, their father took both boys away from their mother to Egypt after she killed herself. Cross returned later and was educated here when he turned seventeen. Whatever he felt for his father had only festered."

Brianna stood at the top of the stairs and listened to the low voices gathered in the library. Dressed in workable muslin, with her hair bound back with a scarf, she'd hesitated at the railing long enough before setting her foot to the stairs. It had been three weeks since the incident with Charles Cross.

When she'd awakened from the ordeal, she found herself back at Christopher's house. Charles Cross had reentered her life and nearly stolen everything, yet for all that he'd done, she didn't hate him. She'd pitied him and had wept for him, for babies are not born monsters.

She'd not seen Michael for two days afterward, as she sat like an invalid in bed, eating everything given to her. Praying that her baby was all right. Selim had not died but had been held over for prosecution. He'd provided a wealth of information, spilling the details of caravan attacks they'd carried out over the last two years, as well as the location of the gold they'd stolen. She could not fathom the depth of his insanity, the tragedy of his life, and for all that he'd talked and pointed fingers at others, that he'd not saved himself from the gallows.

Outside, her brothers' children played, their laughter cleansing her thoughts. Amber had come up last week. Caroline was in town for the start of the Season. Parliament began session three days ago and Michael had taken his seat.

Life continued.

Brianna now stood in the doorway of the library, the familiar smell of leather-bound tomes hidden somewhere beneath the smell of bourbon and cigars. On a low table in front of the settee and high-back chairs, an empty captain's decanter sat on a polished silver tray surrounded by cut crystal. Colin and his family had arrived last night from Carlisle. Wearing tall riding boots, he looked as if he'd just returned from the stables. Johnny sat beside him. His oldest twins were tearing up the yard. David, who was just below Christopher in the Donally pecking order, would not be in from Ireland for a few days. And Ryan sat beside her husband, one booted ankle lying casually across his knee.

A breeze from the open French doors pulled gently at her skirts.

Looking across the room at her husband sitting among her brothers, Brianna watched as his gaze lifted to her, and felt the same constriction in her throat she always felt when his eyes touched hers. She'd been upstairs with Johnny and Colin's wives all night. Christopher had taken his place beside Alex this morning as he anxiously awaited the birth of his children, for he was the new father of twins. The concern she glimpsed in Michael's gaze transformed as he saw what she held in her arms.

Brianna's gaze lowered to the swaddled bundle she cradled to her chest. Those blue eyes held her in a trance as the miracle of life revealed itself in the sudden vent of protest that could be heard all over the house. The plump, round features scrunched in fury. Already this new Donally was wreaking changes on the world around him.

"Where is the new father?" Ryan asked.

"He is with his wife upstairs."

"Hell, Chris is going to be needin' this more than we are!" Johnny laughed, setting down the bottle of bourbon in his hands.

Her family suddenly surrounded her, but it was to the grandfather who stood off to the side that she handed the little boy, and his watery eyes seemed unable to lift from the tiny being that filled his awkward hands. "Your granddaughter has just made her entrance and will be down shortly." Brianna thought of her own mother-in-law, and realized sadly that some chasms might never be spanned, but this one possibly could.

An arm was wrapped around her waist and Brianna let herself be pulled from the crowd.

Michael brought her hand to his mouth and rubbed her knuckles over his lips. "Maybe it's time I put your mind on something else."

"Like what?" Her back pressed to his chest.

"Like this." He pulled her against him. "Maybe we should announce that we've made one of our own." His laugh was warm and close to her ear.

Leaning her head back against his shoulder, Brianna closed her eyes as his mouth touched her temple and moved lower.

Brianna loved her proud, aristocratic husband, but she knew beneath the fervor of his lover's embrace that this was no happy ending to their life. Instead, it was the promise of a new beginning.

Theirs would not be an easy course to traverse. The future by its very definition meant uncertainty, but both of them had the ability to make a difference in this world. Whatever lay ahead, they were far stronger walking this road together than alone.

And since when had either of them allowed adversity to stop them?

His mouth drifted from her temple to the hollow of her throat. "I love you, *amîri.*"

Smiling to herself, she stopped thinking as his lips pressed seamlessly to hers.

She wanted him to take her home.

Home, where dreams were like the rolling, golden dunes of a desert dawn, ever changing and infinite.

Where the foundation for the finest house could be built from the tiniest grain of sand and a touch of moonlight.

Where the magic they'd discovered one enchanted evening in a faraway land would endure to grow and nurture generations to come.

Indeed, the possibilities were endless.

Keep your resolution to get more passion with these irresistible love stories coming in January from Avon Romance!

Sin and Sensibility by Suzanne Enoch

An Avon Romantic Treasure

Lady Eleanor Griffin's overprotective brothers fully intend to choose her bridegroom, and Eleanor knows she might as well enjoy herself now, before a man dull enough to satisfy them appears. But when she meets her brothers' best friend, her idea of enjoyment takes a whole new turn, and her brothers ꞏꞏꞏꞏ are the last thing on her mind ꞏ ꞏ ꞏ

The Protector by Gennita Low

An Avon Contemporary Romance

After a covert mission goes awry, Navy SEAL Jazz Zeringue has no doubts he'll be rescued, but he's certainly surprised when his savior turns out to be the mysterious and beautiful agent Vivi Verreau. Vivi doesn't trust him and is trying very hard not to like him, but they'll have to work together if they're to escape from dangerous enemy territory alive.

Seducing a Princess by Lois Greiman

An Avon Romance

Having set out to avenge a great wrong, William Enton, third baron of Landow, finds himself with nowhere to turn in the most lawless part of Darktowne. Then a vision appears from the dirty alleyways, a woman who seems to know him at once. But she is the princess of thieves, and nothing is as it seems, including the woman he is quickly coming to love.

What an Earl Wants by Shirley Karr

An Avon Romance

Desperate for employment, Josephine Quincy dresses as a secretary would—as a man—and lets her new employer, the rakish Earl of Sinclair, make his own assumptions. But he is no fool, and just when she thinks her game is up, she realizes she has a bargaining chip she never dreamed of—the powerful Earl's attentions . . . and perhaps he in turn is gaining possession of her heart.

REL 1204

Have you ever dreamed of writing a romance?

*And have you ever wanted
to get a romance published?*

Perhaps you have always wondered how to
become an Avon romance writer?
We are now seeking the best and brightest undiscovered
voices. We invite you to send us your query letter to
avonromance@harpercollins.com

What do you need to do?

Please send no more than two pages telling us
about your book. We'd like to know its setting—is it
contemporary or historical—and a bit about the hero,
heroine, and what happens to them.

Then, if it is right for Avon we'll ask to see part of the
manuscript. Remember, it's important that you have
material to send, in case we want to see your story quickly.

Of course, there are no guarantees of publication,
but you never know unless you try!

*We know there is new talent just waiting
to be found! Don't hesitate . . . send us
your query letter today.*

*The Editors
Avon Romance*

Avon Romantic Treasures

Unforgettable, enthralling love stories,
sparkling with passion and adventure
from Romance's bestselling authors

Discover Contemporary Romances at Their Sizzling Hot Best from Avon Books

WANTED: ONE PERFECT MAN   by Judi McCoy
0-06-056079-7/$5.99 US/$7.99 Can

FACING FEAR   by Gennita Low
0-06-052339-5/$5.99 US/$7.99 Can

HOT STUFF   by Elaine Fox
0-06-051724-7/$5.99 US/$7.99 Can

WHAT MEMORIES REMAIN   by Cait London
0-06-055588-2/$5.99 US/$7.99 Can

LOVE: UNDERCOVER   by Hailey North
0-06-058230-8/$5.99 US/$7.99 Can

IN THE MOOD   by Suzanne Macpherson
0-06-051768-9/$5.99 US/$7.99 Can

THE DAMSEL IN THIS DRESS   by Marianne Stillings
0-06-057533-6/$5.99 US/$7.99 Can

SINCE YOU'RE LEAVING ANYWAY,
TAKE OUT THE TRASH   by Dixie Cash
0-06-059536-1/$5.99 US/$7.99 Can

A DATE ON CLOUD NINE   by Jenna McKnight
0-06-054928-9/$5.99 US/$7.99 Can

THE THRILL OF IT ALL   by Christie Ridgway
0-06-050290-8/$5.99 US/$7.99 Can

www.AuthorTracker.com

Available wherever books are sold
or please call 1-800-331-3761 to order.   CRO 0804